#  Waldwick

Waldwick...Survivor

Kenneth Linde

Waldwick Books
www.waldwickbooks.com
McHenry, Illinois

*Waldwick: Survivor, Death and How It Saved My Life*

*Kenneth Jon Linde*

Waldwick Partners, Inc.
dba Waldwick Books
www.WaldwickBooks.com

June 2023



Printed in Wisconsin, United States of America

ISBN: 979-8-9852613-7-0

**ISBN: 979-8-9852-6137-0**

## What the cover is all about....

As an author, one of the biggest challenges is cover selection as it's the first impression readers have when considering its contents.

For the first seven books in the Waldwick Series, we chose photos. For "Survivor" I turned to one of America's premier pen-and-ink artists by the name of J.P. Schmelzer who has been a dear friend for over 60 years.

When the underlying theme of a book is death, I turned to John and he created what lies in your hand. At first, I didn't understand what it meant and then John explained that the practice of toasting someone's grave was a tradition with roots in ancient Greece and Rome and continued in Europe during the Middle Ages where it was believed the dead could hear the living and, by offering them a drink, the living would help the departed pass on to the afterlife.

While John's artistic genius seems attuned to observations showing the enhanced or diminished features of the subject, his attention to so many of the "little things" is almost immeasurable.

Look again at the cover and you'll discover so much more than you initially thought was there. George Terrill is seen holding a wine glass in one hand and a bottle in the other. Look closer and you'll see that the headstone is blank. George is not there to toast the departed, but celebrate his fleeting victory over the eventuality that face us all.

My goal as an author is to have you also find more than you expect. As an individual who has had a very-near-death experience, my only wish is that the following pages provide the same depth-of-thought as its magnificent cover.

**There are no hearses with trailer hitches on the back**

### Assumptions:

Assumptions - we don't know we're making them. They're easier than dealing with facts and certainly take less time. We make them every day. We assume today will be like yesterday. We assume good will happen or perhaps bad. We assume the day will end as it began. Yet, in an instant, it can all change! The other car that runs the red light! Black ice on the driveway! The electric spark! In an instant the assumption we made can take our world and turn it upside down.

My name is George Terrill. For me, it happened on a flight back from France to our home in Milwaukee. As we were getting close to landing I had a weird feeling, unlike anything I'd ever felt before, and it wasn't pleasant. The plane landed, the door opened and I made it down the steps in the hangar. The next thing I knew, I was in intensive care at Milwaukee General Hospital with IV's in my arms and feet, sandbags between my legs and straps totally immobilizing me to the point all I could move was my right thumb to press the nursing station call button taped to my hand.

My mouth and nose were covered by a mask and I could hear the thump/woosh, thump/woosh, thump/woosh of the ventilator next to me as it delivered air and then allowed it to escape from my lungs. My God what happened? My mind cleared as I stared at the ceiling and slowly pushed the call button as a nurse came rushing in.

"Mister Terrill!"

I attempted to nod my head in the affirmative.

"Mister Terrill, do you know where you're at?"

I slowly attempted to move my head from left to right to indicate I didn't but sandbags held it in place.

"Mister Terrill, you're in intensive care at Milwaukee General Hospital."

My wide-open eyes must have communicated my disbelief.

"Let me call the doctor, he'll fill you in."

With that, it was back to total singularity and thump/woosh with the profound realization something major had gone wrong.

A few minutes later a doctor, about my age, walked in and looked at me, while glancing at the electronic chart to see my vitals…blood pressure, 105/60, pulse 82, oxygen level 92%. In other words hypoxemia.

"I'm Doctor Goodman. Do you mind if I call you George?"

Unable to move, nor talk, I couldn't communicate it was fine. Doctor Goodman saw the dilemma and offered, "Why don't we do this…if it's yes, quickly blink twice. If it's no, hold your eyes closed. Do you understand?

I quickly blinked twice.

"George?"

Two more quick blinks.

"George, you suffered a pulmonary embolism that exploded in your lungs in what we call 'showering' and you have 60 small blood clots there."

I blinked and held my eyes closed for an extend period of time.

The doctor took a deep breath and added, "Beyond that, we've identified five relatively large blood clots in your heart and three DVT's, or deep vein thrombi, behind your right knee and two in your left leg."

I simply turned my eyes left and right in then closed my lids tightly in disbelief.

"George, right now you're in critical condition. We've administered what is called a thromboidial dispersant that has taken your blood viscosity down to that of water which is why you're on the ventilator. We've totally immobilized you to minimize the chance of another blood clot breaking loose. At this point in time, if you move, you will die. The next twenty-four hours are critical concerning your survival."

I closed my eyes and felt a tear trickle down my cheek. I opened them and blinked twice quickly hoping Doctor Goodman should come closer.

There was no response.

Again, I blinked twice and slightly nodded. This time Doctor Goodman realized I wanted him to come closer.

Through the plexiglass face mask I mouthed. "Chances?"

The doctor understood and leaned back, reticent to reply.

I opened my eyes wide as if to show my impatience and mouthed "chances" again.

Doctor Goodman closed his eyes for a moment as if to ponder whether to break the code of silence and then looked at me paused, took a deep breath and reluctantly stated "less than five percent."

I blinked twice indicating I understood that my chances for survival were less than five percent.

Doctor Goodman offered. "I'm sorry George."

I blinked twice again as if to infer I understood.

The spell was broken as Doctor Goodman offered. "Mrs. Terrill is out in the hall and will come in for a few minutes but it's really important you don't move. Because of the dispersant we can't give you any additional sedative and it's imperative you remain totally still."

I opened my eyes, blinked twice and Dr. Goodman was gone. I closed my eyes for a long moment and when I opened them Amy appeared - distraught, disheveled and in disbelief. "Oh baby, I'm so sorry. You seemed fine and then just collapsed. They're doing everything they can. The kids want to come but they won't let anyone in, not even Mela and she used to work here."

The nurse came in and urged Amy to leave. Amy looked into my eyes, brushed the hair off my face and said, "Hang in there. We've got a lot more life to live. I love you!"

My eyes tried to follow the love of my life walk out the door as the nurse turned off the lights and I listened to thump/woosh, thump/woosh, thump/woosh until I fell back into a deep sleep.

For six days I was totally incapacitated while Amy was only allowed to visit for fifteen minutes each day. For twenty-three hours and forty-five minutes, I was alone, totally immersed in my own self-pity. It's amazing what you ponder when you think you're going to die. You don't consider the things you did, you contemplate the things you didn't do and make promises that, should this not be the end, you'd make things right.

### Regrets Redux:

One of my greatest regrets had been not sharing my values with my wife and our family. Initially, I'd been too busy trying to show the world I didn't marry Amy for her money. After that was resolved, I was too busy trying to show the world I'd changed by starting the foundation. Then, Tommie and I started Terrill B&B for beef and bourbon and, with the kids grown and gone, I invested too much time getting B&B off the ground.

With 85,500 solitary seconds every day, I had plenty of time to do a lot of thinking about things. My first thoughts turned to those with ALS or quadriplegics and I realized how lucky I was. After the first few hours it seemed that, with great caution, I was actually on the road to recovery and my incapacitation was temporary and not the horrific permanence they faced forever.

When you're lying on your back, unable to look out the window or even the walls, you begin to stare at the ceiling. At first, I counted the squares of tile and then began focusing to see if I could actually count the small holes in each panel, thereby seeking a pattern and correlation. Were the ceiling tiles structured or was it a random pattern like life? There was a pattern! Every sixth tile had the same embossed pattern. Life's certainly not like that! There are similarities but no pattern. It was then I finally realized the center of my existence was me...physically, mentally and spiritually.

The highlight of each day would be when the nurse came in to check my vitals or answer my call when I needed the bed pan. Amy told me there was a sign at the nurses' station announcing, 'Check your modesty at the door' and I began to realize I was just another body filling up time and space until I departed one way or the other. What had been personal and private was nothing more than a name and condition to those who dedicated their lives to the wellbeing of others, referred to simply as 'the patient'.

The time alone was brutal. You can only count the ceiling tiles so many times. After surveying all the things I hadn't done, I began making a mental list of things I wanted to do if I made it and one of them was sharing my values with our kids. Each day painstakingly blended into the next and then the next and then, well you get the image.

I began to examine my values and realized there should be a structure of values in terms of levels of importance if you want to lead a fulfilling life. I realized, without being egotistical, at the center of my existence was me…all of me…physically, mentally and spiritually.

Next came my wife, without whom my life would have no meaning. Next came the kids who represented our, greatest achievement. Next came my job, then non-nuclear family and friends, hobbies and interests and, finally the universe. I began to comprehend where I'd made my mistakes. I began to understand who and why the pieces fit together the way I'd organized them. I began to vow, if I made it, I'd adjust, readjust and glue the pieces together in that order…self, spouse, children, jobs, external family and friends, hobbies and interests and finally all others.

On day four Doctor Goodman came in with a smile on his face. My vitals were improving and the probability of my demise was gradually being reduced.

"Good morning, George. How are you doing?"

I blinked in the affirmative as he continued. "Good news. We're going to take you off the respirator and put you on oxygen. How does that sound?"

Doctor Goodman left and the nurse came in who removed the mask to which I proceeded to offer a huge sigh of relief.

"George, you're not out of the woods yet."

"Odds," I whispered through my parched throat.

"Fifty-fifty," was the reply.

I must have had a forlorn look on my face at Doctor Goodman responded. "George, we don't really know why you're alive. You were in such bad shape when you got here, the other specialists and I didn't have our standard conference call. We never thought you'd make it through the night.

"And now?" I hoarsely whispered.

It was great to have the mask off and I hoped the inside of my mouth would recover quickly.

Doctor Goodman seemed to not be in his normal hurry and so I asked him, "was it really as close as you said it was?"

The good Doctor looked at the ground and then at me and thought for a moment and replied. "George, someday I'm going to have to write you up for the American Journal of Medicine. You shouldn't be here, but you are. With 70 blood clots in you, your vitals didn't reflect how bad it was. The main risk was one of the blood clots breaking loose and going to your heart or brain and either killing you or you having a stroke. That's why we put you on the thromboidial dispersant and totally immobilized you."

"OK. So I was dying?"

"Not really, but the risk of dying was one of, if not the highest I've ever seen.  When a person starts dying, their circulation reduces so it can focus primarily on the body's internal organs.. This process reduces blood flow to the hands, legs, and feet, which is why a person nearing the end of their life often feels cold to the touch, or might complain of feeling cold themselves."

"So this is why people kept grasping my hands and feet?"

"Yes."

I was all making sense now.

Doc stopped for a moment and then added. This change in blood flow can also cause the dying person's skin to appear yellow, or waxen and some will also develop what's referred to as "mottling," which is a purple or pink pattern forming on the skin. There's nothing that can be done to stop these changes to the body, but attempts to  make the person more comfortable can be made by adjusting the room's temperature, or providing extra blankets."

"Which is why I had the extra and weighted blankets?"

Again a nod in the affirmative.

"What's really different in your case is the fact you remained totally lucid which is why we did the blinking routine. When approaching death, a person's brain starts to shut down in certain areas, to focus on only the most necessary functions, much in the same way the rest of the body does. As the brain begins to change and starts to die, different parts become excited, and one part is the visual system ... where people begin to see light."

"You mean like ghosts?"

"No, not really, just that light becomes more intense. You see, the sudden release of neurochemicals in a brain beginning to shut down can cause a person to have "amazing experiences.""

"This whole ordeal has been an amazing experience," I offered.

Doctor Goodman continued. "Those who specialize in hospice care report many patients claim to see loved ones who weren't actually there have dreams of loved ones during their final days, or smell a familiar smell such as cigars or a certain perfume."

"Wow!"

The good doctor continued. Instead of constantly talking about keeping people alive or fixing the problems, he was giving me insight into the end which I found incredibly interesting as he continued. "A natural death can seem like it's dragging out forever, because there's a lot taking place before a person is actually dead. It's certainly not like it is in the movies."

"Until about 100 years ago most deaths happened quickly, because there were no medical measures set in place to properly care for patients. Due to modern advancements in medicine, death can be prolonged for quite some time."

"Today, a lot of us call it "active dying" which is the final, rapid slide that happens in roughly the last few days of life. First hunger and then thirst are lost. Speech is lost next, followed by vision. The last senses to go are usually hearing and touch which is why we hold the hands of those near the end, to simply let them know they're not alone."

"How do you determine someone is dead?" I inquired.

Doc continued. "In standard medical terms, there are two ways a person's death is determined. The most commonly accepted form of death is cardiac death, which is the absence of the heart contracting and pumping blood due to a disturbance in its electrical activity. The second, less common, is brain death, which is defined as the irreversible absence of all brain activity. Once a person becomes brain dead, the heart can continue pumping, when hooked up to medical equipment, but would not be able to do so on its own."

"Before the invention of ventilators and medications to help keep the body's functions active, there wasn't a need to factor in such a thing as brain death. In earlier medical days, patients with no brain function quickly succumbed to cardiac arrest. This presents a difficult situation, both for family members, as well as medical professionals who have to make the call whether to keep a person who's been diagnosed as brain dead on a ventilator, or to pull the support and let their heart follow the brain to death. If death is no longer a single, specific moment in time, everything gets complicated."

This was really interesting as Doctor Goodman continued. "After the heart stops there's often a surge of brain activity which could cause a person to experience brief moments of near clarity to the point a person's brain can sometimes remain active even after they pass away, long enough to hear their own time of death announced. Some of the patients that were 'dead' and then recovered report hearing full conversations, and even viewed the room they were in, after their death had been called by medical professionals."

"Well, miracle man, right now, we all think that, if you continue the progress you're making, in a few days, we can get you out of ICU and on the road to recovery."

"How long?" I whispered again.

"Healing is never a linear progression. There will be good days and bad and so I can't quantify your recovery period."

I took a deep breath and it felt good to be off thump/woosh and even the racket from the nurse's station sounded good.

"When can I see my wife and family?"

"Amy can visit but we need to make sure you're healthy enough for the kids and so we'd like to wait a few more days."

"Understood"

"Any questions?"

"Can I tilt my bed up so I'm not looking at the ceiling? I've counted the tiles a hundred times."

"It should be all right, but let the nurses do it and please remain immobilized. We need to make sure the clots are receding and don't want one to break loose and explode in your heart or brain."

Doctor Goodman looked at his watch and realized time was of the nigh. He smiled a somewhat laconic expression and finalized. "Well George, I think we've had enough talk of death today and, in your case, not something you need to worry about right now."

The thoughts of that, after four days, made me realize I couldn't rush things.

By day six, I was ambulatory. No more bedpan! Hooray. It was still a porta potty set next to my bed and my thought became 'one small poop for George, one large poop from my behind'.

Amy arrived and filled me in on all happening in the world. With so much time on my hands and accepting the treatise I was the center of my personal universe, my quiet time allowed me to focus on my personal introspection. In other words, about who I was and what I would do over if given the chance.

I looked at my wife and thanked her for all she had done.

I'm sixty-one years old and told her that, when you go through life and never have an experience of thinking you're going to die and then it happens…the experience that is…you know God is real and there's power in prayer, and miracles do happen.

Amy smiled a shy smile as if to indicate she agreed. Never having been religious, it was then she admitted every day after our visit, she would stop in the hospital chapel and say a prayer.

I was grateful not only for the results but the prayers and realization she too had turned to God, not as a last resort but for comfort. For the first time, I sensed she was believing there was a greater being who looked down upon us all with goodness and compassion in a world so wrought with pain and suffering. As Amy was about to leave, I asked her to bring a notepad so I could write down some of my thoughts. Television was atrocious and I wanted to see if I couldn't begin to capture all that had been swirling in my head.

## The Physical Self:

The next day, Amy brought two lined tablets and a couple of those fancy liquid gel pens and placed them on my nightstand. I asked her to bring a couple more tablets as I had a lot to write. She looked at me and smiled, knowing I was on the road to recovery.

I took pen in hand and began. Within a few sentences I realized no one, including me, would ever be able to read what I wrote. My forever girlfriend Ceclia, who had been my administrative assistant, had retired with her husband John and moved to Phoenix. Only she could make out my scribbles. I vowed, if I made it, I'd simply scan the pages and have her type them. For someone who wanted to be a writer, my punctuation and grammar is probably on the same level as a sixth grader and so I know my Ceclia would clean it all up and make me seem like some kind of wizard, which I'm not.

Amy called Ceclia and told her what happened. Ceclia said she and John would pray for me and agreed to take my chicken scratches and make them legible.

I hope my passion for life and what I surmised doesn't come off as preaching. I'll do my best not to make to it sound like some sort of Sunday sermon. Six days of isolation, immobilization and incapacitation constantly believing it will be your last does something to not only your body but your brain as well. The only thing that kept me from going crazy was the hypothesis of relationships and realization I'd failed. Through repetition hour after hour and challenge after challenge of their validity... self, spouse, children, job, non-nuclear family and friends, hobbies and interests and the universe, became chiseled in my soul. The repetition and self-challenge of validity resulted in a self-administered covenant to serve as a guideline to make me a better person...more compassionate, more caring, more involved in the lives of others and not just myself. I can only hope what I write makes sense.

"Birth: No person has ever made the decision to be born. It was the act of others who brought us into this world. Yet, when life begins, we initiate the journey that will eventually result in our demise. I believe what we endure, accomplish and achieve along our life path is the unique combination of genetics, environment and divine intervention."

"For some the journey will be short. For others, the duration can be long. What matters isn't the length of the journey but what transpires in its duration. I think back to the Duke and the study of telomeres and realize, beyond calamity or malfeasance, we're all somewhat controlled by our genetic makeup and need to ride the ride as long as we can."

"Life and near-death has taught me the cliché is true...'It's not the destination that matters, it's the journey". While we can look back at where our family came from like Will Terrill did, I now know all we can do is observe and comprehend the consequence of each generation on our today. From their trials and tribulations, victories and defeats, greatness and humility, we hopefully can better define who and what we are and put our own existence into better perspective and begin to develop a set of suppositions I hope will be the cornerstone of the next chapter of my life."

"After all I've been through, I now accept life as fragile where the foremost concept we can't escape is the reality our existence is incredibly frail. From my experience, I truly know, in an instant, it can be over...lost forever as we know it. With this underlying thought, I've vowed to live each day as if it's my last. Not in terms of lack of prudence but making certain I share the feelings I have for others and crafting my emotions so they are aware. It's been said countless times, if we all knew the world was going to end tomorrow, we'd be on the phone calling those near and dear to us, telling them we loved them."

"When you're told you have less than a five-percent chance of living three hours, you not only think about yourself but those who lost the battle. The most tragic thing is a life taken, abruptly, without the ability to express feelings of love and gratitude. As I lay with the blood clots, I kept thinking about things I should have, would have done differently."

"I look at who I am today and realize now life is malleable. While death is the end of this phase of existence, there were and are constant forces that altered 'who' and 'what' I am. Forces, both good and evil, which impacted my being so my consequence is modified, altered and even diminished, based not only on my own actions but those who have come before me and those from whom I have no common bond...other than to have had my life path cross theirs for some inexplicable reason. The great teacher I had as a child. Rodney, my caring friend, who showed me the beauty of acceptance. Amy, who made the sun shine and me feel special. All of them altered my own self-concept and modified my perception of what and where I am."

"I've travelled the world and met an incredible number of really neat people. Sometimes people came into my life, and I knew right away they were meant to be there, to serve some sort of purpose. None of us will never know who these people are - possibly a roommate, neighbor, co-worker, long lost friend – or someone we accidentally sat next to on an airplane. Like Rodney, when I locked eyes with him, I knew at that very moment, he would affect my life in some profound way. Great Grandfather taught me many lessons and helped me figure out who I am and still who I really want to be."

"It's not always great. Sometimes, at first, things happen that may seem horrible, painful and unfair. However, in reflection, you find that without overcoming those obstacles you'd never realize your potential, strength, willpower or heart. Without darkness, we'd never appreciate the light."

"I sincerely believe everything happens for a reason. Nothing happens by chance or by means of good luck. Illness, injury, lost moments of true greatness and sheer stupidity all occur to test the limits of our soul and those we're associated with. Without these small tests, whatever they may be, life would be like a smoothly paved, completely straight, perfectly flat road to nowhere. It would be safe and comfortable but also dull and utterly pointless. It's the people we meet who affect our life and the success and downfalls we experience that gives it meaning. These people help create who we are and who we become and, for that matter, our destiny."

"I've learned, even the bad experiences can be learned from. In fact, they're probably the most poignant and important ones. If someone hurts me, betrays me or breaks my heart, I do my best to forgive them, for they have helped me learn about trust and the importance of being cautious when I do open my heart. In business, if someone attacks my well-being, I try to remember they're only trying to accomplish the same mission as me. I think back to my brother and his ex-wife and shake my head. Yet in the end, Tommie and I grew closer for which I will always be thankful."

"I now believe, if someone trusts and respects me, I need to trust and respect them back, unconditionally because, in a way, they're teaching me their meaning of trust and respect and how to open my heart and eyes to things around me. The Duke always said, "If someone assists you in attaining a level of success, make certain they also bask in the radiance of accomplishment and share the reward, for they too took the risk of the journey."

"By what has happened these past days, I've really learned we all need to make every day count. I need to appreciate every moment and take from them everything I possibly can, for I may never be able to experience that moment again."

"I want to slow my life down and talk to people I've never talked to before, and, above all else, actually listen. I'm doing everything to break free and set my social sights high. My life has been blessed and yet, there have also been many times when what I did wasn't the right thing to do. Yet, I still want to hold my head up because in the end, I think the good has outweighed the bad and I therefore have every right to do so."

"If there's one thing so many of us do, its redundancy. I want to make certain my life doesn't become routine, where I rely on just the same people and relationships to try and make it grow. New people mean new circumstances, new ideas and the freshness that comes with it. At the same time, I also feel I need to be certain my social life does not consume me. It's only one segment of my existence."

"For so long, I've felt inferior and tormented by the things I didn't do. As I lay in bed looking at the ceiling, I began to tell myself I can be a great individual if I can believe more in myself. I've come to one conclusion, if I don't believe in myself, it will be hard for others to believe in me as well. Even though life's round of golf is on the back nine and I'm closer to my eighteenth hole, I now believe I can make life anything I wish. I can transcend my being into whatever is prudent and wise. My goal is to make certain those who rely on me, sense my belief in what I do and the light at the end of the tunnel is truly sunshine."

"My life has been so much more than I ever thought possible and yet I sincerely have some regrets...the woulda's, coulda's, shoulda's we all have. Nowhere is that greater than work and, if I'm allowed to, I need to help those around me understand the value they provide and there's certainly more to life than what happens at the office. It took me a long time to accept the refrain, 'Work to live and never live to work! Have fun and make certain those around you do too'."

"Most importantly, if I appreciate someone, I need to tell them. As I quickly learned, you never know what tomorrow may have in store and I need to always make certain I learn a lesson in life each day. I sincerely believe it's ultimately critical we all understand our position and role, not only as it relates to our own life and those with whom we interact, affect and modify, but how our life dramatically affects those generations who follow in our genetic footsteps. We inherit the assets of those who came before us. Should it be the case their expectation, accomplishment, aspirations were fraught with mediocrity and indifference, then, to the best of our ability, we need to overcome that shortfall for our progeny, elevating them to a position above where I began."

### Not-So-Good News:

On day seven, Doctor Goodman came in and his jovial smile was gone. I thought, 'Holy shit, now what?'

"George. As you know, we've been monitoring your blood ever since you arrived and while the blood clots appear to have begun to dissipate, we're still having issues with stabilizing the coumadin levels and need to keep you here until it's at a safe level."

Doctor Goodman had a very pregnant pause and then added, "We also ran some other tests and determined your PSA has increased from 3.8 to 8.2 since your last physical exam."

"And?" I inquired.

"While not a comprehensive conclusion, an elevated PSA might mean you have prostate Cancer."

The six-letter word was like sticking a needle in my heart as I caught my breath and whispered, "Cancer?"

"George, it's the second most common form of Cancer in men. If caught early enough, it's highly treatable."

I repeated. "Cancer, now what?"

"We need to run some more tests when you're out of the woods with the blood clots. If the numbers are accurate, we'll need to have you see a urologist and perhaps a urological oncologist."

"Will I still be here in the hospital?"

"Nope, prostate Cancer is normally a slow growth situation and delaying a few weeks won't make much difference, so we need to first focus on your initial stabilization and then proceed."

"Why now?"

Doctor Goodman looked out the window and then at me and added. "There was a doctor by the name of Hamer in Germany who correlated 5,000 Cancer patients and found they all had some form of physical or emotional catastrophic situation that preceded the onset of their Cancer. This might be the case with you and what you're currently going through or it might be a coincidence. Nearly 25% of all Caucasian men end up with the malady, while 40% of African Americans and 15% of all Asians are in the same boat.

Right now, we need to focus on the blood clots and why they happened to make sure they don't reoccur, then we can focus on the other stuff."

In an instant, my few minutes of relief were gone. On day eight, I was transferred to the step-down floor which was half way between ICU and a regular room to allow to me to begin to re-stabilize my life.

I called Amy and shared the PSA news. I needed to share it with someone.

That afternoon Jack and Melia arrived. "You're looking good!" Melia offered.

I took in a very deep breath and replied, "Dodged a bullet!"

Melia glanced at the pulse oximetry and saw a reading of 96% and was relieved. Because of Melia's medical background and her concern for how I was taking it, Amy had already shared with Melia the PSA numbers.

"Dad, mom told me about the other issue. It's very common and quite treatable, if caught early enough."

I replied as I tried to wipe the concern from the corners of her eyes. "I know and please don't worry. Perhaps it's a mistake. They're going to run some more tests when I'm out of here."

The hospital had a fifteen-minute cap on step-down visits and so the conversations bounced from the kids to Mineral Point football to the Badgers and back to me.

Melia inquired. "Do they think the clots are genetically inherent or because of all the flying you've been doing?"

"They don't know. If it were just one blood clot, they'd attribute it to flying. However, with seventy, they don't know."

Melia looked at me with one of those intense looks only a daughter can elicit and said, "Please take care of yourself."

"I will. I promise."

Visiting time was over and the nurse came in to shoo my guests away. Imagine driving over two hours for a fifteen-minute visit in a hospital with a wing named after your Grandmother where you started your residency.

19

"Thanks, dad. We love you."

For the first time since I don't know when, Melia gave me a kiss on the cheek. Melia stopped at the door, turned, smiled and offered. "When you get out of here. We need to have a family get together."

"That sounds great!" I replied as the room became empty, except for the aroma of compassion which had just lifted my spirits by simply thinking about tomorrow only to be quickly smothered by the silence of singularity that re-entered my world. I touched the spot where the kiss had been, softly smiled and thanked God I was still alive.

Amy came and was allowed to stay for dinner. We ordered off the menu and the food was actually quite good. Her dark eyes met mine and a soft smile pursed her lips. "I love you." Amy whispered in a tone I hadn't heard in years. Perhaps, just perhaps, the fear of me leaving had rekindled the spark missing in our lives for such a long, long time.

**Just George:**

The next morning Jane, the phlebotomist came in. I called her Vampira Jones as she sucked blood from my arm. Next it was Sarah Branson, the physical therapist, who went through what the next few days were going to be like with walking the next big step to my recovery.

Sarah dropped by for a very few minutes and outlined the plan of attack to get me up and running as she called it. Phase One was a 'meeting' where she slotted an hour the next day to go through the whole physical aspect and she began.

"Mr. Terrill."

"George, please."

"Please? What?"

Just what I needed, another smart ass. If one in the room wasn't bad enough. Sarah began. "Basically, the human body can be broken down into autonomic systems including the reproductive, endocrine and neurological systems. Beyond which we have the muscular, cardiovascular, respiratory, skeletal, digestive and lymphatic network, which all work in unison to keep us alive."

"Got it," I confirmed.

"We have five critical sense organs which allow us to reach beyond our own existence and participate in the world around us. They are our eyes, ears, nose, tongue and skin."

"What about pipe?"

"Pipe?" Sarah inquired with a frown.

"You know, pipe organ."

Sarah's left cheek compressed as her mouth contorted in pain at my feeble attempt at humor. She continued after I promised not to butt in. "When we use these five elements properly, our world comes to life and find we have vision, hearing, smell, taste and touch who create a pallet of inputs to enhance, adjust or enforce our thought processes and allow us to simply be who we are. Because you weren't ambulatory, your five motor organs...hands, legs, mouth, rectum and sex organs were literally unused and have begun to atrophy."

I thought of the last one on the list and agreed as Sarah continued. "These organs allow us to move beyond here and now and expand our horizons. While controlled by our brain, each system has needs. They can stop working, which can then be somewhat but not totally compensated for by the others."

I nodded in agreement as Sarah continued. "Failure of any one of the autonomic systems can kill you and, yet, we take them for granted until they stop functioning properly. Then, like the motor organs, they become the focus of our attention. My goal is to help you develop a set of goals and diets to assist in sustaining your health within each of the systems through rest, exercise, nutrition and sustenance."

All of a sudden what I thought was a point of potential levity made me realize six days of looking at the ceiling was a whole lot worse than what she was talking about and so I began to listen in earnest.

Sarah continued. "What sets us apart is how all the systems work together to create the physical self and from that, our own self-concept. While vanity is a declining aspect and/or ever-increasing challenge as one ages, it's still a factor that plays an integral part of our own self-concept. When you look in a mirror or examine a photo, you see your reflection and either like or dislike what you see. We all do it and then compare what we see to others and judge what we are by what we think is there."

I nodded in the affirmative as Sarah added. "We all have reference standards...height, weight, hair, eyes, teeth. VERY few of us don't see something we wouldn't like to change about our appearance we sincerely feel would make us more attractive to...who else...the opposite sex. We use air brushed physical specimens to set our reference standards and wonder why we're so frustrated with ourselves."

Sarah asked me to sit on the edge of the bed and I did as she continued in a very introspective tone. "The physical self is about so much more than appearance and the autonomic aspects. It's about how the body integrates neural clues and creates responses therein. Eye-to-hand response plays an integral part in sports. Overall appearance plays such a profound role in social acceptability to the point where people outside the parameters of normalcy, are often ostracized."

"What we are physically is based on a set of genetic footprints laid down by our ancestors. Skill sets are predicated on our genetic code and are one of the few things we can't really control. No one can will themselves to be taller. Men cannot will themselves to have full heads of hair. Eye color is not a selection process. So many of us are challenged by our weight and constantly told that, for health reasons, being thin is critical. We do have the ability to build and/or train muscles to work in unison so we can be better than we would be without the development and that's why I'm here."

There was a pause and then Sarah concluded. "The secret to long term physical health goes beyond genetics and into what we all can do to help sustain our body integrity. Number one on the list is obviously exercise, both physically and mentally."

I realized, for years, my exercise consisted of running to the bathroom in the morning. Researching materials for my dreamed-about book and having very frank discussions with the medical support team convinced me I needed to increase my physical activity level to improve my overall health.

Sarah added. "Walking is a wonderful way to slow down the aging process. The *Journal of the American College of Cardiology* reported people who run less than an hour a week have the same health benefits as people who run more, regardless of age, gender, body mass or health conditions. Statistics from doctors who surveyed 50,000 adults over a period of 15 years, indicate runners had a 30% lower risk of death overall and a 45% lower risk of death from heart disease or stroke than non-runners and lived an average of three years longer."

Sarah's tone changed again. You've been sedentary and we need to get you up and physically functioning where each day we will try to go a little further as we increase while maintaining your heart rate at a level prescribed by your cardiologist. Sarah outlined we'd start with the walking and then I'd go downstairs and start on a treadmill and riding a stationary bike then begin doing a light workout with weights to improve muscle tone and finally swimming. By doing this, Sarah noted I'd be helping my cardiovascular system and improving muscle tone.

Sarah looked at her watch and, like everything else in the hospital, time is money and my time for the day was up. She stood, looked at her I-pad and said. "Tomorrow we begin. See you at ten."

Whoosh! She was out the door, leaving me anticipating the next day and wondering what to do with the rest of the one I still had until Amy arrived.

**Blue Croc Shoes:**

I watched the hands on the clock and, just as she said would happen, at precisely ten, Sarah walked in to push, pull, urge, cajole and coax me out of my dark labyrinth of soft pillows and lumpy mattresses.

"OK, George, time to begin. Each floor lap equals 330 feet and we need to get you up walking," Sarah pontificated.

"Let me see…330 feet to the floor and 5,280 feet to the mile. Bet you want me to have a goal of sixteen laps per day," I offered with a proud grin on my face.

"You got it!" Sarah replied.

"You need to remember, I'm a veteran rehabilitator. When I was young and foolish, I flipped my Jeep and spent three months in Meriter Hospital in Madison where my drill instructor put me through the same boot camp."

"You ready to give it a shot?" Sarah inquired.

"Heh, I can put on my big boy pants and go solo."

"You've been in bed for ten days. I think I'd better go along for the ride, if you don't mind."

"OK but only if you put on a gown and have your bare butt hanging out the back like mine," I snickered.

"Not going to happen. We've got another gown for you to put on backwards so you don't gross out all the nurses and other patients. No more dancing cheek-to-cheek down the hallway."

"Darn! There goes all the fun." I retorted.

"For me or for you?" Sarah inquired.

"That's up to you."

"Do I have to wear the lousy cloth slippers or can you get me a pair of those blue Crocs like you guys all wear?"

"Sorry, they're hospital issued and I can't sneak another pair."

"Hmm. Tell you what. Go down to the big chief's office and tell them George Terrill is getting belligerent and wants a pair of blue Crocs or he's going to cry."

"I know…baby blue…right?"

"All right. You win! I'll wear the slippers this one time but do so in protest."

We began our first lap in what was to become a regular routine as Sarah giggled and shook her head. "I heard you're a real piece of work from the nurses and I can see why you've earned that reputation."

"Sarah, you've got to realize, ten days ago I had a five percent chance of being alive for three hours. For six days I was on a respirator staring at the ceiling, unable to talk, which almost killed me. For the first time since I got here, I'm starting to feel good...perhaps too good…and so I need to celebrate the only way I know how and is by trying to put a smile on your face and everyone else's."

While I tried to include a little levity, I guess it came out pretty intense. Instead of the smile I hoped for, I got a very serious look as Sarah inquired. "Did you really invent Medigolve?"

"No, I didn't. The people on my team did. All I did was put the team together."

"But you won a Nobel Peace Prize".

"No, **WE** won a Nobel Peace Prize".

"Is it true the Pediatric wing of the hospital is named after your family?"

"Actually, my wife's"

"So, Doctor Williams was your mother-in-law?"

"Yup!"

"Was she as great as they say she was?"

"Everyone here saw her in her medical realm. Beyond here, she was my mother-in-law and grandma to our kids and one of the finest people I've ever known. Kind! Considerate! Humble! Generous! Funny! Oh my God, she could make you laugh until you thought you were going to pee your pants."

"Why are you staying in a regular room and not one of the VIP rooms upstairs?"

"Because, I'm just an old farm boy from Wisconsin who doesn't like having his ass kissed. If I went upstairs, everyone would be fawning all over me which would divert some of the attention other patients deserve. I just want to be George, if you don't mind. Just another patient who has hopes, dreams and goals who only wants a few things out of life…simply to feel wanted, needed and loved. Like everyone else who comes through the emergency room doors, I was born and someday, will die. In between, my goal is to make my life and hopefully the world a better place than when I arrived."

We stopped at the end of the hall and Sarah looked at me and smiled. "You're more than just a piece of work. You're kind, generous, gracious and, above all else, humble. I'm honored to work with you."

Wow! I wasn't expecting that and so I countered. "I've got something you need to promise."

"What?"

"I'm just George. Today, tomorrow and always. I only want to blend in. Nothing special! No ooohs and aahs! Just an old man on the mend…a patient who's just like everyone else...except maybe the blue Crocs."

Sarah creased a slight smile. "Well, maybe we could bend the rules one time."

"One more thing."

"What?"

"Do you have any books on basic anatomy and physiology I could read?"

"We have a pamphlet on the subject."

"Anything would be fine."

"Ok, you got a deal!" Sarah replied as we finished lap one and I was gassed. Three hundred and thirty feet and I was tired. Tomorrow I'd try for 660 or even 990, whoopee!

Day two was a killer. Not like seventy blood clots, mind you, as Sarah put on her drill instructor hat and made me push until I thought I couldn't take another step. I was exhausted and she didn't even break a sweat as she offered. "Running and increased cardiovascular activity from walking and riding a bicycle has the ability to balance out other things that increase the risk of early death such as obesity, high blood pressure and smoking."

We stopped in front of my room and I was panting like an old dog on a hot summer's day as Sarah concluded, "Within reason! It's imperative we all accept who we are. We can't make excuses! However, we need to realize no one is perfect and by exclusively modifying our appearance won't make us richer, sexier, happier or more intelligent."

I collapsed into bed and thought about what Sarah shared and surmised there were several challenges to physical health not in your normal book of do's and don'ts. I thought of my self-mantra... physical, mental and spiritual health and realized, without physical heath, nothing else would ever have full value or true meaning. I vowed I needed to accept age meant new and different challenges. Yet, I also needed to realize and continue to focus on maximizing my health through proper mental, dietary and exercise protocols to create a calmer and more serene existence!

The challenge for me consisted of the realization there are so many solutions to so many issues, people simply can't keep up with them all. However hearing, 'less than five percent' meant I really needed to focus on the big ones and hope for the best for all the rest.

**The Discovery:**

When Sarah said sixteen laps I thought it would be easy. Wrong! The first few laps were dedicated to simply reaching 'home' or my new room. As they increased in number so did the boredom and then the curiosity regarding who else was stuck on floor number six wanting nothing more than to go home.

On day four of my not-so-merry-go-round, I peeked in a large room and saw a group of elderly ladies sitting in wheel chairs and it almost broke my heart. So alone! So isolated! So sad! I went to the nurse's station and inquired.

Marge, the head nurse, pointed out the ladies were all stoke patients too sick to be released to a nursing home.

"In other words?" I inquired, almost not wanting to hear what Marge had to say.

Marge nodded. "Several of the ladies have no family except for their roommates. They're here all alone, and have no visitors. They all know what's next and they call the place 'the last stop', as in the last stop before heaven.

My eyes closed as the pain of knowing eight people waiting to do nothing more than die overwhelmed me.

"Is there anything I can do?" I inquired.

"Not really. They're too sick to go anywhere."

"Can I at least talk to them?"

"Sure! I think they'd like that. All they ever see are medical people and social workers and having an outsider come and visit might cheer them up."

"When's a good time?"

"Well, mornings are when we run tests and the doctors visit and they all go to bed early." Marge paused for a moment, reading my level of disappointment and asked. "How about right after lunch?"

"Two o'clock?" I inquired.

"Sure," she said with a smile.

The next day I sauntered down the hall in my hospital gown, still attached to my IV pole, and put on a broad smile as I entered the room. For the next half-hour I told every clean joke I knew, talked about the Badgers, Packers and Brewers and, finally, the weather. When my 'session' was over, I promised to come back the next day and left eight ladies sitting there wondering 'Who in hell was that idiot?'

The next day at precisely two I showed up again and one of the nurse's aides helped put my 'lady friends' in a semi-circle with me in the middle. For the next hour I read the Milwaukee Journal and we kibitzed and joked about all the stories to the point even some of the ladies began to smile.

The next day it was the same routine, except by the time I got there, the ladies were waiting. As we were finishing the newspaper, a lady by the name of Florence asked me if I could read the obituaries. I thought, 'My God, why?' and inquired.

"Well, when the day comes there's nobody older than me, I know I'll be next."

Day four arrived and so did I. The ladies were in a circle and as I unfolded the paper one of them asked, "Are you George Terrill?"

"Yes."

"Did you invent Medigolve?"

"Well I didn't, but people I have the honor of working with did."

"Didn't you earn a Nobel Peace Prize?"

"Yes, we did." I offered.

"Thought so." The lady replied.

"Why did you ask? I inquired.

"Because most people don't want anything to do with old decrepit people like us and you're spending time making us feel better about ourselves and that's special."

"I'm not special. I'm just another patient down the hall who's trying to get better."

We read the paper and joked around and I told the ladies I'd see them the next day.

Amy came every day for dinner and it gave me something to look forward to and would always ask "Is there anything I can bring you?"

"How about a Copps hamburger and chocolate shake?" I replied. "Ask Nurse Ratshit if it's OK."

It was, and the next night Amy and I snarfed down the first real food I'd had in two weeks. While it wasn't Terrill beef, it sure tasted good.

Day three saw Amelia and V drop by. They came by chopper and we talked about all the programs they had going on with the Hochunk, and how quickly the kids were growing. Fifteen minutes flew by and then they were on their way back to their reality. God, it was good to see them.

Sarah had the weekend off and it was good to see her on Monday. She asked for my progress and I told her I was up to twelve laps and only made passes at three nurses per day.

"Still not 100%?"

"Nope, not until I've offended the entire staff," I chortled.

"Was the pamphlet any help?"

"Sure was! I learned a lot about things I took for granted."

"Any other things you want to learn about?"

"Only, how do you keep your sanity here."

"We've got a pamphlet on sanity and I'll have it brought up to you."

Another pamphlet! Whoopee! Sure enough, a couple hours later someone put the pamphlet on my table while I was taking my afternoon nap and quietly slipped out the door. I woke up and read it and began writing again. My hot dinner date was still a few hours away and I thought I could write down some more words of wisdom.

Amy and I had dinner ala cafeteria that turned out just like when we were first dating. No pretense! No hoity toity! Simply my wife and I enjoying each other's company.

"Any progress on your book?" Amy asked.

I smiled and handed her a few more sheets.

### The Mental Self - Part One:

Quiet time meant more writing. I'd received copies on mental health, took a whole bunch of notes and began writing. I realized there were actually two aspects to the mental self. As I sat pondering my own health, Cassandra Johnson knocked on my door.

"May I come in?" she inquired.

"Sure, why not?"

"I'm the hospital's Occupational Therapist."

"Huh? I don't need a job."

Cassandra or Cassie as she asked me to call her, smiled and replied. "An occupational therapist helps people participate in the activities they want and need to do through the therapeutic use of everyday activities... occupations... where my goal is help people regain, maintain, or improve the skills they need to do those activities.  Our basic protocol has certain parameters concerning patients who have spent extended periods of time immobilized or suffered traumatic experiences."

"You mean like seventy blood clots and six days, strapped to a bed on a respirator, looking at the ceiling?"

Cassie pointed her finger at me, smiled and said "Yup!"

"I think I need a psychiatrist more than an occupational therapist." I countered.

"Well, you're scheduled for both."

"You mean I got a two-fer?"

Cassie frowned as I responded. "Two for the price of one."

She politely smiled, nodded in agreement and began. "Well, I'm here to talk about the basic mental part to make sure you can function the way you could before."

"OK. Let me have it."

"The mental self is the part of us that's responsible for our thoughts, emotions, and memories which combine to makes us who we are and allows us to interact with the world around us. It's complex and ever-changing and is influenced by our genes, environment and experiences while being influenced by our thoughts, emotions, and memories. It's essential for our survival and well-being and allows us to make sense of the world, to learn and grow, and to form relationships with others."

"In other words, it's a lot different than being here, right now?" I inquire.

"Not really," Cassie responded. "This place is simply a microcosm of the world except it's more structured and personalized. Yet, for the sake of those who work here...who by the way...are also people who have their own mental selves, it's somewhat institutionalized and depersonalized simply because the people here deal with life and death and therefore can't allow their emotions to override their professional duties."

I pondered her explanation and saw what she was talking about made sense. I was in a life or death situation and for me it was obviously quite important. They see it every day and acclimate to the drama, if that's what the right word is. If they let every patient tear at their heart strings, they'd end up like Mela who simply personalized everything.

Cassie continued. "I've heard you're very intelligent."

"Compared to who or, for that matter, what?"

My response caught the evil eye as Cassie added. "There are many factors that contribute to intelligence, including genetics, environment, and personal experiences. Because of your... uhh... experience and the fact you were restricted by the respirator, we need to make certain your faculties are consistent with what they were prior to your attack."

"Ok, but why are some people more intelligent than others?" I asked thinking of Peter and the Madcity Boys in particular.

Cassie smiled and began. "The first component that determines your mental acuity is genetics. Studies of twins and adopted children have shown intelligence is about 50% heritable. Numerous genes come into play and there's no one gene which determines intellect."

"How about Levi's?" I interrupted.

Cassie took a deep breath of exasperation and continued. "It's important to note genes alone do not determine intellectual destiny. Even if you have smart genes that might make you more or less intelligent, you still can't use them or, if you weren't born with the right genes, develop your intelligence through environmental factors"

Right away I'm thinking of the forest as Cassie added. "The home environment in which you grow up can have a significant impact on your intelligence. Factors such as nutrition, education and exposure to stimulating experiences can all help boost your intelligence."

After having the joy of knowing Sir Francis Bacon and his training regimen, I realized I could learn a lot more than I already had, thereby motivating me to do what I call tunnel learning...taking a subject and digging into it until I know more than I did before and hopefully more than many other people.

Cassie continued. "Another key element can be your personal experiences. For example, if you're exposed to challenging problems and are encouraged to think critically, you're more likely to develop your intelligence."

My mind wandered as I thought of Peter, Luke, the MadCity Boys and how Amy always made me strive for more as Cassie added. "It's important to remember intelligence is not a fixed trait. It can be developed and improved through both genetic and environmental factors."

Cassie paused, smiled and looked at the pile of papers on my night stand, nodded and continued. "People learn in many different ways. Some people learn best by reading. Others learn by listening, watching or doing. There are many different theories about how people learn, but most experts agree learning is a complex process involving both cognitive and affective or emotional factors."

I was getting impressed. This lady knew her stuff and I decided to keep my smart-ass mouth shut.

"There are some important factors that influence learning. As an example people are more likely to learn something if they are motivated to do so. Motivation can come from a variety of sources, such as curiosity, interest, or a need to achieve a goal."

Or hanging around with a bunch of really intelligent nerds, I thought.

Cassie recited. "People need to be able to pay attention to what they're learning in order to learn it effectively. Attention can be difficult to sustain, especially when the material is boring or difficult to comprehend. In addition, people need to be able to remember what they've learned in order to use it. Memory is a complex process that involves both short-term and long-term progressions."

This was making sense and I vowed I'd write it all down and send it to Ceclia to add to my dossier.

Cassie wasn't done as she noted. "People need to understand what they're learning in order to use it effectively. Understanding can be difficult, especially when the material is complex or abstract and they need to practice what they're learning in order to master it. Practice can help solidify memories and make learning more automatic."

I morphed farther into my serious mode and realized I needed to pay more attention and stop minimizing what this lady knew.

Cassie smiled and continued.  "Learning isn't a one-way street. People need feedback in order to know how they're doing and to make corrections as needed. There are several different strategies that can be used to improve learning. One is called active learning which involves engaging with the material in a meaningful way through reading, writing, discussing or doing something with the material."

My mind flashed back to college where I went from being the village idiot to doing relatively well as soon as I learned how to learn, which in my case was writing everything down. For me, if it went through my hands to my mind, it stayed. If it just went through my eyes, forget it...which is what I originally did.

Cassie continued. "Repetition helps to solidify memories and make learning more automatic as well as organizing the material which can help to make it easier to understand and remember while visualization can help make learning more concrete and memorable."

"Finally, there's what's called metacognition which is the ability to think about one's own thinking. This can be helpful for identifying difficulties in learning and developing strategies to overcome them."

I realized my six-day introspection actually had a name... metacognition and I was relieved to learn I wasn't wacko.

A smile crossed Cassie's face as she realized she'd hit a homerun in terms of getting my attention and more importantly my respect as she concluded. "Intelligence only happens through learning which is a lifelong process. As we learn new things, we change our brains and our minds. Learning can be challenging, but it's also rewarding. By understanding how we learn, we can improve our learning and achieve our goals."

"In other words, knowledge and wisdom," I surmised.

Cassie slowly shook her head 'no' and continued. "Knowledge is the accumulation of facts, information, and skills. Wisdom is the ability to use knowledge to make sound judgments and decisions. Knowledge is about what you know. Wisdom is about how you use what you know." "Knowledge can be acquired through education, experience, or both. Wisdom, on the other hand, is more than just knowledge. It's also about understanding, insight, and judgment. Wise people are able to perceive the big picture, understand the implications of their actions and make decisions in their best interests as well as the best interests of others."

While I'm certain it wasn't her goal, Cassie had put me in my place. I initially had little respect for occupational therapists when she first walked through the door and a profound amount of respect when she left simply because she taught me something that made me realize the value of what she did.

The session was almost over as Cassie and her obedient patient went through a litany of coordination and word assimilation exercises as she concluded the patient in room 620 hadn't suffered any long term or permanent setbacks during his hospitalization.

As was always the case, the proverbial time machine, better known as her I-pad, went 'ding' and she knew she had to go work with another inmate as I began calling myself. I thanked Cassie for the lesson in learning and the answer to my own self-proclaimed mantra regarding the mental self...or at least the intellectual part of it.

### The Mental Self  - Are You Nuts?:

The days were blurring and actually becoming a daze. Goals were set and routines established. I got to know the nurses and they got to know me. In other words, I was becoming institutionalized.

After seven daze on the rehab floor, I thought I had it all down until Doctor John Haugen strolled in.

"Good morning, Mister Terrill. I'm Doctor Haugen, the hospital psychologist."

"I've been waiting for you Doc. This place is driving me nuts." I joked.

Not even a smile, nor any twinkle in his eyes, just the incessant need to bite the purple bulge on his lip and push his glasses up his nose.

"Mister Terrill, after a patient has a near-death experience there can be instances of emotional instability and my role is to ensure that you understand the circumstance and provide guidelines regarding regaining any possible lost positive mental momentum.

I thought, positive mental momentum? What the hell does that mean?

Doctor Haugen sat down, crossed his legs and began.
"Good mental health is essential for a happy and fulfilling life. It allows us to cope with stress, maintain healthy relationships and achieve our goals. There are many things we can do to improve our mental health, including eating a healthy diet, getting regular exercise and enough sleep, which are all important, not only for our physical, but mental health."

I thought he and Sarah went to the same college and took the same class except Haugen had about a half dozen pens in his lab coat chest pocket that made me wonder, why in hell do you need six pens with you?

Haugen continued. "The World Health Organization defines mental health as 'a state of well-being in which the individual realizes his or her own abilities, can cope with the normal stresses of life, work productively and fruitfully, and is able to make a contribution to their community'. Today, there are many different types of mental health problems, some of which are common, such as depression and anxiety disorders, and some not so common, such as schizophrenia, bipolar disorder and dozens more."

"OK?" I thought as my mind flashed to my wife and my complete understanding of what it's like to live with someone who's bi-polar.

Up went the glasses as Haugen continued. "The most important thing is to be happy and that's what I'm here to talk about. How does one become happy?"

I wanted to say, by being left alone, but thought I'd better not. They still had dull needless and straight-jackets."

Haugen continued. "Spending time with loved ones and building strong social relationships can help us feel supported and connected and make us happy. While stress is a normal part of life, it can take a toll on our mental health if we don't find ways to manage it. Exercise, relaxation techniques, and spending time in nature are all great ways to reduce stress. If you're struggling with your mental health, it's important to seek professional help. A therapist can provide you with the support and tools you need to cope with your problems and improve your mental health. By following these tips, we can improve our mental health and live happier, healthier lives."

I thought, so far what he said could have been printed on the back of a Rice Krispies box.

The legs uncrossed, Doctor Salt leaned forward and seriously inquired. "Mister Terrill, are you happy?"

I sort of cringed and thought. Let's see. I almost died. I spent six days looking at an f--ing ceiling, haven't seen my kids in nearly three months and just learned I've got Cancer. Based on that I replied. "I'm happy to be alive."

"Well, that's good, but what about the rest of your life?"

"What rest of my life? I get to see my wife for 30 minutes each night. I'm awakened to the sound of bed pans rattling. I've already memorized the breakfast menu and talk to eight old ladies every day who are simply waiting to die. Ain't life grand!"

Legs crossed, glasses pushed up his nose, lip bit and it's time for Georgie to lay it all out. "There are many things that can make a person happy. First are good relationships with family and friends which I have. You see, I believe strong relationships with people we care about are essential for happiness because they provide us with love, support and a sense of belonging."

I was on a roll. Perhaps I shouldn't have, but the weeks of terror and frustration had reached a boiling point and this poor guy was getting the net results. "Next are meaningful work or activities. When I'm engaged in work or activities I find meaningful, it gives me a sense of purpose and satisfaction which is why I started the Derrick Williams foundation and Terrill B&B. Third is good health which, until I took a nose dive into the tarmac at the airport, I thought I had, only to be surprised by *'you've got Cancer'*. You see, Doctor Haugen, when people are physically and mentally healthy, they're better able to enjoy life and experience happiness."

I looked at Doctor Haugen and pronounced.  "Right now, I guess I'm batting two for three, right Doc?"

Haugen looked at me with a sense of disbelief. He was being challenged instead of being considered all-knowing and I'm certain he'd been told our family donated millions to the hospital and so I continued. "Fourth is a sense of security. When we feel safe and secure, we're less likely to experience stress and anxiety. Being institutionalized doesn't help promote that sense now does it?"

I sensed I was being facetious and so I calmed it down as I added. "Another really important practice is gratitude or simply taking time to appreciate the good things in our lives, like the people here. This helps me focus on the positive and allows me to forget the Cancer growing in me and my recent near-death experience."

"I won't deny I'm scared. I won't deny everything I do isn't an act that allows me to hide what's really going on. But it's really tough to have a positive outlook on life when it's been threatened. Because I didn't die and because of all the people here, I can see the good in every situation, even though things are tough."

I was on a roll and didn't want to stop and so, being somewhat brave and totally an ass, I continued by asking, "Why didn't you ask about joy instead of happiness?"

"I...I consider them the same," Haugen replied.

I gave him a look of surprised derision and noted. "Joy and happiness are often used interchangeably, but there are some key differences between the two. Joy is a deeper, more lasting emotion than happiness. Happiness is often fleeting, while joy can last for a long time."

Haugen's mouth dropped open and let his glasses slide while I added. "Joy is more spiritual than happiness. To me happiness is associated with pleasure and good times while joy is associated with a sense of purpose and meaning making joy more resilient than happiness."

I leaned back on my pillow and added. "Doc, happiness can be easily shaken by negative events like seventy blood clots, while joy is more resistant to change like having a family who loves you and eight old ladies who wait for the clock to strike two each afternoon."

"I might feel happy one day and sad the next, but I'm more likely to feel joy even when things are tough. Ultimately, joy to me is a more profound and lasting emotion than happiness. It's an emotion rooted in my sense of purpose that can help me to weather the storms of life."

Doctor Haugen sat with his mouth agape. He came in as the teacher and became my student as I stripped away the facade and let him see what it's really like to nearly die and then be told you won the battle but not the war.

It was time to go for the closing statement and so I did. "From all the above, I should consider myself blessed to the point

I'm trying to give back to others, such as the ladies down in the stroke patient ward. Helping them is making me feel good about myself and making their world a little better. Sadly, so many people today only think about what it takes to make themselves happy. When you live in the present, you're less likely to dwell on the past or worry about the future. So you see Doc, ultimately, what makes each person happy is unique to that individual but the consummate sense of happiness can pervade all the trials and tribulations of life that can evolve into a sense of joy **IF** one sincerely feels wanted, needed and loved."

Doctor Haugen scratched his head, uncrossed his legs and stood. He looked at the old man lying in bed and simply said, "thank you."

I looked at him and replied. "You're welcome," as he walked out the door. My brain was tired. It was almost time for my dinner date and so I stopped for the day. It certainly was good to go from ceiling staring to literally being busy all the time with pamphlets and papers, strewn across my room even when I had visitors who wanted to find out if I was nuts.

**Lighting the Candle:**

Amy arrived and it was wonderful to see her. After so many years together, I think we both had been taking each other for granted. Each afternoon, I'd do my writing and then look at the clock and count the minutes until she appeared.

As was the case whenever Amy literally materialized, the staff stood at attention and did everything they could to make her feel welcome as they attempted to stand out amongst the masses. I guess money can do that and it was the last thing either one of us wanted and was probably the reason why Amy loved France so much...simply because no one knew who she was.

We had yet another gourmet meal from the cafeteria. Just the two of us, as she offered.  "George, I've been reading what you're writing and it's simply wonderful. Please don't stop."

I was honored to think she liked it and promised to keep pen in hand even though it would have been easier to use my laptop. There's something about the swirls of emotion that can't be duplicated by pressing on some buttons in sequence to take thoughts and emotions and place them on a screen.

"I heard you gave the staff psychologist a tough time."

I shook my head in dismay and apologized to her as I noted. "I didn't mean to but he got me going on this ephemeral stuff about whether or not I was happy and I simply gave him my opinion that happiness is transitory while joy is longer lasting."

"George, you can't give the staff a bad time.

"Perhaps I was tired. Perhaps I was frustrated. Perhaps, perhaps, perhaps and I should have known better than to euphemistically compete with authority, but I did.

"What did you say?"

"Good and bad are two concepts that have been debated for centuries. There's no one definition of either one. What's considered good or bad can vary depending on culture, time period and individual perspective as can the concept of giving someone a bad time. To give someone a bad time means to annoy, tease, or harass them. It can also mean to make things difficult or unpleasant for them. All I did was show Doctor Haugen there could be greater depth to our conversation if he would allow it."

"But you offended him!"

"Because he sat in that chair and pretended to be all knowing when all I did was ask a rhetorical question about the difference between happiness and joy. The guy asked me if I was happy. What a stupid thing to ask. Of course I'm not happy being here, being almost dead and learning I've got Cancer. You know what it's like. You know how it feels. Were you happy?"

I didn't wait for Amy to answer as I continued. "Yet, there's still joy in my heart because I have you and three great kids I love. If that's bad, then I'm bad.  Good and bad are defined by society and culture that are constantly evolving as society changes. I think, there are different factors that influence how we define good and bad that include our family and friends, religion, beliefs, education and experiences, the media and the laws and regulations of our society and our government and when someone walks into a hospital room and asks you if you're happy, I think they're bad. I didn't give the psychologist a bad time, I just challenged his logic and he got pissed.'

"But you shouldn't have."

"Why not? If we all sublimely sit and listen to bullshit, the bullshit becomes fact and then decree. All I wanted to do was make him think and not be so...so arrogant. If I gave him a bad time and everyone thinks that, I'm sorry. However, ultimately, it's up to each individual to decide what they believe is good and bad.

I was on a roll and should have stopped but mighty mouth kept going. "In general, good is often associated with positive qualities like kindness, compassion, honesty, and integrity. Bad is associated with negative qualities such as cruelty, selfishness, dishonesty, and lack of integrity. This guy's supposed to help and not come in and question the obvious. If I insulted or offended him, I'm sorry. I'm going crazy here and he came to see if I was already there."

I looked at my wife and became sincere. "Amy, mental health is more than just emotional balance. It's also intellectual sustenance that allows a person to grow while remaining both physically and mentally healthy and capable of logical reasoning. The physical therapist briefly outlined our five senses but I believe there are four more...the sense of being, the sense of belonging, the sense of purpose and the sense of humor. These aren't autonomic responses, nor intellectual, nor do they come about from reasoning. They manifest themselves only in the spiritual self that can lead to our one true goal – joy...not happiness which is transient. Sadly, joy is profoundly difficult to achieve because every time we think we're there, something else pops up and we have to move the marker!"

I took one last sip of my now-dreaded, apple juice and added. "Doctor Haugen and I talked about the mental self but skipped the part about dreams and the role they play in our lives, where dreams have a profound influence on motivation. Because dreams allow us to "see" beyond the immediate we're all inherently susceptible to being unhappy. Our dreams tell us it can be better. Our reality tells us it's not. Whether its loneliness, dependence, failure or being ostracized, we all seek those elements we interpret as needed to satisfy our existence and make it complete."

I slid one elbow down to my knee and looked Amy right in the eyes. She knew what I was about to add, was something I truly believed in. "If we act as benefactors of our heritage and have truly improved our moral, ethical, spiritual, empirical and intellectual standards we inherited, then we need to transfer more than our genetic structure to those who follow. These become our dreams of what can be. Whether it's as simple as looking better, feeling better, acting better or evolving to such things as accomplishing something that's never been done before, we all have hopes of what will happen, should the change be made. If this is the driving force, then it can serve as the engine that works for the betterment and modification of our position in life and our spiritual self. But what happens to our current existence?"

Amy's mouth was open as she and I hadn't talked like this in years simply because deep, deep thoughts had become coated with the fine layers of daily life, like dust upon the dresser, that held so many other things we never had time to pull out and explore.

I was now in an intense philosophical mode as I literally stared and added. "For some, dreams and aspirations are so weak and shallow they create no action whatsoever and they become mired in 'now'. For others, dreams become so intense, they become narcotizing and those dreamers find the scope of their existence narrowed like a white-hot spotlight, to a very fine focus, to the point they begin to feel as if the accomplishment of a single objective will serve as nirvana."

I leaned back in my chair and continued. "Obviously, there are different magnitudes of dreams...those of grandeur, retribution, accomplishment and dominance are but a few that permeate us all. Equally important, our dreams take on different perspectives in the different stages of our life to the point where age isn't determined by years on the calendar but more by attitude. When we're young, we dream about the future. When we reach middle age, we dream about today. When we're old, we ponder yesterday and what could have been".

I leaned back further in my chair as Amy did likewise signaling a change in intensity. "God didn't provide us with the same sense of satisfaction the Chimp, elephant or gorilla seem to enjoy. He's given us the ability to believe we can do something about it."

"It's our interpretation of what we need to do to make ourselves happy that moves us to action. So, in the name of happiness, we move on...in our jobs...in our social existence...in our personality...in our marriage or interpersonal relationships and finally, in our expectations of where we want to be and how we each define the word 'success' and, although biased, this becomes our personal definition and measurement of our accomplishment with one ultimate goal, simply to bathe in the majesty of joy. It's amazing how those goals can change. Until two weeks ago, I had a grand set of goals, then it became only to wake up alive the next day. Now, it's to get out of here and back to some sense of normalcy."

It had been a long, long time since my wife had heard me expound. At first, I thought I was going to catch holy hell until Amy simply shook her head, smiled, wiped a tear from her eye and whispered. "Welcome back. I've missed you, my love."

### Isms:

Another day, another set of laps, another meeting with the ladies. I made it back to my room and had a stranger waiting for me. Her name was Gladys Johnson who was from the hospital's executive team. We had a pleasant conversation and she asked why I was in a regular room and not one of the suites. I told her my goal was to be treated like a regular patient without all the fancy stuff. I think she was surprised. I really didn't know why she was there. I think Doctor Haugen's experience made it all the way to the deep carpet section and she'd come to see if I was still ranting and raving. Perhaps to butter me up and ensure the Wilco gravy train was still making its annual stop at their front door. As I lay there thinking about Mrs. Johnson, I knew what I wanted to add to my folio and began writing.

"ISM'S! Socialism, Communism, Materialism No matter what our age, we've all lived through a period of personal and social peril...a period I'll call an 'ism' when social dynamics have been challenged to the point they have or had the potential of affecting the way we think, act and are perceived within our own society."

"While the Great Depression serves as nothing more than a point in history, profoundly, it defined our society and economic structure that has continued into the twenty-first century. To have and then to lose, is much weightier than to never have at all. The great depression ripped away the pretense of wealth, stripped away the concept of security and obliterated a sense of well-being. In its place, it left a country suspect, fearful and insecure. For nearly a decade the issue was not economic growth but sustaining one's life against what must have seemed to be incredible odds."

"Newton's third law of motion states that for every action there's an opposite and equal reaction. This law applies not only to physics but economics, sociology, politics and life as well. The Great Depression resulted in the development of economic, social and political structures designed to protect the masses from themselves and, in the end, created America's first threat to success and our first 'ism'... socialism, where, for the good of many, there are limits put upon the success of a few."

"While the ideal world had everyone sharing in the effort and reward of the system, the net result of growing socialism is a limitation on individual reward and potential curtailment of ambition. Socialism is an economic system in which the means of production are owned and controlled by the people, either directly or through state control. The goal of socialism is to create a more equal society by ensuring everyone has access to basic necessities such as food, housing, and healthcare."

"While this has tremendously assisted the overall well-being of our society, it has come at the expense of lowering the reward for effort invested for those fortunate, talented or lucky enough to succeed. Socialism then became the first 'threat' to our personal achievement.

"The second 'ism' that faced many did not come from within but was an incipient threat to our well-being and that was communism which is a more extreme form of socialism in which the state owns and controls all aspects of the economy, including production, distribution, and consumption and the goal is to create a classless society in which everyone is equal and there is no private property."

"While not directly exposed to its wrath, we were still emotionally bludgeoned by the threat of nuclear war that had millions of kids in air raid drills in elementary school trying to hide their bodies and souls beneath their desks, all the while having flashbacks of the devastation seen from films of the American atomic attacks on Japan."

"The ideological conflict between the United States and the Soviet Union saw our country attempt to prepare us for nuclear war while trying to convince us we might possibly survive. The net result was a profound sense of angst which permeated lives and innocence, burning an incredibly powerful image in minds, hearts and psyche... leaving those most affected feeling as if there was no future... subconsciously believing there was no long-term existence... having people sense tomorrow would truly never come as they all knew and understood was culminated in total oblivion from a nuclear warhead less than thirty minutes away."

"While there are many points and events in time that are evolutionary, there are truly few which are revolutionary, changing our thoughts and habits and the way all of us live. I call them tectonic moments where an abrupt shift results in an earthquake of social change. The 1963 assassination of President John F. Kennedy represents one of those instances. Not only did it demonstrably mark the end of the age of innocence for America, it created what so much of our world has become today...a nation of exploiters who take the smallest nuance, expand upon it, create an issue and then reap its bounty. While the assassination riveted all of those alive to their television sets for the very first time, it also showed the broadcast industry that a total news format could not only exist but thrive."

"Instead of the newspaper or thirty minutes of daily TV news, America became a nation and then a world of non-stop information. With this, the demand for immediate information gratification began as people no longer found it tolerable to wait for the morning edition, we needed to know 'now'."

"While this has been both good and bad, the reality that the media had to satisfy 24 hours of content, instead of 30 minutes, began a downward spiral which has yet to reach bottom. Stories that once would never made the news become national headlines repeated over and over and over again and again and again, until every minute detail is drummed into viewer's heads. Today, events, circumstances and situations that reflect the abnormal are propagated until we begin to believe they're the norm and do so to the point that each passing year, our beliefs and values, concepts and elocutions have been devastated such that the core beliefs in our culture, society and way of life have been eroded and degraded to a politicized level of dissatisfaction, disarray and disbelief."

"The 1970's was an era filled with the response to two decades of profound social, cultural and political change that's almost impossible to comprehend! None reflected the growing changes more than the Viet Nam War brought into our homes in living and dying color. The battles in Viet Nam made people challenge our government and leadership and took them away from being a people who trusted and respected to one challenged, disregarded and simply disobeyed those who had established the system for their own benefit."

"In the end today's success is measured as an antitheses, where bad is good and good is bad, victory means defeat and America's social heart and soul was shredded into thousands of pieces, each representing a life, a thought and an intention, well-meant but gone asunder. Compound this with the social revolution that brought about action without consequence and total disregard and respect for authority in a liberated world and the table is set for the continuing profound re-modification of our own definition."

"What an incredible time! For sixty years America has lived in a state of revolution...social, political, ethical, sexual...all intersecting at one point called 'now' in the most formative state for three generations who sincerely believe Newton's Law does not apply...and taking everything and pushing it to the extreme until the extreme becomes the norm that is then pushed even further."

"I've read that the sixties really were times of intense excitement, fear, frustration, fornication, experimentation and revelation where everyone truly assumed they were important and could 'change the world... rearrange the world'. I can only imagine these times and imagine periods of distrust, disbelief and fear, that fomented social uneasiness remaining today. For the generations who came after them... I believe the time was an age filled with stories and acceptance of what was and what is and realization that earlier times were times  truly changed their world... opening many doors... good and bad, that had never been opened before."

"I've often wondered why so much happened in such a short period of time. It would be difficult to go back and piece together all of the different parts of the puzzle that made everything happen as it did. I guess we would have to look at the sociological impacts of the post-war baby boomers, television, birth control pills, the cold war and threats of nuclear holocaust, Viet Nam, race relations and even the Interstate Highway System and then try to inter-connect the pieces to see how each impacted our existence, expectations and relationships, whose dots were connected by one thing…music which led the way for so much of what changed and how this form communication not only reflected upon, but helped perpetuate the upheaval society created, participated in, and survived."

"When my parents were in school, each of these people and concepts were introduced, accepted or rejected and became part of the normal set of values by which all people in our society are now judged. I really don't know what happened, but the thriving excitement simply folded as that generation molded and 'We' became the 'Me' generation...uptight, selfish, materialistic... a lot like their grandparents, except perhaps more cynical."

"How did it affect the following generations? As the snow quietly settles upon our temples, I wonder if what our parents did really made any difference. Are we any better? Is our world a better place in which to live? Are their children and our children any happier? Again, Newton's third law prevailed. Again, we witnessed a society changed, incorporating a new sense of purpose, values and dynamics which established what was right and wrong for all of us to strive for."

"One of the saddest consequences lies in American government that has morphed into nothing more than a group of individuals who've become brands, where the promise of popular representation is elusive, if not illusory. Choices for President are scant, government agencies hoard public power and interest groups and political action committees easily determine the fate of those without money and therefore the power over those who disagree with them. Our national elections are filled with bloated promises, staged deference to the voter and flashy debates that prize spectacle over substance with political parties simply hawking a commodity - namely the candidates, where voters are simply shopping among the available merchandise."

"As the final decades of the final century of the last millennium came into place and the overt threats that pervaded our society, government and psyche began to subside, we began to live without the focused external threats we had become accustomed to.

"Instead of tranquility, we found ourselves embroiled in the largest, most incipient threat to our existence...a pervasive enemy so powerful and so dynamic as to shake our social order and threaten our virtual existence. This threat is so powerful and yet so pervasive, it challenges our social, political, economic and even religious foundations, shaking them as they've never been shaken before... threatening all that we have cherished for eleven generations... challenging our values and our goals...redefining who, what and where we are in recorded history."

"This 'ism' is profound and, yet, evasive...elusive and yet so blatant that it stands before each of us day after day... questioning who, what and where we are in our existence, redefining our concepts of accomplishment and success while narcotizing the entire populous into following the rhythmic beat of its drummer."

"It's more profound and more pervasive than all that have come before. It's more threatening and potentially more damaging than all we've faced. It has the ability to simply destroy our way of life and do so in a manner that will leave the populous divided and defeated, unable to achieve any form of social peace and welfare. This 'ism' has started from within...an economic model we export around the global village we call earth. This 'ism' is materialism... the acquisition of 'things' for the sake of ownership."

"In one generation the bar has been raised concerning every single element within the basket of our existence, making each of us longing for more and larger items to maintain what we perceive to be a 'basic' style of life. Such things as single car garages and one-bathroom homes now seem quaint and obsolete when 70 years ago, garages and even indoor plumbing were still beyond the reach of many. Our accumulation of physical things has transcended into our basket of accumulated experiences where elements such as vacations become expected and items as innocuous as children playing soccer and baseball have become paid-for, organized "experiences" that connote different degrees of acquisition."

"Sadly, for some reason, our concept of care evolved to a point that we attempted to protect our children from anything negative. To play games without losing and awarding trophies for simply participating might be all right for little ones but that's not how life works and the generational expectation of entitlement is really hurting our country."

"Today, our world has become one of 'packages' such as packaged homes meeting certain socio- economic criteria based on income, lifestyle and age, to package experiences, also based on the same set of criteria. We've become a meringue society…a great deal of fluff but little or no substance."

"We live in huge homes with rooms we never use, next door to people we hardly know that we never think to talk to. We take our children to soccer or football or ballet as we text someone we hardly know, never realizing that our occupants are also strangers in our lives…simply appliances used to measure our social credibility factor… married/divorced, big house, two children, two cars, one dog…ain't life great!"

"Once again, Newton comes into play. The cost of the extreme is the extreme cost. We run our economic race, always uphill. We find ourselves over-extended financially to the point that 35% of all Americans are past due on their bills and make the only available sacrifice they can… giving up precious time to sustain our 'dream' world and our 'dream' existence…now working more than any other society on earth…now more hassled, more frustrated, lonelier and isolated… and more emotionally devoid of the spirit that we aspired to. Add to this the fact that, in twenty years, our society went from 61% considered middle class to only 50%… a sad barometer on what and where we are going."

"Our short-term costs are profound…lost time, lost energy, lost senses of accomplishment, purpose and well-being. Our long-term costs are pathetic…social strangers who have brought isolation and loneliness into the area that deserves our highest sanctity...our family!"

"Gone is the sense of being special. Gone are the redundancies that only come from repeated encounters at the breakfast and dinner tables interspersed by social solitude as everyone ponders their most recent text upon their phone. Gone are those quiet moments when people gather only for the sake of each other! All replaced by harried schedules where strangers meet in the name of tradition."

"We idolize equality and individualism, yet the unrealized dreams of women, Blacks, and Native Americans and belie the concept of 'equality of condition' simply because the family has been hollowed out. This 'equality' has led to loneliness, hedonism, broken families and disaffected, disenchanted, disinterested young adults, while those who have done what they could to sustain their family wonder if those in loose-knit groups can ever be conducive to social progress and continuation of our democracy."

"Where are these issues most exacerbated? In our children! Imagine a high school with 1,000 students. Now visualize about 450 of them saying they are persistently sad or hopeless, 200 saying they've seriously considered suicide and nearly 100 saying they've tried to end their own life **in the past year.** "

"At one time, school was a sanctuary where goodness prevailed before assaults turned them into fortresses of fear exacerbated by the daily onslaught of those who want to die and take innocents with them using assault weapons made for war and not little children. When little girls, who dream of being princesses and little boys of playing football are cut down and become nothing more than horrifying statistics, we all should admit that what we have and who we've become as a society is simply wrong!"

"And what is the result of this insanity? We're all aware of its persuasiveness and yet we find that it has defined the concept of success and simply moved the bar of expectation that much higher, eradicating another share of what was once 'middle class' and delineating it to either lower middle or upper middle, depending on whether we're a two-income professional or two-income blue collar family. Beyond that, with 40%-50% of all first-time and 60% of all second-time marriages ending in divorce, we find 35% of all children under the age 18 living in a single-parent, single income homes and 25% living in households with a mother alone, where one income devastates the concept of well-being on a daily basis, fomenting anger, frustration and isolation in tomorrow's populous."

"Defining our roles by where we shop...Target or Wal-Mart... what we drive...used car or new SUV...and where we vacation...Europe or Branson, Hollywood or Dollywood we see the divide between the rich and poor degenerating into political polarization and rampant populism that appeals to ordinary people who feel their concerns are disregarded by established elite groups. Profoundly, the disaffected are attracted to a group of smooth-talking politicians who don't lead the same lives, don't face the same challenges and don't understand what it's like to be challenged daily by the anxieties of American expectations because they're well educated, wealthy and privileged and have structured politics to ensure they remain that way for the rest of their lives through special pensions, special health insurance programs and special perks many populists don't even realize exist."

"In our germane world, I believe we all live in a state of 'anticipatory expectation' meaning we make adjustments and modifications to our natural selves because we anticipate the expectations of others and society with only one real goal...to better 'fit in'. To accomplish this we relinquish some of our uniqueness and freedom to garner the approval that we all need. In so doing, we create a 'protective wrapper' that insulates us from life's bumps and bruises. It's this protective wrapper that defines 'what' we are instead of 'who' we really are to our children."

"For people to truly understand each other, they must be accepted... warts and wrinkles, habits and foibles, beliefs and expectations for who and what they are."

"When people are truly attracted to each other physically, mentally, emotionally, intellectually, socially, acoustically and spiritually, then the evolution is natural and the risks mutual while 'being visible' evolves with comfort and joy as the lives of people become intertwined, based on trust, acceptance and the sincere belief that it's special and forever."

"In order to be truly successful, I now realize I must be capable of standing completely naked in front of myself and those I cherish. It's only then that both they and I can understand what I **really** am... without adjustment, without anticipation...without calculation of what others will think."

"And so, I think I have it...a changing definition of the concept of success and how that definition affects, controls and dissipates roles as parents, teachers and mentors as well as the mental self by controlling our own self-concept. All of this is predicated on the mental self. Yet, in order to succeed, a definition must be developed if I'm to refine not only what I am but who I am as well. From these self-concepts, I believe I need to develop a plan to ensure my life's journey and that of our children such that it is wrought with pleasure, joy and satisfaction. If I can achieve this, my final destination will be blessed with a profound sense of fulfillment called joy, that includes or results in the creation and nurturing not only the mental self but my spiritual self as well."

My dinner date arrived and told me she was really impressed by what I'd already written. I handed her the next epistle, which she read and then asked her if she thought I was pontificating. She noted there were spots where I was probably a bit too rancorous but realized it was simply my passion showing through. I thanked her for the comments, kissed her goodbye and then it was time for her to leave. She told me she loved me which was the best medicine I had that day.

## DRE:

As I got involved with the ladies and waited for my numbers to balance, I almost forgot about my PSA until one night I was asked to drink what tasted like swill and told to keep the bathroom door wide open. I did and boy, you talk about being happy I did. The next morning there was no breakfast as I needed to have what was called a DRE which I learned was short for digital rectal exam. NOT FUN!

The next day, Doctor Ramine walked in and introduced himself. He was the urologist assigned to me.

"Well, George, we've examined the samples of your prostate and determined you do have prostate Cancer and your Gleason's, which measure the type and veracity of your Cancer, are seven/eights, which means your Cancer is moderately aggressive. We have several options we want you to consider. The first is radiation therapy which is broad based and would probably slow your Cancer. The second type of treatment is proton beam therapy, which is more finite but requires 37 treatments over a six-week period. Finally, there is a nerve sparing radical prostatectomy where we surgically remove your prostate. Each option has its pluses and minuses."

"The proton beam procedure is a one-shot deal and can't be repeated. This means that, if we have to do the prostatectomy and don't get all the Cancer cells, we don't have any reserve insurance."

I looked at Doctor Ramine and I could sense that what he was saying was, "Heh buddy, you've got Cancer that's growing relatively fast and you better get the stuff out of you and keep the proton beams as insurance."

I reiterated this conclusion to the good doctor and he nodded. No one likes to hear that they are about to have a life changing procedure and yet the logic of it all was making sense.

"You need to talk it over with your wife. There's no rush, but you do need to be aware of what's going on."

I looked at this man and could sense the compassion as I replied, "Understood."

With that, reality set in and the good doctor was gone, leaving me alone to consider my fate and bringing me back to the certainty of life. I never professed to being bold and this was one instance when that self-concept was certainly playing out.

**Father Pat:**

Later that morning, after all the doctors, nurses, aides and social workers had departed, a priest walked into my room. At first I thought I'd died, but could still hear the noise in the hallway and concluded he either had the wrong number or had been instructed to soothe the rabid beast who'd upset the resident psychologist.

"Good morning George. How are you feeling today?"

"Not bad!" I lied.

"I heard you had a close one."

"Yup, sure did!" not knowing if he was talking about the blood clots or Haugen salt.

"Well, it appears God isn't ready for you yet. I'm Father Pat. Part of my calling is to work with those who've had a near-death experience and that's why I'm here. I've come to see if I can be of any assistance."

"I'm not Catholic," I replied.

"Well, I'm not from Wisconsin. Does that mean we can't talk?"

"I guess not."

For some reason Father Pat's warm smile was melting the ice between us and it did seem good to have someone who wasn't always in such a hurry to talk to.

"I heard you're a big Badger fan."

"Sure am!" I replied.

"I went to Notre Dame. You won't hold that against me, will you?"

"Only if we were playing you this week." I offered.

"Are you a religious man?" Father Pat inquired.

"Not much. I was raised Methodist in Mineral Point and somewhere along the way, I got out of the habit of going to church." I responded in a somewhat embarrassed manner without realizing the double entendre.

"Church isn't for everyone," Pat replied. "I had the same experience. Got married. Got a job as an accountant and thought I was set for life. Cancer came along and took my wife and with it my life and I really fell down the rabbit hole of self-pity. One day when things were really bleak, I was in Walmart and ran into this old guy by the name of Charlie O'Brien. Charlie was in his eighties, had trouble breathing due to COPD and couldn't pick up a big bag of dog food. I stopped and offered to put it in his cart. Our eyes met and something happened. I don't know what but there was an instant bond between us."

Pat continued with a slight, sanguine smile on his face as if reflecting on a memory he cherished. "I asked Charlie how he was going to get the bag in his car and he said he hoped a good Samaritan would help him. I was about done shopping and offered to get in the check-out line behind him and help. I followed him out to the parking lot and put the bag in there for him."

Pat leaned back and continued, "'How are you going to get it out when you get home?' I asked. Charlie noted that he lived with his sister and they normally took the dog food out one bowl at a time."

"'Do you live far from here?' I inquired. "A few blocks," Charlie replied, as he was already taking deep breaths from simply walking to the car."

"'Do you want me to follow you home and put it in the house for you?' I asked.

"'That would be really nice of you.'"

"I followed Charlie to a small ranch house a few blocks away and watched as he pulled into the garage. I walked up the driveway as he opened the trunk. 'Where do you want me to put the dog food?' I asked."

"'We keep it in the laundry room so Mabel doesn't get into it.' I could tell by the tone of his voice that Mabel had to be his dog. Sure enough, in the kitchen with tail wagging was an aging, profoundly overweight Beagle with white whiskers and droopy ears all happy to see Charlie and this stranger who was carrying her dinner."

"Charlie reached for his wallet and I frowned. 'Please, I didn't do it for money. I did it because you needed some help.'"

"'Thanks but I didn't get your name.'"

"'I'm Pat, Pat Byrne.'"

"'Well, Pat, can I at least give you a cup of coffee?'"

"'That sounds great,' I replied."

Pat paused for a moment to let all that had transpired soak in and then continued. "We sat at the kitchen table and began a conversation that changed my life. You see, Charlie was a retired priest. His hobby was woodworking and all the dust probably caused his COPD. Charlie was far from svelte and actually looked a lot like the cartoon character Ziggy. In fact, he fondly admitted that a lot of the kids called him Father Ziggy."

"I asked Ziggy what it was like to be a priest. He said, everyone thinks the challenge is the lack of sex but you get over that. He said the real problem was the singularity. While he was a firm believer in God, going to bed each night alone was the worst part. He knew he didn't have long until he hopefully would be able to talk to God in person and prayed he'd made a difference."

"I told him about my job and my wife and how I was now alone. I shared the sadness and sorrow and how I, too, felt all alone. We talked for three hours about anything and everything from sports to family, even the politics of the church."

"In that period, I went from being all alone to realizing why God had put me on this earth…to work with people like you, George…to hopefully help you through your darkest hours and see if I couldn't help you realize there  a reason for what transpired."

Father Pat paused and looked out the window before continuing again with tears in his eyes. "I loved that man and when he went 'home' I knew why God had sent me to Walmart…why Ziggy needed help with a bag of dog food and why I'm here today."

"George, I know you've accomplished an incredible amount for mankind. I know you won a Nobel Peace Prize. I know you're held in high regard with the Hochunk Nation. Yet, I also can sense a level inadequacy…a profound sense of disappointment… like you're questioning if there isn't more… more to life…more to what you're supposed to achieve."

"For several days I've passed by your door and didn't stop. Then, a few days ago, I heard the nurses talking about some crazy patient who's ignited the candle of life on a group of lonely, elderly ladies who are simply waiting…and in some cases hoping and praying…to end their lives. I knew then, that I had to meet this man. I vowed I'd stop by, simply to be in your presence to see if the aura of goodness prevailed."

I was humbled. What started as nothing more than satisfying my curiosity was being transformed into a life-changing experience. Yes, I'd started the foundation! Yes, we'd accomplished a lot! However, there was still a yearning inside me for more. Was the foundation nothing more than another business venture? While I was the conductor, wasn't it the Mad City boys who'd created the melody of greatness that changed the world?

Father Pat looked at his watch and I knew it was time for him to go. As he arose from the chair and stood next to my bed he asked me if I would join him in the Lord's Prayer. For the first time since who knows when, I nodded, agreed and recited those long-lost words.

Father Pat shook my hand and asked if I minded that he stop by the next day and my only response was, 'Please'. When I arrived in the ward at two that afternoon, there were only seven chairs. One of my lady friends had departed. Nothing was said but everyone knew and wondered who'd be next. We read the paper and kibitzed but there was still a chill in the air.

Amy came for dinner and we had our evening conversation. She asked how my day went and I told her about Father Pat and the empty chair. There was joy in my heart to have what I just knew was going to be a new friend and sadness as I realized one of my 'lady friends' had departed. I told her about the test scores and she knew I was concerned.

"You're getting the best care there is and they probably caught it early enough, so let's leave it at that." Amy lamented. Amy noticed that the pen and paper were on the table with nothing written on them.

"Not in the mood?" she asked.

"No time," I responded. "Perhaps tomorrow."

It felt good having Amy there and I really wanted to go home but my numbers were still all over the place.

## Dots:

The next morning, the routine was back to what it had been and after Vampira, I thought I was done until Nurse Nancy came in and told me I could take a shower. "Whoopee!" It had been two weeks and boy did it feel good. I had just put on my jammies and crawled into bed when Father Pat walked in.

"Good morning! How are we doing today?" Pat inquired.

"Not bad for an old man. Up and able, ready to go."

"Want to talk about religion?"

"Uhh!" I replied.

"Come on, let's see if we can't break down the barriers between us so that you're not so...so constricted."

"OK."

Father Pat glanced at my table and asked if he could have a sheet of paper. Generous me handed him the entire tablet upon which he put a small dot and asked, "What does the above small spec represent to you?"

"Uh, very poor penmanship," I replied.

"Is it a black dot on a white page or a white surface surrounding a black hole?"

"I give up."

Father Pat continued. "With only one surface, there is no reference except to the other! No direction! Virtually no meaning! Add another dot and the entire thought process begins to change. Now there can be direction and the dots become the point reference. Connect the dots and you have a line from the beginning until the end."

With that Pat drew a line between the two dots and showed it to me. I remembered it from Uncle Will, but thought I should be courteous and allow him to continue which he did. "Such is life! We all have two dots...our birth and death. It's the life path that we follow between the dots that matters and our belief in the consequence of our existence. Along that path, we all need to develop many things...a concept of self in terms of our relationship with others, right and wrong, good and bad, permanence and temporal existence, which is where spirituality comes in, and what men have interpreted. You see, George, religion is simply a structured form of spirituality interpreted by a bunch of men who, like you and me, have or had, strengths and weaknesses and were both good and bad."

"Today's humans are not unique in this! As long as man has been able to escape his here-and-now in both time-and-space, the questions of who, what and why have lingered. There are a plethora of varying ideas ranging from profound belief in an omnipotent to the belief that there's nothing beyond this instant."

"Like everything else, there are extremes for a few and the middle for the rest of us. When attempting to grasp the concept of the spiritual self, explanation becomes a real challenge as it's incredibly difficult to develop any sort of philosophy that transcends all the different concepts with any degree of equity."

"While the science of the human body is based, for the most part, a cause-and-effect hypothesis, the perceptions of human existence are not so. Instead, we all end up with a myriad of different hypothesis that, when homogenized into one treatise, is not a soliloquy but a summary, not a mandate but a set of alternatives; done so, not as fact, but an interpretation from which one, and one alone, can deduce their own conclusions."

I offered Father Pat the chance to sit down and he did. Through a little string pulling, I'd arranged for a second chair in my 'office' for my dinner date and sat across the small table from the man who was quickly impressing me.

"I heard you almost died."

"Yup!"

"I heard they don't know why you're still alive."

"Yup!

"I heard you're a real piece of work."

"Yup."

"I also heard that every nurse on the floor wants to take care of you because you make them laugh and feel alive."

"Can't answer that one."

Pat looked at me, stopped for a moment and then asked. "What do you think happens when you die?"

"I don't know. Do you?"

"Nope!"

"I do know what happens when you think you're going to die?"

"What's that"

"You think about all the things you didn't do and not the things you did.

Pat inquired. "What do you hope happens when you die?"

"People miss me."

"What about you?"

I thought for a moment and took a deep breath. When you think it's going to happen, it gives death a whole new perspective. "I hope it's not the end, but a transition from one form of existence to another."

Pat smiled and nodded in the affirmative.

"Then you believe in God?"

"Yup"

"Would you agree that God is a being who is worshipped as the creator, sustainer and ruler of the universe and is often described as being omnipotent or all-powerful, omniscient or all-knowing, and omnipresent all-present?"

"Are you talking about God or my wife?"

Pat chuckled and added, "God is also often described as being loving, merciful, and just."

"Well, one of the three leaves Amy out."

"Which one?"

"Merciful." I replied with a wicked grin.

Pat looked at the floor, paused to catch his train of thought and then noted. "We all use the words nothing and everything all the time and yet, they are absolutes representing the two extremes of existence. Nothing is the absence of anything, while everything is the presence of everything. Nothing is a difficult concept to grasp, because it's something that we cannot experience directly. We can only experience the absence of something, such as when we're in a dark room or sound asleep. However, we can't experience nothing itself."

"Everything, on the other hand, is something that we experience all the time. We are surrounded by everything, from the smallest atoms to the largest galaxies. Everything is constantly changing and evolving, and it is impossible to take it all in. The difference between nothing and everything is a matter of perspective. From the perspective of nothing, everything is just a collection of meaningless particles. From the perspective of everything, nothing is just an empty void."

"However, from our own perspective, we exist in a state of both nothing and everything. We're made up of particles, but we're also more than just the sum of our parts. We have thoughts, feelings, and experiences that are unique to us. We're part of something larger than ourselves, but we're also individuals. The duality of nothing and everything is a mystery that we may never fully understand. However, it's a concept that's worth thinking about, because it can help us better understand the nature of existence."

Pat continued. "There are many different religions in the world, and each religion has its own beliefs about everything and nothing, life, death and God. Some religions believe in one God, while others believe in multiple gods. Some religions believe God is personal. Others believe that God is impersonal. Some religions believe that God is involved in the world, while others believe that God isn't. There's no one right answer to the question of who God is. Each individual must decide for themselves what they believe about God. However, for many people, the belief in God is a source of comfort, strength and hope."

"What about heaven, eternity and sin?" Pat rhetorically asked.

I replied, "Heaven is located fifty-two miles southwest of Madison, called Waldwick. Eternity is how long it seems I've been in this hospital. Sin is having the Badger football team play Ohio State in Columbus"

Pat shook his head and added. "Heaven and eternity are often used interchangeably, but they're actually two different things. Heaven is a place, while eternity is a state of being. Heaven is the place where God dwells. It's a place of perfect peace, love, and joy. It's a place where we will be reunited with our loved ones who have gone before us. It's a place where we will be able to worship God and serve Him forever. Eternity, on the other hand, is a state of being that's characterized by everlasting life. It's a state of being that's free from sin, death, and suffering. It's a state of being full of love, joy, and peace."

I thought, 'I certainly hope so. With my luck, I'll go to hell, be with my friends and there won't be any bars to go to.'

Pat asked. "What do you think sin is?"

I paused for a moment and gave my response. "Sin is anything that makes someone else unhappy even if it makes you happy and transgresses all living beings."

"Including animals?"

I thought of Francis and nodded in the affirmative.

"But you're not a vegetarian."

"Nope, but I make certain that the living beings around me are given a higher quality of life to compensate for a shorter quantitative existence."

Pat continued. "To me, sin is a transgression against divine law or the law of God. Each culture has its own interpretation of what it means to commit a sin. While sins are generally considered actions, any thought, word, or act considered immoral, selfish, shameful, harmful, or alienating might be termed 'sinful'."

Pat continued on. "In the religious context, sin is a transgression against divine law or a law of God. Each culture has its own interpretation of what it means to commit a sin. While sins are generally considered actions, any thought, word, or act considered immoral, selfish, shameful, harmful, or alienating might be termed sinful."

"In Romans 3:23, sin is defined as 'missing the mark' or 'falling short of the glory of God' In other words, sin is anything that goes against God's will. This includes things like disobedience, rebellion, selfishness, and unforgiveness. With this interpretation, sin has a number of negative consequences. It can damage our relationships with God, others, and ourselves. It can also lead to guilt, shame, and condemnation"

"However George, there's good news for those who have sinned. Jesus Christ died on the cross to pay for our sins. He rose from the dead, conquering sin and death. By trusting in Jesus Christ, we can be forgiven of our sins and have a restored relationship with God."

"But who decides God will?"

Pat paused as he knew where I was going.

"It's an interpretation of right and wrong." He replied.

"Who decides what's right and wrong?"

Pat took a deep breath. "Well, that's where it gets sticky."

"I know, I read my uncle's book about how things were uhh...interpreted in Medieval time. Let's just say no one should demand perfection until they're perfect themselves."

"I totally agree."

"Instead, I have my own rules....what's right is what makes you happy without making anyone else unhappy. What's wrong is what makes either you or them unhappy."

"That's a really broad statement."

"It's a really broad subject. The difference is that my rule allows for change, your rules were set by a bunch of old guys centuries ago who thought the earth was the center of the universe and flat."

"How about having a soul?" Pat asked.

I hadn't had discussions like this since college philosophy and answered. "Some people believe that your soul is a spiritual or immaterial being that's separate from the body. Others believe the soul is simply a product of the brain and that dies when the body dies. If I'm going to be baked and still believe it's a transition, I've got to have some part left and I don't know of a better name than soul."

"Pat nodded again indicating we both were thinking along the same lines as he asked. "Where does the soul fit in the universe?"

I interjected. "Hmm. Like I said, the soul is a difficult concept to define and there's no one answer to the question of where it fits. Steven Hawking said the net sum of the universe was zero. If so, where would the soul go and what would need to be given up? Having said that, Hawking also said the universe was expanding and so it might be doing so to give more room for all the souls. Beyond that, we only perceive our universe and it might be that we can simply go through one of the black holes to a whole bunch of universes and into a megaverse which would have more than enough room."

Pat responded. "There's no scientific evidence to support the existence of the soul, but there's also no scientific evidence to disprove it. Ultimately, the question of whether or not the soul exists is a matter of faith."

"If the soul does exist, then it's possible that it fits into the universe in a number of ways. It's possible that the soul is a part of the fabric of the universe or that it's a separate entity that interacts with the universe in some way. It's also possible that the soul is something we can't fully comprehend, and that its true nature is beyond our understanding. The soul is a mystery, and it's something we may never fully understand. However, it's a concept worth thinking about, because it can help us better understand ourselves and our place in the universe."

After almost finding out first hand, I asked. "How does the soul affect spirituality?"

Pat offered. "The soul is often seen as the spiritual or immaterial part of a person. It's believed to be the part of us that connects us to something larger than ourselves, such as God or a higher power. There are many different ways that the soul can affect spirituality. For some people, the soul is the source of their religious beliefs. They believe the soul is what allows them to connect with God. For others, the soul is the source of their sense of purpose and meaning in life. They believe that the soul gives them reason to live and strive for something greater than themselves."

"The soul can also affect spirituality in more subtle ways. For example, some people believe that the soul is what allows them to experience love, compassion, and forgiveness. They believe that the soul is what makes us human and connects us to each other. Ultimately, the way the soul affects spirituality is a personal matter. There's no right or wrong way to experience the soul and its effects on spirituality will vary from person to person."

"So you don't believe animals have souls?" I asked.

Pat shrugged his shoulders while I refrained from sharing how Francis, our pig had expressed that animals did. I'd already met with one psychologist and didn't want to spent time with another.

The discussion was getting pretty intense when Pat deflected it by asking, "What about spirituality?"

"You mean the spiritual self?"

"Yes."

Now we were getting to the real meat of what I wanted to know as my treatise about oneself dealt with the physical, mental and spiritual self. I asked Pat, "Tell me what you think."

Par replied. "The spiritual self is the part of us that's connected to something greater than ourselves. It's the part of us that knows our true purpose and meaning in life and therefore determines right and wrong, good and bad and should serve as the foundation for our life's premise."

I nodded in the affirmative, visually urging him to continue.

"It's the part of us that's connected to the divine, universe or to whatever we believe in. The spiritual self is often seen as the part of us that's most authentic and true. It's the part that's not afraid to be who we are, no matter what others think that's filled with love, compassion and understanding. It's not always easy to access and can be buried deep within us, hidden by our fears, doubts, and insecurities. But it's always there, waiting to be discovered."

Pat paused for a moment to gather his thoughts and then added, "I believe the spiritual self is the part of us that's connected to something greater than ourselves. It's the part that's aware of our own mortality that seeks meaning and purpose in life that's compassionate, loving, and forgiving. While often associated with religion, it doesn't have to be. Spirituality is a personal journey and there's no one right way to experience it. Some people find spirituality through prayer, meditation or spending time in nature. Others find it through their relationships with others, their work, or creative pursuits."

Pat smiled and continued. "George, there are many benefits to connecting with our spiritual selves such as finding the meaning and purpose in life, allowing us to cope with stress and difficult time as we develop stronger relationships and live a more compassionate and loving life to the point we experience greater happiness and well-being and experience joy. The most important thing is to find what works for you. There is no right or wrong way to connect with your spiritual self. The important thing is to be open to the possibility of something more."

I had my answer. I'd been pondering how to express my feelings and he had it and gave it to me as I became somewhat introspective as if Pat had opened a locked door that had been closed for a long, long time.

Pat continued. "When we connect with our spiritual self, we feel a sense of peace, joy, and love. We feel connected to something greater than ourselves. We feel like we're part of something special. It's one of the most important things we can do in life. It helps us to live a more fulfilling and meaningful life. It helps us to find our true purpose and meaning in life. It helps us to become the best version of ourselves."

Father Pat smiled and added. "As you can see George, this entire philosophical exercise has no end to the point that it's my proposition that the spiritual self is the establishment of relationships from man-to-man and if you so believe, God-to-man, through man's belief in something greater than himself as reflected in his relative position within the absolute order, not only of mankind, but the universe as well."

"In so doing, spirituality takes into consideration all forms of relationships by creating a set of parameters that address right-from-wrong, good-from-bad and what is expected by our family, society, culture and, again, if so believed, our God."

"The spiritual self goes way beyond the rational self to address the question of, 'Why?'. Why do I exist? Why must I act the way that I do to be accepted? Why am I doing what I do and for how long will I do it? Finally, what are the consequences of my actions?"

"If you want to reflect upon yourself and see these consequences, you must delve into the spiritual self and create a form of manifest destiny that provides a pathway to the accomplishment of a single objective...true happiness that must include not only your own happiness but that of others and not only your own security also that of those whose lives you touch! In other words, determining a physical, mental, emotional and rational sense of wellbeing!"

"The critical precursor is that life and happiness are already within you and readily available. It's only the question of learning how, when and where to open up your life to broader horizons that will allow you to reach that higher plane of individual, social and spiritual security and satisfaction so that you have a more profound sense of wellbeing and consequence."

The nurse came, saw that we were deep in discussion, simply nodded and walked away as Pat continued. "While this might seem somewhat simplistic, it really isn't, because it encompasses so many different variables including not only our relationship with our fellow man but our entire universe and then our concept of the consequence of our lives. The spectrum is broad and based on each and every set of life's permutations transcending not only philosophy but time as well."

Pat paused and then added. "There are many factors that go into our own sense of wellbeing but most of them are predicated on relationships. Amongst them are such variables as being healthy, rested and maintaining a good diet, having a positive relationship with our partner and a network of close friends, along with a beneficial level of self-esteem without being narcissistic."

"Add to good health, having an optimistic outlook on life, in general, along with realistic and achievable goals, a sense of belonging and purpose and meaning, supported by some sense of belief beyond here and now. Many of these components center around having a meaningful and fulfilling career and enough money to ensure you're not worried all the time while being able to adapt to change as it happens. All of these are interrelated and yet dynamic so that changes in one component affect changes in others while deficiencies can have profound consequences on other elements as well."

"What's really important is to accept that money is NOT linked to wellbeing. All money does is expand the options, improve living conditions and increase social status. It does NOT ensure happiness. It's the quality of personal relationships that predicate our sense of wellbeing and not the size of our bank account."

Pat smiled and sort of shrugged his shoulders while quietly admitting. "George, I know that an inadequate amount of money is never an issue with you and your family but what about having too much? Personal wellbeing is an extremely difficult accomplishment. In America 25% of all people report they're depressed, while only 20% said they're happy. This means 55% of all Americans were neither happy nor depressed...taking each and every day as it came, like walking on a treadmill. Step-by- step but going nowhere."

Pat paused for a moment and looked out the window again and then asked. "How does one achieve a sense of wellbeing?" And then continued. "When Virginia died, I was a wreck. I hated the world and God and everything he stood for. I blamed the hospital, doctors and even the Church. It was everyone else's fault until one day I looked in the mirror and realized I was as much to blame as they were to the point that I needed to give myself a broad-based level of intrinsic comprehension, where I reviewed not only beliefs predicated on a supreme being but those basic thoughts cemented in hypothesis of agnostic, humanistic and atheistic premises."

75

"Even after all the study I can't say which is the right set of thoughts, nor what my own personal inclinations are. In fact, I find myself in a maelstrom of provocative thoughts unleashed like never before. As my duty to those I come in contact with, all I can do is reflect on my conclusions and apologize if you find them confrontational to your own acquired deductions."

"What then are our boundaries? At what point have we traversed beyond what is considered normal? How do we, as social animals, create and maintain a set of parameters by which we can successfully interact with those around us from whom we need acceptance and social approval?"

"If we were isolated, this wouldn't be an issue. However, this ability to extend beyond ourselves remains profoundly difficult throughout life because most of us were socialized by people who never learned how to relinquish the reins and be physically, emotionally, socially and spiritually free."

"I became a priest to help people. When I chose my life path, I took the vows of chastity and obedience, to lead a life of simplicity consonant with the people I serve. There are things in the church, I don't agree with. However, underneath the structure and tradition lie inherent cornerstones which include the sincere desire to help others. We know those who weren't perfect. We know that when they're made examples of, it affects our ability to do good. Yet, because of our faith we persevere."

Father Pat was done for the day and so was I. He filled my mind with so much to think about, I really didn't know if I could write another word and then it all came to me. I quickly scribbled some notes as it was time for my evening 'date' who arrived precisely at six like she had every day where I shared what Father Pat brought to me to which Amy simply replied "Holy Shit!" which I felt was an apropos summation of the day.

**As Life Goes On:**

The one thing about hospitals you quickly learn is that there's a schedule and routine for everything. In the 'step-down' ward, Milwaukee General had what they called 'tandem nurses' who were 'matched' and worked three consecutive twelve-hour shifts and then had four days off. The nurses were 'paired' based on their personalities and many of them became great friends.

With the three-on, four-off, twelve-hour schedule, the patient – namely me - got familiar with the pair and if you were there long enough, learned the routine. Pair number one was Angie and Bree who were like peas in a pod…both young, all smiles, full of energy and compassion.

Pair two consisted of Samantha who everyone called Sam, and Regina who I learned her family called Gina but everyone at the hospital called Reggie. Reggie's tall for a woman. Not as tall as our Melia, who's taller than most men, but still above average height. She has the body of an athlete without being lanky, light brown hair pulled back in a pony tail at work along with piercing blue eyes and an effervescent smile.

Sam's African American with almond color skin and naturally curly hair. She has a beautiful face that's almost like some Egyptian goddess with high cheek bones that become accentuated when she smiles, which is often, that literally lights up the room. I particularly loved her hands with long lean fingers whose nails were always manicured but never outlandish.

The two were a little older, a little wiser and a little less idealistic. They were just as professional and caring, yet, you could tell they'd been around the block a few more times than Angie and Bree as the stars in their eyes has faded a bit. While they all treated me with care and compassion, I looked forward to the Sam and Reggie Show the most because they always had smiles on their faces and enjoyed my cut-ups where every smart-ass comment or double entendre I threw at them was volleyed back with an answer that made me smile.

Now two-times-three makes six and so, on the seventh day, you got what they called 'floaters' who filled in for the 'Three-Bees,' as everyone called them. The floaters could be anyone who were only there for a day before the cycle began again.

The teams either worked from 7:00 AM to 7:00 PM or vice versa. At the shift change, they'd come in together and report on your condition, explain what was going to transpire in the next twelve hours and then ceremoniously erase one name and add the other to the white board.

After ICU and thump/woosh, thump/woosh, thump/woosh, they could have sent a gorilla in and it wouldn't have mattered. However, as my health improved so did my wit and with it my sarcastic interaction and anything else I could do to make them laugh. My goal was to add a little levity to their lives so they enjoyed the few minutes we had together while giving me something – anything to look forward to. While I appreciated all the nurses, I repeatedly shared my satisfaction with Amy about Sam and Reggie as they certainly made my stay better than it would have without them and hoped we could do something special for them as a way of showing our appreciation.

On day number nine Amy called and said she was running late and wouldn't arrive until around six-thirty or eighteen-thirty in hospital time. I told her not to rush. I wasn't going anywhere. Around eighteen-forty-five, Amy walked and, as she entered, there was the familiar smile on her face that made me feel she was glad to see me.

"How was your day?" Amy asked.

"It was interesting," I replied.

"Tests?"

"Not really." I lied. "Just trying to climb the mountain."

We perused the dinner menu and I ordered meatloaf with cooked carrots, the obligatory Jell-O and more apple juice. God, I wanted some Terrill bourbon!  Amy ordered the chicken breast, peas and a slice of white cake.

The food went down and the clock hit nineteen hundred hours or 7:00 PM. Amy hadn't been there during a shift change and so she didn't know the routine. As we sat looking at each other, the highly acclaimed Reggie and Sam team walked in.

"Good evening, Mr. Terrill."

"Amy, this is Reggie and Sam and they're the three-bees who drew straws and got the short one and have been taking care of me."

Sam looked at Amy and smiled. As an African American, Sam immediately identified with her as one of the 'sisters' as Sam offered. "Good evening Mrs. Terrill. It's an honor to meet you. I knew your mother and have the greatest respect for all she did and what your family has done here at Milwaukee General."

"Thank you." Amy replied.

Sam went to the white board and erased her name. As she turned, she looked at me, smiled and added, "We don't get many patients like Mr. Terrill."

"You mean with his malady?" Amy inquired, while also garnering a smile.

"Well, if you want to call it that, yes," Sam responded.

"I hope he hasn't been too 'difficult'".

"Not really. I worked in Peds and I think he's about one step from there."

"Above or below?" Amy retorted, which brought a chuckle from everyone in the room.

It was Reggie's turn as she wrote her name on the white board and offered. "My name is Regina Heck but everyone calls me Reggie. I'll be Mr. Terrill's nurse tonight."

"You mean, warden, don't you?" I countered.

"It's nice to meet you, Reggie," Amy responded.

Reggie looked at Amy and then at me and offered. "If there's anything I can do to be of assistance to you or Mr. Terrill, please let me know."

"Well, thank you."

Reggie reached in her pocket, pulled out a business card and said, "Here's one of our cards. Please feel free to contact Sam or me if we can be of assistance. Amy went to the dresser opened her purse and handed both Reggie and Sam one of her business cards.

Reggie examined the content and saw that it was in French as she inquired. "You live in France?"

"We have a home there and I'm on the Board of Governors at the local museum which is why I have the cards. If you flip it over, I have our Wisconsin information and my cellphone number."

"France! I've always wanted to go there," Sam offered.

Amy replied. "You'll have to visit sometime. We also have a home on St. Martin as well."

I thought I knew where this was going but kept my trap shut. I'd shared with Amy how much I missed Sam and Reggie on their days off and what great care they'd provided where I didn't feel like just the patient in room 630 and more like a real person.

Amy looked at me and I nodded. I knew what was about to transpire and couldn't have been happier as she noted. "We have a guest house on Saint Martin and, for the wonderful care George has indicated you've been providing, we'd like to welcome both of you as our guests."

Both Sam and Reggie's mouths dropped open.

I'm certain they'd received gifts from grateful patients or their families before, but never a vacation trip.

"Really?" Sam inquired, incredulously.

"Yes, of course," Amy replied.

Amy paused for a moment and then inquired. "You work the same shift, correct?"

"Yes, we're what are called tandem nurses." Reggie replied

"You're on three days and off four, correct?" Amy inquired.

"Yes," Sam enthusiastically responded.

"We could fly you down and you'd have four days and fly you back or you could use vacation time and stay longer. The guest house is empty most of the time. It's up to you."

"Really?" Reggie excitedly inquired.

"Sure! You're welcome to bring your husbands or significant others, too. There's plenty of room and we have a car you can use. George has been treated incredibly well by everyone but has particularly felt your care and compassion and it's one way we can express our gratitude for all you've done for us and do for other patients."

Amy paused for a moment and then added. "We know how difficult your job is. Our daughter did her a residency here before meeting her husband." Amy lowered her voice and added, "I only have one request. This is for only you two. We don't want to set a precedent or want others to feel shorted."

Both Sam and Reggie nodded in the affirmative as they glanced at the wall clock and Sam announced she needed to excuse herself and get back to reality. With that, Reggie's attention turned to me as she noted. "Mr. Terrill, had a close one but things are looking better. If you need anything please feel free to call me.

Reggie turned back to Amy and offered her hand. As the two of their hands intertwined, Reggie noted, "It was very nice meeting you Mrs. Terrill."

"Please call me Amy."

Reggie said thank you again.

With that, the handshake ended and Amy's left hand went to Reggie's right shoulder as she stated. "I hope we can meet again and thank you for taking such good care of George."

The spell was broken and Reggie turned to leave. Pausing at the door, Reggie looked back at me and then at Amy and repeated, "It was an honor meeting you and thank you."

"Nice girl," I offered.

"Quite pleasant." Amy added as I returned to my solitary confinement.

### What's It All About:

Seven AM gradually arrived and the dynamic duo re-appeared with smiles on their faces and excitement in their hearts.

"Do you really have your own plane?" Sam asked.

"About thirty, the last time I counted."

"And we'd get to fly in one?"

"Yes."

"You're serious?"

"About as serious as seventy blood clots but you need to get me out of here first."

"You mean, you'd be going with us?"

"No, of course not. I've been grounded for six weeks until my body stabilizes. The two of you can go and take your husbands or boyfriends and everything will be arranged."

"Could it be just the two of us?" Reggie asked.

"If that's what you want," I replied.

"A whole house to ourselves?"

"Yes! It's called 'House on the Hill'. It was Amy's mom and dad's. We built a new home a couple miles away and decided to keep 'House on the Hill' as a guest residence for our friends, employees and very special people like you."

Reggie just stood there, somewhat in shock and then looked at me and said. "I've never been anywhere. I've only flown on a plane twice to Florida. Do we need passports?"

"Yes."

"How long does it take to get them?"

"I don't know. I've always had someone at our company do it for me. Tell you what, you and Sam go online and complete the application, get your passport photos and bring them here and I'll have someone take care of it for you in our travel department."

"You'd do that for us?"

"Sure, why not?"

Reggie simply shook her head in disbelief…a trip to St. Martin, a private jet, a house and a car and all for free.

"Yup. Except you will have to pay for gas."

"For the car?"

Smart ass me couldn't resist. "No, the plane"

Reggie's mouth dropped open in consternation until I let out a loud guffaw and offered, "Just kidding. It's all included.

In typical ladylike fashion the next question was, "What do we wear?"

Well depending on the time of day and where you're going, it can range from nothing to what we call Saint Martin dress casual consisting of longer shorts and a top."

"No dresses?" Sam asked.

"Only if you want to and then probably casual sun dresses. Mrs. Terrill can fill you in."

I paused for a moment and then remembered. "We award four trips a year to our company employees and I think there's actually a brochure personnel put together that explains everything. I'll text the office and have them send over a couple of copies."

"What's the weather like?" Sam asked.

"Right now it's hot and humid. The weather in the fall is when it starts to get beautiful as the temperature and humidity levels decrease and the breeze picks up. Temperatures from November to May range from a low of about 75°F at night to about 82°F during the day with plenty of sunshine. A couple of days you might have brief period of clouds and rain showers but they don't last long. Sometimes, there's a strong enough breeze to go parasailing, kite boarding and hang gliding. Jet skis are also available. We don't partake in any of these activities anymore as we're usually on a rest-and-relaxation vacation but we'll have it arranged if you want to do it."

"Sounds wonderful," Reggie offered.

"We love it there," I replied.

Sam needed to make her rounds and excused herself as Reggie stood at the end of my bed and continued. "What's it like on St. Martin?"

"Well, it's half Dutch and half French. Obviously, from Amy's business card, you saw we have our house in France and Saint Martin on the French side. Our side, as we call it, is really laid back and the food is incredible. We like the lifestyle in that it's very French in terms of great food and profound lack of outward judgement and social restrictions."

"Do people speak English?"

I replied. "The island gets about one and a half million cruisers every year and another half million come by plane. Because of the number of American cruise lines, about 75% of the people are from the US, 20% from France, and the remainder from elsewhere else. You hear German, Dutch, and Portuguese being spoken. On the French side, it's probably 60% French, 40% American, but I'm just guessing."

"I do know that the overwhelming majority of beachgoers are middle-aged or older. We normally only see children on the beach on weekends when the locals come out. We're not party people and there's not much night life in the Orient Bay area, so we generally get to bed not too long after dinner."

"I heard there's a nude beach," Reggie offered.

I reluctantly replied. "All beaches on St. Martin are topless and Orient Beach, which is just down the road from the house, is the only official clothing optional beach. Visitors sometimes go nude on other beaches that are less populated and there are a few where no one seems to care. On the Dutch side nudity is common on parts of Cupecoy Beach. Although not officially allowed, it's tolerated."

"So, people are all running around naked on Orient beach?" Reggie inquired.

"Not really. There used to be Club Orient at the south end that was the nude resort. Hurricane Irma wiped it out in 2017 and that area is still designated as the clothing optional area. The rest of the beach is European, which means topless if you want, but there's no pressure either way."

Reggie seemed interested and so I went into further detail. "Saint Martin is almost fully recovered from the devastation and there's still some reconstruction in process. Orient Beach has largely returned to its former state, though with some notable exceptions. Pedro's Beach Bar no longer exists and Club Orient including Papagayo's Restaurant is gone. However, the beach south of where Pedro's stood and in front of the former Club Orient, remains a designated nude beach. An umbrella and two lounge chairs can be rented there, although the lounge chairs are the old-fashioned kind with vinyl straps."

Reggie smiled and so I kept going. "At the northern end of the developed beach area, Coco Beach has re-opened. It'll be interesting to see if Coco Beach ever restores the nude section it used to have. It's a little hoity-toity for us farm boys. The main part of Orient Beach allows nudity until eight a.m. Many people claim the time limit's nine but either time is merely a guideline. We're early risers and yet Amy has walked as late as 9:00."

"What happens if you break the rules?"

I looked at Reggie and noted that there aren't any lifeguards and normally few beach patrols. Swimwear is 'regulated' by the various beach bars/restaurants."

"The major beach bars that have 25 or more umbrellas are Kontiki, Wai Plage, Bikini Beach, La Playa, KaKao and Coco Beach. All have umbrellas and lounge chairs lined up several rows deep and they will politely ask you to wear what's appropriate for their customer base. Every now and then, and I mean like rarely, do the beach police show up and either warn the walkers or give them a twenty Euro ticket.

From Kontiki south towards the Ozone, as Melia calls the clothing optional zone, there are a number of small vendors who rent umbrellas/chairs for as little as $15."

"Do you have any favorites on the beach?"

"Amy and I spend the majority of our beach time at KaKao and use the lounge chairs and umbrellas because they have 4-inch pads which are very comfortable."

"What should Sam and I wear?" Reggie inquired.

"That's really up to you. The old adage, 'If you've got it flaunt it, if you ain't, hide it,' is apropos.

"What about Mrs. Terrill? She's in fantastic shape."

"When Amy came down with Leukemia and they said there wasn't any more they could do for her, she went to Saint Martin to die. Between her annual T-cell transplants, then getting really involved in holistic medicine and a rigorous exercise program, she's in really great shape."

"She's got a great body," Reggie offered.

"She does one-hundred push-ups and sit-ups each morning and goes to the gym three days a week where she runs three miles and does twenty chin-ups."

"My God, no wonder she's in such good shape."

I looked at Reggie and lamented. "She's got a six-pack, while I'm working on a half barrel."

Reggie laughed and replied, "You're in great shape."

"For somebody my age!" I retorted.

"No, for any guy. I mean, you're really in good shape."

I returned to the apparel line of thought and offered. "There's been a big transition in what people wear on the beach. When I first went there, the young women wore bikini bottoms and probably half the young girls were topless. Today most young women wear those, I think they're called, Brazilian suit bottoms where the term 'half-assed' has a totally new meaning."

"Surprisingly, toplessness today is fairly rare. When it does happen, it's normally a few middle age French women. The other big change is in body art. When I first started going, the only people with tattoos were sailors who went out, got drunk and woke up with 'mom' on their arm. Now, virtually all the women have some sort of ink. For some, it's a little. For others, it's a lot."

"How about you?" Reggie asked.

I looked at her as if she was some sort of dolt. She'd been taking care of me and seen everything. Instead I replied. "It's up to the person. If they want to add ink to their bodies, why not. Some of it, I find attractive and some, well, I think is a bit much."

"What do the men wear?" Reggie inquired.

"Some men wear sports bikinis. If they're in trunks, you can almost tell where they're from by their length. Those from Europe are usually in mid-thigh while those from the States are what I call knee-knockers. In general, the beaches and the island as a whole, are less crowded and more mature than when I started going there and seems to be a bit more conservative. I think it's because the tourist mix has changed and more Americans are visiting."

"What difference does that make?" Reggie asked.

"Americans are just more conservative than Europeans and more hung up on their bodies. The American media correlates the human body with sex, while the Europeans are much more casual about the whole thing. It's like being here in the hospital. You take care of people and see their bodies and think nothing of it and that's the way the Europeans are."

Reggie looked at me and asked, "Are there any stores where Sam and I can buy bathing suits? We'll want to fit in."

I just said, "there's plenty of stores on or near the beach and in Phillipsburg."

"How about you? Do you wear one of those Speedos?" Reggie inquired with a smirk.

"No," I replied with a nervous giggle.

"Chicken?" Reggie asked.

"Not really. If that's what a guy wants to wear, it's fine. If that's what he's comfortable in, why not? Most men, including me, don't feel comfortable. Not because of social pressure but because I don't think I have the body for it. If I did, I would. It's really one of the great things about Orient Beach. No one's forced to do anything and no one particularly judges you if you don't. At first you look at guys in bikinis and you think it's strange. Then after a couple of days you realize it's no big deal."

"What do you mean strange?"

"Well, if a guy wears a brief bathing suit in the States, people probably think he's gay. I always thought it was hypocrisy to think that and then cheer on the male Olympic swimmers who wear the same suits. My thought is, 'what difference does it make?' We've been socialized to think that anything short of knee knockers is exhibitionistic on a man.

"So you would if you wanted to?"

"Sure, why not?"

"What about going to the Ozone?"

I repeated. "Sure, why not?" more for effect than anything else and then continued. "I grew up on a farm and we had a pond. The house was over a mile from our cousins and they didn't own a telescope. My mom was one of those farm wives who busted her butt helping dad in everything from farming to housework. We saw calves being born when we were little and mom wanted to make sure we were comfortable with how everything worked."

"In the summer mom would do the wash on Thursdays and hang the clothes outside, including those we were wearing. My brother and I would run around naked, play in our sandbox, swim in our little inflatable pool and thought nothing of it."

I smiled at the memories of Tommie and me playing in the sand and continued reflecting, "Dad took an old tractor tire, filled it with sand and that was our playground along with a rope swing on the oak tree we'd swing on."

My mind returned and I added, "Even when we got older, I don't think I ever wore a bathing suit in the pond and only wore old gym shorts when we went to town and swam in the Mineral Point pool."

Reggie nodded and smiled, realizing I was probably more liberal than she thought.

"What about at your house on St. Martin?" Reggie inquired.

"The 'House on the Hill' and our house are totally private."

I think Reggie was a bit relieved and so I added. "The first time I was there, I had the same trepidations you seem to be having. I quickly learned it's not nearly as erotic or neurotic as imagined. What's really cool is that, because the parameters are so wide, you can wear whatever you want and no one will care."

"How about dinner?"

"I'm not hungry right now!"

"I mean in Saint Martin."

I smiled and replied. "We go into Grand Case for dinner. There are several five-star restaurants in a row."

"That's where you need to be dressed up?"

"Everyone wears shorts to even the five-stars but they're the longer dress shorts than the ones you wear to the beach."

"How about you?" Reggie inquired.

I smiled and said with a lascivious grin, "I have a pair of booty shorts. Sadly, with my knobby knees, skinny calves and boney butt, I try to wear dress shorts in the restaurants. No sense scaring all the patrons thinking there's a large chicken on the loose."

Reggie giggled at that and made me wonder if it was my wit or my physique.

I paused for a moment and then added. "If you like, we can make appointments for haircuts and massages at the house. We also friendships with the owners of our favorite restaurants. We can make reservations for you if you like, or you can go on your own. We normally only make dinner reservations because the beach restaurants all have great lunches where you can sit and people watch if you like."

"What are the beach restaurants like?"

"They literally transition from the Les Jardins area, which means 'the gardens', that has some really good night time restaurants to Le String, which is down near the old Orient Beach Club."

"What do you mean?"

"Well, let's see. On the north end you've got Coco Beach, KaKao Beach, La Playa and Bikini Beach who attract a lot of cruisers with their black socks and cameras. Those staying nearby are a little older and more conservative in terms of attire, meaning people will either be in street clothes or cover-ups.

"Mid-beach you have Kontiki and Wai. The foods good and the clientele is a mix of toters and locals."

"Toters?" Reggie asked with a frown.

"Camera toters."

Another giggle from Reggie.

"On the south end you've got Le' String, Sun Beach and Chez Leandra, which are adjacent to the old Club Orient and the rocks, as they're called, which represent the delineation between the French beach and the Ozone."

"Which one do you like best?" Reggie asked.

"They all have different personalities and different clientele. The more mature crowd seems to end up on the north end. Your age group usually ends up on the south end near the Ozone. All of them have great food. Our daughter, Mela, who's about your age, ended up hanging out at the south end a lot."

"It sounds wonderful."

"Other than Waldwick in the summer, it's my favorite place on earth."

## Experientialism:

After a day of walking the halls, meeting with the physical therapist and social worker, insulting the psychologist, studying and then entertaining my lady friends, I thought my day was done and wasn't expecting any other visitor except Amy. It was lights out at ten and I woke up at four as Reggie was making her mid-night rounds.

Instead of quietly checking my vitals she saw I was awake and whispered, "Hello".

"Good morning."

"Are you having trouble sleeping?"

"Not really. I'm an early riser and I'm wide awake."

Her normal in-out, see-yah, goodbye demeanor had been replaced by a more casual and less stressed atmosphere as she offered. "I've got some questions, if you don't mind."

"Of course not. Pull up a chair."

"I can't, it's against hospital policy."

"Understood."

There was a long pause as if Reggie was pondering her next statement and then looked at me and confided. "Sam and I are what's now called Experientialists."

"A what?"

I'd never heard the term and so Reggie filled me in. "Experientialism was initially coined as an educational term dealing with activities from a learner's prior experience that's used to implement a new skill. While the generations after War II focused on acquiring things, derogatorily called materialism, my generation's goal is to experience as many different things as possible. While big houses and nice cars seem like they'd be wonderful, taking those same dollars and investing them in memories are really important to people my age right now."

I must have had a frown on my face as Reggie continued. "There's a group of us who do things together. Most of us live downtown and don't own a car, as we haven't needed one."

"How do you get around?" I asked, somewhat perplexed by the situation.

Reggie smiled and said, "Walk, ride a bike, take Uber or public transportation. When we need a car, we rent one. I don't have the $10,000 annual cost of the car depreciation, insurance, upkeep, maintenance and parking and use that money to do things."

"A lot of what we do is based on sports, but it's only a part of what we try to experience. In the past two years, I trained and ran a half marathon, ski jumped, parachuted, bungy jumped, went snowmobiling, body surfed at Hilton Head and did the polar plunge in Lake Michigan on New Year's Day."

"Wow! How many are involved?" I asked, realizing Reggie had done more in a year than I had in thirty.

In my darkened room I could still see Reggie shrug as she continued. "The group's dynamic. I don't know, right now, twenty, thirty. We don't keep track and keep in contact through social media. What's really neat is that our group, if you want to call it that, consists of black, white and browns, straight, bi, trans and gay, religious and non-religious, who are mostly professionals in their mid-to-late twenties or early thirties, who live around here and have a few things in common where we never, and I mean never, push our social, political or sexual agendas on the others. This eliminates a lot of friction and potential confrontation that allows for a sense of wellbeing and acceptance."

I realized that Reggie's Experiealist group was what I sincerely believed in...simply accepting each other for who they were and I was interested, even in the middle of the night and so I asked. "Who decides what you're going to do?"

Reggie shrugged her shoulders again and replied. "Someone gets an idea and we text each other to see who's interested.

"What about, you know, dating?

Reggie lowered her voice and glanced towards the door, indicating what she was about to offer was personal. "I enjoy the group and the events. If I uhh...well, if I need the physical experience, I've got friends with benefits outside the group who have the same outlook on life I do."

"You mean?" I whispered as I thought I knew it meant, but didn't want to overstep my bounds.

Reggie paused as if deep in thought and then offered. "It's not as random as you're probably thinking simply because of my inherent belief in the true meaning of friendship. To me, friendship is a relationship based  on mutual affection between people that's a stronger form of interpersonal bond than an "acquaintance" or "association" which is what our Experiealist group is."

"Your generation had friends who were or are normally delineated along gender lines. Men have male friends. Women have female friends. Rarely do I see in your generation where men or women have close friends of the opposite sex. Where my generation is different is in the fact that these friendships are non-binary which means I have close friends from not only both defined sexes, but those in between, where the ultimate friendship goal isn't physical, but social."

I liked where Reggie was going with this, but still thought it odd that she'd be sharing it with me. Reggie looked down at the floor and then at me and, in all earnest, noted, "Friendship is characterized by a number of qualities, beyond mutual affection that include respect, trust and loyalty to the point we enjoy each other's company and have a willingness to help and support each other."

Reggie glanced at the door again and continued. "As for the physical part, it's not like it was when you were our age. Back then, there was emotion involved in terms of either being romantic or a sense of conquest. Having FWB's is simply a non-exclusive relationship where people are friends to the point of total trust that allows for intimacy without a romantic relationship."

I was surprised and yet curious as Reggie again cautiously eyed at the door and lowered her voice further. "There are a lot of reasons why people have these types of relationships. Some simply want to...uhh...you know...without the emotional baggage.

Others may be looking for companionship and intimacy without the pressure of a commitment. Still others, may be trying to avoid the pain of heartbreak or rejection."

I was incredulous and also curious and so I asked. "How do you take it from a plutonic friendship to one that's physical?"

Reggie looked at me, took a deep breath, and replied. "Most guys get the signal and are more than willing. Women are bit more restrained. For men, it's part of your nature. For women the reticence seems to be part of our socialization as well as the threat of unwanted results. The net result is NOT the physical act, but the emotional aspect afterwards where the friendship remains without the pressures that are normally involved in a physical relationship."

I simply shook my head, somewhat in disbelief, while regretting things weren't like that when I was her age and before I met Amy.

"So people just find a person and begin?"

"You don't 'find a person'. You develop trusting friendships with a person or persons." Reggie replied, allowing me to question if this meant concurrent or consecutive.

"What happens if a friend with benefits becomes emotional?"

"If they agreed in the beginning what this was all about, then they're really not friends are they?"

I nodded and smiled at the logic and inquired. "Do any of the relationships end up in marriage?"

"Sure. Several couples I know have and that's great for them."

"So there are always guys to meet the…uhh…needs?"

"You said guys. Let's leave it at that."

"Do you think this will be forever?"

"Probably not, it's just the phase I'm in. We're all well-educated, have good paying jobs and aren't ready to settle down."

I was both surprised and shocked. Surprised because I had no idea situations like this existed and shocked that Reggie was so open about it. I inquired. "What about the future?"

"Someday, I want to experience the majesty of having a child grow within me. When it's born, I want  the pleasure of nursing something I created while filling it with love and kindness."

"In other words, get married and have kids?"

"If I find the right partner, yes. However, I don't know if I'll ever want that. Marriage is a lifelong commitment...it's longer than anything else you ever do and only ends one of two ways...divorce or death. Isn't it better to be committed with such passion you willingly stay together with nothing binding you except your passion for each other?"

I thought of Amelia Earhart and her marital requirements, 'I shall not hold you to any medieval code of faithfulness to me nor shall I consider myself bound to you similarly. If we can be honest I think the difficulties which arise may best be avoided should you or I become interested deeply (or in passing) in anyone else.'

'Please let us not interfere with the other's work or play, nor let the world see our private joys or disagreements. In this connection I may have to keep some place where I can go to be myself, now and then, for I cannot guarantee to endure at all times the confinement of even an attractive cage.'

'I must exact a cruel promise and that is you will let me go in a year if we find no happiness together.'

Reggie continued, "Right now, I want to try things that allow me to expand my horizons. I see death every day and am profoundly sad for those who die filled with regrets they've never lived life. We only have one chance and I want mine to be the richest it can.

"What's at the top of the list?"

A broad smile crossed Reggie's face as she simply exhorted. "Wanderlust! I want to visit all seven continents and experience as many different cultures as possible. I want to meet and talk to people who have different perspectives on life than I do. I want to share the joy of living and experience what makes others happy. The physical part is just a small portion of the entire experience and

I want to keep it that way. Right now, I have the luxury of deciding who, what and when. As long as I have that ability, I want to sustain my control."

I smiled and was envious as I appreciated her outlook on life as quite liberating. Reggie glanced at the clock and I realized time was of the nigh and so I revisited the subject of Saint Martin. "Regarding your vacation experiences, we can make arrangements for you to go scuba diving, snorkeling, sailing, parasailing, or deep-sea fishing if you like. There's also an island called Lle Tintamarre you can take the ferry to. It's a very short ride and has a great beach where you can snorkel and perhaps see some of the sea turtles or Gladys, the nurse shark."

"Shark?" Reggie said with a combination excitement and concern to the point I didn't know if she was in her experiential or alarmed mode.

I continued. "Reggie, it's all a reaction to the movie *'Jaws'* that came out before you were born. There are normally less than forty unprovoked shark bites and five deaths in America each year out of ninety million people who swim in the ocean. I can't do the math but I know that around twenty-five people get hit by lighting and ten die which means you have just about an equal chance of being zapped and bitten. I don't know what the odds would be about getting zapped and bitten at the same time but I don't think they're too great."

Another giggle.

I continued. "Young tiger sharks, who haven't learned the difference between humans and regular food do most of the biting. When they do bite, it's normally only once because they don't like the way we taste. As for nurse sharks, they rarely bite humans, even by mistake. In fact, in the past three years, there's only been three unprovoked nurse bites in the whole world."

"Are you still talking about sharks?" Reggie questioned with a smirk.

"I hope so," I countered, realizing how the word *nurse* now had two meanings. I continued. "Almost all the time the Nurse

Sharks are sedentary and simply looking for food on the ocean floor. Gladys is about ten feet long. She's quite amenable to human interaction and actually appears to like seeing humans every now and then, so don't worry about becoming a peanut butter and Reggie sandwich."

Another giggle then Reggie retorted. "I know a few nurses here that fit that description."

I laughed and continued. "If you want to shop in some of the designer stores, we can arrange for you to go over to Saint Barths but I'm warning you, it's REALLY expensive over there."

"Isn't it a long way to the other islands?"

"About twenty miles and so we can have you there in less than an hour by boat."

"Really?"

"Yup. However, if you only want to go into Phillipsburg you'll have a car and it's about seven miles from the house. We suggest going on a day when there are the fewest ships in port as the crowds can be massive."

"When's that?"

"The ships are in port every day. However, Tuesday, Wednesday, Thursday are the heaviest days...especially Wednesday when the 'Oasis of the Seas' docks that can have as many as 5,500 passengers. This means, with the other ships, over 10,000 toters converge on a small commercial area."

Reggie looked at me and got quite pensive as she asked. "How will Sam be treated?"

My tone quickly changed from laidback to one of profound seriousness. "My mother-in-law was of African descent. My wife has African heritage. Our kids are one-fourth African and were taught to be proud of it. If anyone demeans, degrades or mistreats Sam, it will be taken care of. We've been through the bullshit and it's simply not tolerated."

At that point, I knew I needed to make a decision and offered, "We'll also provide you with Wilco identification cards for the restaurants and activities. We can make the reservations and you simply provide the cards. Trust me, you and Sam will think you're in heaven and there will be total respect."

"I'm just concerned for Sam. She's so kind, sweet and incredibly sensitive."

I took a deep breath and continued. "When Hurricane Irma devastated the island, Amy's mom and dad not only rebuilt several properties on Orient Beach but provided monthly stipends to keep the restaurants from going out of business. People on Saint Martin have long memories and always express their gratitude for what the family did. There's one place you will have to be careful though."

"Where's that?" Reggie asked.

"Down near Club Orient there's a store called 'Lucille's' where the owner sells bathing suits to nudist and could sell ice cream to Eskimos."

I smiled at the memory and continued. "Our daughter Melia was there with Amy. Lucille convinced Melia her bathing suit was old fashioned. From the way the story goes, by the time Amy and Melia left, Melia had three suits…one called Itsy Bitsy, one called Teenie Weenie and the other she called OMG!"

"OMG?" Reggie inquired. "You mean, 'Oh My God!'"

"Amy said it consisted of three triangles and some string."

"In other words, a micro bikini?" Reggie inquired and simply shrugged as if indifferent.

"I guess so." I replied. "Story tells, at first, Melia stuck to Itsy Bitsy. Then, when Amy left and Melia's crazy friend Annie showed up, things got a little more uhh…liberal when Annie talked Melia into wearing teenie weenie."

Another shrug, as I paused and pondered whether I should explain why the change and added. "It all began because the family rarely travels without security and Melia was upset when she discovered the Saint Martin security team spying on her to which Melia decided to rebel against the structure."

"Will we have security?"

"Only if you need it."

"Let's hope not." Reggie replied as she asked, "What did Melia do?"

I paused for a moment and then thought, *'what the heck, she'll never meet Melia anyway'.* "Annie's a real free spirit. I mean REAL free. She'd readily fit in your Experientialist family and probably be the leader. One day, the girls went over to Happy Bay, which is a secluded beach. Annie went naked and talked Melia into going topless. As they were walking down the beach, Melia spotted the security team hiding in the bushes, got really pissed, and she and Annie passionately made out on the beach in front of them."

"That's it?"

"Well, Melia's a very conservative person and to be topless and making out with a naked woman on the beach was way, way beyond her persona. When they sent the skiff to pick Annie and Melia up, Melia was still so pissed she called Amy and told her off. It was a real cat fight!"

Reggie was now grinning as I continued. "The next day, Melia was still riled up. She and Annie went into Phillipsburg where Melia supposedly got a small tattoo and blew over two thousand dollars on retro clothes."

"Tattoo?"

"Yup"

"Of what?"

"I heard a small rainbow."

"Have you seen it?"

"Not where it's located."

Reggie's eyebrows arched as she commented reluctantly offered. "Ooooh-K."

I continued. "Melia's six-feet-two and bought some of those platform shoes making her nearly six-feet-five in the get up. She's got frizzy hair, except it's light brown and had it cut really short. In the end, my 'milk toast' daughter, who'd always toed the line, rebelled."

"Is the retro store still there?"

"I think so. Why?"

"I love retro clothes."

There was a pensive pause and then Reggie inquired. "Were you upset?"

"Heck no! It's what Melia needed. She'd gone through a terrible experience during her residency and it broke the ice so that my distraught, despondent, dejected daughter came back to me."

"Did she ever wear OMG?"

"I don't think so. I think it's still at the house. Anyway, they ended up down at Club Orient a few times."

"What did Mrs. Terrill think?"

"Amy? Well, I think she's the one who told Melia to go there."

"As I said, Amy had Leukemia and went to Saint Martin to die. Obviously, she didn't, but while she was there, she went through a transformation that included a great deal of holistic adaptations including diet, exercise, breathing, stress reduction and re-socialization including three really critical relaxation programs."

"What are they?"

"Let's see if I can remember…Uh…Mindfulness?"

"Breathing and relaxation," Reggie offered.

"Wim Hoff?"

"Environmental adaptation," Reggie added.

"Shin Rin Yoku."

"Japanese Forest Bathing for Sensory awareness," Reggie stated and then added, "In other words a form of personalized Yoga."

"I guess so, but I don't like yoga. I never acquired a taste."

Reggie had a look on her face and then it clicked…*yogurt*!

I continued. "In addition Amy shared that when she was taking the first steps to recovery, she did a complete evaluation of her physical self and realized that half her problems centered around her lifestyle consisting of the wrong foods and little or no exercise resulting in a stressed-out individual who sincerely feels that it was the stress that brought on her leukemia."

Reggie looked at me and nodded as she added, "There are a lot of studies going on about stress related cancers simply because stress elicits higher levels of cortisol in the body that generate false reads on rogue cells and never sends T-cells to destroy them. The rogue cells are given a chance to survive and Cancer begins.

I added. "As Amy recovered, she began both diet and exercise programs that consisted of the right foods and walking the length of Orient Beach, that eventually evolved into her running it. Amy told me that to go from weighing seventy some pounds when she arrived, where everyone looked the other way because she reminded them of death, to regaining her health and appearance was the most liberating experience of her life."

I looked at Reggie and didn't know whether to continue but felt in the medical environment we were in it made sense to lay it all out and so I continued. "Amy said that, with all the doctors, tests and treatments, she got to the point she realized her body was nothing more than an electro-chemical device used to power the brain and she only felt 'whole' when her entire body was fully relaxed and naturally stimulated."

Reggie smiled, nodded in agreement and then introspectively added. "Shin Rin Yoku is based on the combination of nature and realization that 80% of our out-of-body sensory information comes from our eyes."

"By going out in nature or simply closing them for a longer period of time and relying on our other senses, our entire body begins to receive impulses that would otherwise be overridden. Add in Mindfulness for relaxation and  Mrs. Terrill is spot on! The entire staff here is taught about Mindfulness to help clear the brain. I just need to add the Forest Bathing to see if I can't relieve some of the stress this job puts on me but it's tough when you live in downtown Milwaukee."

I felt I needed to continue and so I added. "With that assumption, Amy became completely aware of the social bonds that impede most people. She began experimenting with the different holistic methods and started her journey back to today. Along the way, she released her inhibitions and with it the trepidations regarding what people thought when it came to achieving her ultimate goal of inner peace and tranquility. By becoming aware, it cleared her mind, cured her spirit and cleansed her soul. By incorporating a healthy diet and adding the exercise regimen, she delayed many of the physical challenges that affect people our age."

"I know, she looks incredible," Reggie offered.

I continued. "Beyond the looks, you find a person who's at peace with herself. There are times, but they're few and far between, when things stress her out as her inner peace truly helps her maintain her wellbeing."

Reggie stopped for a moment and reluctantly inquired. "So Mrs. Terrill practices her form of yoga on the beach?"

"Like I said, before eight in the morning, you can walk the entire beach naked if you want to. They only enforce what we call *'bottoms-up'* after eight."

"Any weirdos?" Reggie asked.

"Only when I'm around," I replied with a snicker which broke the ice and minimized the conversations intensity.

"You ever do it with her?"

"We walk the beach, but I don't run anymore. My knees are shot."

"I mean go naked on the beach."

I just smiled and shrugged my shoulders to let her think whatever she wanted.

Reggie, added. "Mrs. Terrill is in great shape! A lot of people think she's your daughter."

I didn't know whether to take that as a compliment for Amy or a diss on me, and so I took it as a compliment.

Reggie paused for a moment and then asked "How about the Leukemia? We all know how Doctor Williams died."

"She went through T-Cell harvesting and gets her injection at the Carbone Center every year in Madison. Thirty-five years! So far, so good."

"You mentioned re-socialization, what did you mean by that?"

I didn't want to go into all the details and simply replied. "When your family is wealthy and your father is as dynamic as The Duke and then being of mixed race, Amy had a lot of internal expectations that really affected her own self-concept. In going to St. Martin and being accepted for who she was, where no one knew about the wealth and the racial issue was never as weighty as Milwaukee, Amy was able to free herself of a lot of the self-induced stigma she'd carried for so many years."

"In other words, socially liberated?"

"In many different ways, yes." I thought the rest should remain between Amy and me as I added. "The only mistake Amy made was meeting some idiot farm boy who fell madly in love with her. They did it the old-fashioned way...got married, had three kids that allowed Amy to be a mom and now a grandma and live the life many people only dream about."

Reggie smiled and offered. "I don't think it turned out too bad for either one of you."

I looked at Reggie and continued. "Trust me, it hasn't all been a bed of roses and you have to realize and accept there are always thorns. I hope and pray, I've allowed my wife to lead the life she wanted and deserved. At the same time, I thank her every day for the life she's given me."

"Marriage isn't easy. It's two people who need to bend their ways to make it work. I think we've done a pretty good job. We both have our strengths and weaknesses... good points and bad. Yet, because we profoundly love each other, we accept each other as life partners."

"So that's why Saint Martin's so special," Reggie concluded as she glanced up at the clock.

I looked at Reggie, smiled and reiterated one of my silly slogans. "You asked me what time it was and once again, I told you how we build watches."

Reggie paused for a moment and then smiled. "Mr. Terrill, most times, we refer to the individual in this bed as 'the patient'.

We're taught to build the emotional wall so we don't get too close them."

"You've touched the lives of so many people here with your sense of decency, level of generosity and humility that no one calls you 'the patient', they call you Mister Terrill."

A pleasant smile crossed Reggie's face and then poof, she was gone, needing to hit her PPH or Patients Per Hour as I thought, 'As life goes on, as life goes on.'

**Sam I Am:**

I fell back asleep but was awakened to the clanging of dishes or bedpans they both sounded the same to me. It was 6:15. I got up, did what I needed to do, took a shower and put on the clean pajamas Amy brought the night before. At 7:05 Reggie and Sam walked in for the symbolic changing of the guard with Reggie erasing her name and Sam adding hers.

It was Sam's turn to report. "Mr. Terrill, your numbers are improving and today you'll be having a chest x-ray and cardiac CAT scan to see how the clots are doing. Because your $O^2$ level is 97%, they also want to see if you can make it to sixteen laps on the floor…that is, as long as you don't bother the rest of the patients like you did yesterday when you were singing the melody to 'Chariots of Fire'."

I smiled and went, "Tah, dah dah. dah duh, dah," and got a look of exasperation from Nurse Sam.

Reggie said goodbye, smiled and told me we had a 1900-hour date. I told her, 'Have a good day, and don't let the bedbugs bite", as she walked out the door.

Sam looked at the blank breakfast menu on my table and inquired whether I'd ordered food.

"Nope!"

"Why not?"

"I'm tired of oatmeal and don't like cream of wheat. The eggs are always cold by the time they get here and the bacon is overcooked."

"You have to eat something, Mr. Terrill."

"I'm hungry for pancakes or better yet a waffle smothered in strawberries and whipped cream."

Sam got one of those looks on her face and said, "Let me see what I can do."

"Really?"

Sam went into a southern drawl and continued. *"Y'all see, it's my sisters working down in the kitchen and they do me favors every now and then. I'll see if I can rustle up some pancakes!"*

We both chortled simultaneously at her decrepit imitation and then I got serious. "That doesn't really happen, does it?"

"Every now and then," Sam replied.

"What do you do?" I asked, looking directly at her.

"Brush it off. What do you and Mrs. Terrill do?"

"It's been so long since we've had an overt situation, I really don't know what I'd do anymore. Amy and our daughter, Melia were in Saint Barths once and it happened there. Amy was so pissed, she wanted to buy the store and burn it down."

I paused for a moment to simply allow the conversation to change course and added, "I think I know the feeling and I'm sorry. I hope I haven't been like that."

"Oh God, no! All the black employees loved Doctor Williams. She was the first woman of color to head a department here at the hospital and was world renowned. Whenever I'm in the lobby and see her picture on the brass plate by the elevator, I rub it and thank her for opening the door. She's been an inspiration for the rest of us. We don't get *it* that much anymore. It's still there and still hurts but it's not like it was for my parents or grandparents."

I responded "Believe it or not, I had a relative who married a slave girl in Virginia in the 1860's. You can imagine what it must have been like for them. They literally escaped with their lives to Wisconsin and she taught school outside Mineral Point."

"So, you've got a little soul in you?"

"Nope, she would have been my great, great aunt but not part of the bloodline. With three kids who are mixed race, I had to learn about *'the look'* and teach them to keep their heads up high. Because of our...our socio-economic level...they didn't have it as bad as other mixed-race kids and I'm happy for that."

"Any of them married to someone of color?" Sam inquired.

"Well, Melia married a white school teacher. Derrick married a German girl. George, who we call 'V', married a Native American girl and they live in Wausau."

"Are you talking about George Terrill and his wife Amelia?" Sam asked almost incredulously.

"Yes."

"Oh my God. I never put the pieces together."

"What?"

"The Derrick Williams Foundation paid for my college education. Without them, I'd be down in the basement."

"No, you wouldn't. You have more dignity and compassion than hardly anyone I've ever known. You would have made it some way."

"Thank you. There are a lot of others of color who have the same feelings as me, if only given a chance."

"I know. I've seen it! I've felt it and I'm proud to say I've done everything I possibly can to make people realize it's 'who' that matters and not what. Underneath, our DNA is 99.5% the same."

Sam switched subjects and asked, "You're serious about St. Martin, right?"

"Yes."

"Reggie said we get to use a house and car."

"Yup!"

"What should I expect?"

"Which way?" I inquired.

Sam had a look about her and I knew what she was referring to as I answered. "Well, first of all, it's very European and quite affluent so that a lot of the indirect B.S. you get up here doesn't happen. Second, the island gets a lot of cruise tourists, including many of color. This means that once they realize you're not a local, they'll quickly shift to the tourist mode."

"What's that?"

"The phony baloney sweet crap to try and get more of your money. I told Reggie we're giving you Wilco ID Cards for the bars, restaurants and activities. As soon as you flash those, trust me, everything will change. If they ask how you're related to the company, tell them you're Assistant Vice President of Personnel and involved in the corporate rewards program. They all know each year we award four employee trips for outstanding service and if it looks like you're one of the decision makers, the B.S. will be lathered on like you won't believe."

"Really?"

"Sam, money talks and in our case, on Saint Martin it literally hollers."

"What about Reggie?"

"Tell them she's your assistant. Tell you what, I'll have Wilco business cards made up that have your title on them and let Jermain Johnson, who heads up personnel, know what's going on. You still need to be a little careful. Reggie said that it's going to be just the two of you, correct?"

"Yes."

"I'll have Jermaine contact Wilco Security and there'll be two Google watches at the house. Wear them and read the instructions on what to do if you're in need. We have our team in place as we provide most of the hotel security for the island."

"Anything we need to be worried about?"

"Three things. First, the sun. It's intense. Second the French guys. They're intense. Finally, Lucille if you go in her shop, she's intense and she WILL sell you something," to which I began to laugh thinking about Melia.

"Reggie said there's a nude beach."

"Yup! In fact, there are several. You're not offended by that are you?"

Sam looked at me as if I was some sort of dolt. "Mr. Terrill, I see naked people every day. I don't think seeing naked people on a beach will be that different."

"That's a good attitude. The beauty of the clothing optional section of Orient Beach is that it widens the parameters of acceptance elsewhere so that anything above being naked seems all right. The clothing optional section is only about twenty-percent and there's a pile of rocks that serves as the delineation. In true European fashion, you can wear clothes there or go topless on any beach. The beach restaurants prefer you cover up while eating but beyond that, it's totally up to you."

"What about you?" Sam inquired.

"Well, I go topless all the time." I smirked. "No one has ever said a word."

Sam looked at me, simply smiled at my smartass response as she added. "If I were your daughter, what would you expect?"

I got serious. "Sam, if you were my daughter, I would be incredibly proud of what you've accomplished and your compassion that shows every time we're together. As for Saint Martin, our daughter Melia was there and did what she wanted to do. She and her mother had a little tiff and it pushed Melia a little over the edge in terms of revolting but I think it did her good. The reason Amy and I are giving you and Reggie the trip is because we're proud to know you and grateful for how you've helped me recover."

"So, Melia went a little wild and crazy?"

"For Melia, yes, but you need to understand, her reference point for wild and crazy was probably the same as most nuns. For her, rebellion was getting a tiny tattoo, having Lucille talk her into wearing brief bikinis and hanging out down by Club Orient."

"That's it?"

"Yup, that's it!"

"That doesn't sound that bad to me."

"Then go for it!"

Sam knew time was of the essence and got back into her professional mode as she smiled and excused herself. As she reached the door, she turned, smiled and said, "Thank you".

I was alone again, hoping I hadn't been too open about Melia but the words were out and couldn't be retrieved. Me and my big mouth...time for the hall laps and my lady friends but first, eating a heaping pile of pancakes that were delivered, smothered in butter with enough maple syrup to take a bath in and squiggly bacon just the way I like it.

**Socialization:**

The carbs did me good and I finally did my sixteenth lap while feeling quite satisfied. Once again, I hummed the tune from 'Chariots of Fire' but did it softly. I went back to my room, and was about to begin writing when Father Pat stopped by and invited me to the visitor's lounge.

Pat was in civilian clothes which meant it was Wednesday and, as he crossed his feet, I noticed he was wearing tennis shoes and no socks. We made it to the lounge and a point where I never thought I'd see the day when I would get into a discussion on religion with anyone, let alone a priest. We were always taught there were three things you never talked about...politics, religion and money, yet here I was talking religion with a priest. Not just any priest, but a guy who'd lived and loved only to have his wife depart, making him angry, frustrated and sad who turned to God because he helped an old man with a bag of dog food. This was like going back to college and debating so many philosophical things all night long only to realize there were no quick answers.

As we were sitting in the empty family room I looked at Pat as he wanted me to call him and asked.

"What do you think would have happened, had I died?"

Pat was quick to respond. "Your soul would have gone to heaven."

"But what's a person's soul?"

Pat looked at me and said "Woah!"

I knew this was going to be difficult, but after some self-evaluation, Pat added. "The soul is a complex concept that has been interpreted in many different ways throughout history. In general, the soul is seen as the immaterial essence of a person that which makes them who they are that's often associated with the mind, emotions and spirit."

"There's no scientific evidence to prove or disprove the existence of the soul. However, many people believe that the soul is a real thing that survives the death of the body that allows us to experience love, compassion and other spiritual emotions."

"George, the concept of the soul is a personal one, and there's no right or wrong answer to the question of what it is. In religious terms, the soul is often seen as the part of us that's connected to God that is immortal and will continue to exist after the body dies. It's often seen as the seat of the mind, where our thoughts, memories, and emotions reside. To me, the soul is my true self and the essence of who we are beyond our physical bodies."

I nodded in the affirmative. Father Pat and I were getting into some deep stuff and I asked him what he thought heaven was. Father Pat smiled and replied. "In general, heaven is a place of eternal happiness and peace, where people are reunited with their loved ones and live in the presence of God where there is no pain, suffering, or death and surrounded by God's love and grace where they can experience all the good things that life has to offer, without any of the bad."

"In other words, Camp Randall Stadium." I joked and then realized that Father Pat was being serious as he continued. "The Bible doesn't give a detailed description of heaven, but does offer some clues about what it might be like. For example, in the Book of Revelation, heaven is described as a city with streets of gold and gates of pearl. There are also rivers of living water and trees of life and the air is filled with the sound of angels singing."

"Still sounds like Camp Randall to me."

Pat continued as if the smart ass was fully attuned. "No one knows for sure what heaven is really like. But for many, the idea of a place where they can be reunited with their loved ones and live in the presence of God is a very comforting one."

"Do all religions have a heaven?" I asked, now gathering in the serious nature of Pat's dissertation.

"In Christianity, heaven is usually described as a place of perfect beauty and harmony, where there is no pain, suffering, or death. In Islam, Heaven is called Jannah. Those of the Jewish faith call heaven Gan Eden. The Hindus call heaven Swarga while the

Buddhists call heaven Devaloka. What's neat is that all religions describe it as a place of peace and happiness."

I looked at Father Pat and asked him, "Do you believe in the devil and hell?"

Pat paused, took a deep breath as if to collect his thoughts and then answered. "The devil has many faces and multiple meanings. In the Abrahamic religions the devil seduces humans into sin or falsehood. In Judaism, Satan is seen as an agent subservient to God, typically regarded as a metaphor for the yetzer hara, or "evil inclination". In Christianity and Islam, he's usually seen as a fallen angel or jinn who has rebelled against God, who nevertheless allows him temporary power over the fallen world and a host of demons."

"In the Book of Revelation, Satan appears as a Great Red Dragon, who is defeated by Michael the Archangel and cast down from Heaven. He's later bound for one thousand years, but is briefly set free before being ultimately defeated and cast into the Lake of Fire."

"In the Middle Ages, Satan played a minimal role in Christian theology and was used as a comic relief figure in mystery plays. During the early modern period, Satan's significance greatly increased as beliefs such as demonic possession and witchcraft became more prevalent."

"For some people today, the devil as a literal being who exists in the spiritual realm. For others, the devil as a metaphor for evil and a symbol of all that is evil in the world. For still others the devil as a psychological force and a representation of our own inner darkness or the temptation to evil. Finally, others see the devil as a social construct and therefore a product of human imagination, rather than a real entity."

"What about hell?"

Pat shook his head, put on a little frown and continued. "The concept of hell is also a complex one that has evolved over time. In the Bible, it's often referred to as Sheol, which is a Hebrew word that can mean "grave" or "pit". In the New Testament, hell is referred to as Gehenna, which was a valley outside of Jerusalem where garbage was burned. In Christian theology, hell is typically seen as a place of eternal punishment for those who have rejected God."

Father Pat looked at me and asked, "what do you think?"

I looked at him and honestly answered, "I don't know. I think that heaven means finding the happiness we all seek and hell are the roadblocks to acquiring that happiness."

I paused for a moment to think about what I wanted to add and then sort of blurted out something that had been hidden inside of me for a very long time. "I think we all have the devil inside of us and that hell is simply the consequence of doing wrong and it all begins with our own ego."

"Having been blessed with a life full of opportunity and luxury, I've worked as hard as possible to not become egotistical. Egotistical people are those who have an inflated sense of their own importance. who believe that they are better than others and deserve special treatment. Egotistical people often have a need for attention and admiration, and they may be boastful or arrogant. I don't have a high opinion of myself nor do I believe that I'm better than others, and am embarrassed when people remind of my accomplishments. I hope I'm not boastful or arrogant and don't want to be the center of attention."

"Living a strange life compared to others and having a social circle filled with those who have 'made it' I look at some of the people I meet and see arrogance and a sense of superiority and self-importance and, for some reason, a huge sense of entitlement."

"I think what's really sad is that these people are selfish. I mean, they've made it materially and now they want more. They want everyone to think like they do, act like they want them to act and be socially subservient, unwilling to help others, who are always taking but never giving and always, always, always putting their own social, political, ethical and financial needs ahead of others."

I looked at Pat, took another deep breath and added. "These people are living hell on earth, because they often lack empathy and understanding, compassion and forgiveness the rest of us have simply because we're happy with what we've got. They're inherently unhappy and simply looking for the event, circumstance or person that will lead them to happiness which they never really find simply because of the drive they have that takes them financially, socially or politically above the masses and beyond self-satisfaction."

Pat's mouth dropped open because the joker was serious and the shroud removed and he was seeing what lie within my heart and soul as I continued. "What makes for the living hell is the innate inability to forgive and refusal to let go of anger, resentment, or bitterness towards someone or something that has wronged them. Instead, the sinners spend their lives trying to get even and prove to the world they're better than the next guy thereby creating isolation, sadness, and despair that leads to stress, anxiety and depression as can be seen by the lack of healthy relationships."

"Power, authority and money don't buy happiness, they buy expanded parameters that allow you to seek out what you want out of life but not satisfaction or happiness. To me, happiness only comes when you sincerely feel wanted, needed and loved. It doesn't come from houses and cars, trips and women or having people make you feel important and certainly not from having power over others to make them do what you want. I have it all, seen it all and been exposed to it all and it certainly isn't what makes life great."

We started out talking about death and ended up talking about life. I don't know if this was where Father Pat wanted the conversation to go, but it was like the final act in some play where all the previous scenes lead up to what I thought was the grand finale when in fact it was just act one.

"Do you mind if I talk about the spiritual self?" Father Pat inquired

"Not at all," I replied.

"George, as children we're all programmed so that specific situations require a certain range of responses, experiences and behaviors that are considered acceptable. In a world filled with so many variances and changes, how do we interpret those parameters and make them applicable to our today?"

"While we've discussed the physical aspects and social boundaries, the social and spiritual elements are co-joined in a sense of propriety that permeates all that we are, all that we do and all we believe."

"There are two segments to externalized spirituality...belief in a supreme being and then the structure that creates the order by which that belief is practiced. I'm not here to tell you to believe in God, nor am I here to talk about any of the 4,200 different religions in the world as being more accurate than the rest. That would be like telling someone how to drive from Milwaukee to Los Angeles and saying which is the best way to get there. There are dozens of possibilities. All that matters is that you get there. What one can profoundly say is that what a person believes is up to them and not up to you! All religions can help provide a conscience AND help a person traverse through any crises, including their own death and no one should ever attempt to take away that strength from another human being."

Pat looked at me with a very sincere expression and continued. "One of the most profound events is seeing a photograph of yourself and realizing how much you've changed. As you peer out at the camera lens and your reflection is splashed upon the paper or screen, you wonder when did this all happen? When did I go from what I thought I was to what I am today? This doesn't just happen in how we appear but how we think, feel and act as well."

"Mortality is an eventuality. If you sincerely feel that there's a God, death is only an event and not a circumstance. I believe we all wonder if there's an 'other side' and whether the prophets, evangelists, pontificators and enunciators have it right."

"Father Ziggy once told me, 'When you've been around as long as he had, you'd heard all kinds of stories about the afterlife and what's 'over there'. He added, 'No matter what your faith, you go to church, temple or mosque not only to acquire that ever-important conscience, but hoping that what has transpired in your life is more than what there really is.'"

"I once asked Ziggy 'What is conscience?' and he said 'Catechism of the Catholic Church defines *conscience as a judgment of reason by when a person recognizes the moral quality of an act.* Accepting this definition, conscience then represents the ability we have as humans to know what is good and bad while also providing direction concerning what we should do or defining what we have already done.'"

"Reflection is an incredible thing as it makes you think about the elements that transformed you from what  you were to who you are. You're the culmination of the thoughts and ideas, events and circumstances that altered your life course and hopefully made you better...things that have REALLY moved you and made you wonder."

"There were countless people who made me better...my mother, wife, associates and friends. But there are also two books that changed me....'*Passages*' because it outlined the different phases we ALL go through and '*Awakening at Mid-life*' which added depth and meaning to the last few years. Both books I profoundly recommend as they will add more meaning to where you are."

"The second phase of transition revolves around the people you meet who open their hearts to you and share their innermost thoughts and emotions. Ziggy said he always believed in God and that, in the end, we'd see those who had come before us. He made me feel that it wouldn't be so bad because first, there was absolutely nothing we could do about it and second, because he sincerely believed he would retouch those who'd come before him that he truly missed."

"The movie '*Ghost*' simply touches on the afterlife. Until we reach that point when it's our time, we can only wonder. My vote is to believe in God because he's interpreted by my fellow man to teach greatness...through honesty, integrity, humility, generosity, forgiveness and kindness."

"George, I can't prove there's a God, nor could Ziggy. All I can do is share experiences that outline why I believe there must be more to life than what we have 'down here'. Thomas Kuhn's book, *'The Structure of Scientific Revolution',* points out that all humans have a really difficult time dealing with infinity and the universe due to its complexity and profound vastness. What we do then is reduce it down into smaller segments or portions to the point that we develop theories, structures and opinions of the world that Kuhn calls *paradigms or 'universally recognized scientific achievements that, for a time, provide model problems and solutions for a community of practitioners'."*

"Such things as a flat world or the earth being the center of the universe were all paradigms that now seem quite quaint. However, when people were burned at the stake, at the behest of the church for believing in something that was not a popular belief, it became quite serious, especially to them."

"Next, are the stars! If you've ever been away from the city lights, I mean like really, really far away and peered into the heavens, you can get lost in the beauty, lost in the expanse and, above all the magnitude that lies beyond. Imagine ten stars and now multiple that number to the 100$^{th}$ power. That's how many stars astronomers  believe there are. Where did they come from? How did all of this start? You can keep going back and back and back to yet another source to the point of incomprehension and wonder where it all began."

"Like you, one of Ann and my favorite places to go was the Caribbean... not only for the sun, but the stars. There are so many more to see, there's so much more of life to ponder. There's no better place to imagine your insignificance and perishable existence that make you reconnect with your inner-self and how you fit into this universe. Ask any astronaut and they all say it's a religious experience that makes you realize how small we all are and how great the universe really is."

Simply take a small, long tube and point it at the daytime sky! As you peer into the tube, you'll see that the stars are there, even during the daylight. God isn't there only in our hours of darkness. He's there on our brightest days as well."

The conversation ended and it was agreed that it would resume the next day. There was no way I was going to share the Saint Martin offer we gave to Reggie and Sam with the other members of the staff. They were prompt, polite and professional but not personal like Reggie and Sam. However, if Father Pat wanted to take a religious pilgrimage to visit one of the Saints he could visit Saint Barthelemy that was named after Saint Bartholomew, one of the twelve apostles of Jesus Christ. Saint Kitts that was named after Saint Christopher, a legendary saint who carried a child across a river. Saint Lucia that was named after Saint Lucy, a virgin martyr who was killed in the 4th century AD. Saint Vincent and the Grenadines were named after Saint Vincent, a 4th-century saint who was martyred in Sicily or Saint Martin, named after Saint Martin of Tours, a 4th-century saint who was known for his generosity and Patron Saint of Horses, equestrians, cavalry soldiers, beggars, geese, poor people, alcoholics, people who run hotels, and those who make wine.

**The Heebie Jeebies:**

Another day and more laps. Pat and I met in the lounge and had just sat down as another couple came into the waiting room. Father Pat didn't know if he should continue.

I urged him on and he proceeded. "I took the time to study the primary religions of the world to learn what lies at their roots. In all instances, there's a God or supreme being. In all instances there's a focus on the unexplained which revolves around death and what happens after we die. Most primary religions came from some sort of myth or story shared from generation to generation. Christianity, Muslim's, Hindu and Buddhists all believe in a life hereafter that will be determined by what we do during this life."

"The beginning of time almost always is perceived as that point when great chaos achieves a sense of order, such as in the Hindu religion. Some religions believe that, with an infinite past and an infinite future, there would be no beginning. The Bible differs from most religions in that there was an absence of an initial state as is outlined in the Book of Genesis."

"We Christians believe that we will lie in waiting for the return of Christ. Muslims believe that if you have lived by the faith, you will go to heaven. The Jewish faith does not believe in the afterlife. Hindu's feel that you will be reincarnated over and over and over until you lead a good life where you will be finally freed to go to heaven. Buddha taught that you're reincarnated and are a basically good and it's your errors in life that determine if you need to have a do over."

"What's remarkable is that all the primary religions seem to teach the same four basic tenants...humility, generosity, compassion and forgiveness, as personified through their apostles... Jesus, Moses, Mohammed, Buddha or whomever, while their lives and teachings center around these basic elements."

"In expanding beyond the 'big five' we see that all other religions follow the same criteria and that death can be compensated for through leading a life that follows these rules. Once again...New York to Los Angeles!"

"What's so incredibly profound is how much of our world has come about because of religion...art, music, architecture. What's also so incredibly sad is how much pain and suffering has come about because of man's differing beliefs regarding right and wrong, good and bad and the ways to get to heaven. As Rodney King once profoundly stated, *'Why can't we all just get along?'*."

The other couple left and I think Father Pat was relieved. I don't know why except to think that our conversation was personal...one-on-one and from the heart and not some discourse intended for the masses.

"George, in my religious studies, I learned that all religions are formalized interpretations laid down by people. There is no direct communication with some form of omnipotent being! Regardless of the faith, almost all religions have as their goal, the creation of conscience that teaches the results of not abiding by the four precepts. Christians, Jews and Muslims have rules about things you should **not** do such as the Ten Commandments... (*'Thou shall not covet thy neighbor's wife'*) while Eastern religions focus on things you should do."

Pat got up, went to the vending machine and got two cans of Sprite, brought them back and sat down as he continued. "I took it upon myself to delve into the primary structures to see what appeared to be the cornerstones of each. Whether it was the big five or one of the 4,195 other religions including Taoism...which believes that the only permanent thing in life is change...to Confucianism who believes in Yin and Yang... complimentary forces that make up all aspects of life, organized religion is about how we treat others."

Pat took a sip of his now, almost-flat Sprite and continued. "Religions such as Sikhism are very explicit about what man needs to overcome...greed, anger, false pride, lust and the attachment to material goods, while the Shinto faith purports that all humans are inherently good and that evil is caused by evil spirits and they are all about setting rules of behavior that go back to the four cornerstones...humility, generosity, compassion and forgiveness."

"The fall of Rome, the dark ages and the Gothic wars of the mid-sixth century profoundly affected the direction of mankind and the atomic philosophy of the universe. Charlemagne in the late 700's brutalized what today is most of western Europe but did so in the name of God, standardizing the Catholic faith, bringing education to the masses, creating Cursive, our still-used writing system and developing a basic representative political structure still in effect. Was he right or wrong?"

"Did I ever tell you, he was a relative?" I inquired.

"Really?"

"Yup! My great uncle spent about twenty years doing our genealogy and was able to take it back to before the birth of Christ. He even wrote a book on it."

"Incredible!" Father Pat responded as he continued. "Consequent to Charlemagne's realm, the Crusades, beginning in 1095, allowed for a profound transformation of thought and the initial establishment of contemporary religious protocol that took the precepts established by Charlemagne one step further by establishing consequence for one's actions, in other words, conscience."

"Based on Dante Alighieri's 14$^{th}$ century writings, '*The Divine Comedy*', which describes Dante's descent into the underworld through purgatory and eventual arrival in paradise, the segment entitled *Dante's Inferno* literally redefined perceptions of damnation. His writings were so profound they not only changed the Catholic Church but precipitated one of the world's most famous painting, Botticelli's *'Map of Hell'* that visualized the consequence of one's acts. In the history of mankind few, if any other instances, have the words and imagery of two independent artists combined to materialize one abstract concept."

"Working in conjunction with each other, the 'Inferno' and 'Map of Hell' clarified the results of sin in a terrifying vision of Satan and the consequences of not living a life filled with humility, compassion, generosity and forgiveness as interpreted by the Catholic church and did so to the point that, together, the poem and drawing became a profound watershed moment for an entire religious movement that dominated the world from that point in time through most of the 20th century."

Pat leaned back, took a deep breath to not only provide air but give me time to mentally digest what he'd said and then continued. "To the contrary, Lucretius concluded that all religions were superstitious delusions where humans projected concepts of power, beauty and security that they aspired to achieve, creating Gods to personalize those aspirations. As was written in the 2012 Pulitzer Prize winning non-fiction book 'The Swerve', *'Everyone is subject to the feelings that generate such dreams: they wash over you when you look up at the stars and start imagining beings of immeasurable power; or when you wonder if the universe has any limits; or when you marvel at the exquisite order of things or experience an uncanny string of misfortunes and wonder if you're being punished...'"*

"Recently we've seen the beginnings of a tectonic shift in religious participation in America. Fewer and fewer western societies have a preponderance of people attending church on a regular basis. A recent report noted that, while 86% of Americans report that they grew up Christians, only 70% still claim to be such. There appear to be dramatic shifts as more people move out from under the auspice of a set doctrine of one faith and shed their spiritual connections along the way."

Father Pat arose, stuck another dollar in the slot and pressed the Sprite button again. He returned, took a sip and continued. "A recent Gallup poll noted that the percent of the population attending services regularly is at the same percentage as it was in the 1940's. It concluded that what's happening is that the truly devoted continue to go to church, while the former ancillary members have stopped going. For some it's because many faiths no longer satisfy their spiritual needs and the human failings of those who profess religion have turned some believers away."

"For others it's because life has been filled with what I call anti-Sikhism and the once-believers are overwhelmed with greed, anger, false pride, lust and the attachment to material goods that comes from living in our materialistic society today. What appears to be gone is a sense of guilt for not going to church, just as there are so many other social aspects that previous generations felt guilty about that today's American society does not."

"In an ever-increasingly complex, stressed-out world, many people are reverting back to where it all began...personal spiritualism. This is the original faith, as there is no starting person or point when it began. In prehistoric times, people were motivated to seek out unseen and unknown forces that controlled things. Whether it was the sun or moon, summer or winter, light or darkness, they didn't know why and so they believed that there was a force or forces that controlled what they could not. Here the highest possible goal is the enhancement of happiness and pleasure and the reduction of pain, not only in ourselves but in all things living and inanimate that we come in contact with. Sadly, the greatest obstacle to happiness is not pain but delusion of achievement of more than we're capable of attaining, sustaining or regaining. Because we're inherently gripped with these delusions, the challenge of true happiness is profoundly difficult to ever attain."

"Today, Spiritualists believe there are other planes of existence...like heaven with loved ones waiting for us to join them. To this end, Spiritualists believe that humans are an indivisible part of the Devine and that God is the spirit within us all, where meditation and prayer are used to activate that spirit within each of us so that free choice and personal responsibility can allow individuals to transcend from a normal existence to one which, through the advancement of others, people better themselves. Spiritualists affirm the premise, similar to Christian Scientists, that modern beliefs mean following natural laws concerning personal growth from intellectual, spiritual and social perspectives and that love and the seeking of truth from science are critical to our existence.

"Spiritualists do not have a governing body or rules and regulations but a generalized set of precepts that state that they believe in infinite intelligence, the phenomena of nature, where both the physical and spiritual aspects are indications of infinite intelligence, where communication with the so-called dead really happens. There were and are prophets who did or do have the ability to show others the way people should truly interact."

"As a Catholic priest, it probably sounds like blasphemy. It's not! It's just that, to me, what Spiritualists have done is personified what all religions have at their core by stripping away the structure and developing a free-form method of conscience which, for me, and I think a lot of others, would be difficult to maintain. It's very easy to justify instead of rectify."

Pat put his second Sprite can on the table and continued. "As we spoke of both the physical and mental selves, neither has meaning without the spiritual self. To some the word 'spiritual' immediately conjures up a vision of religion. If so, which religion? In the troubled history of mankind, more people have unwillingly died simply because they had a different religious concept than for almost any other reason."

"Spirituality is **not** about religion. It's our concept of good and bad, right and wrong, proper and improper. Religion is simply the structure by which these elements are formalized where each religion has at its core, a fundamental belief that permeates into a series of premises about how we should act towards each other and the world in which we live. Religions then summarize the consequences of our thoughts and actions and then the personification of those actions."

"While going to church, temple, mosque or any other physical entity serves as a reinforcement of our basic needs, it's what happens in our daily lives that fulfill that profound need of the understanding of good and bad, right and wrong, so that we establish a code of conduct and the ability to properly function within that realm. Mankind inherently knows what it should be doing to the point that what's right is what makes a person happy but does not impinge upon the happiness and overall wellbeing others. What's wrong is what either makes us unhappy or transcends to other beings, both human and non-human, in such a manner as to make them unhappy."

"Sadly, our society continues to see the decline in importance of organized religion in America along with the traditional family. In some instances, these are replaced by individuals who are either too aloof or too indifferent to care about understanding the basics of life or those who shun organizations in the name of independent thought, action and belief."

"With our growing intellectual independence, it's extremely difficult to ascertain all the cannons of any religion and sustain a strict abidance to their intent, custom and/or objective. We all have the right to challenge. We all have the right to question. We all have the right to ask if the intent of another is the good of all. For many, they're simply looking at religion as a smorgasbord where they pick and choose the items they feel they need to sustain their lives and emotional balance."

A deep breath and an expression of resignation and Pat added. "All that matters is that there's a belief. Not in a supernatural but in honor, integrity and goodness that can only from having a conscience."

Father Pat stopped for a moment and looked at me intently as he added. "I sincerely believe that every single human being has some degree of spirituality and it's something everyone can, and I believe, must have. Spirituality then is simply the quest to discover what's sacred. It can be anything, as long as it has a grip on an emotional level rather than the cognitive or rational one. Spirituality is a sense of awe, a sense of wonder, a sense of profound unity with the universe in which we live can only happen to the fullest when we sincerely feel what's transpiring is good...good for us...good for others...and good for the universe, in which all beings live."

My head was bobbing in the affirmative as Father Part had hit home and he summarized, "For many, this spirituality is a personification or God. For others it's a sense of wonder at the magnitude and/or beauty of the universe, the complexity of life or the duration of time as we know it. In the end, the spiritual self is not about premises and postulates, it's about emotions and experiences that profoundly alter our being and transport us with awe to create a profoundly overwhelming sense of peace and wonder. For me this sense of awe comes from the people I meet with whom I can have conversations like this. When we're at that apex, then and only then, is our spiritual self at rest. Then and only then, will there be a fulfillment of our dreams! Then and only then will the tranquility of self-satisfaction permeate all that lies within us so that we bask in a realm of contentment, bathe in the cool blue waters of internal peace and know that our being has purpose and meaning."

There was a pause and then Pat added. "While most people perceive the spiritual self, to be that dynamic between the individual and some supreme being I hypothesize that all religions and personalized interactions between a person and a supreme being have, as the final objective, the establishment of a personalized level of ethical criteria concerning one's interaction with all creatures great and small that can be summarized as the establishment of one's character."

"To define character is a profoundly difficult assignment as it transcends social, cultural and religious parameters that permeate all levels of one's existence and are therefore spiritual in nature. In one concise summation, the establishment of one's character is predicated on the establishment of a set of criteria based on one profound aspect...respect! For oneself! For others! For all things great and small to which a person is both dominant and subservient!"

"Character begins with the little things in life that are then tested, revealed and further developed by the decisions we make in the most challenging times. It doesn't come from following a set of rules, regardless of who has made them...government, church or family, but from the small acts of responsibility we take upon ourselves every single day including the ability to stand up for what you sincerely believe in."

"In order to have spiritual character, we must know right and wrong and choose what is right. This is how character is developed. By facing tough decisions and choosing the right ones because we're honest, forgiving, trustworthy, understanding, reasonable, thoughtful and individually accountable for our actions we act in a way that's important enough to create character to the point that, in the end, it's not what we do but how we do it, that really matters!"

"Our spiritual character is the sum of our personal integrity where integrity is doing what we do when no one is watching and doing the right thing, even when we could get away with something that's wrong. Spiritual integrity is critical to every single thing we do because it's the foundation of trust in our own eyes and those around us. If you don't have personal integrity, you can't truly love yourself or others This then is formulated in our spiritual self...that point in our brain that understands right from wrong, good from bad that inhibits our transgressions."

"George, the beauty of spiritual integrity is that it's blind to all other things...age, wealth, fame or social circumstance. From the moment you're born only **you** can determine whether you'll be a person of integrity and it's not something to which there are levels...either you have it, or you don't. You can garner spiritual integrity through changing yourself from within but this means that you first must recognize and admit that you need to change, which is a profoundly difficult thing to do. Few sane people believe that what they're doing is wrong, even when it is. There's always some justification that make it right within our own mind and this is what makes it so profoundly difficult."

"At the end of the day it's not your reputation that matters it's what you honestly, sincerely and, in an unbiased manner, think of yourself. It's your spiritual self that will make that decision."

"All any religion does is create a conscience. Rather than wondering why people don't respect us, we need to respect others simply for what they are...people...people trying to do the best they can. When we accomplish this, we have begun to build or rebuild our own personal integrity."

"When this part of our existence comes to an end, if we have time to look back, we'll all be disappointed by the things we **didn't** do more than by the things we did. The woulda's, coulda's and shoulda's of life are what create more sadness, frustration and disappointment than all the failures we've accumulated along the way!"

I looked at Father Pat and asked, "Do you believe Jesus was the son of God?"

Pat looked at me, smiled and replied. "We're all God's children, and if that's the case, so was Jesus. If he was or wasn't, really doesn't matter. What matters is that he was a great teacher who changed the world with only one goal...making it better."

"Was he the only son of God?" I inquired.

Pat smiled and offered. "Muslims hold Jesus in high regard, believing him to be a prophet of God and the Messiah. They believe that he was born of a virgin, performed miracles, and was raised to heaven by God. However, Muslims don't believe that Jesus was divine or the son of God. They believe that he was a human being who was chosen by God to deliver his message to humanity."

My God! What a powerful conversation that put everything in perspective. By nearly dying, I was beginning to feel alive. In other words, death and how it saved my life...not physically, but emotionally, psychologically and most important of all spiritually.

How could I ever write what was spoken? There was no way I could say what Father Pat said and do it any justice. Father Pat had an uncomfortable expression upon his face. He looked at me and expounded. "George, I've really got to pee!"

We quickly shook hands and said goodbye. I went back to my room and took out my pen and began. I'd written about physical and mental health. Now I needed to add something - anything - about spiritual health. I took looked at the paper and simply wrote. "I sincerely believe happiness only comes to those who accept themselves for what they are…imperfect, temporal beings willing to grant there's a benevolent force greater than themselves. This force understands and allows weaknesses and infirmities, while providing the essence needed to understand right from wrong, good from bad, and tolerance from intolerance while practicing humility, compassion, generosity and forgiveness. When we have all four, then and only then, will the physical self, mental self and spiritual self truly be alive."

**Release Relief:**

Father Pat visited every morning and I visited my lady friends as well. In both instances, I watched slight smiles turn into grins as strangers became friends and someone to look forward to. For those nine days I did my best to make our time together better for all of us. With each day, I was feeling a little better. With each day, I was feeling stronger. With each day, I felt both my body and soul starting to heal as I began to realize that all I'd done with the foundation was give my resources and not myself and for the first time in my life, I felt the profound joy of giving, not judged by material things but by the wealth of goodness within me.

On the tenth day, Doctor Goodman came in and did something I'd never seen before, he sat on the edge of my bed and announced I was being released while calling me Wonder Boy, saying it's a wonder I was alive. I looked at him and replied I didn't leave because God wanted me to see the majesty of giving of myself.

Doctor Goodman wasn't aware that it had been me going to visit my 'lady friends' and inquired, "So it's you who's done what we could never do."

"What's that?"

"Give hope to a group of old ladies by putting a smile on their faces and joy in their heart and something or someone to look forward to each and every day. George, you truly are a great man."

"No, I'm not." I retorted. "You see, those ladies put hope in my heart and gave me something to look forward to and I'll never forget the majesty of giving I received."

"George, I received a call from Mr. Rodney Whitehorse, president of the Hochunk Nation who inquired about your wellbeing. He told me they call you Little Spirit and I asked why. He noted, it was because of your inherent goodness and generosity of spirit. At first, I thought it was a hyperbole and, yet, as I've gotten to know you, I've begun to realize you're special in so many ways. I can't thank you enough for reassuring me there's goodness in the world

130

as people like you are what made me become a doctor and continue to allow me to reap the rewards for what I do. By the grace of God, you made it. Be careful and don't forget about the *other* problem. You can go when you're ready. Make sure you follow the guidelines the nurses go over with you."

With that, the euphoria of getting out of the hospital was gone and reality set in as I offered, "I've got to stay until two. I need to say goodbye to my lady friends."

We stood as Doctor Goodman at first, shook my hand and then pulled me in and gave me a hug before saying, "I normally don't do that but you've restored my faith in what seems like an endless journey for many of us. Thank you."

I sat back down on the edge of the bed and reflected on all that had transpired. From the edge of death to a future… still somewhat clouded… but brighter than it had been for a long, long time. I looked out at the cityscape and realized I hadn't been outside in over three weeks. I hadn't heard a bird sing or a dog bark. I hadn't smelled the scent of summer or felt the soft grass on my bare feet and, yet I wasn't remorseful for my hiatus. In fact, I was grateful as there was a new perspective on life that made me realize I'd taken so much for granted that made me promise I would never, ever forget again.

Father Pat came in and I gave him the news. He already knew! We promised to keep in touch and I asked him when was his day off. He said Wednesday, even though he still came to see me even then. I offered to take him fishing. A huge smile crossed his face as he noted it had been a long time since he had done that. I told him there was one condition. He asked what it was. I replied, "Unless it's winter, don't try walk on it." He almost split a gut laughing and it was great to see a different side to him as he inquired, "Do you mind if I gather the fish? I once heard about a guy who went fishing and caught 153 in one day and that's my goal." One more hug and then Father Pat was gone…out into the world…on to another lost, lonely soul too frightened and concerned, aware that all stories must have an end, including mine.

After lunch, I packed up my get-well cards, thanking God they weren't expressions of sympathy and put them out of the way, until Amy was scheduled to arrive. I then went down to the gift shop and bought eight red roses. At exactly two, I went back up and gave seven ladies kisses on the cheek and thanked them for saving my life. I then took the remaining rose and placed it on the pillow where Mary had slept, as I slowly slid my hand across the bedspread and whispered, "Thank you, Mary."

As I was walking out that ward door, I turned and smiled one last time at my 'lady friends', knowing the faces I touched would be for the very last time. Within seven months, all that was left were memories. They'd all joined Mary, leaving me with only the recollections of days gone by where the warmth of giving of myself prevailed and provided new meaning to my life.

## Heading Home:

Amy arrived, came up to the floor to thank all the nurses and caregivers, simply duplicating what I'd already done. Even though it was almost 3:00 PM and their day off, both Sam and Reggie came to say goodbye. It seemed strange to see them in 'street clothes' and was thankful for the care given, yet anxious to get out of prison.

We rode down on the elevator and Amy got the car and we headed for home. It felt good to see the world again. You take so much for granted when you're in it every day.

"Anything you need?" Amy inquired.

"Le' Duc's!" I replied.

A smile crossed Amy's face as we went south on Highway 83 at the 287-mile marker. As always, there was a line. I sat in the car and watched my wife order my strawberry shake. We'd been married 35 years and she'd birthed three kids, yet she was still as slim and trim as the day we met. I guess the one-hundred push-ups and sit-ups each day really did matter.

She opened the driver's door and slid in next to me, handing me my shake as she began slurping down her chocolate custard with marshmallow topping. After two bites, she looked at me and smiled mentioning, "Glad you're home."

"Me too," as my left hand slipped across and squeezed her right in a gesture of gratitude.

We ate our treats and headed north to Pine Lake. Amy pushed the button and the gate opened and I was home. I opened the passenger door, stood for a moment and felt the breeze. I took a deep breath and smelled the lake. I looked at the lawn and realized Amy had someone mow it and was grateful. We made our way in the house and it was as if time stood still. Everything was as it had been on the day I almost went away. One day, we'd agreed not to say the word 'died' and I kept my promise. Amy had lost her mother, dad, brother and Aunt Julia and couldn't fathom another departure.

The events of the day and over three weeks of inactivity had taken their toll and I was tired. Amy asked if I wanted dinner and I politely said, 'No.' We went into the family room, sat on the couch as I looked at the photos of the kids and grandkids on the fireplace mantel and thanked God to be alive. I closed my eyes for a moment and was gone…a deep sleep without the beep, beep, beep and clamor that had been a part of my twenty-three-day existence.

Around ten, Amy awoke me and told me to come to bed. Still tired. Still worn out. The thing I wanted and needed the most wasn't going to happen. I knew it. She knew it. We knew it. Instead, I kissed her, told her I loved her, whispered 'Goodnight Moon' and fell asleep.

We come into this world programmed to do one primary thing...sustain our genetic heritage. We have primal and learned behaviors that transcend that single objective... propagation of the species. As mankind became socialized, the period of bonding became extended and with it, the entire spousal concept. No one can expect it will be easy! Marriage is a very difficult task, and, yet, it's one of, if not the most important jobs in a person's life, if they expect to be happy and satisfied. I awoke around four and listened to Amy breathe, spending my reflective time peering at the ceiling and trying to figure out why my wife lived with me, tolerated me and what were the key ingredients in our, or any marriage.

In the hospital, I came up with seven components that seemed to add up regarding creating and sustaining a viable relationship with someone to whom you were legally bound. They are attraction, association, communication, understanding, trust, compromise and forgiveness and that's what marriage is all about.

Long term marriage is NOT easy! First, there's familiarity that breeds commonplace instead of exception. Add to this the media making you think that if you only did this or purchased that or went here or there, you'd be happier, more glamorous and more attractive to others, including your spouse.

After breakfast Amy said she had some errands to run and I simply nodded. The thoughts in my head were swirling and I wanted to get them down on paper. While the computer was there, I looked at the sheets I scribbled at the hospital and decided I wanted to continue to hand write my thoughts and e-mail them to Ceclia. From my heart to my mind, to my hands, to my fingers, to the paper before me, my goal became nothing more than an expression of my emotions. When I reached a point where I didn't really have enough depth of knowledge, I acquiesced and turned on the computer, googled my perceptions until I had what I thought made sense.

As I looked at the photo of Amy on my desk, I reflected on why I fell in love with her and why that love remained. I pondered why and realized there were four critical reasons why I was and remain attracted to her. The first was and remains a physical component. We are often attracted to people we find physically attractive that goes beyond their shape. For me, it was Amy's eyes and smile. I can remember where, when and how we met. I could take you back to the exact spot and how the glisten in her eyes and smile literally stopped my beating heart.

Experts say that attraction is a combination of factors including our genes, culture, and personal preferences. I don't know about the genetic aspect, I do know that American culture, normally places a woman's physique at the top of the list. While our first encounter was brief when she appeared as the UPS driver, it was probably, no make that, because of her looks, that sparked my interest. That lithe body! That light caramel colored skin and hair! All that I could have imagined was there. Yet, it went far beyond her body to her eyes and smile as they were the most beautiful eyes and smile I'd ever seen.

However, it was our second encounter at the Nitty Gritty that placed the bait in my mouth and made me swallow - hook, line and sinker. It was then I realized that, while we came from different backgrounds and were partially of different races, we literally laughed the night away, filled with double entendres and madcap innuendos.

Dating is like a play where you portray yourself in a manner you hope will appeal to the other person to the point they want to witness the next act. As our relationship grew I realized Amy's outer protective layer was a lot like mine and yet, below those protective wrappers, we were both so much more sensitive and introspective than our exterior persona provided. As we grew closer and closer, the facade began to thin as our real inner cores became exposed such that, in many ways, we realized we complemented each other yet had different strengths and weaknesses that have helped us grow and learn in this thing called life.

Finally what attracted me to Amy and has kept me there all these years is the chemistry between us that I really can't explain. I learned that initially it's a neurochemical cocktail that lit the fire and believe kept the bond as strong as it is where the attraction sustains itself not by chemical elicitation but by the garnering of mutual trust, mutual respect and mutual reward simply because there's a singular point of reference we both can rely on through good times and bad, happy times and sad with a profound sense of security that we are there for each other, forever.

The concept of nothing is an absolute as is the concept of forever and neither can happen, simply because there are no absolutes in life. Because of this fragility, it's important we always remember that attraction is a complex thing where there's no one reason why we're attracted to some and not others in both conscious and unconscious ways that need to be recognized and nurtured day-after-day, week-after-week, month-after-month, year-after year till death do us part.

**Desire:**

Amy came home with lunch…KFC. One would think that eating in hoity toity restaurants all over the world, while selling some of the finest beef, would make me some kind of connoisseur, yet every now and then I love KFC and Amy remembered. As we sat finishing off the ten-piece bucket with mashed potatoes, gravy and kernel corn, I looked across the table at my wife and understood why, after all these years, I still yearned for her.

We finished lunch, cleaned the table and, as Amy was putting the dishes in the dishwasher I came up behind her, turned her around and gave her a deep kiss. As we embraced, my hands slid down until they reached her lower back and I pulled her in as a slight gasp of expectation escaped from her lips.

"I love you," I whispered.

"Me, too," Amy replied.

"Well I'm glad you love yourself but what about me?" I sarcastically countered.

"Smart ass!" Amy retorted.

"I know…everyone likes a little ass but no one likes a smart ass," I responded.

Amy leaned back and looked deep into my eyes and offered. "How about tonight we put candles around the hot tub, get all relaxed and then….?"

As we embraced, for some reason I remembered my wedding vows when I took a personalized version of the First Letter of St. Paul to Corinthians and whispered to myself, the final few sentences.

*"When I was a child, I would talk as a child, think as a child, reason as a child. When I became a man, I put aside these childish things but was still not whole. Until I met you, I only partially knew life and what it meant to live. Now that we are together, I am complete because I know and accept that while our marriage will rely on faith, hope and love, the one that will always carry us on forever and is the  greatest of all is love!"*

The spell was broken when the phone rang and it was Melia calling to see how I was feeling. I looked at Amy and smiled as I made my way into my office and turned on my computer. I had printed articles from the day before and began organizing them as my mind kept jumping ahead to the hot tub and our adventure. Even with my mind in split decision mode, I was able to write.

As Amy and Melia were on the phone, I remembered Amelia Erhardt's wedding vows and how different they were and realized that my marriage was structured more like hers that what I had professed.

*"If we are to have an existential relationship, we both must accept the foundation of a free will and the ability to think, act and be what we were or are!"*

As I thought of these words and what they meant, I surmised that the real key was commitment and partnership and how they are constantly being challenged in any marriage by changing times, changing circumstances and changes in life and our perspective of the meaning of just one word…*'happy'*.

Amy had things to do and so I went to my office and began writing.

"For all of the waywardness blamed on this controversial four-letter word, lust is actually one of the most practically useful urges of human expression. Chemistry, appearance and our own learned predispositions for what we look for in a mate play an important role in who we lust after as well. Without lust, we might never find that special someone. While lust keeps us "looking around," the one we lust after isn't always the one we're actually in love with and it's our desire for romance that leads us to fall in love."

"Love is expressed as an action and experienced as a feeling. Love has an essence that resists defining in any single way that encompasses compassion, determination, tolerance, endurance, support, faith, and much more. At its core love is attraction... physically, emotionally, sexually and yes, chemically."

"If you've ever been in love, you've probably felt it was some sort of addiction, because it is! Humans are wired for romance in part because we're supposed to be loving parents who care diligently for our helpless babies. Romantic love both exhilarates and motivates us. It's also critical to the continuation of our species. Without the attachment of romantic love, we would live in an entirely different society that more closely resembles some social circles of our sibling species. This stage is intended to be "love for the duration" where we passed fantasy love and  entered into real love, I came to realize that the bond must be strong enough to withstand the many problems and distractions that come from this thing called life."

"If you're a proponent of the theory of acclimation, where the human species acclimates to its environment to the point that it no longer produces the chemicals found in the inception of any event, circumstance or surrounding and things then return to "normal", real marriage begins."

"If you don't believe the hypothesis, think about all the things that were once special that became mundane due to repetition in your life, houses, jobs, cars, events, people! With repetition, the neural responses began moving through the same synaptic channels and chemical production in the brain is either dramatically reduced or dissipates entirely."

"Studies have shown that passionate love fades quickly and is usually gone after two or three years because the procreation chemicals   -   adrenaline,   dopamine,   norepinephrine, phenylethylamine, etc. - dwindle. Suddenly your lover has faults. Why has he or she changed? Actually, your partner probably hasn't changed at all. It's just that you're now able to see them rationally, rather than through the blinding hormones of infatuation and passionate love."

"If the relationship can advance, other chemicals kick in. Endorphins, for example, continue to provide a sense of well-being and security. Additionally, oxytocin is still released when you're having sex, producing feelings of satisfaction and attachment and vasopressin also continues to play a role in attachment."

I took a deep breath and hoped I wasn't pontificating. I looked at the clock at it was nearly five realizing someone else in room 630 was about to get their dinner.

There's nothing better than a warm August night in Wisconsin, sitting out in the screen porch listening to the sounds of summer, drinking a cold beer. Man, that's what makes Wisconsin God's country. I offered to grill and cooked porterhouse steaks. After dinner, Amy put her arms around my neck and whispered, "Remember Lake Wingra? Let's go for a swim." It was already getting dark and the yard had been sprayed by the mosquito company and so I slyly smiled and said, "OK".

Quietly, we went to our beach, slipped out of our clothes and slid into the cool refreshing water of Pine Lake. While most 'Pine Lake people' have both the lake and a pool, the freedom of skinny dipping in the lake was just the right mood maximizer as Amy and I swam, hugged and slipped into one of those physical modes you only dream about. Finally, we made our way to the pool and walked in holding hands and then each other. Sadly, nothing transpired. I was embarrassed, ashamed and frustrated. Amy vowed we'd 'save it for the next time'. What a sad, pathetic reminder to 'welcome home'.

## Interpersonal Attraction:

Morning came and Amy said she needed to go to Wilco. The after effects of the previous night remained and by the time the gate closed, I already missed her. My world was still thinking of our relationship and the interpersonal attraction. As I sauntered into my study, I turned on the light, re-read the details from the day before and continued.

"Interpersonal attraction can be defined as the attraction between people which leads to friendships and romantic relationships. The entire process is actually different from perceptions of physical attraction, which involves views of what is not considered beautiful or attractive and is why cross-gender friendships can flourish without having the relationship turn sexual."

"Interpersonal attraction is a major area of research in social psychology that is related to how much we like, dislike, or hate someone. It's perceived to be a force acting between two people that tends to draw them together and resist their separation. When psychologists measure interpersonal attraction, they refer to the qualities that create the attraction including, not only the physical aspects, but the other components such as personality and situations as key ingredients. Repulsion is also a factor in the process regarding one's concept of 'attraction' which can vary from extreme attraction to extreme repulsion."

"Propinquity is probably an unfamiliar word to most people. According to Rowland Miller, a propinquity effect is defined as 'the more we see and interact with a person, the more likely he or she is to become our mate.' In the initial attraction of two people components such as physical attractiveness, responsiveness and propinquity to those who are similar and responsive to us, along with those who like us are paramount."

"So far, most of what I've studied has dealt with the physical aspects of a relationship, without all the other components of attraction, such as, the intellectual and social elements, without which the physical part wouldn't be there. Another bazillion books, give or take a few, have been written by a whole lot of experts and so what I write is pretty basic."

"One really neat theory is called 'the interpersonal attraction principle'. In this concept, social psychologists identified several factors that influence why two people are attracted to each other including affection, respect, liking, friendship or physical partner. This effect is very similar to an exposure effect in that the more a person is a receptor of a stimulus, the more the person will like or dislike - social allergy - that stimulates them."

"Until recently, familiarity was perceived as only happening when two people interacted. However, with the advent of the internet, studies now show that familiarity can also occur without physical exposure, where the same patterns can be created to resemble those developed face-to-face, in terms of quality and depth, as if the persons had actually met."

"Similarity is also a crucial determinant of interpersonal attraction. Studies about attraction indicate that people are strongly attracted to those common to themselves in physical, intellectual and social levels, which can encompass everything from physical characteristics to life goals, ethnicity and appearance. This attraction goes beyond the physical elements as people are attracted to others who are similar to them in demographics, attitudes, interpersonal style, social and cultural background, personality, interests, activities, preferences, socio-economic status, communication and social skills. With the advent of the internet, people are turning to online internet dating sites which is changing everything VERY fast!"

"When attraction evolves in a positive manner, it normally turns into a more profound sense of caring about the other person to a degree that's more intense than that experienced with other people. The question then becomes, what differentiates caring from attraction?'

"Caring is a feeling of concern and affection for another person. It's a willingness to help and support others, even when it's not convenient or easy and is an important part of any relationship, whether it's with a family member, friend, or romantic partner. Caring is a way of showing that you value the other person and you are committed to their well-being."

"Caring is a critical part of life and its happiness. Without caring we would all be indifferent and there would be no peaks...only valleys. Caring could, in its purest form, be classified as 'passion'...a passion for life, a passion for love and a passion for other beings, both animate and inanimate. While many people would call passion for others compassion, I don't! To me, that word sounds didactic, elitist and condescending. With passion [caring] there becomes greater value and, therefore, the chance of a greater loss and sorrow."

"Perhaps that's why so many people remain passion-impaired. With passion comes risk, where the loss can become greater, the disappointment more profound, the emptiness even deeper. When something for which we have passion suddenly dissipates and we feel pain, today's plastic world tries to minimize it so that we're never allowed to be sad. One MUST be passionate, caring and enthusiastic."

"Without these attributes we're only a shell, walking, interacting, functioning in a world like some plastic snowman sitting on a neighbor's lawn at Christmas. There but not really...glowing but not really...dynamic and three dimensional...but only as what they represent and not what they truly are."

"Caring is part of our self-concept. It must be a segment of our inter-personal definition that gives us dimension. We care because we want to fully integrate ourselves with other people and other beings...to make ourselves better and hopefully make them better... to think, feel and act...in such a manner they too walk away from one of life's intersections better, more positive and in some way moved by meeting us."

"When you've led a life of 'the look' simply because I'm white and Amy is mixed race, the article by Sharon Johnson that summarized a study of 5,000 young recipients by Match.com found that 86% of today's younger generation find nothing wrong with interracial relationships, 80% with interfaith and 65% with same-sex marriages. Perhaps, finally, our stigma is going away with the hope it won't be there at all for Derrick, 'V', Melia or our grandkids."

"I can only imagine what it was like for Amy's parents and thank them for their dignity in tolerating what they had to go through. Genetically, there's a 99.9% similarity between Caucasian and African humans. This means that the two groups share 99.9% of their DNA. The remaining 0.1% is responsible for the differences in physical appearance, such as skin color, hair texture, and eye shape."

"I once told our kids, it's important to realize that the concept of race is a social construct, not a biological one. There's no scientific basis for dividing humans into different races. All humans belong to the same species, Homo sapiens and the concept of race was developed by Europeans in the 17th and 18th centuries simply as a way to justify slavery and colonialism."

"Life's too difficult as it is to have to endure ostracization simply because of the color of our skin and when you're attracted to someone, it shouldn't be limited by social constricts predicated on race, religion or orientation. It's your life and the goal is to make it as meaningful as possible and that means finding someone to share it with."

It was late afternoon when Amy arrived and asked how I'd spent my day. Without lying but also not telling the whole truth, I said I was simply doing research and trying to add to what she read from the hospital. She asked if I was up to going to the Five O'clock Club for dinner and I simply smiled which meant yes, and so we went where I was honored when everyone asked how I was doing, which made me feel good.

## Curveball:

Another day of reading and writing. I'd already used up the ink in one of my pens and my eyes were blurry as the afternoon was quickly coming to a close. I stood and stretched and heard the gates open and hoped it was Amy. It was. She came in with a bag of groceries and a harried look on her face.

"Are you OK?" I inquired.

"Sure! Why?" she inquired in a very short way.

"I don't know, you seem a bit frazzled."

"Traffic was terrible."

"Do you want to go out for dinner?" I asked, trying to take some of the sting out of her day.

"Not really. I just got home." Amy replied in a somewhat abrupt way.

"How was Wilco?" I asked.

"A mess!" she responded.

Two words…two lousy words and that was it. In the old days, we'd go through the details, now the subject and Amy, both seemed almost unreachable.

"What's on your agenda for tomorrow?" I asked.

"I need to go back to the office," Amy replied in a very tacit way.

"OK. Do you want to talk about it?"

"What's there to talk about? Things aren't going well and I need to be there."

"Anything I can do to help?"

"Not really."

I knew that when she got in one of her 'moods' to back off and so I let her quietly make dinner and we ate in almost abject silence. After probably ten minutes she asked, "What did you do today?"

"I worked on my manuscript."

"Do you want me to read it?"

"Not yet. I've still got more I want to write."

"What do you think you're going to do with it when you're done?"

"I don't know. Hopefully give it to the kids."

"Do you think they have time to read anything? They're so busy, they hardly have time to even call."

That brought up a sore subject. Amy had come to the hospital every day. Melia called every other day. 'V' came to visit and called once. I got a plant from Derrick but that was it. He'd always been the distant one and so I didn't think anything of it.

After dinner Amy went to her office and me to mine. I thought long and hard about what to write and this is what I came up with.

"Rewards are the part of a relationship that makes it worthwhile and enjoyable. Costs can be anything that can cause irritation. Comparison levels are also taken into account during a relationship suggesting people expect rewards or costs depending on the time invested. If the level of expected rewards is minimal and the level of costs is high, the relationship suffers and both parties may become dissatisfied and unhappy."

"While there can be a degree of permanence, there's always a comparison of alternatives going on in a person's brain meaning that satisfaction is temporary and conditional. This subconscious maelstrom is predicated on the inherent feeling that another person could replace the current relationship with one the individual perceives to be more desirable.

It's this underlying similarity principle that applies to both friendships and romantic relationships that's important. There appears to be a high correlation between the proportion of attitudes shared and degree of interpersonal attraction. As an example, happy people like to be around other happy people and dour people would rather be around other dour people or themselves. When an individual perceives characteristics similar to themselves in on-going relationship, bonds are more easily formed either in self-serving - friendship - or relationship-serving - romantic - relationships."

"The look-alike effect also plays an important role in what is called 'self-affirmation' where a person typically enjoys receiving confirmation of every aspect of their life, ideas, attitudes and personal characteristics. It seems that most people are looking for an image of themselves to spend their life with."

"To say that two people would only be attracted if they were the same is ludicrous! So many factors go into the equation including not only all the social dynamics but personalities, as well, where the term 'personality' refers to individuals' characteristic patterns of thought, emotion and behavior. What creates an individual's personality is actually a combination of nature and nurture...nature - genetics - and nurture - environment. The genetic aspect correlates with our own chemical composition along with the creation and elicitation of all the brain chemicals."

"Simply stated, the daily balance of brain chemicals have a profound effect on our entire mental process and therefore our moods and core attitudes. In psychology, this is called 'temperament' and usually refers to those aspects of psychological individuality that are present at birth, or at least very early on in child development, and are related to emotional expression that are presumed to have a biological basis."

"There is generally, a recognizable order and regularity to behaviors. Essentially, people act in the same or similar ways in a variety of situations. Personality is psychological in nature but is influenced by an individual's neuro-chemical processes that influence how that person moves and responds in their environment and how they act or react regarding thoughts, feelings, close relationships and other social interactions."

"When the attraction of a marriage moves beyond the 'chemical phase', the length of the average relationship becomes related to perceptions of similarity (called convergence) where the couples who remain together longer are seen as more equal as they become more alike through shared experiences. At the same time, the attraction is enhanced when long-term couples are more complementary of each other. Studies found that people would be more satisfied with their spousal relationship if their partners differed from them, at least, in terms of dominance, as two dominant persons may experience conflicts, while two submissive individuals may have frustration as neither member take the initiative."

"In the end, the attraction part of the relationship is based on the melding of personalities, convergence and complementary roles and relationships that create a unified bond called 'we' instead of you and me."

"As a marriage, or partnership continues, the entire concept of the theory of acclimation takes hold. What's special becomes common, what's common becomes mundane! What's mundane becomes intolerable! Here's where the marital physical challenge really begins and where seven critical factors required to sustain a viable marriage come into play."

"From all of this, we can quickly see that the secret to a long-term spousal relationship is the maintenance of attraction. We need to be TRULY attracted to each other physically, mentally, emotionally and spiritually."

"We all change and the 'honeymoon' chemistry will dissipate! We get older and change in the different aspects. When the core attraction is there, the spouse remains special... continues to be placed in a position of awe and remain the light to which we can confidently turn when we find ourselves in a realm of darkness. This is the real attraction and why, through thick and thin, people stay together."

At eleven, I crawled in bed and Amy was already asleep. I turned off the lights, stared at the ceiling and woke up at seven the next morning. The house was quiet and when I went into the kitchen, there was a note on the table telling me Amy couldn't sleep and went to the office early. I didn't think anything of it as she'd done this dozens of times before.  I ate breakfast and went to the computer. I wanted to finish the segment on spouses and so I began where I left off.

**Now What?:**

I did research and worked all day. My eyes were tired. You can only do so much computer time and then you've got to stop. I looked at the clock and it was 6:30 PM. I'd been reading for over ten hours. Where was my wife? Why hadn't she called? I was now upset and concerned when I heard the gate open and assumed it was her.

Amy walked in the house and looked frazzled. Her normal perfect hair was askew as was her make-up, which certainly wasn't like her.

"Tough day?" I inquired, to which I got a cold stare and reacted with, "Sorry."

"I don't want to talk about it. Ok?" was her terse response.

"I was just trying to see if I could be of any help."

"I'm tired. I've had a rough day. I'm going to have a drink, take a hot bath and go to bed."

I stood there and realized I was not part of her evening plans. I went to our video room, turned on the big screen and watched a Packer pre-season game. "We interrupt these commercials to bring you one play of football!" At eleven, I crawled into bed and listened to the silence of nothing…nothing said, nothing felt, nothing but the emptiness of feeling alone.

Morning came and once again, there was a note on the table that she'd left early. Once again, I rattled around the house and went to my study and began again.

I needed to take a break and decided to go for a walk. When you live in the country it can be a bit difficult as no one seems to want to come across some old guy walking on the highway and the days of avoiding them are gone. I took my chances and made it out to Highway 83 and back again just as Amy was pulling in the driveway.

As she pulled into the garage, I know she saw me and, yet she closed the garage door with me outside. Now I was pissed as I pressed the security code and the door opened.

I walked in the house and Amy was in the kitchen with her head in her hands. While normally, I'd be in some sort of consoling mode, I was upset by the garage door incident.

"Didn't you see me walking down the road?" I inquired in a somewhat irritated manner.

"Without looking up Amy said, "No, I didn't see you walking down the road."

"Well, I was and I was walking up the driveway when you closed the garage door."

"And?"

"And? And you simply ignored me."

"I didn't ignore you. I didn't see you."

"Bullshit!"

"Fuck you!"

"Gee, thanks for the invitation." I retorted.

"What's that, another one of your smart-ass attempts at being cute?"

"You said 'fuck you' and wouldn't that be what two people do?"

"Two people make love and not fuck. When I said fuck you, I meant, go to hell."

"What's your problem?" I shouted.

"My problem? My problem? How about our problem?" Amy castigated.

"What?"

"You…why did you tell the nurses about Melia in Saint Martin? It's none of their fucking business that Melia and I had an argument."

The shit hit the fan. Amy was always very protective when it came to our family as I replied. "Is that what this is all about? Me telling two nurses about Saint Martin."

"People don't need to know our personal business. Telling Reggie what Melia and Annie were doing on Happy Bay is inexcusable."

"What?"

"Well, isn't that what you told her?"

"Hell, no! I said Melia was angry about the security and kissed Annie to express her anger."

"Reggie said that you told her Melia and Annie were naked."

I thought for a moment and realized I'd indicated Annie was naked and how that could be construed and finally tried to explain. "Reggie wanted to know about the beaches and decorum, that's all."

"It didn't come out that way and what about the tattoo? Why did you tell Reggie about that?"

I looked at the floor and then at Amy and replied, "sixty-five percent of all people getting tattoos today are women. Fifteen percent of men and thirteen percent of women already have them. We don't live in a gilded world. You've got one and I'm thinking about one for myself."

"You? Why would you get a tattoo?" Amy challenged in a sarcastic tone.

"Because, I'm sick and tired of being so…so fucking conservative. I just about died! Now I want to live. I'm from a time past and now, I want to do things that bring me up-to-date."

I paused for a moment and then simply asked, "What's this all about?"

Amy glared at me and answered, "I don't want you sharing our family life."

It was then everything came into play as I spun the table and asked, "How do you know I told Reggie about Melia?"

There was a long pause before Amy could reply. "Because."

"Because what?"

"Because, I had lunch with Reggie and she filled me in."

"You had lunch with Reggie? I thought you were going to Wilco."

Amy knew I had her in a lie as the emotions drained from her face.

"I was there and then Reggie called and we decided to have lunch."

"Lunch and what else?"

"She had some questions about Saint Martin."

"Questions you couldn't answer on the phone?"

I paused for a moment and then simply asked her, "Is this another Karen episode...or Sydney?"

Tears gathered in Amy's eyes.

"It is, isn't it? Errands and Wilco two days in a row. Instead its Reggie. I saw it when you two first met. Beneath it all, I knew it was there."

Amy looked at me with a sympathetic plead and then down at the table and then back at me. "You don't understand. I try! I really, really try and, yet I can't." With that, the tears flowed and she literally convulsed in remorse.

I stood, not knowing whether to be angry, hurt, frustrated or compassionate. With what I'd been studying, I felt I knew more than before and, yet one still feels as if they're not enough. After a long pause, I inquired, "What about the other night? Was that real?"

"Oh, George, it was real. I love you. I hoped that by making love with you, the urge would go away. When I met Reggie for lunch, it was just that. Nothing more! Can't I even have lunch with someone without you being jealous?"

"Jealous? How can I be jealous when I didn't even know about something?

I looked at the floor and pondered what I should do or say. As the silence became deafening, it was Amy who spoke. "Reggie just had questions because you said too much."

"What does that mean?

The tears were flowing as Amy looked out the kitchen window at Pine Lake and replied. "I would have but didn't."

"You're the one who said we've always got to be careful. Remember Karen? Remember what it took to shut her up? I shared a few things about Mela and you go ballistic and yet you...you!"

I left it at that. When you're standing in a hole, stop digging. I guess we were both wrong. But then what had Amy really done?

Had lunch with a woman? I need to be more reticent about what I say. God, a mountain out of a mole hill!

No dinner was served and none expected. The silence in the house was deafening as I went to my study, turned on the light and worked until I thought Amy would be asleep.

**Revelation:**

I knew that the boiling pot would not stop overnight and morning breakfast was anything but cordial. I also knew we both needed time to cool down and so I went to my study and began writing again. Little did I realize that by day's end, I would have, in an indirect manner, accepted what I'd professed so long ago, finally realizing I was the one out of step, where the only issue was one where I felt violated by the events and not the circumstances.

It took me a long time to realize what a couple does together help makes marriage better. I began to regularly find things I liked about Amy's appearance, character and abilities that I sincerely appreciated and took pride in telling her and showing I'm truly grateful for all she does for me. Things aren't perfect! However, my number one caveat has been loyalty! I don't say negative things about her behind her back. I defend her if anyone speaks negatively about her. I never ever undermined her authority in front of the kids and I don't mess around!

I try to recognize and make allowances for times when we're tired or upset or not our usual self. I read and now understood the consequence of being bi-polar and try to respect Amy's mood swings and opinions. We might not always agree but I try to. I sincerely try to consider her views and understand her needs. I'm a long way from perfect, but I try. For major decisions, we try consult each other before making them. I love the fact that we continue to share our plans and dreams and are open and honest with each other about every aspect of our life. It's not easy! There are things I don't like and yet my commitment to Amy and dedication to her are so strong that the commitment and allegiance usurp my dissatisfactions.

It took a very long time before I realized what I enjoy isn't what Amy likes and how she experiences something isn't the way I do. I believe that, at the core of all satisfaction is learning about oneself so that you can derive pleasure simply in being. I don't know if this is the case for other couples. However, when I see this happen -

when two people do unite, they do so out of profound emotional desire and not out of a sense of physical, or social starvation. When this happens, and only when it happens, can a union be one that is a creative blessing and not a form of dependency.

Sustaining attraction for each other isn't easy. Our life is a journey where the experiences along the way give it meaning and no experience is more profound than inter-personal intimate experiences that shape, define and meld who and what we are to ourselves and our loved ones.

In all aspects, living life to the fullest means looking over the horizon to see what's on the other side! By discovering you learn. By learning you expand your knowledge and increase the parameters of thought and deed.

It was three-thirty in the morning. Perhaps I was over-reacting. Perhaps, I was simply tired of fighting and making her so frustrated. Perhaps, just perhaps, my mind was changing, like so many others and what transpired was something I could accept. It was going to be difficult and, yet, as I thought back to that first time I learned of her proclivities and pronounced my vows of acceptance, I realized that tacitly, I hadn't lived up to my side of the bargain. I'd told her then that I would accept her. I'd told her I would share her. I'd told her I would still love her and for all these years she'd resisted what now seemed to precisely be what she's needed all along, and did so, simply to satisfy me.

**Results:**

The weeks were literally roiling by. I was now five weeks out from being released from the hospital. During the week, I had appointments with the cardiologist, phlebotomist, urologist and psychologist. Fortunately, there wasn't an appointment with a gynecologist thrown in.

Doctor Goldman, who'd been my primary at Milwaukee General, came first and scheduled a stress test. All systems go! Whoopie! One more week, and I could fly again as long as I wore compression socks.

Next came Susan, the phlebotomist, who stabbed me and literally sucked me dry when I called her Vampira Jones. Why did they need five tubes of blood?

Next came, Doctor Thompson, the urologist, who looked at my numbers from the DRE and most recent PSA and noted we needed to do something and recommended discussing it with Amy as the results were indicating I needed to have a nerve sparing radical prostatectomy. The virulence was such that it appeared I might have conditions that would exacerbate the prostate Cancer to evolve from Stage Two to Stage Three and that was not good.

I asked what the difference was and the good doctor indicated that stage one simply meant cancerous cells within the prostate. Stage two meant more cancerous cells that were still in the prostate that had not reached the wall. Stage three meant cancerous cells that had reached the wall of the prostate, while stage four meant the Cancer had spread beyond the prostate.

I swallowed hard until Doctor Thompson noted, "George, today, more than two million men in America who have had prostate Cancer, are **ALIVE**!"

To some men, the reality of hearing what lies ahead can signal a profound 'change' that can be emotionally debilitating. They feel their manhood is about to be taken away. They feel as though the one natural instinct common to all will be removed, eradicated, erased in a few snips and stitches.

I was directed back to Thompson's office for the pre-surgical orientation. Angie, one of clinics PA's appeared. She had to be in her mid-thirties and was very professional in her demeanor. I think she knew most men were embarrassed by the topic of conversation.

Her first topic was the statistical aspect of my malady. Angie noted that 25% of all Caucasian, 40% of all African American and 15% of all Asian men got what I had and that, normally, the situation was such that the Cancer was slow growth.

Angie handed me a packet of pamphlets and I was instructed to read them while adding "The reason you're having surgery and not radiation or brachial seed implants is due to the virulence of your Cancer, measured in what are called your 'Gleason's' which are moderately to fully aggressive. The oncologist feels any other method beside removal won't work. Without removing the cancerous prostate, things can become morbid. However, by removing the prostate and therefore the Cancer, your probability of living a longer life increase significantly." Slam, bam, thank you mam, as is the case with most physicians today, no time for small talk as Angie rose and walked out the door.

I drove home and opened the packet. Each pamphlet was staggered in height from small to large and included in one master packet to indicate the reading sequence. The first was about anatomy and physiology regarding how the male reproductive system works where the testes create the sperm and the prostate creates semen and what happens to create and erection and climax. The pamphlet also addressed what happens as we age and how the prostate functions in terms of not only sexual response but urinary control.

Next, came a pamphlet regarding the DaVinci Robot and the surgical procedure regarding not only the process but the recovery period and what I would need to do to prepare and finally what to expect during the recovery period. It seemed amazing that I'd have the surgery one day and be released the next.

The third pamphlet dealt with the consequences of the procedure and noted that removal of the prostate interrupts the process and the patient is literally sterilized. It went on to state the reason the procedure is called a 'nerve sparing radical proctectomy' is that the surgeon *attempts* to save the parasympathetic nerves that run adjacent the prostate. These nerves control the smooth muscle in the penis which regulates blood flow to the corpus cavernosa which are a pair of sponge-like regions of erectile tissue.

The corpus cavernosa consist of a network of blood vessels, smooth muscle, and connective tissue where, when a man is sexually aroused, the smooth muscle relaxes allowing blood to flow into the tissue causing the corpus cavernosum to swell and become erect.

While nerve sparing is the goal, the ability to do so, considering the delicacy of the nerves, that are like wet tissue paper, compounded by age, results in a decreasing probability the nerves can be spared. The net result is erectile dysfunction or ED."

If being sterilized and suffering from erectile dysfunction aren't bad enough. The pamphlet stated that, "Like any other part of the body, when not used, the corpus cavernosa and penile structure begin to atrophy and patients experience penile length shortening or PLS, that affects both length and girth of the penis.

Concurrent with this, the frenulum, or nerve endings that communicate through the sympathetic nerves that are not affected by the removal of the prostate become less distended and therefore less sensitive to stimulation. While climax and pseudo-ejaculation can still take place, it becomes more difficult to create the necessary arousal.

The next segment noted that removal of the prostate also means elimination of the prostatic sphincter which is the valve between the bladder and the urinary tract. With its removal, the body has to learn to use the perineal muscles located between the legs for bladder control. By incorporating what are called Kegel exercises, the body quickly learns how to primarily control bladder function. However, the same muscles are used for balance, lifting, profound laughter and coughing and when one of these takes place, there can be the discharge of small amounts of urine called urinary incontinence, or UI, commonly called 'dribbles and drips'.

The next consequence of prostatic surgery may be weight gain. This may be due hormonal changes, psychological issues or lack of physical activity. This can be compensated for by a more stringent awareness of diet and exercise.

Let's see...sterilization, erectile dysfunction, penile length shortening, urinary incontinence and potential weight gain. In medical terms...Sterilization, ED, PLS, UI and weight gain. The only good news was that the probability of living five years after the surgery increased to 90%.

The final pamphlet dealt with the psychological aspects and was virtually a sales brochure from a psychologist named Michael Sternberg, specializing post-prostatic depression.

After reading all this I was about as enthused as I was going for my DRE. This was serious!

**Not-so-great Expectations:**

Amy and my verbal altercation slowly subsided and we were back to square one. She appreciated my written details and was more than supportive when it came to what lie ahead. A timetable was set for something that sounded so urgent, yet it was still five weeks before Robbie the Robot would be available for my surgery.

With summer turning to fall, I looked at the Badger Football schedule and had some strings pulled so that I would have three weeks between Camp Randall visits in which to recover and the day was set.

I hadn't done much writing and then the urge was upon me, to write that is.. I'd left off with attraction and still had spousal association, communication, understanding, trust, compromise and forgiveness to cover. I was about to address the subject of association when Amy had a proposal. "Let's go to Saint Martin." It sounded great to me even though I was going to miss sitting in Camp Randall watching the Badgers play East/West, South Carolina State.

I asked her if Reggie and Sam had ever taken their trip and she indicated she didn't think so as they wanted to wait until the weather was more amenable than the heat and humidity of summer. I mean, why leave Wisconsin in the summer when you can go in fall or winter and escape the cold?

"What would you think if we went down the same time they were there?" Amy inquired.

"After the summer escapade I was tentative and, yet, after what I'd written, I would have been a hypocrite if I let one circumstance get in the way and acquiesced. Amy called 'the girls' as we began calling them and Reggie informed her that they were on their duty cycle and would have four days off.

Amy asked if they could skip a cycle and go for a week. Reggie indicated that she'd love to but didn't think personnel would allow it. Amy asked if she and Sam really wanted to. If so, Amy thought she could pull a couple of strings and have their shift moved. A telephone call was made and miraculously Reggie and Sam's shift was deferred and they would have eleven days in a row off so the trip was planned. The threesome was excited. I was filled with trepidation. How was this going to work out, even though we'd be at two different houses. I thought about it and all that was about to happen and went into my study and did some more research and wrote the following.

**Association:** "A comprehensive relationship transcends the attraction aspect and incorporates doing things together and not just in the physical arena! Association means that both parties take their interests and dislikes and modify them so that there are times, circumstances, events and situations they share. An association is defined as two or more individuals who voluntarily enter into an agreement to accomplish a purpose. The purpose obviously is life, yours, theirs and your offspring's."

"The biggest failure of marriages starts when couples begin living separate lives, no longer sharing activities, thoughts or their inner world. 'Alone together! Alone apart! If they began all over, they'd never start!'"

Amy is and will always be my number one priority. With work and children demanding both of our attention, it was easy to ignore the other adults in our lives. I try to take a moment each day for Amy to let her know I'm thinking about her.

Is our marriage perfect? Hardly! Have there been 'bumps in the road?" Of course. Yet, when someone asks me, overall, how has your marriage been, I give in an eight out of ten. I don't think anyone ever has a ten. I learned my lessons the hard way and so, when I was asked the secret to our marriage, I said. "Your spouse MUST be your best friend! The word 'friendship' conjures up thoughts of honesty, vulnerability, companionship, and mutual respect. It also implies a certain outlaying of time and energy... TOGETHER!"

"Association, is about building that true friendship through common experiences by doing things together. This is when friendship begins in a marriage. It can be anything...movies, dinner, simply walking, household chores and fighting shoulder to shoulder. Friends look in the same direction at the same time. Marriage without friendship cannot work in our culture. Friendship has to be nourished and nurtured regularly or it faces the danger of becoming a business relationship. Couples that don't give attention to developing their friendship often come apart."

"In marriage, the ultimate question is...'am I investing more emotional energy in my spouse than I am in my job, friend or child?'"

"After all those years of being on the run, I vowed we'd have at least one meal together each day. I realize this **is** association... doing things together.... growing together... experiencing together... creating memories together! We're a very long way from perfect but we're trying! I'm not proposing not doing things apart! Our world must go beyond each other or the mental aspect outlined previously will not happen. We need to have a realm that includes others... other people, other interests, other events and circumstances! What a couple must do is blend both associations and worlds into one classic event that can be shared when needed and done so with a semblance of balance and equity."

## Communication:

After our bout with 'he said – she did' Amy and I were getting along like the old days while my outpouring of acceptance of her for what she needed, opened up a once-closed vault that allowed her to express herself more openly than ever before. From this and before our trip, I was inspired to add yet another few pages to my thoughts.

"When you're attracted and then associate, you're well on your way to achieving the third element and that's communication. It's imperative we speak and listen to each other. Not just words but thoughts and feelings, likes and dislikes, elements that allow us to begin to delve into each other, unlike anyone else."

"One of the best ways to sustain a relationship is by showing true interest in what your partner is saying or communicating. If we show interest and sincerely respond, they will pick up on it and be honored. It's not just the words we say but how we say them that are important. When we use words and actions and deeds and then REALLY listen to what our spouse is saying keeping their words and actions and deeds in mind, then and only then are we really communicating."

"Another precept I read removed the skill sets and breaks communication down into four different components of which we all have varying degrees of proclivity. Some people communicate by seeing and doing. They like activities and gifts. They notice people, places and things with just the slightest glance. They take things at face value and don't look deeper into things. They feel and share love by doing things with or for other people. Some people communicate through talking. They have the natural gift of the gab and are designed to be able to talk for long periods of time. They enjoy talking and listening to other people talk. They feel loved when they're talked to and like to hear the words I love you."

"Digital people communicate through connection and understanding. They find the deeper meaning in everything they think, see and do. Understanding is very important to them. They feel worthy when they share connections with others and are understood.

"Kinesthetic people communicate through their bodies. They move, feel and express through their bodies. Kinesthetics love to touch people and things around them and like physical activities and physical forms of affection. Regardless of the type of person we are, there is some sort of communication channel that can be traveled that will allow us to enhance our relationship with another person."

"Within all the communication modes, we need to feel free to ask our partner how they feel if we're ever in doubt. We just need to keep in mind it's how **<u>they</u>** feel and NOT how we feel or think they would feel that's important. How sad to sit in silence and listen to nothing, see nothing, hear nothing and feel nothing. How lonely to be within a crowded room with someone we care for and feel singular in thought, mind and spirit."

"Life and love are those magic components that allow us to escape the singular mode, the isolation and foreboding silence that comes when we're alone. In our world today. loneliness is one of the biggest issues facing so many people...Young! Old! Somewhere in between! We see their faces peering out from beneath a veil of sadness expecting so much more than what we have… reaching out, trying to touch someone to share this thing called life."

The beauty and joy of a long-term marriage is the combination of attraction, association and communication. I am profoundly blessed! My wife is a wonderful listener and a great caregiver. When I've expressed my emotions, she's been there for me to comfort and console, to direct and even reprimand, when I need it, because she's been with me, understands me and profoundly cares for me. She sees me from the outside and how my actions and reactions affect others in ways that I quite honestly don't see.

I can sense Amy's level of guilt about her orientation and temptation. Even though I completely understand it's what's natural for her and accept it, she feels remorseful about the way she is. I have always accepted and now really understand that we all have strengths and weaknesses, foibles and idiosyncrasies that can upset us when we try to live within what our society and culture deems as normal. Yet, when we don't match up to the rules and regulations compared to who we really are, there can be an overwhelming sense of guilt that shouldn't be there. I not proposing we avoid cultural norms or violate the sanctity of innocence and decency. I'm saying that what's right for one person doesn't always have to be what's right for everyone.

## Understanding:

Reggie and Sam were excited and I think Amy and I were, too, but for different reasons. When you're used to getting on your plane and going anywhere in the world to be sequestered for nearly three months, with no travel and little to do, any respite from consistency seemed invigorating.

After all the blood clots, and my now prevalent fear of flying, we were taking one of the speed demons to minimize flight time. As we boarded the plane I announced to Reggie and Sam. "Ladies, welcome aboard Amelia[X.] She's a Spike S-512 SSBJ personal aircraft designed to cruise at Mach 1.6, or 1227 miles per hour, which will put us in Saint Martin in about 90 minutes.

"There aren't any windows!" Sam proclaimed.

I proudly offered. "The edges of the windows create too high of a drag coefficient that affects the intensity of breaking the sound barrier which is simply the speed that an object must overcome in order to travel faster than the speed of sound or 767 miles per hour, which is also called March One. When Spike approaches the speed of sound, the air in front of it has to move out of the way very quickly. This causes the air to compress and creates a shock wave, or sonic boom. This isn't a physical barrier. It's a limit imposed by the laws of physics that include increased aerodynamic drag which is why there are no side windows. Each seat has a screen that allows you to see all the different sights as if you were on the outside of the plane. We have some snacks on board as well as drinks. I don't know if you imbibe or not but we can normally satisfy most tastes."

Even though we'd had our 'travel' sessions at the hospital taking literal strangers to a place where customs are different has its challenges. We really didn't know the girls, as we called them, and I was concerned about propriety. In my experiences of dealing with medical professionals I learned they either were quite modest or had minimized their inhibitions based of what they did day after day and experienced in their careers.

In bringing someone to Saint Martin with its liberal outlook on life, I had no idea what to expect from Reggie and Sam. I hoped they were what I thought or what their outlook would be...young, open-minded and somewhat adventurous, yet socially cautious and somewhat 'proper', if that's the word I needed, without being dowdy.

Amy and I had discussed the cultural differences between Milwaukee and Saint Martin and agreed that she needed to let the girls know there was a difference. On the plane Amy explained, "Like Europe, Saint Martin is a lot more liberal than Milwaukee in terms of attire. At the same time, the island isn't against women covering themselves or being modest. Men and women have the choice to cover or not to cover - be modest or risqué."

"The beauty of the culture is that it's your 'choice' and 'freedom' to dress as you choose and not have one way of dress forced on you by any man, religion culture or government. There might be those who judge you but they'll not only be in the distinct minority, but are people who would have probably judged you anyway. More than likely, it will be people you'll never see again as long as you live."

Both Reggie and Sam nodded in the affirmative. I don't know if it was because they agreed or they understood. All we could do was let them know they weren't in Wisconsin anymore.

Amy had picked up one of the fancy-schmancy leather Wilco folios for me with the tablet inside and with time on the plane and the girls gaggling, I was able to create another chapter in my epistle about marriage. I'd done some research that would serve as my foundation for explaining who my wife was.

With the past regarding Amy's delicate emotional structure, I knew I needed to study what was going on so that I had a better understanding of why she was the way she was. Over my months of study, I really didn't want to share it with her and so I always told her I was working on Terrill B&B stuff and she accepted my explanation as I clandestinely researched social dynamics.

Amy had been diagnosed as having Bipolar II Disorder when she was in college, characterized by episodes of hypomania and depression. We knew her severity was mild and the kids called the bouts, 'her mood'. Yet, we also needed to watch for indications it might reach a higher level as she got older which, we learned was quite common.

I once asked a physician what caused her condition and was told the exact cause is unknown but was thought to be triggered by a combination of genetic and environmental factors. He also said it's more common in people who have a family history of the disorder which might have been the case with Amy's brother Derrick.

I'd known throughout our marriage but could never actually predict when it would flare up except when she was under a lot of stress. For Derrick I attributed it to the drug and alcohol abuse or vice versa which was why Amy always scrutinized her alcohol consumption.

I've accepted Amy for who she is and she me. I'd assured her numerous times I understood her proclivities and physical needs. I also studied and learned there's some evidence there may be a correlation between bipolar disorder and bisexuality where studies found bisexual people to be more likely diagnosed with bipolar disorder than others.

As long as I'd known Amy she'd always been less than inhibited when it came to her body. She attributed it to the psychological impact of her leukemia and how her self-concept was shattered when she lost so much weight and was socially shunned. One can only imagine what it's like to go from a vivacious young woman to a walking skeleton so emaciated everyone associated her with death and would look away as she walked by.

Amy is also left handed and there's some evidence that left-handed people are more likely to develop bipolar disorder than right-handed people. A study published in the journal "Schizophrenia Research" found that 40% of people with bipolar disorder were left-handed, compared to 10% of the general population and may be due to differences in brain development. I was thinking about getting a subscription to the magazine but was afraid our mail lady would think I was nuts.

In my research I found articles stating there appears to be some evidence to suggest there's also a correlation between bipolar disorder and lower levels of inhibition than in people without the malady. The study also found that the level of bi-polarity somewhat determined whether the proclivities remained at a low level of self-consciousness or transcended into exhibitionistic tendencies. Putting them together - mild bipolarity, cultural tolerance and medical trauma - seemed to create the reasons for the lower level of inhibition and sexual orientation of my wife.

Regarding Amy, her condition always concerned me regarding the stability of our marriage. The term bipolar relationships is often thrown around to describe partners that blow hot and cold with each other or are always in conflict. In reality, being in a relationship with someone who has bipolar disorder is a lot more complicated and we've been blessed that our 'issues' never moved beyond a little anger and a few tears or to the point of me ever questioning my profound love for her.

Contrary to many others Amy and I have a successful, fulfilling relationship even though there have been some problems. The biggest problem is that her mood swings and behaviors are often unpredictable, and not all episodes follow a specific pattern. This makes it difficult to know where I stand and I feel worried about her safety when she's acting impulsively or don't seem like herself. I can tolerate the funk, it's the anger and irritability that can be especially challenging.

Fortunately, Amy's condition is such that she's never had the destructive or impulsive behaviors that are hallmark symptoms. We're both cautious about alcohol and/or drugs, excessive spending literally has had no meaning, gambling or, to the best of my knowledge, engaging in risky sex which would cause strain and conflict in most long-term relationships hasn't been there beyond what I've known.

Since we've been together, there's always been a profound sense of honesty between us such that, when her depression strikes, I usually know what to expect. It's not easy, but we get through it and simply move on. To be bipolar must be really difficult. To have it exacerbate or precipitate other tendencies has called for patience, tolerance and understanding...on her part...not mine, and she's been a real trooper in determining her own self.

Regarding the other issue, I wanted to understand the challenges of her situation and did research into it and learned that it's estimated that bisexuals comprise four million adult males and seven and one-half million females in the US. In a study, that examined bisexual identity, current relationship characteristics, feelings about bisexuality and mental health, it found staggering levels of emotional struggles. Fifty-eight percent of the respondents reported either high or very high levels of psychological distress, with histories of anxiety, depression, and eating disorders the most common. Sixty-seven percent reported they had been diagnosed with mental illness by professionals. Almost half of the respondents disclosed self-harm or thoughts about suicide within the last two years. 28% had attempted suicide and seventy-eight percent thought about it.

The numbers were staggering and frightening as I realized the profound level of anger, fear, frustration and disappointment Amy must have felt and potentially continues to feel. My only hope was based on my acceptance and continuing mantra that her orientation wasn't wrong and my assurances seemed to be helping. I love her more than anything and to even imagine she thought of suicide sends shudders up my spine.

One night, Amy and I had a very frank discussion of what *'it'* felt like to be bi-sexual and she replied, "The darkness is darker, and the colors deeper but the path is rougher." She looked in my eyes and quantified. "However, the love is stronger, the passion richer and the success sweeter, simply because I know what love is."

I inquired. "When did you realize your orientation?"

Amy put her finger before her lips and pondered for a moment and then replied. "I think I always knew I was different. When I was little and played with dolls, I had Barbie and Ken and was attracted to Barbie as much as Ken. For a long time, I fought it and thought I was a lesbian, until I realized I still liked guys.

I went from a very diverse grade school with multiracial students to junior high where I was the only mixed-race girl in my class. I didn't want to let anyone know that I came from an extremely wealthy family and so I kept a lot of my emotions internalized. I was a very quiet child, very afraid of being myself, who just wanted to blend in. I was bullied, didn't make many friends and developed a stutter."

"I started to have an identity crisis that only got worse in high school. A lot of kids were going through issues at home or were being bullied at school and it was a very lonely time. I remember feeling very misunderstood and silenced."

"In school, we weren't taught about anything other than heterosexual relationships in sex education. We had no LGBT networks where being gay was something we only saw in magazines or on TV and never anything about being bi. It wasn't something openly discussed. I knew it existed but it was very much a taboo subject. I didn't understand my own feelings. I knew I felt attracted to people regardless of their gender."

Amy had a forlorn look on her face as she added. "One of my few friends came out and her life was turned upside down. She was bullied and quit school. I witnessed how hard she had it and even though she was so brave I couldn't do it. I pushed my feelings to the side, hoping they'd go away and conceal who I was."

"Hiding my sexuality was a lot easier than hiding my race. When I went to Georgetown, I wasn't visibly 'out' and there was a lot of internal pressure to be visible when it really wasn't possible. I mean, at the time, being considered black and having a different orientation at a Catholic School was a real challenge. However, I was living the most authentic life I could where I felt I had no choice but to hang out with my straight friends, hear homophobic language and just blend in. I couldn't be who I really was around certain people. Even in grad school, people kept assuming I was straight because I was never in a different relationship they knew about."

Amy took my hand and continued. "When I was 21 years old, I finally admitted to myself that I was bisexual. I also realized I was having mental health problems with an emotionally unstable or borderline personality disorder and depression. When I found out I had a personality disorder I was shocked and then I read the symptoms and reflected on how I felt and behaved and it all made sense. Because of the family and my fears about how it would affect mom and dad, I knew I couldn't join the LGBT network because the group was bi-phobic. Whenever I was around them, I overheard members using the terms 'greedy' or 'confused' when speaking of other bi's and I realized I couldn't be my whole self."

I sat in profound awe that my wife was allowing me into her inner soul making me both proud and afraid as I reflected on a book I read in English 201 called 'The Picture of Dorian Gray' written by Oscar Wilde. I looked at Amy and said. "Oscar Wilde once wrote, 'It's better to give in to temptation than to resist it. If we resist temptation, our souls will grow sick with longing for the things we've forbidden simply because desires are natural and healthy and when we deny them, we're denying part of ourselves."

Amy sincerely nodded and replied. "My psychologist told me virtually the same thing...desires are a part of who we are and shouldn't be suppressed. Instead, we should find healthy ways to express them and not always let the laws of society dictate what we can and cannot do because laws are often based on fear and prejudice. She added, 'You continue to constantly deny yourself the things you want and have resented yourself and your life and now feel guilty and ashamed which is probably the cause of your depression and anxiety.'"

Amy looked down at the ground as if to reflect on the challenges she faced and then finally at me as she continued. "My psychologist noted that it's important to remember that not all temptations are created equal. Some temptations are harmless. Others can be harmful to your physical, emotional, or spiritual well-being and we need to be able to distinguish between the two and resist the temptations that aren't worth it. My question was, 'how do I know which ones are harmless and which ones are harmful?' I knew what I inherently felt. I knew what I wanted and I knew that until I tried, I'd never feel fulfilled. Yet, I was afraid of the social recriminations and ostracization of being... being... in the middle - shunned by both the straight and gay communities."

There was another pause as Amy collected her thoughts and continued. "Besides the leukemia and being what's categorized as a 'tri bi'....bi-racial, bi-polar and bi-sexual, I came to St. Martin to die, simply because I wasn't brave enough to do it myself, especially after my brother died from an overdose. Fortunately, I realized there are places and people in the world who accept me as me and that's when I fell in love with here and why it's so special."

Amy had a pensive look and then added. "Right before I met you, I decided to come out to my parents. Mom said she already knew and had known since I was little and was totally supportive. I was afraid of my dad finding out until mom told me, she and dad had discussed it when I was in high school and he supported me whatever the consequence."

"When I did come out and tried to associate, others accused me of being attention seeking where my sexuality was fetishized simply because bisexual erasure is and remains rampant. We're gay when we have same-sex partners, straight when we have different-sex ones. Yet, oddly, neither gay nor straight people become asexual when single. As soon as a previously thought of 'straight' a person comes out as bi and is seen with someone of the same-sex, it's described as a 'gay fling' or a 'lesbian crush'. People don't seem to understand, I'm neither. I'm not gay, nor straight. You're the only person who seems to fathom what I'm like and yet I know, deep down, I hurt you. I don't mean to, but I do and no matter how hard I try, I can't change."

A smile erased her former forlorn look as Amy reflected. "George, one of happiest days of my dad's life and mine was when he met you and felt my love for you and you for me. Mom asked me if you knew and I told her we'd discussed it. It was then that she too had joy in her heart as her prayers were answered that was validated when the boys and Mela came along."

Suddenly, tears welled in Amy's eyes. "I know there are days, but things are getting better. Now I know why my moods feel so intense and are highly changeable. I understand why I feel disassociated with myself and the external world because at times, in my youth, I de-personalized who I was simply to feel accepted. Now I realize the more I accept who I am, the less depressed I feel and the less confused about my identity. I'm now able to acknowledge that my emotions, memories and experiences are real and valid and the only person who gets hurt is you."

I simply shook my head no as if to express my disagreement as Amy continued. "Without you George, I don't know if I would have made it. You not only accepted me for who I am but believe in me. Being tri-bi is incredibly difficult. You get it from all sides. Yet, because of you, I've felt the greatest feeling of all and that's true, unrequited love...love of me for simply being me. I know it isn't easy. I know there's always doubt and yet I'll always keep my word to you that I vowed the day we got married."

Amy leaned back and had another sad look on her face. I put both of her hands in mine and tried to be consoling as I offered. "We all have something that makes us different. Yours just happens to make you special."

I was glad Amy shared it with me. She knew more about herself than most people. I'm also proud to say I've acquired a better understanding of who my wife is and can honestly and sincerely tell her there isn't anything wrong with her while I accept her with open arms with all my love. It's just how nature made her and what's natural for her. In my heart I ache, not about her inclinations, but knowing how dreadful it must be to go through life thinking you're bad when in fact you're simply responding to the way God made you.

I'd begun writing about understanding before we departed and simply reflected while the girls excitedly talked about St. Martin. As they laughed and giggled, I put the finishing touches on another aspect of marital success.

Time together, sharing of events and circumstances and inter-personal communication leads to the fourth critical element... understanding, which, through perseverance and caring, results in empathy.

"But how do we acquire empathy?"

"Yup! Our brain is wired for empathy through what are called 'mirror neurons' which are parts of the brain that react to emotions expressed by others the neurons reproduce those same emotions in ourselves. More succinctly, mirror neurons are a type of brain cell that respond equally when we perform an action or witness someone else perform the same action. They were first discovered in the early 1990's when a team of Italian researchers found individual neurons in the brains of macaque monkeys that fired when they grabbed an object and, also, when the monkeys watched another primate grab the same object."

"Here are some generic examples....You're driving home. Out of nowhere, the car in front of you gets smacked by a driver texting and running a red light. Automatically, you recoil in sympathy. You're watching a football game, and you feel your own heart racing with excitement as the tailback crosses the goal line. You see a little kid sniff some unfamiliar food and wrinkle their nose in disgust. Suddenly, your own stomach turns at the thought of the meal."

"Specifically, as we traverse life with our spouse and children and grow to better understand them, we also seem to expand the magnitude of our mirror neurons towards them so that we share their joy and sorrow. In other words, we increase our empathy or the experience of understanding another person's condition from **their** perspective. We place ourselves in their shoes and feel what they're feeling and become a spectator of life! Our mirror neurons come into play!"

"I wrote of intellectual growth that comes from replication and reasoning. What better form of knowledge than the person we're living with? Understanding another person is profoundly difficult and, yet, it's the core of any lasting relationship! It's what allows us to appreciate what's good and accept what is bad! It's what makes today as alive and exciting as yesterday and tomorrow!"

"How can we possibly understand someone else if we don't understand ourselves? There are a million ways we can begin to understand who we're. Life, as it progresses, has a way of showing us what we're made of and provide ways to learn how to accept ourselves for what we are. This is truly one of the genuine gifts of growing older."

"Self-understanding is not something we can sit down and deduce. Most self-knowledge comes gradually and without immediate impact and, yet there can be finite moments of true realization that can end up providing profound levels of release from years of denial, self-doubt or even guilt. It all starts with admission... admission of who we're... strengths and weaknesses, good and bad, fact and foible, little-by- little, until we have a clear picture of WHO we are as much as what we are."

"Alternatively, self-realization can be something more profound. In most cases the experience affirms long- held intuition, which can offer a sense of reassurance. Nonetheless, self-understanding can change the way we think about our past – successes and failures, life choices and relationships so that we're open to understanding our partner that much better. This is why it's so important we continue to learn about each other throughout our marriage. This requires time, communication, persistence, imagination and patience. Sadly, a couple may share their home, lives and love and yet realize we experience and interpret our worlds in different ways that lead to simply not understanding one another."

"People who take their wedding vows with the utmost sincerity and have been staunchly committed to each other can still fall into trouble if they don't grow and change with their spouse throughout their marriage. We need to continually "update" our understanding about our spouse. When we've spent a lot of time with someone, done things together and have truly communicated so that we know the person's beliefs, feelings, inhibitions and expectations, then we can begin to understand who they are and that becomes the next element of the equation. The challenge is understanding is like a moving target as both parties are constantly in a state of flux so what we know today can have little influence tomorrow."

"Just as we understand our job, community or how something else works, understanding another person is profoundly critical to truly bond with that person. Books and articles have been written and columnists remain employed simply to outline the challenges of understanding. The core of this conundrum lies in not understanding how the other person thinks, it's that we all live in our own truth where we're biased and somewhat dishonest with ourselves."

"Think of how many different points of view we get when people witness the same event. These people aren't lying or misled, they're simply relaying their interpretation through the filter of their own experience and perceptions. This means that instead of one set of variables we have two. This makes understanding a moving target where the truth varies as the experience varies to the point that it's important to understand that your partner has their own reality and perspective as they have experienced it."

"We can share all the activities...bonding, convergence and unification but failing to have this perspective can result in a total lack of true understanding. If this is the case, what can a person do about it? If they feel they don't understand how their spouse thinks, it may be a matter of perspective. In many cases in simply means peering through their glasses at the world, while their spouse sees the world through their own unique periscope."

"Being human, we truly can't determine if our understanding of our partner is correct but we can put forth the effort to try. A person should accept the limitations they have concerning the extent of understanding someone else and allow that they may be misinterpreting what their partner tells them."

"Similar to witnessing an event, if there's an incident involving two people that later leads to an argument, each person has their own perspective about what happened. The first person wants their spouse to agree with their view of what happened and their partner wants them to agree with his or her perspective."

"As we experience convergence and grow together, we can learn about the person and what makes them tick. These elements and their personality will be filled with both great and wonderful as well as lousy and sad components that come with the person. There will be things we love and things we hate, things we admire and things that simply drive us crazy. Don't worry, they're thinking, feeling and wishing the same things about us."

"There's no such thing as the perfect person, nor the perfect marriage but it starts with attraction, association, communication and understanding and just when we think we have all it figured out, we realize that, like us, the one we love is changing too, ebbing and flowing with thoughts, emotions, experiences and deeds that change who and what they are. It's important to understand these differences to foster a healthy marriage."

About seventy-five minutes into the flight, our captain came on and requested we buckle our seat belts. We were about to land when all the video screens came to life showing what the pilots saw and we could watch the plane make its approach. I told the girls they could slide the vertical guide on the right side of the screen and it would magnify the image if they so desired. I did and there was Uncle Frank waiting with the Rover by the International Security gate. It was good to see him after the summer I had.

We landed, taxied to the international area as the door opened with the rush of hot, humid October air. We made our way down the stairs as I introduced Reggie and Sam to Uncle Frank. Even at 83, he still had a roving eye and infectious smile as he did a once-over of both girls promising to make certain their vacation would be one they'd never forget. Little did we know then how true that statement would be.

**Trust:**

We made it to 'House on the Hill' and ensured Sam and Reggie were familiar with the floor plan and amenities. As always there were fresh flowers on the table, food in the Sub Zero and all the perks of wealth. The final subject was the watches. We made certain the girls understood that no one would be watching them but assistance was always available.

I asked the girls if they preferred wine or alcohol and both indicated wine. We went to the vault and went through the security protocol and opened the vault to dropped mouths. Picking out some Terrill red and white for their indulgences, throwing in a bottle of Terrill bourbon for emergencies, I told them if they needed more, just let me know.

"We're only a couple miles away and so we're here but not here, if you know what we mean."

The girls expressed their gratitude and we left them to enjoy the week.

Uncle Frank drove us to the 'Lighthouse' and we took the tram to the top. The sun was just setting and so Amy and I went out by the pool and watched the spectacular light show. As the sky darkened the sensors turned on and we were ensconced in the warm glow of their illuminations.

As was the case on virtually every trip, the first night meant dinner at Le Taitu which is a very casual, indoor/outdoor restaurant that's run by two brothers whose love of food is exemplified with every bite. To say dining was casual would be an understatement. Amy opened her closet and took out a pair of old shorts and tank top as I slipped into my traditional t-shirt, baggy shorts and flip-flops.

We were welcomed and shared a bottle wine with a fresh crab salad and then it was back to the 'Lighthouse'. We slipped out of our clothes and took a quick dip before calling it a night.

I awoke at six and the house was empty with a note indicating that Amy had gone for her run and would be bringing croissants from Good Morning. I jumped in the pool to wake up, wrapped a towel around me, grabbed my folio and began writing.

The fifth element only comes from the ongoing repetition of attraction, association, communication and understanding and that's trust. What a unique concept in today's world! If we take the word 'run' for example...we see a word filled with so many meanings and so many different interpretations. Now try the word 'happy'...not as many possibilities but a much higher level of interpretations and references based more on personal experience. Now the word 'trust'...even fewer meanings and fewer interpretations but much greater impact. There are types of 'ions'...degrees of 'happiness'... but only trust and mistrust."

"Trust is a complex concept that has been defined in many different ways. In general, it is a belief in the reliability, truth, ability, or strength of someone or something and the willingness to rely on someone or something, even when there is some risk involved. It's essential for any kind of relationship, whether it's personal, professional, or even commercial. Without trust, it's difficult to cooperate, share information, or build lasting relationships."

"Trust is predicated on a series of activities who's outcome is the anticipated response in result, degree and consequence. An infant trusts its mother to nurture, love and care for them. A child places their small hand in that of their father for guidance and security. A teenager trusts his friend with their deepest secrets. A parent trusts a child with their car."

"When a pattern evolves where an action precipitates an anticipated reaction, then trust can begin to be built with others. It's when the action doesn't result in the anticipated response that we begin to distrust the event, person or circumstance."

"Trust is important but it's also dangerous. It's important because it allows us to form relationships with and depend on others, especially when we know that no outside force compels them to give us such things. But trust also involves the risk that people we trust won't pull through for us. If there was some guarantee they would pull through then we wouldn't need to trust them. Therefore, trust can also be dangerous. What we risk while trusting is the loss of the things that we entrust to others, including our self-respect."

"Because trust is risky, the question of when it's justified is of particular importance. If trust is warranted then the danger of is either minimized, as with justified trust, or eliminated altogether. Leaving the danger of trust aside, one could also ask whether trust is justified in the sense of being possible. Trust may not be justified in a particular situation because it's simply impossible. This is because the conditions necessary for trust don't exist, as is the case when people feel only pessimism toward one another - like in separation, divorce or finding out your spouse has had an affair."

"What value does trust have? Although the value trust has for a particular person will depend on his or her circumstances, the value it could have for any particular person will depend on why the trust is valuable. Trusting someone provides us with benefits beyond those that come with cooperation but, again, for these to materialize trust must be justified. Sometimes trust involves little or no cooperation so the person who trusts is completely dependent on the trustee, although the reverse isn't true."

"Total trust would be an absolute. Most people can't perceive absolute anything except, perhaps trust in God. We certainly can't totally trust ourselves, just as there is no such thing as total darkness. We can't totally trust another, just as there is nothing that is totally white. There can be degrees that approach some ultimate point but we can't sense a way that two human beings can ever TOTALLY trust each other. Does this mean we should shirk from attempting to develop such a relationship? Hardly! In fact, trust should reflect the need to constantly strive for the ultimate in any relationship - the union of two people - physically, emotionally, intellectually and spiritually."

"How can one have a successful relationship without trust? Trust is all about predictable results. When we trust someone, we trust their instincts, we trust their behavior and we trust their loyalty. Distrust is when those expected or anticipated responses just don't happen. Trust is truly built on character. If one doesn't have character, one can't be trusted in business, life or marriage!"

"How can two people be bonded together when they don't inherently trust each other? How can two people expect to function as one unified body when one or both sides can no longer precisely anticipate what the other half is going to do, say or act? People change! Experiences change! Trust should never, ever, ever change IF people want the partnership to thrive."

"Trust is a complex psychological concept that has been defined in many different ways. In general, trust can be understood as a belief in the reliability, honesty and integrity of another person or group. It's a willingness to rely on someone or something, even when there's some risk involved."

"Trust is an essential component of all relationships, from personal relationships to professional relationships. It's also important for social and economic interactions. Without trust, it would be difficult to cooperate with others, to make commitments, or to take risks."

"Trust is built over time through repeated interactions. When someone is trustworthy, they keep their promises, they are honest, and they act in a way that is consistent with their values. When someone is untrustworthy, they break promises, lie, and act in a way that is inconsistent with their values."

"Attraction, association, communication, understanding and trust. Five down, two to go...compromise and forgiveness."

**Compromise:**

Amy returned from the beach to report nothing had changed. The crowds weren't there because of the time of the year and she was able to get her run in and then stopped at Good Morning.

After thirty years I still was surprised by how good of shape Amy was in and no longer surprised by the brevity of her Saint Martin attire. I didn't know if Amy's suit would fall in in Melia's Itsy Bitsy or OMG categories. I was doing everything I could to 'contemporize' my thoughts and, after so many years, accepted that, in Saint Martin, she could wear whatever she wanted. She was comfortable and indifferent and that's all that mattered. She wasn't trying to entice, seduce, enthrall or objectivate anyone, including herself. It was just what she felt met her needs for the time and place we were at.

We sat and ate our croissants with Irish butter and strawberry jam and proceeded to simply sit out by the pool all morning. Around 11:00, Amy asked, "Where do you want to go for lunch?" This meant, which restaurant on Orient Beach.

"I don't care, you choose today and I'll choose tomorrow." We'd played this game for years and so it was nothing new.

"I'd like to go down to Le' String."

"OK."

We made our way down behind the new restaurants and parked behind our building with the activity store, Lucille's and Le' String as tenants. Amy and I were warmly welcomed as we began enjoying a wonderful lunch while relaxing on the beach loungers, swimming and drinking bargain beers for the hell of it. I had delicious mahi-mahi with coconut rice, leeks and vegetables. Amy had grouper in tomato sauce with risotto, topped off with some beautiful rose wine from France.

As we were about to leave, Reggie and Sam appeared.

"Hi girls!" I offered, waving at the two of them as warm smiles crossed their faces. Reggie and Sam walked up and there was the traditional small talk as they told us about how wonderful everything was and how much they appreciated the house and laid-back atmosphere. We stood and talked about the different restaurants and what each one was known for. I felt that I was with a human rainbow… light, medium and dark brown women all contrasted by good old pasty white me.

Reggie looked at Amy and said, "Mrs. Terrill"

"Make that Amy, please."

"Amy, I love your suit. Did you buy it down here?"

Amy smiled and noted that she'd purchased it from Lucille as she nodded towards the store that was virtually next door.

"Do you want to see if she has anything you like?" Amy inquired.

"If you don't mind." Sam replied.

I interjected. "Remember, ice cream to the Eskimos!"

Amy grinned, shook her head and asked. "George, why don't you watch our things while the girls and I do a little shopping?"

I got the message. "George, this is serious and men aren't welcome."

I snarfed down a couple more beers and watched the human parade. I don't know how long the girls were gone but when they came back, I had a whole new leader board as both girls came back carrying plastic bags with more suits designed to entice the boys and pay Lucille's rent.

For October, it was still hot and muggy and Amy suggested we go for a swim. Now, there are dreams and they are DREAMS and to think I would be cavorting with three great looking girls would be any guy's fantasy except the aspiration was thirty-six years too late and all I could do was pretend to be a dirty old man for a little while.

For the next half-hour we goofed around in the gentle waves and then got out. I grabbed the beach towel and wrapped it around my waist as the three girls simply hung out in more ways than one, oblivious to the looks, smiles and stares of the passersby. Gee, to be young and good looking. I'd add the caveat 'again' but it never happened in the first place.

A couple more beers, a little more wine and it was time to go...not only in terms of departing but bladder wise and any reservations I think the girls once had.

Amy and I began walking to the Rover as I glanced over my shoulder at the two somewhat inebriated nurses and thought to myself, 'Welcome to Saint Martin,' while inquiring, "Were the girl's suits itsy bitsy or teenie weenie?"

"Does it matter?" Amy replied.

"Guess not." I responded, realizing that only the cruisers, camera toters and newbies ever seemed to care.

Amy and I went back and jumped in our pool. Amy then curled up on the couch and began reading, I opened my folio and wrote.

The next element seems to be the one that kills most relationships and that's compromise. Both parties must realize that in a partnership neither side should 'win' and always get their way. One of the key precepts of business is that a good negotiation is when no one is happy. Marriage shouldn't be like that but it should be where both sides bend so that there is unity in thought, action and achievement."

"So many people I've talked to who've gone through a divorce roll their eyes and nod their head in affirmation when I say that one of the key elements to marital demise was the lack of compromise. This lack can be physical, sexual, social, financial and/or familial. It can be predicated on doing things that the partner doesn't like to do. It can be as mundane as sharing tasks or as profound as having interests that are so divergent that so much time is spent apart that the saying, 'alone together, alone apart, if they began all over, they'd never start' becomes apropos."

"Like the Rolling Stones intoned so many years ago, *'You can't always get what you want.'* Conversely, we can't always succumb to the wishes of our partner. The fulcrum beneath the teeter totter must remain in the middle. What really challenges the entire concept of compromise are children when they are used as a reason not to do something. We can't go here, we can't do this, we can't, we can't, we can't, because of the children."

"In a marital relationship, compromise is the process of finding a solution that spouses can agree on, even if it's not their first choice. Compromise is important in relationships because it helps to build trust and respect. When both people are willing to compromise, it shows they care about the other person's feelings and needs. There are a few things to keep in mind when compromising in a relationship. First, both sides must be willing to give up something. Compromise isn't about getting everything you want. It's about finding a solution that both people can live with. In order to accomplish this, one must be respectful of the other person's feelings."

"Even if we don't agree with the other person, it's important to respect their feelings. We've discussed communication and, yet, I need to reiterate that communication is key to any successful relationship. When you're trying to compromise it's important to talk to each other about your needs and wants. Finally, we all need to realize that  compromise takes time and we can't expect to find a solution overnight."

"When children arrive, BOTH parents should be involved and work on developing a logical, equitable and reasonable set of parameters that address many subjects including physical, social and recreational aspects. Sadly, in our society the mother assumes the burden and responsibility and all too many times uses this responsibility to move the fulcrum so that it favors her wishes."

"Periodically all relationships need an equity checkup. Couples often hold different beliefs about what's fair and when we feel we're being wronged resentment builds up. But fairness isn't an accounting system! Rather, equity is a flexible balance of give-and-take that we agree upon in the context of our relationship based on communication, understanding and trust."

"When we have an understanding and agree to the profound responsibilities of raising a child, then and only then can we come up with a set of compromises that address the wants and needs of both parties. This can only happen if we associate, communicate and understand. This can only happen if we trust our partner's judgment and realize that adding another person to the equation will have tremendous consequences on every single aspect of our life... physically, emotionally, financially and socially."

"When I hear about individuals who are in challenging relationships one key issue that seems to come up repeatedly deals with finances and perceived equity. If any relationship is truly a partnership, it shouldn't matter who makes the most. What should matter is that there's a sense of fairness on how the pot is split. To this end, I'm a proponent that bill paying should be a mutual endeavor where all income is put into a 'general' fund from which all bills and investments are taken. When this is done, the difference should be then split evenly. While monetary measurement is one factor that will probably never be equal, time is always equal, commitment should always be equal and sacrifice be equal as well and that means that the life invested is also very, very equal."

**Forgiveness:**

I don't know what it is about Saint Martin that draws Amy and I so much closer. Perhaps, it's because we're alone, singular and doing everything together. To have the girls with us but living in 'House on the Hill' while we're at the 'Lighthouse', made the trip somewhat exclusive as we vowed we wouldn't intrude on their vacation.

Amy asked the girls if they'd like massages and both concurred. Amy made the reservation with Felix and Claude and asked if I minded if she went and had one, too. I said I didn't mind at all. Amy then asked if it was all right if she had Florence come and cut everyone's hair. I thought, "sure, why not?"

Now a massage takes about an hour each and three women getting their hair done another three and so I figured Amy would be gone around four hours. It was ten in the morning and so I said, "Why don't you make it a day and bring the girls to Anse Marcel and I'll meet you at three for cocktails?"

Amy thought that was a great idea and so she departed. Quiet time, allowed me to peruse what I had written and continue on. Just before three, I pushed the button for the tram and listened to it slowly make its way up from the base of the hill. I got in for the two-minute drop and entered our garage expecting to see the Rover there. It wasn't. Amy hadn't returned and simply walked the hundred feet to the restaurant.

I made my way to the bar and said hello to Pierre. The staff always made certain Amy and I were warmly welcomed. I had my usual glass of Pino Noir and waited and then waited and then waited some more. I looked at my watch and it was nearing four.

Pierre came to my table and announced. "You have a telephone call from Mrs. Terrill."

I went to the bar and said "hello".

"Georgie!" Amy only called me Georgie when she either wanted to make love or was drunk which was extremely rare as

Amy was always, and I mean always, in control of herself. With the word slurs, I knew what was going on.

"Georgie, why don't you come to the house and party."

"What party?"

"The girls and I."

"Are you sure?"

"Why not? Let's have some fun."

Amy had the car and I could tell she was in no condition to drive and so I agreed.

Pierre called a taxi and I went to 'House on the Hill', pressed the security buttons and watched the gates slowly open while being serenaded  by some sort of music blaring from the outdoor speakers.

I made my way around back and stood in shock. The girls were in their bathing suits while Amy still had the towel she probably wore during her massage wrapped around her. All three were sitting on chaise lounges, empty wine glasses by their sides and new hairdos on the heads.

The bathing suits didn't surprise me, nor did Amy in the towel. The hairdos? Well, it certainly wasn't what I expected. Reggie, had always worn her hair in an old-fashioned ponytail. During my stay in the hospital, Sam, had a shaped Afro to accentuate her face while Amy, always kept her naturally curly light brown hair, straightened.

I really don't know what got into them. Reggie and Amy had, what I learned later were called Boy Cuts that were really, really short on the sides and just long enough on top to have the hair lie down. Sam literally had what we called a Buzz or crew cut when I was a kid.

With the new doo, Reggie's long neck was accentuated and she looked fantastic. Sam's cut was probably the least appealing, yet her soft facial features and infectious smile overcame her new look. Amy was the biggest shock. She looked like Derrick...almost masculine...as her square shoulders and muscular arms stood out like never before.

Amy looked at me and smiled, as her hand slid down to her stomach in an almost luring manner and said, "Georgie, I forgot the vault combination and we're out of wine. Can you please get some more for us?"

Amy'd already had too much, yet, I knew to say no could potentially cause a scene. With that, I went to the vault, punched in the combination, did the retinal scan, spoke to Wilco Security and listened as the tumblers turned and the vault door opened. I grabbed four bottles of Pinot Noir and another Terrill bourbon just in case, reported the quantity to Wilco and closed the door.

"Pour us a drink, dahling!" Amy giggled in her awful Zsa Zsa Gabor accent. "Bring them out to the pool."

I did as directed and brought the four glasses poolside.

Amy looked at me and smiled an almost lecherous grin as she announced, "We want to go skinny dipping".

The girls looked at Amy with a stunned look on their faces and I could tell, the 'we' meant 'I'.

Amy continued. "The girls knew you were coming and didn't want to make you feel uncomfortable if we all were naked."

I thought, "My God, them being naked wouldn't have made me uncomfortable half as much as seeing them  drunk"!

"Georgie! Are you going to come skinny dipping with us?" Amy slurred.

The girls saw the reticence in my face as Amy said. "Come on, Georgie, the girls saw everything you got in the hospital. Are you chicken?" Amy giggled and then crowed..."Chick, chick chicken," as the girls started laughing, as well.

Wisconsin is known for its imbibing to the point that Amy and I actually created descriptive levels for how drunk someone else was...level one was called 'loose'. Level two was simply 'drunk'. Level three... 'shit-faced', 'blasted', 'totally tanked', 'f---ed up', or whatever. Amy had gone past levels one and two and was blurry-eyed. I only hoped she wasn't so drunk she'd get sick. The cool water would have felt good and I actually thought it would help sober her up but I didn't have my suit and read the expression on the girl's faces to say, 'please don't'.

"Georgie, we all had wonderful massages. You should have one. Sooo relaxing and so...so sumptuous, right girls?"

Both Reggie and Sam nodded with somewhat embarrassed looks as if secrets were being divulged.

Amy smiled at me and recited. "Too bad Felix and Claude are gay. Claude is beyond handsome...I mean like beautiful. That hair! Those eyes! That body! That tight butt! If he was straight, I think I would give him a massage in all and I mean ALL the right places."

The girls cringed as I considered the source and condition and let it slide.

Amy was beginning to weave and I was getting concerned. She finished her wine and attempted to set the empty glass on the table next to her. The girls slowly did likewise and I think we all knew they'd reached their limit.

"I think we should let the girls get some rest, don't you?" I asked.

Amy slurred. "Don't you want to party?

Pausing and looking at the pool, Amy repeated, "I want to go swimming!"

Amy arose while looking at me with a blank stare. "We're going skinny dipping aren't we? Just like Lake Wingra?"

Amy slid her hands around my neck as her towel fell to the ground and she enticed. "Come on Georgie, get a little wet and wild for a change."

Amy looked at me and smiled before offering, "I don't have hang-ups about being naked but sadly, I know you do."

I didn't know how to take that. Was she complaining or simply stating a fact.

There was a long pause until Amy realized it simply wasn't going to happen and inquired. "Where are my clothes?" Then sardonically stammered. "Oh, yah, in the bedroom where I came to die. Guess I didn't, did I? Lucky me!"

"I'll get them," Sam offered.

Sam departed quickly, simply to escape the scene playing out, while Reggie stood almost statue-like wondering what in hell was happening.

Sam returned with Amy's clothes in her hands. I took them, had Amy put one hand on my shoulder for balance and knelt down. I took a quick look at 'my' rose tattoo now within inches of my eyes and helped her step into her shorts. As I stood, I slid the shorts up until they were at her waist.

Like a spoiled little brat she briskly announced. "I don't want to wear a shirt. I want my boobies hanging out."

God, was I embarrassed, as I somewhat tersely replied, "why don't you put your shirt on?"

"Why do women have to wear shirts when men don't? We all have nipples. It's simply not fair."

I rolled my eyes and succinctly indicated it was really time to go.

Amy nodded, as if surrendering. With that, she staggered over to Reggie, smiled, leaned in, slid her hands below Reggie's waist and gave Reggie an extended kiss on the lips or what we called a lip lock back in college. Amy leaned back, squeezed Reggie's behind and slurred in an atrocious British accent. "Thanks for a great afternoon daaahling. We must do this again sometime."

I think Reggie was a bit shocked and somewhat disconcerted to have a completely inebriated woman passionately kiss and fondle her.

Amy turned to Sam and smiled, pulled her in and gave her a long hug and tried to repeat the lip lock. Sam's eyes went huge. It wasn't what she expected as Sam pulled back and I knew she'd had enough.

Amy finally turned to me and slurred. "Are you driving or am I?"

"I am," as I shook my head in disdain and declared, "Get in the Rover", in a less than gentle tone.

The girls looked at the two of us and simply winced. It was time to go. Reluctantly, Amy slid into the passenger seat and pulled down the passenger visor, looked at her new haircut and simply questioned herself, "Do I look butch?" shrugged and whispered, "Maybe I am, but who cares? My husband certainly doesn't!"

We weren't even down Hope Hill before Amy was already zonked. I drove back to the 'Lighthouse', helped Amy into the tram. Being small in size, there were no seats and so watched her sway as the tram slowly made its way up the hill. I simply stared at my half-naked wife whose eyes were glassy who was still woozy but didn't seem to care. The two-minute ride seemed to take an hour before we made it to the entrance where I pressed the cylinder sensor and listened as the security bolt moved to let us in to the edges of our own privacy.

I'd never seen Amy like this in my life - walking, stumbling and weaving, ambivalent, unaware and most certainly unconscious of her missing attire. Amy gave me an unfocused stare and announced. "I think I need to get some sleep."

I nodded in the affirmative until Amy proclaimed. "I gotta pee."

I took her into the bathroom and closed the door. Ten minutes later, I knocked on the door and there wasn't any answer.

"Amy! Amy!"

Total silence.

I opened the door to find Amy asleep while sitting on the throne. I slipped off her shorts from around her ankles, walked her into the guest bedroom, and toppled my naked wife into bed, all the while wondering what in hell happened?

It was early and I decided to write.

"Forgiveness is the process of letting go of anger, resentment, and bitterness towards someone who has wronged you. It's a conscious decision to release the negative emotions that are holding you back from healing and moving on. There are many benefits to interpersonal forgiveness. It can help to reduce stress and anxiety, improve one's physical and mental health, strengthen one's relationship, promote personal growth and development and increase their sense of well-being."

"I learned that there are many different ways to forgive someone and there's no one right way to do it simply because what works for one person may not work for another."

Forgiveness for me is when I allow myself to feel the emotions and don't try to suppress my anger, sadness, or hurt. When it happens, I try to understand the other person's perspective. It doesn't mean that I have to agree with what they did, but it can help me to see things from their point of view."

"I always try to make a decision to forgive. This doesn't mean that I have to forget. However, it does mean that I'm choosing to let go of the negative emotions that are holding me back."

"I'm a knee-jerk person who over-reacts. When I'm trying to forgive someone, I try to give myself time simply because forgiveness is a process that takes time to heal from a betrayal or hurt. I know and accept it's not always easy, but it's always worth it because it can help me heal, grow, and move on with my life."

"Forgiveness is one of the cornerstones of religion and a treatise on our relationship with all others, including our spouse. To forgive a spouse means to restore a bond of love and communion when there has been a rupture."

"Anger, lust, lying, cheating, all the 'traditional' sins challenge our relationship with others. When the bond is broken we tend to objectify them and judge them, not seeing them as a person, only as objects of our anger and hurt. This is a normal reaction. It's too bad because it only causes more harm."

"We categorize people in terms of their transgression against us. Tonight I was embarrassed and quite honestly, somewhat ashamed. The woman I love had made a fool out of herself and embarrassed our guests. I knew I need to get over it. I knew that the longer I nurtured the anger and alienation, the more deeply the resentment would take hold and the more it would feed on my soul.

Resentment is a Cancer that will destroy us if we don't forgive! It also leaks out and damages our relations with others when we slander and gossip about those who've offended us and try to draw others to our own side."

"Forgiveness means overlooking the transgression and restoring a bond of trust. Today, there was a lot to overlook, that's for sure. It doesn't mean I should justify the offensive action or accept it as right, nor does it mean I should justify my anger or reaction. Forgiveness simply meant laying aside my judgment and reaction, accepting Amy for who she is, or anyway who I thought she was."

"We all screw up! It's human nature! We make mistakes in what we say, think and do. These can be so big, so stupid, so profound as to affect the rest of our lives. There are many times when we hear about how a person has acted and asked ourselves, *'What were they thinking?'* It's not just them! It's all of us! Our wondrous brain takes us beyond here and now and things we think are logical are just downright stupid. Words, actions and deeds become so wrong we, for all intents and purposes 'screwed up'!"

"When mistakes affect our spousal relationship...which by the way, they will...it's only through the strength of the other six elements that we can forgive or ask for forgiveness. This is the true test of a marriage."

"People shouldn't try to test the hypothesis, nor should everyone be forgiven for what they do. No one's perfect. We all make mistakes. The key is recognizing that there has been an error, admitting an error, apologizing and then ensuring that it doesn't happen again. When the time comes, I'm certain Amy and I will discuss what happened."

"On the reciprocating side, Amy must also accept the fact that I'm human. She must respect the fact that I'm not the perfect person who only filled her body with oxytocin. I, too, make mistakes and when I do, hopefully,  Amy will use the EXACT same set of parameters with me."

"The questions then become, do we recognize our errors? Was it truly a mistake or something we think was wrong? Did we admit it? Did we apologize for it? Did we learn from it? If yes, we need to move on! Don't harp on it! Don't bring it up every time we have a disagreement! Don't use it as a sword to stab each other in the heart every time things aren't perfect. Life is full of errors!

Over the years, one of the things I'm most proud of is that fact that I've learned to live with mistakes, learn from them and accept them as part of our relationship. And so, once again, I repeat the seven critical components to a successful, long-term marriage... attraction, association, communication, understanding, trust, compromise and finally forgiveness. I'm doing my very best to include these in our marital portfolio so that final all-so-critical element...love...will also be there, without words, flowers, gifts or anything else."

## The Big Truck:

With Amy in her 'condition', I decided to sleep alone in our bedroom, awakened early, got up, went downstairs, made coffee and waited for the guest bedroom door to open. A little after nine, the door opened and Amy sheepishly made her way to the kitchen table wearing the tee-shirt she wouldn't wear the night before.

"How are you feeling?" I asked.

"How big was the truck that hit me?"

"You really got blasted."

"How big of fool did I make of myself?"

"Well....," I sort of flinched and let it be.

"That bad?"

"Uh huh!"

"Oh, my God!" as Amy simply shook her head in regret as her hands slid up to her forehead in remorse.

There was a pause and then Amy took a deep breath as if to expel some more of the toxin before adding. "I don't remember a thing."

"Do you remember calling me?"

"No."

"Do you remember demanding all of us go skinny dipping?"

"What?" Amy expressed incredulously.

"Yes."

"Did we do it?"

"No."

"Thank God!"

What an answer. Was she glad I didn't because I would be naked in front of the girls or because she was embarrassed by the way I look. With that, Amy went to brush back her hair with her right hand as she habitually did whenever stressed and got a concerned look. She took her left hand and repeated the process before asking, "Did I get my hair cut?"

"Oh, yah!"

"Do I dare look in the mirror?"

"How about a cup of coffee first."

"That bad?"

"Not bad, just different."

"You mean like weird?"

"No, not weird, just a completely different look for you."

"What do you think?"

"Well, at first I was shocked but now I'm getting to like it." I didn't really know what else to say.

Amy got up and went in the bathroom. When she came out, she announced, "I look like a boy."

"A lot like Derrick?" I inquired

A frown came over Amy as she replied, "Yes," and then sort of smiled.

Amy sat at the table with her head back in her hands before asking, "What about the girls?"

"Well, they both were a little, uh, loose, but not nearly as loose as you."

"Their hair?"

"Like yours."

"And?"

"For Reggie, an improvement. For Sam, well...not quite as great."

Amy took a deep breath and commenced. "I don't know what happened. I let the girls go first for the massages. When Felix started on me, he noted I felt really tense and needed to relax. I tried to, but he said it wasn't working. He offered a small envelope with three jelly beans in it that he said would help, then went to help Claude fold up his massage table and that's about the last thing I remember."

"Jelly beans?" I said, now knowing what happened.

"Yah, you know like the Easter Bunny brings."

"Were they laced with THC?" I asked.

"You mean marijuana? In jelly beans? Do they make those?"

"Yes."

"Oh my God!"

"How many did you eat?"

"All three?"

"I thought I was supposed to."

"The girls?"

" I don't know. I think they each had one."

"Well, that might be what happened. When I got there, you were certainly relaxed and about as giggly as I've ever seen. In other words stoned, with no, and I mean absolutely no, inhibitions."

"More than skinny dipping?"

"Well, sort of. You expounded on Claude. How good looking you said he is and inferred what you wanted to do to him."

"Physically?"

"Yes!" I replied with a degree of compunction.

"Oh, God! I'm Sorry." as Amy's shoulders sagged as she began to physically wither.

Amy paused and then inquired. "So you think I ate marijuana jelly beans?

"Yes! All the symptoms were there. THC produces levels of euphoria, relaxation, altered perception, and increased appetite.

"How do you know so much?"

"Where did I go to college?"

There was a significant pause and then I offered, "I'll bet you had the wine, then the massage and jelly beans before Florence arrived, didn't you?

"Yes."

"Well, I think we've solved the riddle. The drinking on top the THC affected your coordination, reaction time, and judgment and certainly impeded your decision-making.

Amy got serious. "Was I being a jerk?"

Whew! "Not a jerk, but a lot more, uhh...ostentatious than I think the girls were expecting."

"Why, what happened?"

"Getting naked was going to be one thing. Wanting me to get naked was another. The Claude description was something else, but the passionate kisses goodbye probably went over the top."

"I didn't..."

"Yes."

"Both?"

"Only Reggie. Sam wasn't up for it. I don't know about when you were massaging Reggie's butt though."

"Oh my God!" Amy winced.

"The argument about wearing your shirt topped the cake."

"What?"

"Oh yah!" I said with a tone of slight disdain. "You refused to put on your shirt because you said it wasn't fair since I had nipples too."

"Did I put in on?"

"This morning!" I replied in a somewhat laconic way.

Amy sat, head in hands and simply shook in repentance. I countered. "Heh, the girls were partially stoned and will probably let it slide."

Amy looked at me and then out at the pool and inquired. "Do you think I should call them and apologize?"

I pondered the question and replied. "Why don't you wait a little while and then call them. You can explain what happened and see how they respond. If they're upset, apologize. I'd explain you'd never done any drugs before and had no idea what was going on and never want to again, especially after what happened to your brother."

Amy looked at me with sorrowful eyes, touched my hand and asked. "Will you ever forgive me?"

I smiled, laughed a somewhat reserved expression and added. "My only disappointment is that I didn't tape it. I could have used it for blackmail. God, were you out of it. Now it all seems funny, especially when you didn't wear a tee-shirt home because I have nipples."

Amy swallowed hard and then asked. "What about my hair?"

"It looks great and if you don't like it now, it'll grow back. Until then, make the most of it."

"Do you like it?" Amy asked again as if in need of confirmation.

I smiled and looked at the new Amy, raised my eyebrows, smiled…"And so, I get to see what my wife would look like as a boy. Should I start calling you Andy?"

Amy looked at me, pursed her lips and earnestly inquired. "You really don't mind that I look like a boy?"

"Not at all." I added with a chuckle.

Amy was loosening up, getting over the shock of both her escapade and new appearance, and got one of her pensive looks I hadn't seen in years as she flippantly inquired. "If I look like a boy, should I dress like a boy?"

"You mean, go Butch?" I retorted.

"Huh?" Amy had a surprised look on her face, not realizing I was a little more socially adept than she perceived.

"I'm fine with it." I responded in a somewhat sardonic way as if to challenge her proposition and then laughed as I offered. "You know, flannel shirts, jeans and boots, that kind of stuff. Oh don't forget the Doc Martins and leather biker jacket."

"Better yet, a big tattoo of a Harley on your back and white tee-shirt with the sleeves rolled up and a cigarette stuck behind your ear and always without a bra. Just don't get more assertive because you'll scare me!"

I knew the issue of wearing a bra was a moot point. In our years together, I'd come to accept Amy's penchants and one area that remained consistent was her aversion to the undergarment, which she called her holsters."

At first, I found 'sans-a'bra' somewhat erotic. Years dulled the sensuous nature and allowed me to accept her choice in the name of comfort. In Milwaukee, she kept 'the girls' as Amy called them in their holsters whenever in public, simply because of social decorum. However, when we were at home, the holster always came off simply because she didn't feel comfortable. On St. Martin, I don't think she even had holsters with her. Her apparel choice and attire was intended for the casual nature of the island devoid of and ambivalent to, any form of exhibitionistic intent.

I was jokingly rubbing it in to the point that Amy got the giggles as one of those mocking looks crept across her face. With that, she shook her head, ambled upstairs and returned minus the shirt, wearing only my gym shorts and proposed, "Let's go down to Anse Marcel and have lunch. If I look like a boy, I'm going to dress like one, too."

Needless to say, what had been an embarrassment was turning into one of those moments we could laugh about.

"Come on! Let's go, big boy!" Amy pressed as she put her hands on her hips and projected a look of impatience before starting to giggle.

Instead, I stood up, took off my shirt and offered. "Now we're twins. You see, I've got nipples, too."

Now we were both laughing as I looked at my wife and simply admired her physique. While most women begin to 'soften' as they age, the combination of diet, genetics and exercise allowed Amy to sustain her youthful figure.

Other than her amazing smile what really defines Amy's body is it's proportionality. Not too tall. Not too short. Not too thin but balanced and accentuated by her breasts that are neither diminutive, nor pendulous while having retained their youthful consistency where, for her age, make that any age, she was in great shape.

In the end, I simply smiled at the woman I loved, pulled her close and felt her breasts against my bare chest. I held her and reflected at Amy's, 'I Love Lucy'esque' demeanor. My mind went into a contemplative mode realizing it was Amy's way of saying she was sorry. In one fell swoop she'd broken the morning melancholy and allowed the sunshine of love to appear once again as all was forgiven thereby allowing me to understood that the woman who'd always been so adamant about drugs, had learned you only take one jelly bean and then, it should always come from the Easter Bunny.

## Recompense:

Amy took a dip in the pool as I sat at the kitchen table working on yet another chapter of my never-ending epistle when she came up behind me and gave me a hug before saying, "I love you George Terrill more today than yesterday, but not as much as tomorrow. I don't know how you tolerate all my peccadilloes and yet, because you do, I love you all the more."

I stood and gave Amy a deep kiss as I said "I can, because I love you and care for you more than anything else in the world. Yesterday was just one of those days. I'm already smiling about it and hope the girls are too. What's crazy was to see you unwind the way you did. You've always been so... emotionally tight and I think it did you good to let go. While I've always understood some of it, I guess yesterday was actually a way for me to look deeper into who you are and, in so doing, get a better understanding, and therefore greater acceptance. We come here to unwind and be ourselves without all the social limitations we have at home. To simply have you release some of that deeply seated decorum and let your frustrations go was actually blameless to see."

I stopped and looked Amy in the eyes. "I know the past few months have been stressful. My near-death experience didn't just affect me, it affected you. You have no idea how much I appreciated your daily visits, our dinner 'dates' or our fifteen minutes together when I was in ICU. For me, I was the patient and  psychologically, institutionalized while you sustained reality and the emotional toll must have been simply profound."

Amy looked down at the floor and then at me as tears welled in her eyes. "I thought I was going to lose you. You can't leave me! You're the rock that keeps me stable. I don't know what I would have done, if...f...well if, you know."

"But I didn't."

"But I can't get it out of my head that you almost did."

"It will happen to all of us someday, it's not a question of if, but when and how and then the only recovery for those left behind is knowing why. Death is a natural part of life. It's something we'll all experience at some point. Amy, it's important to remember that death isn't the end. It's simply a transition from one state of being to another and I'm not afraid."

"Don't go, please don't go!"

"I'm not planning on it."

We hugged and then all of the tension that had built up came flowing out in a torrential flood. Tears and gasps for breath, then more tears and tremblers. For a long moment we stood, singular, and yet, as one, until the last vestiges of her emotional equity expired. There was a pause as Amy gazed at me through her sadness as I took my thumb and slid it along her cheek wiping away the sorrow and placing her salty existence within my mouth. We hugged as Amy provided a reluctant smile.

"I think you'd better call the girls," I whispered, not wanting to break the serenity that enveloped us.

Amy nodded in the affirmative and got her phone. I knew this needed to be a private conversation and so I went to the control center and looked at the weather report. A few minutes later, Amy returned and was all smiles. She'd spoken to the girls and apologized. Amy noted that Reggie asked 'For what?' which meant the day and circumstances were minimized.

Amy noted she'd offered to take the girls to L'Auberge Gourmande for dinner and it was accepted. She then called Uncle Frank and asked him to call Mary and reserve the back alcove and tell her there would only be four of us. She felt we needed semi-privacy.

Dinner was scheduled for seven and Amy thought it would be nice if we got dressed up. We went out on the master deck and showered together. Even after all the years, it was still a special way to say 'I love you'. Amy got out her fancy casual dress that highlighted her physique. I think I was a little envious. She had all the different clothes options, while I got out my one pair dress shorts and a button-down shirt, realizing men really don't have the choices women do in more ways than one.

We'd agreed to meet at the restaurant and the girls already knew where to park as they'd been eating their way down Boulevard de Grand Case. Amy and I arrived ten minutes early and were pleasantly surprised to see that Mary had removed the second table and had a red velvet rope across entrance with a sign that said 'reserved' hanging on it. For a restaurant as well respected as L'Auberge Gourmande, or '*The Gourmet Inn*', to have them take out a table when the waiting list for dining could stretch into months was an expression of gratitude for our family and our belief in them.

We sat in the room and through the entry I could see those dining in the main area. As I was about to take a sip of wine, I noticed every head in the place look up and men's mouths literally drop open as Reggie and Sam made their way back to our little room.

As Pasquale escorted them into our small setting, my mouth dropped open too. The two 'Plain Janes' were simply breathtaking. Gone was the basic 'hospital look'. In its place were two spectacular looking young ladies as a flicker of regret for not abiding by Amy's skinny dip wish flashed through my lecherous mind.

Both Amy and I stood and smiled as the girls broadly nodded in acceptance. The girls were about to sit when Amy shook her head 'no' and motioned to pirouette and exclaimed, "You're both simply gorgeous."

Sam nodded and bashfully smiled in an almost innocent way. I sensed there hadn't been too many times in her life when someone told her she was beautiful. With her somewhat round face, Sam had added gold stud earrings and matching gold necklace and had just the right amount of pink eye shadow to highlight her sensuous brown skin. She, too, had chosen a dress to wear what was tastefully cut to accentuate her figure. Above it all was her effervescent smile that simply lit up the room.

I looked at Reggie and realized what Florence had done was simply pull the inner beauty out of its shell. Her boy cut was simply enchanting as her long neck was accentuated by long gold earrings that matched her necklace. Wearing a low-cut top that highlighted her shoulders which had taken on an almond color almost matching that of Amy's and a mid-thigh miniskirt that probably came from Melia's Retro Store and emphasized Reggie's long legs, making her look simply ravishing.

As the girls sat down, Pasquale re-appeared and asked what we preferred to drink. I suggested Dom Perignon and he knew it was a special evening, asking if there was a vintage I preferred. I told him it was a special evening and bring what he thought would mark the event as he inquired. "Ten or twelve degrees?"

"Ten please."

Living part time in France and owning a winery, was teaching me to appreciate the nuances of fine wines and I knew that a two-degree centigrade difference from twelve to ten or 54 to 50 degrees Fahrenheit affects Champagne in three  ways. First, the bubbles are smaller and more delicate because the bubbles need more time to form and rise when the wine is colder. Second, the flavors of the Champagne will be more pronounced because the cold temperature helps preserve the aromas and flavors of the wine. Finally, the Champagne will be more refreshing because the cold temperature helps to numb the taste buds, making the wine seem crisper and more invigorating.

Four crystal goblets were set on the table as a 2006 bottle was presented. With a very professional tone to his voice, Pasquale noted. "Dom Pérignon is a produced by the Champagne house Moët & Chandon in Epernay, France. It's named after Dom Pierre Pérignon, a Benedictine monk who was a pioneer in the production of sparkling wine. The wine is made exclusively from grapes of the Chardonnay and Pinot Noir varieties and is known for its distinctive flavor and finesse."

I tasted its sweet nectar and nodded in the affirmative and so it was poured. We looked at each other and I said, "I believe this calls for a toast."

Everyone raised their glasses as I pronounced, "The beauty of friendship comes from understanding and accepting that none of us are perfect and all of us, by caring for each other, puts joy, not only our hearts but our lives as well."

The crystal was delicately touched and we each took a sip.

Reggie spoke next. "Sam and I want to thank you for the vacation. It's simply incredible. We're being treated with generosity that goes above and beyond what we could ever expect."

Turning to Amy, Sam offered. "Mrs. Terrill, I don't know how we can ever thank you for having Irene take us over to St. Barths this afternoon for shopping. Your generosity is so much more than we can ever accept."

Amy smiled and responded. "Girls, it was my way of saying thank you and well....let's leave it at that."

Everyone knew what *'that'* meant and it was the end of the chapter of one crazy day when things sort of got out of hand.

As we settled in, Pasquale introduced the girls to Henri who was the head chef who inquired whether they preferred, fish, fowl, lamb or beef? The girls both shrugged as Henri' offered, "if you like seafood, we have fresh lobster I will cook especially for you. If you prefer fish, we have sea bass caught this morning. If you enjoy lamb, we have some spring lamb I can make any way you prefer. We are known for our duck and also chicken. However, if you would like beef, I have both veal and Kobe beef filets that are my favorite."

The girls shrugged as if they didn't know. Henri then asked, "Is there anything you wouldn't prefer?"

The girls both replied lamb and I was glad as I didn't like it either.

"Why don't you allow me to make something special for you. I think you will enjoy what I have in mind."

All four of us nodded in the affirmative as Pasquale poured the last of the Dom in our glasses and I nodded for another.

"Would 1972 be acceptable?"

Once again, I nodded in the affirmative and ordered a chilled seafood appetizer for the table consisting of iced crab, shrimp, scallops and lobster on a bed of ice with a Conch shell in the middle. The conversation evolved regarding how different St. Barths was compared to St. Martin in terms of cost and attitude. No mention was made of the last time Amy was there with Melia and I hoped the clerk learned a lesson.

When the seafood centerpiece was empty, Henri personally presented his creation consisting of a medley of the items he'd outlined, except the lamb, consisting of lobster, sea bass, chicken breast and filet of Kobe beef. We all ate and ate and then ate some more. As we sat languishing in gluttony, Mary presented small cart with four servings of Baked Alaska which she remembered was Amy's favorite. The girls grinned as Pasquale arrived and lit the ensemble and served us dessert saved only for special occasions.

The meal ended and I simply nodded to Mary and said thank you for a wonderful evening. We adjourned and made our way back to the parking lot and paused to say goodnight. To do so, we'd become accustomed to kissing another person on both cheeks which is called '*faire la bise*' and a sign of affection and respect. To faire la bise, two people stand close to each other and touch their cheeks together. They then make a kissing sound, but do not actually kiss.

Sam and Reggie had it all figured out and we did the official French goodbye to which I pulled back, smiled and said, thank you for a wonderful night. Amy and Reggie were next as Amy's hand went behind Reggie's back and held it there for an extended period of time as Amy acknowledged, "You simply look marvelous."

I have no idea what the day cost. Between shopping on St. Barths and a very, very special dinner, I'm certain Wilco accounting was going to wonder what in hell happened, to which Amy would simply say, "None of your God damn business."

Amy and I made it back to the house and rode up the tram. Amy went in and took off her dress and slipped back into my shorts and returned with a devious smile simply to denote that what  started the day as a proclamation of defiance, became a mode exemplifying her inherent desire.

"Want a night cap?" I inquired.

"I have something else I'd prefer."

"And what that might be?" I lecherously inquired.

"One thing I do remember from last night."

"Which is?"

"My offer."

My mind rolled back to the night before..."Tonight, you can have me do whatever you want...anything Georgie...anything!"

It wasn't long until...well...let's leave it at that.

**Whatever:**

One of the few risks of the Caribbean in the fall are potential storms. Between hosting the girls, eating and simply relaxing, we were oblivious to the news, weather and sports…other than Badger football, which I watched on my laptop. Damn Hawkeyes!

Amy called Wilco Ops who said Amelia[X] would tentatively arrive on Saturday around 1:00 PM. They also noted there was a Tropical Depression about 500 miles east of Saint Martin and would let us know if there was any development.

Having witnessed Irma and experiencing her rage I took it upon myself to study Caribbean weather and knew that a tropical depression is actually a tropical cyclone with maximum sustained winds below 39 mph. Once a tropical depression forms, the National Hurricane Center (NHC) gives it a number based on its order of formation during the hurricane season such as Tropical Depression One, Two, Three, etc.

A tropical storm is simply a tropical depression with maximum sustained winds from 39 to 73 mph that can result in flooding, storm-surge, strong winds and tornadoes. The first stage of a hurricane begins with a disturbance created by the evaporation that occurs over tropical ocean waters. Once it begins to evaporate a cloud of warm air begins to form heating the air around, creating even more densely packed clouds as air rushes in. As the air continues to heat up a large mass of rain clouds begin to form over the ocean and start their journey towards someone's potential demise

The NHC assigns names to tropical storms using the official name list for that season that's developed by the World Meteorological Organization or WMO which sounds like a radio station to me. The tropical storm name lists rotate every six years, unless a particular storm is so destructive and/or deadly that the WMO votes to retire that name from future use which they did with Katrina in 2005, Sandy in 2012, Harvey in 2017 and Michael in 2018.

Once a tropical storm's winds reach 74 mph, it's called a hurricane and considered a Category One that maintains the same name. If a hurricane's sustained winds reach at least 111 mph it's classified on the Saffir-Simpson Hurricane Wind Scale that can range from one-to-five depending upon sustained winds. After 111 mph it's classified as a category three as it and anything more powerful are named 'major' hurricanes.

While the media usually plays up wind as the culprit, water is the number one safety hazard, mostly by drowning in either the storm surge, flooding or high surf. Studies of deaths from 1963-2012 found that storm-surge flooding claimed nearly half of the fatalities while rainfall-induced freshwater floods and mudslides accounted for about one-quarter. High surf is responsible for about six percent with another six percent occurring offshore in marine incidents within fifty nautical miles of the coast

After Irma, we and everyone else on Saint Martin, knew taking a cavalier attitude could be fatal. When we designed the 'Lighthouse', we had goals of beauty, functionality, safety and security. From a visual perspective the house was all white and literally carved into the top of Bell Hill at an altitude over 600 feet above sea level. The side facing the ocean was semi-circular in design and done so, not only for the view, but to remove any flat walls and edges.

In order to bring the 'outside in' and the fact that the house was literally cantilevered, we designed the north-facing hurricane wall such that, instead of being sliders that went sideways, with a touch of a button, the windows literally lowered into casings located below the floor and out of the way. In addition to the glass, there were also perforated stainless steel security panels in the casings that could duplicate the same process so that when there was a storm or we weren't there the windows and house were secure.

With the climb and structural design, breaking into the house would not only require mountain climbing skills but also figuring out how climb over the ledges which were erected like a ship's prow such that the top edge of the railing was six feet out from the railing base and constructed at a 45-degree angle so that the outer edge was thirty feet off the ground. In doing this we had six-foot railings on the outside that were only three feet tall on the patio. This not only provided safety and security, but created storage areas beneath the prows that could hold all the furniture and 'flyables' as we called them, which was anything that could be blown away.

The primary floor consists of two bedrooms, each with their own half bathrooms and a great room that serves as the living/dining and kitchen area with a master stone fireplace between. Behind the kitchen is the inner sanctum that not only has a room containing the  controls for the house but functions as a small office, as well.

Within the inner sanctum is a vault door it that opens to a concrete-lined cave dug into the hill that encloses all the electronics for both security and communication and then a vault for our liquor and valuables similar to the one on 'House on the Hill', except it's a walk-in instead of requiring a ladder. With the semicircular design, few right angles and everything reinforced and designed to withstand winds up to 200 miles per hour, we felt secure.

Above the main area is the master suite with half bath and smaller cantilevered, semicircular deck where the windows are pocket doors that slide on a track and literally disappear into the side walls. As is the case on the main floor fitted the showers are outdoors, overlooking Anguilla.

Some visitors wonder about the outdoor showers until I tell them that the annual mean temperature of Saint Martin is 80°. Others worry about getting wet and, like a warm summer rain in Wisconsin, it's simply wonderful to be massaged by the raindrops which can actually happen quite often in October which the wettest month, but hardly ever in February.

The master shower is simply a faucet and shower head ensconced in the outer wall with a floor drain that takes the water to the filter and purifier before returning it to the cistern. The main floor shower is located near the outer edge of the deck and consists of a 'privacy wall' that stands from about eighteen inches off the ground to around five feet high and is open to the Anguilla side. With so few visitors, it's hardly ever used. When it has been, some people are a bit skittish until they realize they have all the privacy in the world and yet the pleasure of a warm shower outdoors.

Above the second level is the actual 'Lighthouse' or beacon room, that reminds me of an old cupola you enter through a door in the master bedroom and ascend by using a circular stairway. The beacon room walls are all curved glass with air vents under the roof that provide a 360-degree vista of the entire island which is how the house got its name. Whenever I climb the circular stairs and seek out Hope Hill to the south, sunrise to the east, north across the bay to Anguilla or sunsets to the west, the view reminds me of life in general from birth-to-death and from always looking towards tomorrow to looking back at yesterday.

The beacon room windows are all tempered glass that open from the bottom to allow a little air in and the sounds of the ocean breeze intercepted by the roar of the prop planes taking off at Grand Case-Espérance Airport. Because we're on top of the hill and near the airport, the 'Lighthouse' is required to have a flashing red beacon installed on the roof which, can readily been seen from across Anguilla Channel at night.

At the base of Bell Hill and down near the Anse Marcel parking lot, we have our garage that not only houses our vehicles but is the bottom stop for our tram that takes us to and from the house. We also installed an inground LP fuel tank and stand-by generator that automatically comes on, in case the power goes out, that can operate for fourteen days. With rebar-enforced, foot-thick walls, steel window coverings and a backup power system, we felt we were secure.

The Duke had designed the 'House on the Hill' like a fortress. While not attuned to contemporary safety and security technologies learned from Irma, the vault the Duke created was such that admission into the inner sanctum was equal to being in a fall-out shelter in times of a hurricane or nuclear war with food, water, lighting, sleeping accommodations and enough really, really expensive booze to make one forget about what was going outside for up to a month.

We hoped none of it would ever be needed. However, after Hurricane Irma and the surprise it made on Saint Martin, no one, and I mean no one, took hurricane warnings casually. On the French side it took over five years to recover and the entire island is planning to bury the power lines to minimize the potential interruption of electricity while mandating solar panels be added to the roofs of all buildings. It will take years but should someday resolve one of the biggest problems on the island.

After the Wilco call, Amy texted Reggie and told her what our flight schedule was and there was a tropical depression 500 miles away. We'd intentionally let the girls have some time to themselves and reports came back they were having a 'grand' time and had become acclimated to the French way of life.

The next morning Amy got a call from Wilco and was told we needed to hunker down. Princess Julianna Airport was being closed and neither Amelia[X] nor any plane, would be allowed to clear Saint Martin airspace as Hurricane Mariah was already a Category Two and heading our way.

The question became, what do we do with Reggie and Sam? It wasn't right to have them stay alone. Amy and I debated - go to 'House on the Hill' and stay there or have the girls come to the 'Lighthouse'? Amy called the girls and told them she thought it would be best if they came to the 'Lighthouse'. Needless to say, they were concerned.

Amy then called Uncle Frank and asked him to bring one of the Wilco Security trucks simply because deep water was very difficult for cars to drive in. Uncle Frank noted that even a modest amount of water -- anything over the axles - could cause big troubles and he would bring one of the Toyota Tacoma's that had been modified for high ground clearance that included a high-mounted air intake and an engine-management computer that had been re-installed in the roof pillar and not under the seat.

Uncle Frank indicated we could drive through water up to four feet deep and we thought that was deep enough. He noted he'd have one of the mechanics exchange the vehicle and take the Rover back to the dealership until the storm was over. I asked him to put a chain saw, gas can and some chains in the back of the Tacoma. If the roads were blocked, I wanted to be able to pull fallen trees off the road so people could get through.

Our next concern dealt with airport damage. After Hurricane Irma, it took years for the Princess Juliana terminal to be fully functional again. Uncle Frank noted that the revised design was set for winds up to 130 MPH and should be OK. Those with private planes, were instructed to fly southeast to Guadeloupe as the hurricane was heading for Saint Martin and would then probably 'hook' northwest, following the warm water of the Gulfstream, before blasting somewhere in the States.

The Duke had done his homework when he elected where to build 'House on the Hill'. As hurricanes continue to glide over warm tropical waters, they continue to gather strength and speed. Once they make landfall, they stop gaining power because they no longer have warm water to regenerate themselves.

On land, hurricanes become less organized as wind speeds fall drastically. Eventually, the hurricane starts to break into thunderstorms before falling apart completely. With most islands as small as they are, the eye of a hurricane floats over the island with its high-speed winds and heavy rains and can cause tremendous damage, possibly leveling entire towns in the process.

H-O-H was located further inland on Hope Hill with an elevation of 209 feet above sea level and we knew, after Irma what she could handle weather-wise but remained concerned about looters and therefore, the girl's safety.

We didn't know what the integrity of the 'Lighthouse' would be. It had never taken a direct hit from a hurricane before. Sitting on top of Bell Hill we weren't worried about the water surge but still wondered if the architects and engineers in Wisconsin had fortified it enough.

We chose the 'Lighthouse', went to get the girls and told them what our plans were. They were concerned about work and when we got back to the 'Lighthouse' they called staffing at Milwaukee General. Amy had Wilco call Jim Hendersen, CEO of the hospital, and explain the situation. When you're one of, if not the biggest benefactor, people usually tend to listen.

Using Wilco flight ops, we had a much clearer idea of what was happening than what the media was saying and it still didn't look good. Mariah had been reclassified as a Cat-Three Hurricane and headed right for us. Jesus!

With twelve hours warning I called Uncle Frank and went to H-O-H to help Wilco Security hunker it down. The grand old dame had been through a lot and she'd survived before. We put the pool furniture in the house and pulled everything away from the windows. The crew and I inserted foot-tall, waterproof barriers along the floor line and then bolted the steel panels in place over the exposed windows and doors so water couldn't seep in. We then double-checked the vault, turned off the electricity, drained the toilets and covered the floor drains. Finally, we locked the front door, bolted the shield in front of it and said goodbye.

While small, the Wilco Security truck was actually fun to drive with its oversized, balloon tires, roof rack lights and special insulation around the door jambs to keep the water out. I pulled it into the garage, locked the doors, connected the car to the battery system and set the security mechanism such that anyone who tried to break in would have a VERY rude surprise…ZZZZap, as they got a charge equal to that of a cattle prod that would knock them on their ass. After all the looting that happened during Irma, I wanted to make sure we didn't lose our vehicle.

We rode the tram up to the house and locked it in place. No one was getting up the hill on my toy! While the storm was still over 300 miles away the weather was actually some of the nicest we'd had... something about the calm before the storm…with blue skies, a light breeze and 82 degrees. The girls had literally checked out of H-O-H and brought their clothes with them and were out at the pool when I arrived. As it was nearing dinner time, Terrill porterhouse steaks with corn and rice were agreed to, as we sat around the propane fireplace and simply smiled the contented look of good food, good memories and good friends.

It was amusing to see how both girls had acclimated to the Saint Martin lifestyle and no longer had the degree of reticence regarding what they had once considered quite revealing. At the beginning of the week, as we had seen so many times before, people who first arrive and swim in the ocean or use a pool, quickly cover up. With a few days of sun, along with a lot of alcohol and laughter, the ambiance has a way of taking that cover and abandoning it and the attitude becomes 'whatever'.

I took the girls on the proverbial house tour and they loved what we'd done. At first they seemed surprised that the showers were outdoors as Reggie inquired, "What do you do in the winter?" before realizing it got all the way down to 80 on cold winter days.

During dinner, Reggie and Sam shared their week's escapades. Unbeknownst to them, we knew where they'd been simply by checking where they'd used the Wilco card. We didn't consider it spying, just making sure they had a good time and everyone was properly compensated. Wilco was known as 'big tippers' which ensured great service and we wanted to keep it that way. When someone was our guest, we wanted them to feel special.

As we were eating and drinking some Terrill Pinot Noir I asked, "Well, how was your week?"

Reggie just looked at me as if I was some sort of dolt and replied. "Are you kidding me? It's been incredible. I don't know how we can ever thank you."

"You have!" Amy offered. "Simply by being who you are."

"Well, thank you," Sam replied.

"If you could only go back to one place or do one thing, what would it be?" I asked.

Reggie looked at Sam, got a smirk on her face and then a nod from Sam as she replied. "Probably Peggy and Paul's nude snorkel dive."

I must have had a shocked look on my face as I said, "Really?"

Sam giggled and offered. "We did it on a dare and had a blast. It was so much fun. We saw all kinds of fish and were with two other couples about our age and we all drank rum punch until we got silly."

Reggie added. "That broke the ice and we spent most of the week down in the Clothing Optional Area and began using Melia's title 'the Ozone' with the snorkel couples where we all just hung out."

I thought, 'In more ways than one.'

"What would be one thing you wouldn't want to do or go again?"

Sam started and then Reggie sort of butted in. "The French guys. Some of them were really obnoxious and wouldn't leave us alone, or perhaps the cruisers with the cameras. What hypocrites!"

"Food?"

Sam offered. "Are you kidding me? Some of the best I've ever had. Milwaukee can't hold a candle to what they serve down here."

"Service?"

Sam continued. "That Wilco card was like magic. They knew we were coming and when we got there, they rolled out the red carpet. It couldn't have been better."

"Favorite place?"

"Lunch or dinner?" Reggie asked.

"Dinner"

"L'Auberge Gourmand," Sam replied and then added. "Small, intimate, great food, superb service, wonderful people."

"Other than the Ozone, where'd you go?"

"We went out on the Tintamarre Island but didn't see any turtles or Gladys and yet it was still fun. At first, we were the only ones who went topless. Then I guess we set the standard, as a lot of the other women got brave and joined us."

"Sounds like you really melded into the entire French culture," Amy offered.

"Anywhere else?" I asked.

Reggie replied. "We did happy hours at Le' String."

Sam interjected. "The first time we felt out of place. The next day, we joined the crowd and blended right in."

I thought for a moment and realized she was referring to their attire. Melia had shared the same fact that happy hour at Le' String meant 'come as you are' and the folks from the Ozone came as they almost were, where the term 'bottoms up' took on two meanings.

Reggie continued. The first time I pulled out the Wilco card, Filipe got a great big smile on his face and talked about the time your daughter was here and how he got to know her. He said Melia was one of the sweetest people he'd ever met. We didn't know she'd been on 'The Choice'. Filipe said everyone down here was cheering for her and when she walked away, they were proud of what she did."

"This is the way to live. Great food and not being judged. I can see why you love it here." Sam concluded.

We'd polished off two bottles of the Terrill Red Devil as Amy called it and it was time to get some sleep. No one knew what the next day would bring. Reggie and Sam's suitcases were in the guest bedroom and I offered to have them sleep in what we called the bunk house where there were two sets of bunk beds.

Amy said she thought that wouldn't be necessary and we said goodnight and the girls went to bed. Amy checked one more time and Wilco Ops reported that the NHC indicated the winds had become even more organized and begun to circulate in the center of the storm. Mariah was on her way, like a slowly spinning top of destruction… she was heading straight for us, with us praying she'd change her mind and simply go away.

## Mariah:

I always get up early on Saint Martin and probably always will. Because of this, I've become a sunrise aficionado. Amy likes her runs. I like watching the sunrise as I look at how a few seconds can change the entire outlook on the day and, metaphorically, on life as reflections off the clouds send a different thought as to how the day and, perhaps, life will be.

Today was different as I checked the Wilco Ops report and saw Mariah had increased to a Category Four hurricane with winds of 120 miles per hour that was still 100 miles away. I read the national weather service report that indicated she still looked like a smaller hurricane and wasn't considered threatening. I still knew that a tropical cyclone was nothing to brush off, bringing heavy rains capable of causing severe flooding wherever they made landfall.

On this day there was no sunrise! Dark clouds hovered above and beyond as if death was at our doorstep. Slowly the winds began. At first, nothing but bursts and then I knew it was time to hunker down as I went to the control center and pressed the buttons that activated the security panels that slowly arose from their resting place, providing the hoped-for barrier between death and destruction.

It wasn't long before the lights began to flicker and the generator kicked on. I turned to my laptop and the NHC who reported that the true final form of a hurricane had been developed. In other words, Mariah's eye had formed completely.

Amy and the girls were awakened by sounds as if a freight train was roaring by. The girls must have discovered "Retro" as Reggie and Sam took quick showers, got dressed and returned with Reggie wearing a chocolate brown, ribbed short sleeve romper with a deep V-neck and turn down collar and four buttons down the front while Sam was wearing a creme color, six- button, romper that looked like it was made out of suede that was cut in the same style as the brown suit ending high on her upper thighs.

As they came to the breakfast nook I offered. "So far. So good."

With a storm breadth of two hundred miles and traveling at fifteen miles per hour, I estimated we were in for a little over twelve hours of pure hell. With our generator providing electricity, I was able to monitor the onslaught around the entire perimeter and could see the rain literally roaring sideways. My God, Mariah was a beast.

For six hours, we sat and listened to the roar, killing time by playing board games to keep our sanity and then there was silence as the winds died and the rain stopped.

"It's over!" Reggie announced.

I knew better, Mariah's eye was right over us and the calm we were experiencing would only last a few minutes and then her wrath would begin again except the winds would change direction. I motioned to everyone and said, "We've got a few minutes before the winds pick up again, let's get some fresh air."

I unbolted the side entrance door and we walked out onto the patio and bright sunlight. The pool was overflowing from nearly twenty inches of rain. Beyond that, the 'Lighthouse' had survived the initial assault. We relished the sun and calm and then, as the winds began again, went back inside.

With the silence, I used our two-way radio to contact Uncle Frank who indicated our side had taken a direct hit and Mariah was still heading Northwest such that the Dutch side was about to get clobbered from the counter clockwise winds.

For the next six hours, we played more board games and listened to the roar. The cellular towers were knocked out and we had no way of knowing what was going on over on the Dutch side, or for that matter anywhere in the world. If this was what war was like, I'm certainly glad I'd never experienced it.

Around seven o'clock the winds subsided and with it the horrific noise. I poked my head out the door as my mouth dropped open. We'd been lucky. The architects and engineers had figured it out and other than the pool being too full, we had no damage, except for losing two of the four six-foot potted palms which simply disappeared. They must have weighed two hundred pounds each and were simply gone.

I returned and expelled a deep sigh as I announced, "The worst is over."

I went to the security controls, pressed the buttons and the steel panels slid down below the floor as late afternoon sunlight poured in to create smiles on Amy and the girls' faces and then pressed the back-wash button to drain some of the pool, thereby, reducing the water level to normal.

Just then, the radio clicked on and it was Uncle Frank inquiring about our condition. I noted we were fine and the 'Lighthouse' weathered the storm. Instead of a jovial reply, Uncle Frank got quite serious and noted, "George, we really got clobbered on our side. The last surge simply devastated downtown and the hospital."

"Oh, my God." I uttered as I looked at the girls and said. "There are two main hospitals in Saint Martin. The Medical Center located in Philipsburg has been damaged and the Louis Constant Fleming Medical Center in Marigot can't be reached."

"Oh, no!" Amy responded.

"Uncle Frank said all the roads are blocked with debris on their side and the Dutch aren't letting anyone cross the border. The island is in complete lock down."

I turned to Reggie and Sam, then looked at Amy and said, "We just can't sit here. Girls, do you think you could help out? I guess there are injured people."

Both Reggie and Sam nodded in the affirmative.

I responded. "The problem is that the border is closed. I don't know if we'll be able to get through or not."

Reggie looked at me and said. "We've met some incredible people here and now they're in need. The least we can do is try."

The girls were still in their rompers and obviously didn't have their nurse's uniforms with them. I thought, with the border closed, how could they ever get through?"

"Do you have any identification that says you're a nurse with you?"

Both of them nodded yes as they had the Milwaukee General Hospital ID's.

"OK, get them and let's go."

Amy looked at me and said, "I'm coming, too."

I unlocked the tram and we rode down to the garage. I opened the garage door and my mouth dropped open. There were branches and leaves everywhere. I pulled the Tacoma out and the trio got in and we took off. As we were going up the hill towards Red Rock, there was a palm tree across the road. I put my flashers on, got out, wrapped a chain around the tree trunk and hooked it to the front hasp of the truck below the bumper.

Amy slid over into the driver's seat and slowly backed down the hill, turning the palm tree until the road was clear. I unhooked the chain, quickly threw it back in 'Taco' and headed over the hill. Everywhere we looked was a mess.

We made it to N7, did the round-about and went up the hill past Rancho Del Sol and down the hill to the entrance into Orient Beach where we saw part of a roof of the security station lying next to the road and downed palm fronds everywhere. There was no time to stop and so I proceeded up the hill, past the Orient Salt Pond where new houses stood like pimples on the now-barren land.

There were no more surprises as we made our way up the hill and through Orleans. I was feeling confident we could make it until we saw the border guards and a road block where South Quartier Road merged with N7 and put on my flashers as if to signal it was an emergency but was flagged down anyway.

"Where do you think you're going? The road is closed and no one is supposed to be out of their houses."

Amy looked at the guards and replied. "The hospital has been destroyed and we've been informed there are numerous injuries and deaths. These two women are nurses from America who want to be of assistance.

The guard was unimpressed and stood his ground.

I offered, *"Une minute,"* and told the girls to provide their identification cards from Milwaukee General.

The officer took the ID's and examined them, looked at me and Amy and inquired. *"Et vous?"* or "What about you?"

I looked at him as Amy replied. "My husband is the owner of Wilco Security. We're going to see if our team can be of assistance in helping police maintain law and order. We don't want the same looting we experienced during Hurricane Irma, do you?

The soldier was still reluctant until I pulled out the walkie talkie and called Uncle Frank who was a retired captain in the Korps Politie Sint Maarten, and told him where we were and what was going on. He instructed me to hand the receiver to the guard as I watched the once very-confident private become quite concerned as he simply said, *"JA, JA, JA BAAS ALGEMEEN. HET SPIJT HEEL ERG MEE. JA ALGEMEEN, IK ZAL AFSPRAKEN MAKEN OM DE GROEP ONMIDDELLIJK NAAR HET ZIEKENHUIS TE BEGELEIDEN."*

The soldier called to one of his associates and explained what was happening. The associate's eyes got extremely large and nod and said *"Oui, oui,"* as they motioned for us to follow the soldier and his jeep with lights flashing and horn blaring.

We made it to the disaster sight and both Reggie and Sam put on their game faces. We explained to one doctor they were American nurses who came to help and they were warmly received and assigned to triage the incoming injured and take care of superficial wounds.

You could tell the girls knew what they were doing as they examined each arrival and triaged them from one to five with one being minor injuries that needed basic care such as bandages or stitches, up to five being those whose lives depended on immediate attention. Amy and I became herders, you might say, taking the examined and placing them in the appropriate area for attention. For fourteen hours we worked until the arrivals became manageable for the surviving hospital staff.

I asked the attending physician what his most critical need was and he said, besides blood, bandages and either suture glue or sutures were next. Cellphones didn't work and so I contacted

Uncle Frank on the walkie talkie and told him to contact Wilco to see if they could load a plane with supplies and get them here as quickly as possible. We'd done this in the past and there was an operating protocol for the procedure as we kept emergency medical supplies in one of our facilities ready to help out anywhere it was needed.

We learned Princess Julianna's control tower had been damaged and no planes could land. I told Uncle Frank to contact 'V' and see if he could pull strings in the federal government so that the plane could land in San Juan and fly the supplies over by helicopter. Within a couple of hours the procedure was outlined and steps initiated. Within another eighteen hours, the first load of medical supplies were on their way to San Juan, to be transferred to Princess Julianna and the make-shift hospital. The girls looked exhausted, yet proud of being able to use their compassion, knowledge and skills. The staff at the Medical Center couldn't have been more grateful for their help.

**Good Morning:**

As the patient surge became a trickle, we excused ourselves and headed home. The Dutch side really had it worse than ours and I felt sorry for them but was still grateful. N7 was passable but along both sides were mounting piles of branches and building parts already stacked and ready for recycle. While the population density of St. Martin is around 3,200 people per square mile or about half that of Milwaukee, when you live on an island there's really no room for garbage and junk and so everything had to be processed.

In the Caribbean all the islands 'help' each other in times of weather-related calamity and so a US military chopper from Puerto Rico began bringing the supplies, blankets, water and even more medical supplies and so, when I initially asked if we could fly back with them on a military helicopter to San Juan, I was politely told 'no'. A few phone calls later and amazingly, we were told we could get on the chopper in 'a few days'.

We contacted Wilco who said they'd have our 'shipper plane', the Badger Bus as it's called - used to fly the football team, revamped by removing all but four seats. We'd be flying home in two days in less comfort than we were used to but none of us really cared.

We made it back to the 'Lighthouse' and realized the power had come on. With it forecasted to be sunny the next day, I knew it wouldn't be long until many of the homes and buildings equipped with solar panels would collect enough energy to operate houses and stores in case the power went out again.

All of us were beat! We'd been up for nearly thirty hours, had done what we could on the Dutch side and made it back to the house and then to bed. Even though it was only 8:00 PM, we all said goodnight and went our ways.

I slept about ten hours and woke up around 7:00 to the sounds of Amy and the girls in the pool as the sun had already risen. It was another glorious day on Saint Martin.

"Come on, George. Why don't you join us?" Amy beckoned.

I nodded and smiled, changed into my suit and spent time in the pool simply rehashing the events and thanking Reggie and Sam for their efforts.

"For all you've done for us, it's the least we could do," Sam replied.

I suggested driving down to Orient Beach to see how our property was, to which they agreed.

The girls quickly changed with Reggie wearing more clothes from Retro in an apricot color sleeveless and backless bib romper that was cut  more like denim overalls with a hem sitting high enough to reveal a peek at her lower silhouette while Sam was wearing a black romper tailored from some sort of stretch fabric attached to flowing short shorts that accentuated her legs.

As for Megan? Yup! Same as always...a boy's white sleeveless ribbed singlet, better known as an undershirt,  tank top or wife beater, along with her ripped denim cheeky shorts both of which had to be over thirty years old. To say two were over-dressed and one under, would have been a profound understatement statement.

As for me, cut-offs and a tee-shirt with old leather deck shoes. I think I'm the only guy in America who doesn't like thongs...shoes that is.

We climbed in the Taco, made it to the round-about and headed down N7. Turning in, we got a casual wave from the security guard who affirmed the subdivision road had been cleared. We made our way down past Orient Bay Village and the restaurant courtyard yet did so with a great deal of trepidation.

A smile crossed my face as I realized that, after Irma, new codes had been implemented and actually followed, where each beach building was actually constructed like a concrete bunker that could not only withstand Mother Nature's assault, but also hold all the furniture, awnings and everything else that would have otherwise been washed away.

We made our way behind Wai and through the puddled bumps until we got behind our building near the Ozone. To our pleasant surprise, the system had worked with the only things missing were some small palm trees planted two years before.

The few people who were out were picking up leaves and small branches and stacking them for another day while the beach was deserted and, except for all the seaweed, looked as if nothing had happened. We parked behind Le'String to check our buildings and all of us got out.

"Do you mind if we walk the beach?" Amy asked.

"Tell you what, why don't the three of you walk and I'll go check the 'House on the Hill'."

"You don't mind, do you?"

"No, not at all."

Amy and the girls headed down the beach as I got back in and headed for Hope Hill. I arrived and everything looked fine but I wanted to double check. I punched in the gate code and it swung open. I surveyed the exterior and the only thing apparent was the water level in the pool which had overflowed. I went to the control panel and hit back-wash button, which began sucking water out and draining it down Hope Hill.

I opened the side door and walked inside the darkened house. I found the switch and turned on the lights and it was almost like something from a Disney ride, everything was as it had been, except totally silent and completely lifeless. My only worry was the food in the refrigerator and so I opened the Sub Zero and realized the back-up system kept it cold such that the only loss were the wilted flowers on the kitchen table Uncle Frank provided when the girls arrived.

Memories flooded me of our times together and what all had been said and done within the now-quiet confines. I thought of the Duke and how the house was his dream. I reflected on Dr. Williams and how she'd gone from profound poverty to a life filled with material things others could only dream about that were superseded by all that she'd accomplished in her life.

I knew that Uncle Frank would have Wilco Security and property management come when the time was right and so I re-set the security alarm, locked the door, shut off the back-wash, got in Taco, closed the open gate and made my way back to Orient Beach.

I arrived too soon and only saw three specs walking my way. As they slowly got closer, a slight smile pursed my lips. The freedom Amy spoke of so many times appeared to have been transmitted to Reggie and Sam. My mind wandered to my first trip to this very same spot where I saw the smiles on Rodney and Ann's faces. My mind wandered back to when we'd bring the kids here and the Duke simply became Grandpa, virtually bathing each child in so much attention they were literally wrapped in love. My mind wandered to how I'd reluctantly 'adjusted' to a lifestyle that classified people for who they are and did so without all the conflicts that now permeate American society.

I watched the trio slowly make their way up the beach and realized the genetic osmosis…one white, one black and one mixed race who not only were smiling, but accepting each other for what they were…three individuals filled with strengths and weaknesses, goodness and shortcomings who only had one goal, to capture the moment and lock it away in their memory bank to savor on another day.

Perhaps they'd implemented Mindfulness. Perhaps the morning warmth allowed them to adapt as if they were still adjusting to their temperate existence. Perhaps Amy had involved them in Shin Rin Yoku that allowed them to escape their mind and relish their senses. It really didn't matter. All I knew is that they were free…free of the limits that curtail so many. Free of the constraints we put on ourselves. Free to accept the magic of Saint Martin as two more individuals who fall in love with a time, a place and a way of life that brings us back again and again and again.

The trio arrived and reported that, other than the seaweed, the walk had been wonderful. The girls pulled on their clothes and went to wash their hands in the ocean. Amy looked at me and asked. "Have I told you lately that I love you?"

"No, but you show me every day and that's more than enough."

"Can we come again, soon?"

"OK."

"Will you walk with me then?"

"If you want me to," I replied

"I do," Amy said.

Good Morning was open and we stopped, spoke with Roman and casually sat at one of their outdoor tables, where we drank dark Colombian coffee, ate warm French croissants and admired each other for what we'd become...a team that helped people in time of need. I simply smiled, thinking about how something so simple could also be so good.

**Reality:**

With our departure schedule unsettled and then only a short time until we need to meet the military helicopter, the girls elected to stay with us at the 'Lighthouse'. At first I think there was a degree of reticence on their part about 'visiting'. The spontaneous nature they'd enjoyed at 'House On The Hill' was initially supplanted by a more formal and reserved demeanor. Little did we know, it would be at least three days before we would get the go ahead. During that time, we literally functioned as a unit where the girl's initial social reservations gave way as a level of comfort settled in accompanied by a great deal of levity, laughter and bantering between us as indications of affection and acceptance.

On day four we were finally confirmed for the ride to Puerto Rico and given three hours to travel to Princess Juliana Airport. The girls realized it was time to get back to reality as Uncle Frank took us to the airport and we climbed aboard a US military helicopter that was so loud you could hardly hear yourself think. I believe the pilots enjoyed the company as good looking young ladies weren't their normal cargo.

We landed, were waived through customs and boarded the Wilco 'Badger Bus' that was waiting for us. The ride home wasn't Spike but we got home and that was the important thing. When we landed at Mitchell International, our standard protocol had always been to go directly to customs and then the hangar. Because we'd come through Puerto Rico we didn't need to stop at customs which was a pleasant surprise.

As we unloaded the luggage Reggie and Sam stopped and gave both of us big hugs and thanked us for the vacation and memories. Amy's hand lingered with Reggie's and then Sam's and I sensed it wouldn't be the last time they saw each other. The girls looked at us with an air of gratitude and regret, knowing it was back to reality. We told them it had been our honor and if they ever wanted to go again to let us know. I'd arranged for a car to take them to them home and we said goodbye. Our driver took us home to Pine Lake where, like an old pair of jeans, it felt good to be back and, yet, I was already yearning to go back to the 'Lighthouse' again.

With the delay, things had piled up. I'd missed my urological appointment but they'd been notified as to the reason why and it was re-scheduled for the following Monday. That night the phone rang and it was Melia simply saying, 'Hi' and wanting to know how our vacation went. Amy filled her in as I waved from across the room which was my way of saying "Ditto."  The following morning, I received a call from 'V' who simply wanted to make sure we were OK. He uploaded all the photos of the grandkids and asked that I share it with Amy which I promised I would do.

## Love on the Rocks:

Derrick had always been the quiet one. Unlike Melia who was goofy as a child or 'V' who was our rebel, Derrick had been introspective and intense. When he found Andrea and they became involved I hoped she would be able to pull him out of his shell and let him enjoy the majesty of life.

When Amy elected to retire and Derrick was named CEO everyone thought it was a logical progression. He had Amy's intellect, an incredible education in both finance and law with degrees from Wharton and Harvard law school and all the ingredients needed to lead Wilco in the charge into the next generation.

While Melia called her mother almost every day and 'V' contacted us at least every other week, a call from Derrick was rare to say the least. Amy always said he was too busy or made some excuse why he didn't call or visit even when I was in the hospital. Quite honestly I never gave it much thought.

When we returned from Saint Martin and it was getting close to my procedural day, I told Amy I thought it would be good to get the family together for dinner. After being spoiled in Saint Martin on seafood, I suggested Carnivore Steakhouse Moderne as it offered Terrill Wagyu beef and our wine, as well.

I put Amy in charge of the date and time and she called Melia and got her schedule and then 'V' and got their schedule and finally Derrick at the office and gave him the options. The time was set and the chopper arranged to bring Melia's entourage from Waldwick as well as a plane to bring 'V', Amelia and the kids from Wausau. We made it an early Sunday dinner so that everyone could get home and the kids to bed.

Amy and I arrived to find Derrick already there, sitting at the bar nurturing a dirty martini. As always, he was impeccably dressed in tan slacks, black golf shirt and shoes that even his spoiled father had to admire. On his wrist was The Duke's Rolex Cosmograph Daytona with an ice-blue dial he had inherited and proudly wore.

Around his neck was a thin gold chain. With his one-eighth African heritage, he always looked as if he'd been in the sun with a light tan that made his perfectly white teeth stand out whenever he smiled. With the intelligence, looks, attire and demeanor, Derrick was always, and I mean always, the focus of every female's glances and it showed.

"Where's Andrea?" I asked.

Derrick looked at Amy and then at me and replied. "Mom hasn't told you?"

"Told me what?"

"Andrea moved back to Germany."

"What?"

"Yeah, Andrea moved back to Germany."

I must have had an incredulous look on my face.

"Dad, it wasn't working out."

"What do you mean, it wasn't working out?"

"Well, we just weren't in love anymore."

"So, you two just split up?"

"Yeah."

I was both shocked and disappointed as I added. "But you were so happy."

"Things changed and she got really possessive and domineering."

"When did all this happen?"

"A few months ago," Derrick replied in a very matter of fact way.

"And we're just finding out about it now?"

"Yeah, I guess **you** are."

"What do you mean, you?"

I turned to Amy and looked at her in a very disapproving way and asked. "You knew about this?"

Amy looked at the ground and then me and replied. "I thought they were just having some trouble and she'd be back. With you in the hospital, we didn't want you to worry."

"Jesus! My kid and his wife split up and you didn't want me to worry? Do Derrick's brother and sister know?"

"Yes!"

"So, I'm the only one in the family who didn't know?"

Both of them just shrugged and nodded, "Yes".

"Is it repairable?" I asked.

"I don't think so, she's filed for a divorce," Derrick responded.

"God damn it!" I was royally pissed but when you're in one of Milwaukee's finest restaurants, I needed to hold my temper. Just then Melia and Jack walked in with the kids who came rushing towards Amy and me.

"Grandma! Boppa!" they exclaimed in unison.

The frustration I was feeling, was immediately erased as my grandchildren's innocence pulled on my heart strings.

"How was your helicopter ride?" I asked.

"Oh, Boppa, it was neat. Captain Ann showed me all the dials and told me what they were for. I think when I grow up I want to fly helicopters." Marie responded with the innocence and glee of any three-year-old.

As Melia's kids were settling in, the door opened and 'V' and Amelia and their kids poured in, setting off another round of hellos before the kids settled into cousin talk as we were led to our table with one chair discretely removed.

Amy brought all kinds of coloring books and games to keep the kids busy as small talk centered around Saint Martin, the Badgers and Packers.

The evening went well and when it was time to say goodbye, everyone wished me luck, as surgery was scheduled for the next week. I assured them I'd be fine, I had the best surgeon and he was using the robot and had assured me a speedy recovery.

As we all headed for home, I turned to Amy and said, "Don't ever do that to me again!"

"I thought there might be a chance they'd get back together."

"I don't care. They're my kids, too, and keeping me in the dark was an insult. Do you know what happened?"

Amy was quiet and then took a deep breath as she replied, "Yes."

"Are you going to tell me?"

"Your son was having an affair."

"Jesus!" I uttered and then asked, "Do you know who the woman is?"

"It wasn't just one woman."

I looked out the front window and then realized he'd debased his wedding vows.

I thought back to the seven components of marriage and mentally outlined them once again… attraction, association, communication, understanding, trust, compromise and forgiveness, thought about Andrea and wondered where the cracks first came and how the entire structure finally fell apart.

"Yes, Derrick is separated and that's why he didn't say anything."

Now I felt like a total ass when I realized my family didn't think enough of me to let me know. All the pieces started falling in place as I inquired. "Now, what?"

"Andrea moved back to Germany and they have a financial settlement in place," Amy offered.

"Whose fault?" I asked…already knowing, already upset, angered and frustrated as my mind went through the mantra I hoped I'd never have to repeat concerning our children. "Alone together, alone apart, if they began all over, they'd never start."

After a long pause I finally said. "OK. I understand and will love him for who he is and what he is…our son."

"You sure?"

"I'm totally certain."

"He's been afraid to tell you."

Now I was reflecting on myself and wondering why he would be afraid and was deeply hurt as I took a deep breath and stared out the front window.

I thought about Melia, 'V' and Derrick and pondered the consequence of profound wealth. I asked myself if the reason they turned out the way they did was because of me and did a mental supposition of each one.

Melia…kind, sweet, generous Melia, who only wanted to fit in and be 'normal.'

'V'…my initial rebel who turned out to be the one with the warrior personality willing to give of himself for the good of others.

Derrick…all my trepidations were coming true…not from the sexual thing…that's his business and if he's happy, I'm happy, but from my profound frustration at his sense of entitlement. He'd always had this 'you owe me' attitude where he took our family wealth and turned it into perks others could only dream about. Our son, who thought the rules didn't apply to him.

Derrick's perceived sense of entitlement drilled down into my conscience as I wondered whether it was due to social factors like living in our house where the main treatise was that rules didn't apply to our family. Was it because Derrick got everything he ever wanted where physical possessions were handed out simply because emotional gifts of love, concern and caring were missing while Amy continued to sustain the Duke's economic empire? Was it because he was a twin? I quietly shook my head and realized, I simply did not know.

I took a deep breath and concluded that children who are never told 'no' or who have parents that give in to every demand grow up believing that's how the world works learn that, with enough fuss or manipulation, they'll get their way and that was Derrick.

None of us intentionally try to screw up our kids, yet, the environment they are raised in affects how they see the world and what they expect from other people. Derrick is CEO of our company and responsible for our wellbeing and his attitude towards others directly and indirectly affects his personal and professional relationships.

All of sudden, the light over my proverbial head flashed on as I realized that people like Derrick, with an entitlement mentality, often see themselves as superior to others. It's no surprise that this way of thinking affects interpersonal relationships.

In work, a career may suffer. Entitled people often interview well and can land leadership roles because of their confidence. However, they often lack team spirit and avoid problem-solving in the workplace. Most of the decisions an entitled person makes are self-serving. This can quickly become apparent to their co-workers.

We pulled into Pine Lake and got out of the car. Amy headed for the family room and some innocuous television program designed to fill time but not her mind. I went to my office, turned on my computer, went to the browser and typed in 'entitlement' where the following summary jammed itself into my heart and mind.

Feeling entitled to something and the disappointment that follows when they don't get what they want can reinforce entitled behavior. This typically follows a vicious 3-step cycle:

- When a person is entitled, they're always vulnerable to the threat of unmet expectations.
- When those expectations aren't met, it can lead to dissatisfaction and other emotions like anger and a sense of being cheated.
- When a person is distressed, they try to fix the situation and console themselves. This results in self-reassurance that they deserve everything they've ever wanted, which reinforces the same entitled behavior.

If a person finds they have a sense of entitlement, there are ways to change their mindset. Practicing gratitude and humility can help them become more responsible and considerate. If they're trying to overcome an entitlement mentality, start treating others as they would like to be treated. Regardless of social status, we're all human.

If they're in a situation they think is unfair, they should pause for a minute and think about the greater good. Consider how the world would look if no one else had to work for what they got. Use respect and kindness when interacting with others. Everyone is a human being with feelings and struggles of their own. Go easy on others. Be sympathetic to their needs. Learn from their mistakes. Treat failure as a learning tool. Failing isn't the end of the world. Mistakes made can be corrected the next time. Never stop learning, and look for value in failure.

I vowed to have a man-to-man with Derrick. The following morning I called Wilco and asked to speak to my son. I identified myself and told the receptionist to put me through. After a pause, she came on the line and told me Derrick was in an important meeting.

I lost it!

"Get my son on the phone now. I don't care who he's talking to."

"But, Mr. Terrill."

"Don't give me any of the Mister Terrill shit. I'm a board member and  primary stockholder in the company and I need to speak with the CEO who happens to be my son. Now you've got two choices, either get him on the phone or put on your coat and leave the facility. Do you understand?"

"Yes, sir."

"I'm waiting. I'm going to count back from ten and if he isn't on the phone, you won't be either. Ten... nine... eight... seven..."

"Hello".

"Derrick, when I call, which isn't often, and I know you're there because your car is in the parking lot, I need to speak to you."

"How do you know that?"

"What?"

"That I'm here."

Because I started the security division and have access to all the security cameras, that's how."

"Jesus! Big brother is watching."

"I don't know about Big Brother, but your father is."

"Tuesday? Wednesday or Thursday? Which day is your least busy?"

"Ahh..."

"Don't give me any shit...Tuesday, Wednesday or Thursday. At the count of five, I'll decide... One... two... three..."

"Wednesday."

"OK, clear your Thursday afternoon calendar. You and your father are going to have a long talk."

"But!"

"Derrick, don't even go there. Talk to me now or at the next Board meeting."

"Jesus, dad!"

"I'll pick you up at noon and no excuses!"

My blood pressure was probably through the roof as I sat at my desk and began writing.

"I've gone through our relationship with ourselves and our spouse and how society changed activities and expectations regarding the two longest running events in our life. The third significant relationship is with our children. We made them! It's our responsibility to nurture them, teach them and above all else, love them, guide them, assure them and defend them as need be. We cannot walk away without regret! We cannot ignore without shame! We cannot deny that they are ours simply because we were the ones who brought them here!"

"Boy, did I make some mistakes! In trying to prove to the world I didn't marry Amy for her money, I gave up the one thing that's the most precious commodity we have and that's time…time with my children, time to share their laughter and joy, to console them in their sorrow, to watch them grow and change literally before my eyes. If asked what is the biggest regret of my life, I'd say, not spending more time with our kids."

"Having provided my confession and putting it in perspective, I believe I can begin. I only hope that whomever reads this understands that I screwed up and now try to make amends by sharing what I believe are the key elements of parenthood. There's a saying that those who can't…teach. Perhaps, that best summarizes what I am about to elicit."

As I noted before, the primal objective we all have is to propagate. To bring children into this world - offspring who will carry our genetic seeds forth until it's their turn to replicate our actions and those of their ancestors. That's our primal goal! Having children in America is an expensive proposition. The cost to rear a child to age 18 BEFORE COLLEGE is over a quarter of a million dollars.

When carried full term and a child is born, everything changes. First and foremost, are the internal parental changes from elation, to a lot of stress, uncertainty and dramatic changes. Where once there were two individuals, now there are three. The combination of hormone-related changes, sleep deprivation, breast-feeding, and role and identity issues, all compounded by a change in the relationship between mother and father can be both incredibly awesome and profoundly frightening."

"For women, the feelings of becoming a mother are the most powerful feelings in her life. These emotions can, at times, be overwhelming for both parents and yet it begins. Like the dot upon the paper that began our introspection, we provide a child their meaning through our actions and reactions. This is our relationship to them! They come into this world profoundly innocent and then, through our own experiences and foibles, we share with them, we alter that innocence and affect what was once pure."

"Without reference, we cannot define our responsibility to our children. Without having the foundation of understanding, how can we possibly reflect on why things are so profoundly different today than when we were children? What happened to our innocence? Did it really morph into today's culture or is it just that it's under a microscope so much more today than ever before?"

"Our responsibility to our children and our children's, children's children is to bequeath an existence that has been improved upon for the generations that follow. This betrothal is not monetary. This inheritance is not physical but one based on learned values of caring, hope and trust, communicated through deed and action so that our heirs refer our existence as the base from which to grow."

"The challenge in our helter-skelter world is having enough time for them to really be the nurturer that we aspire. We cannot be Rockwellian in terms of thinking that everything was so pristine in the past, because it wasn't. What we need to do, as a parent, is understand the dynamics of the relationship with our children and how, over time, it too will change, just as that with our spouse has done."

"Family structure, like society at large, has undergone significant changes since World War II. While the nuclear family - with dad, mom, and offspring happily coexisting beneath one roof- remains the ideal, variations in family structure are plentiful - and often successful. I cannot emphasize enough that any particular family situation will have tremendous influence upon a child's happiness, development and future but parents hold all the trump cards when it comes to creating a family. The '*Father's Knows Best*' (Google it! Robert Young, the late 50's) Nuclear Family almost seems quaint. Though this is the most basic family arrangement, it's also rife with complexities."

"Today it's a compound-complex set of relationships. My most profound moment was when I heard two women talking and one said 'my second husband's third wife.' How do we keep it all straight? Times have changed and with it the entire concept of how to raise a child. What happens if we get divorced and we don't like the ex-spouse's new spouse or don't agree with the way they're raising your children? There's really not much we can do about it."

"Today's families can be complex units that are bonded by strong emotional connections. The ways in which members of a family interact with each other and in relation to the group as a whole are often referred to as family dynamics, where dynamics refers to change. In all families, things like traditions, communication styles, behavioral patterns and emotional interdependence all influence the relationships between family members."

"Despite the changing lifestyles and ever-increasing personal mobility that characterize modern society, the family still remains the central element of contemporary life. Families should offer companionship, security, and a measure of protection against an often-uncaring world, where the integral element is attachment to each other. In addition, to coin a phrase from Crosby, Stills and Nash...parents need to *'teach their children well.'*"

"A recent survey found 58% of respondents say that values and morals are the most important thing a father can provide his children. Emotional support came in second, with 52% of the adult respondents giving it top priority for fathers. Just 41% indicated that income was a father's key responsibility."

"With mothers, values and morals tied with emotional support for top billing followed by discipline at 46% and income at just 25%. What's making this so tough is not only the lack of fathers in the home but the exposure to so many things that can truly challenge values and morals."

"Today's digital and social media era is wreaking new and unseen challenges on all aspects of society, including, and particularly, childhood. With the internet, the day a person posts the sonogram of their child is the day the world identifies his or her digital identity and have access to them."

"For the rest of a child's life, people will be talking about them, researching them, affecting them, challenging them, doing everything they can to speed up the process of maturing, simply through expanded exposure to both good and bad."

"Parents must be the gatekeeper to their innocence! We must control what they see and learn from the predators that roam the electronic back alleys! From the early onset, their digital identity will be formed they will have less and less and less control over their privacy as people describe them directly or indirectly, overtly or covertly, through cookies and other electronic tracking methods. This is a profound challenge to innocence and only parents have the ability to ensure someone they care about is shielded from all there is to see in this ever-increasingly connected world. The internet can be a profoundly wonderful tool for communication, learning and sharing. It's just deciding when and to what degree parents allow children to be associated with it that's paramount."

## "Cats in the Cradle":

The day came and I got out my Sunday pants and sports coat, got in the Corvette and drove to the Wilco offices arriving at 11:55. At noon, I expected Derrick to appear. He did not.

At 12:15, I'd had enough, got out of the car and walked into the building. The receptionist looked at me and inquired.

"May I help you?"

"Who are you?" I inquired.

"Sir, I'm the noon receptionist."

"Gee, I would have never guessed that. I have a 12:00 o'clock appointment with Mr. Terrill."

"Is he expecting you?"

"How long have you been here?"

"Six months."

"Ok, let me make this perfectly clear. My name is George Terrill, Mrs. Amelia Terrill is my wife. Derrick Terrill is our son. I am on the Board of Directors of Wilco Corporation and a primary stockholder."

"Are you sure you have an appointment?"

I took a deep breath and reiterated the relationship. Expelling the frustration I was holding, pausing and then offering an alternative. "OK, let's do it this way, please contact Jermaine Jackson and tell him George Terrill is in the lobby."

"Is he expecting your call?"

"No!"

"I'm sorry, sir, Mr. Jackson is not taking calls right now."

Now I was pissed and simply turned around, took out my cellphone and called Amy.

"Hello."

"Amy, are you in the building?"

"Yes."

"I'm in the lobby and the receptionist won't let me in."

"Oh, my God! I'll be right down."

I curtly smiled at the noon receptionist and waited until the door opened and then watched the little girl's eyes get as big as saucers.

"Amy, please inform your noon receptionist who I am and that I've come to go to lunch with our son."

"George, it's only company protocol to keep those without appointments out of the facility."

"I'm a major stockholder and sit on the Board."

"Anyone could say that."

I started calming down, took yet another deep breath and announced, "Derrick was supposed to meet me at noon for lunch."

Amy turned to the noon receptionist and said. "Angela, please call Mr. Terrill and inform him his father is in the lobby waiting for him."

"Yes, Mrs. Terrill."

Angela made the call and two minutes later Derrick was in the lobby as he apologized. "Sorry dad, I thought the lunch was tomorrow.

"Today is Thursday isn't it?"

"No dad, today is Wednesday."

"What?

Amy nodded in the affirmative and I felt like a fool.

"Are you all right?" Amy asked.

"I'm embarrassed as hell. I guess all that's going on and sitting home alone got to me. Derrick, I'm sorry, I'll see you tomorrow."

"OK, dad."

With that Amy and Derrick were gone while Angela had a disconcerted look on her face that probably matched mine.

I drove back to Pine Lake and began writing while realizing I needed to digress and review the dynamics of emotional association.

"First of all, when there's emotional balance, there can be emotional bliss. When one party is more emotionally involved than the other by a profound amount, things happen. The party more involved doesn't understand why the other person doesn't have the same level of intensity regarding feelings and is sometimes jealous or suspicious of the other's independence. Concurrently, the lesser involved person can feel thwarted and emotionally smothered as *the emotional fulcrum*' - the point of balance - is too difficult to function properly."

"The goal is always emotional balance whereby simply moving the fulcrum, we can change the dynamics. Move the fulcrum closer and we need more effort to achieve balance. Move it farther away and we need less! It's as simple as that. Apply this to emotional involvement and we can quickly see that when the emotional fulcrum shifts towards a person, they need more effort to sustain the feeling. Conversely, when the fulcrum of involvement moves away, there is less emotional effort and therefore less risk."

"The second point is that children truly need consistency in their lives. They must be able to comprehend cause and effect. Without this supposition they will remain confused and somewhat intimated by the variances they experience. This consistency can actually be classified, where the parents set the rules based on their parenting skills."

"If the father is only a spectator and not a participant the challenge of achieving a coveted secure relationship is very difficult. A secure relationship is where a child feels they can depend on their parent or provider. They know the person will be there when they need support. They know what to expect and this is the type of relationship children want! Learning can be a scary thing and a child needs to be confident that their parent will be there to back them up when they need it."

"A not-so-good relationship is the one that includes avoidance which is where I believe Derrick and I currently reside. This is at the other end of the spectrum and will lead to problems as the child grows. Here, the child is insecure because he or she has learned that depending on their parents won't get them that secure feeling they covet and so they learn to take care of themselves."

"Another type of relationship is one of ambivalence and is somewhere between the two. Here the child may be insecurely attached to his parents because he or she has learned that sometimes their needs are met, and sometimes they're not. Children are smart and they notice what behavior got their parents' attention in the past and they'll use it over and over until they get their way. The child has a need and they're simply looking for that feeling of security that, sadly, they get too infrequently."

"The final type of relationship can be called the 'disorganized phase' because children receive mixed messages and really don't know what to expect from their parents. They're confused, disjointed and perplexed which leads to all kinds of problems as they grow because all of us end up like our parents in many ways."

I now had the afternoon, evening and morning to prepare for my lunch with Derrick. As noted earlier the way I learn is eyes-to-hand, hand-to-brain and so, I spent a lot of the time looking at studies. In so doing, I came up with the following regarding the dynamics of the parent-child relationship and how things change in the different phases of life - a parent's and their child's.

"Those first few years a child is totally reliant on their parents for everything to simply survive. Until about age four, the father's brain also produces chemical levels of oxytocin that create that parental bonding. Fathers couldn't be happier! Then things begin to change!"

"There are also phases in relationships with children. At first, parents are their teachers to impart right and wrong, good and bad. They must mandate, dictate and teach through example. The child begins school and their realm expands. They're still reliant, but in other ways. This is the phase where they need emotional reassurance that they are wanted, needed and loved, that they hold a very special place in our hearts."

"This is where having the secure relationship really comes into play. It's also that point for men, when it's easy to usurp those parental duties to the spouse in the name of income generation to retain the life to which we ascribe. The oxytocin is gone and it costs an awful lot of money to raise a child."

"The challenge for men is that period when little boys need their fathers and little girls need their mothers the most - from about age eight to fourteen - when they're looking for leadership, companionship, paternal guidance and approval - when the fulcrum still is in the parent's favor."

"Little boys need their father's attention and love. If the father has relinquished these roles to his spouse or a neighbor or some form of organized activity, where the only parental involvement is driving them to the event, those days of non-participation will never be forgotten by the child and not in a good way."

"Young fathers need to make certain they pay attention to their children as they associate, communicate and, above all else, accept them for what they are…children in a crazy, mixed-up world that forces them to grow up too soon, and be exposed to thoughts and things they should never have been. Children today become so much older younger and remain younger older than ever before. The frustrations! The confusion! The angst associated with their social perceptions have resulted in a society filled with unequivocal yearning simply to be accepted that evolves into sadness and depression to the point that over half of American young adults report being so."

"Studies were done in the 1990's of children ages 10-13 that were then paralleled to previous generations. It was determined the 1990's children had the same psychological profile of children from the late 1940's. The same beliefs! The same social skills! The same outlook on life! The big difference was that the children from the 90's were from traditional families while the children from the 1940's were orphans! What does that say about how we're raising children today?"

"In the snap of a finger, that little boy is a young man and the fulcrum has naturally shifted. If we've not been there for him, we may have lost him. He may resent our absence for the rest of his life. Now it's too late. He doesn't need us anymore! We need him! We need his love! We need his respect! Above all else we need to know that he honors us as his father!"

"As the child develops their independence continues to grow and somewhere around puberty, the emotional playing field seems to be in total balance. We need them and they need us but they just don't want to let us know it. You see, it isn't 'cool' to be associated with your parents when you're in junior high."

"The man/boy or woman/girl is going through a profound period of change physically, emotionally and socially as hormones begin to kick in. The fulcrum of dominance has reached the exact center and there can be a war of independence."

"As the child matures a parent's role changes, too. We move from a position of teacher to one of counselor. As decisions become an aspect handled by the child, our position becomes one of showing alternatives. If we attempt to mandate, the child **will** rebel."

"As the child progresses the emotional fulcrum continues to move away from them and therefore in their favor. They seek independence as parents seek reassurance. The child has reached a point where they *THINK* they no longer need their parents and their wisdom. In reality they do, they just don't think so. At this point, the parents have become spectators more than participants - watching them play sports, watching their music concert, watching them go to prom!"

"The book '*Passages*' by Gail Sheehy is about the predictable crises of adult life in which there are seven major life passages that everyone goes through: the trying 20s, the catch 30s, the freedom 40s, the midlife crisis, the empty nest, the encore career, and the final passage. In her book '*Passages II*', there's a profound statement about American boys. It specifically states that today young men get older younger but remain younger longer."

"Physical maturity sets in earlier but the social maturity needed to actually function in life in some form of logical, cognizant way has slid to some point later in their 20's. Why? Because, all of the responsibilities of the former generation, such as having a job and marrying early, have dissipated."

"Today there are few jobs for teenagers. They've been taken by people who need the work to live, who are willing to sacrifice the time it takes simply to provide some sort of sustenance. It's not that children are less committed, it's just that they don't have the opportunity to work in the adult world the way generations before them did and therefore don't have the chance to become exposed to the real world."

"The second element of deferred maturity deals with delaying marital commitment. Previous generations got married when they were in their late teens or early twenties. Today, the average age in America for men to marry is 28.9 and women 26.9. This change has been brought about by the sexual liberation of our culture and also by the deferred maturity discussed."

"This phase means that the twenty-something's have a period of profound independence where they try to live life to the fullest, which normally means they're away from home and living on their own and the emotional fulcrum with their parents moves to its farthest point in their favor."

"The child's busy lifestyle and more '*liberated*' mores are having profound effects on parents who feel they're becoming even more distant spectators, cheering on their offspring, hoping and praying they will someday grow up. Most of them do! It's just taking a little longer than it used to."

I paused for a moment to think of Reggie and Sam and Reggie's statement they were Experientials and realized the term, experience and outlook represented an entire generation and not a few individuals as I continued writing.  "The little boy becomes a young man! The little girl, a young woman! Both are totally independent socially, financially and emotionally. Then it happens! One day they wake up and realize their parents weren't so stupid after all. Children begin to realize the sacrifices made for them and the fulcrum begins its slow slide back towards some degree of equity."

"As time continues on the fulcrum normally comes back to a point close to equity but never quite makes it. The child has their life and the parents remain spectators. When those special events are planned, the parents look forward to them with a much higher degree of anticipation because they'll simply be spending time with their children and, perhaps, grandchildren as well. This brings comfort and joy to the grandparents along with the satisfaction of knowing their genetic responsibility has been met."

"As time passes on roles change as society changes. At some point, the child becomes the counselor to his parents, keeping them appraised of new sets of social dynamics that do not match those with which the parent established his own set of values."

"If time passes even further and parents become more dependent, adult children begin to assume the role of teacher as they help their elderly parents traverse the rapids of an ever-changing, ever-accelerating world. What makes this all so challenging is that we now live in a 'no fault' society where everyone blames everyone else for their problems. If it's not the government, it's the neighbors, co-workers or strangers. They're the ones with the problems, not us and certainly not our children! Sure!"

"Add to this the degree of legal complexity within which we live, where the litigious culture has so exacerbated our freedoms many feel encumbered with rules, regulations and reprisals and are socially afraid to act for fear they'll be sued. In their homes, people are afraid to provide the necessary rules, restraints and consequences for violations that once existed."

"The results of this fear are that we now have some members of a generation or two undaunted by authority and disrespectful of others. This narcissistic segment of the population has taken our society, culture and quality of life and simply thrown it in the trash because of their self-indulgence predicated on their upbringing."

"What's profoundly frightening is that these people are now having children who have taken this lower level of social skills and achievement and passed it on to an even lower level of aspirants who are clueless about how to act and achieve, who look at the world and sincerely believe it owes them something. Nowhere is this more apparent than in today's schools."

"Teachers who want to teach can't because of the rules, regulations and restrictions placed on them by administrators and school boards who are so afraid of losing their jobs and being sued for this or that, to the point the objective is no longer developing educated, socially responsible members of our society, it's simply to process children pursuant with guidelines set by federal, state and local politicians."

"Teachers can't teach! They live in fear of reprisal. They no longer have authority! They no longer garner respect! They no longer have that innate compulsion for the betterment of the child! It has all been replaced by self-preservation in the name of job and financial security predicated on the ominous threat in a lawsuit for abiding by the rules."

"This sad state of affairs transcends so many different professions! Examine the world of medicine and you see a compound-complex situation dominated not by intellect and intuition, through the minds of some very intelligent professionals but through the rules, regulations and risks associated with laws and regulations imposed by the government, insurance companies and lawyers. Physicians are now programmed to do what the insurance companies command and not what's always best for the patient. Physicians live beneath an umbrella of fear where one false move can result in being sued. Sure, there are quacks and yet most doctors and nurses are there to help and not spend their time fighting with lawyers, insurance companies and the government."

"What are the consequences? A society that's limited in intellectual and social skills where propriety and decency are simply being obliterated. I could talk about public manners but this book would double in size. We've become a social embarrassment where the influx of cell phones and texting when walking, places the user at what they believe is the center of the universe and it's our job to pay attention to them and get out of their way."

"There are still countless young people who are true, honest, sincere and polite. Sadly, they appear to be a shrinking majority and the dichotomy is simply profound. We all sit in silence and observe and shake our heads. Where in hell did we go wrong?"

"Nowhere does this degradation seem more paramount than when it comes to communication skills. We spend more time typing than ever before but we spend less time writing and creating. What has our world come to? We cannot, must not, should not rely on the media...not radio, nor television and especially not social media. They are theoretically the fifth estate. One can never forget they're a business with one ultimate goal...to make money and maximize the highest possible return on investment. In order to increase their revenue they need more readers, watchers or listeners. In order to do this they need to sensationalize the message to lure us into their cauldron."

"For decades, the media has made Americans feel socially insecure because it sells. Death is one of their biggest draws and so they amplify it to the point that extreme issues seem commonplace and we all begin to assume they represent the norm. Nowhere is that more prevalent than with the issues of guns...not any guns...assault weapons designed to kill, not maim. Assault weapons so powerful that a small child's head can be completely blown off from a single shell where their remains are identified only by the clothes they wore to school that day. Assault weapons designed for war and not against small children who only want to be just that...children.

"In America today there are 120 guns per person, where 44% of all homes have at least one and nine million guns are sold each year. The murder rate using guns is eighteen times greater in America than any other wealthy nation in the world. Statically, America ranks 77$^{th}$ out of 100 countries in murders per capita and fourth in the total number of homicides with 16,214 reported in 2018."

"When the countries surveyed are similar to the US, the numbers become much more pronounced. We see that America's murder rate is 3.5 per 100,000 which SEVEN TIMES greater that of any of the 22 other countries included. There's a heartbreaking footnote. America ranks 61$^{st}$ in terms of per capita total murders of children in all countries. However, it is the most violent country in the world in terms of the deaths of children due to gun violence."

"Tragically gun violence is the number one killer of children. Not Cancer! Not car accidents! It's the blatant disregard for purity. Catastrophically, we not only take the lives of the innocent, we allow murderers to destroy the emotional virtue of our children, forever branding them with the scars of mortality as they witness and experience the terror, realizing it could have been them."

"While politicians argue, fight and get rich debating things like abortion and orientation our children suffer. While they pontificate about what our children should not be able to see, read or understand, our children's childhoods are being ripped apart, corrupted by the fear that they or their friends, teachers or those they love will be next. Schools should be safe havens for learning, not fortresses built to protect our children and grandchildren from the distress of social, emotional and irrational war."

"Guns are invading our children's psyches and shaping forever their sense of safety, belief in humanity and  understanding of our priorities as a nation, society and culture. When a country averages more than one mass murder PER DAY, where nearly twelve PER DAY are children, something is wrong. One can only the fathom the trauma associated with the loss of a child and the sadness of that first night when one enters a child's bedroom filled with teddy bears and dreams, where there was once joy and laughter, and now nothing but the deafening silence of tomorrow and tomorrow and tomorrow."

"Is it the availability of weapons? It is the stress we all live under? How do we shelter our children from not only the danger, but the insipient fear of their demise? The threat of nuclear war in the 1950's had profound effects on children of that era. What is the threat of death in schools doing to our children today and what can we as parents and grandparents do to insulate them from the calamities facing our society and culture?"

"Flowers and teddy bears appear almost on a daily basis as does the mantra 'never more' until the next round of terror brings back the stark reminder our country, society and culture is now based on death and not on life, on survival and not happiness. How can we justify teaching and children how to play dead or where to hide when the gunman comes and do so to the point the innocents no longer believe it's something that MIGHT happen, but something that WILL HAPPEN while those who have acquired the throne of power sit by and debate what's in it for THEM!"

"Our society has changed! Our culture has changed! Our families have changed! With it has come the profound need for parents to play an ever-increasing role in the growth and development of their children because, sadly, no one else has the ability or authority to do it without the fear of being sued. It seems today in America it has become almost socially acceptable to not be part of rearing of a child. Some men justify in by paying child support either by decree or by sleeping in a house where they really don't live and providing financial means to support the children."

"Parenthood is **not** defined by money. It's defined by love and guidance, care and nurturing through example. Growth is not only physical but emotional, spiritual and ethical. It's important as a father to do things as a family. First, for the experience in the near-term! Second, because we serve as a model regarding our behavior towards our spouse in front of our children."

"Through our actions and interactions with our spouse, we're setting the behavioral parameters under which our children will act when they're adults. This area represents a profoundly important role parents play in a child's growth and development and the wrong actions or their absence, will play an integral role in determining how their children and their children's children respond to those who come into their lives."

"Children, regardless of age, are ALWAYS looking for affirmation - for the security that they matter to their parents even when they screw up. A few kind, loving words can go a long way towards restoring those broken dreams - that pervading sense of sadness that comes when one doesn't feel wanted, needed and loved. Children need to know their parents are there to help pick up the pieces of their shattered dreams. They must show them they're OK and they're there to help them traverse the abyss that lies before them and, most important of all, failure is not the end, simply the beginning of a new adventure."

"Life is what happens when we're making other plans. No matter what's going on in life - major, minor, insignificant - it's not as important as sitting back and listening to that gentle reminder to enjoy the present for these are the moments memories are made of with those we love, especially our children. They're children for such a short, short time and then their childhood will be gone, like dandelion seeds blown in the wind, leaving behind only yesterday when hands were small, eyes lifted up towards ours, filled with love, trust and devotion so innocent, pure and dedicated. Savor the moment! Cherish it with your heart and soul. It's profoundly too precious to waste on anything but the love of a child."

"I finally admitted that becoming a great parent starts by looking in the mirror. It truly may take looking beyond the mirror and back into your life to see things as they really are - at those things that we're still trying to compensate for. We're all victims of our past. We're all subject to the peaks and valleys created by those who came before us that shaped us, molded us and adjusted us to what we're today. Unresolved bitterness affects us much more than it does the one we're bitter toward. Bitterness holds us back from becoming all we can be."

"Forgive! Forget! Learn a lesson and move on! We must all sincerely believe that we're here for a reason and that our future lies in front of us and not behind. My father used to say that there were three ways to learn - by, seeing, by doing and by the mistakes we made. We learn the most from the mistakes and we can truly change our future and make it better for those around us and also for ourselves IF we give it a try."

"We won't be able to do anything about eliminating life's distractions. What's important is to focus on where we want to go, not where we've been. We truly do control tomorrow, if we began laying plans for it yesterday and then if, and only if, we allowed our heart and mind to embrace that direction."

"We must never forget that our children are the results of us. We need to make them comfortable and confident in themselves and their relationship with us. If others, besides me, have a near-death experience and still have the opportunity to reflect on life, act now so that you don't have to spend that time making excuses for the degree of involvement in our children's growth and development socially, ethically, intellectually or morally. This is OUR job! There are stages! There are pivot points! There are times and events that will profoundly affect how our children will integrate into our society so that they are truly good people that all begins with US!"

"The odds **ARE** against us! There are so many people who don't have a clue about right and wrong, good and bad that it seems simply overwhelming. Yet, if we don't take parenting personally, if we don't take those steps to show our children we love them and, through example, reflect on respect for each other, God, and our society, who will? It's a lonely battle that begins at the breakfast table where the meaning of the word 'no' is profoundly understood. It transcends social morays to the point that expressions of gratitude and respect become automatic. It fosters a sense of being, belonging and pride that constitute an acceptance of decency and humility, generosity and compassion that supersedes the concept of self in a selfish world."

"When this happens, when these attributes show up in our children, then and only then, can we consider ourselves successful, not only as a parent, but in life itself. It's never too late to begin! It's never too late to show our children that we love them, respect and honor them by being their parent. We brought them into this world with an expression of passion. Remain passionate about them and their existence and the rewards will be multiplied beyond your own level of comprehension."

I leaned back in my chair, pulled out my cellphone and sent Derrick a text that simply said, "I love you and am proud of you. You will always be my son...Love, Dad"

Two minutes later, there was a ding. "Thanks, dad. I love you, too...always your son, Derrick."

"See you tomorrow for lunch?"

"Dad, I've got a lot on my plate right now. Can we revisit the subject another day?"

My mind went to Harry Chapin's *'Cats in the Cradle'* and it hit home as a depiction of Derrick and my lost relationship and the importance of spending time with your children. The song tells the story of a father who's too busy to spend time with his son. As the son grows, the son becomes more and more distant to the point that, as an adult, he has no time for his father and the two of them are estranged thereby serving as a reminder that time is precious and we shouldn't take our children or it for granted.

## Work:

I made it to my pre-operative exam, took all the preliminary tests and was mentally trying to prepare myself for what lie ahead. I'd done enough research to know what the probable consequences were and accepted that what was about to happen would be life-changing and also life-saving. To keep my mind occupied I went to the folio and continued writing. I'd covered my self-relationship, that with my spouse and children and it was time to address the salient point that almost cost me my marriage, namely, my job or career. Speaking from personal experience meant my thoughts and attitudes are more detailed than other sections. This is because what we do for a living consumes so much of the most precious resource we have...time. Here's what I sent to Ceclia...

"I sincerely feel that a rewarding career is one that provides a sense of purpose, satisfaction, and fulfillment that allows you to use your skills and talents, make a difference in the world and earn a good living. One of the sadist things is to be passion-impaired about what you do. If you're passionate about your work you're more likely to be engaged and motivated. You'll also be more likely to stick with it through the tough times. Not all of us are fortunate enough to have a father-in-law who takes us under his wings or be able to start at the top of our profession. A rewarding career provides you with opportunities to learn and grow including new challenges, learning new skills and advancement. What's sad is when a person is trapped in a non-supportive work environment where they don't feel valued and respected and are uncomfortable asking for help when they need it nor are any part of a team."

"American society is such that when we have a conversation with someone new, one of the first questions asked is, 'What do you do?' This is particularly true of men. By informing someone of what we do for a living we're establishing a social level. Responding as a professional... doctor, lawyer, etc....results in a completely different set of responses than from saying we work at McDonalds. Sadly, most Americans judge people by what they do not who they are. In many instances, American corporate structures are simply power modules where people only have power over us and then only to the degree we think we need something from them. Take away the perception of need and we erode the power base!"

"The biggest problem today is that we're living in a dichotomous world where we aspire for independence in a system that's stacked against most of us. With the way our country is going, very soon only two types of Americans will exist: the uber-rich and the ultra-poor."

"Our socio-economic profile was formerly similar to a Dromedary camel. As we evolved from manufacturing to a digital and service economy, our society has been transformed into what looks like a Bactrian camel with a lower and upper middle class and few precisely in the middle."

"America is supposed to be the land of opportunity which is why so many immigrants continue to arrive in our cities. For some it's simply to get a better job or, hopefully, more security. For others it's to build their dream business. We've all seen it dozens of times where a creative entrepreneur starts a company and, through the forces of talent, dedication and the ability to inspire others, he or she builds an empire. As the company increases in size so does the founder's ego. Things that used to be dreams…cars, homes, trips, perks and most of all people catering to them… become commonplace and their ego begins to get in the way of progress or they get involved in a political scheme that protects them from the rest of us. Tragically, big banks, corporations and politicians have never been richer and more interconnected as the average American struggles to keep a good-paying job and their own sense of values."

"In 1969 The Peter Principle was introduced by Laurence J. Peter which observes that people in a hierarchy tend to rise to '*a level of respective incompetence*' where employees are promoted based on their success in previous jobs until they reach a level at which they are no longer competent, as skills in one job do not necessarily translate to another. The Peter Principle is often used to explain why there are so many incompetent people in positions of power and why companies periodically make bad decisions while others lose track of social, technical and cultural changes and simply fade away."

"In America we spend more time working than any other society in the world. Not only do we invest the normal hours of the workday but we transcend what was formerly our personal time with the extensions necessary to simply keep up. The challenges upon us and demands are now so great that, in many ways, they're hard to comprehend."

"In addition to doing the tasks for which we're employed the entire internet scenario takes countless hours of our time to simply respond. Hearing tales of people receiving 100, 200, 300…1,600 e-mails **a day** seems ludicrous. How can one function under such pressure? How does someone accomplish anything? In order to succeed at understanding the role of our job in our life it's critical to understand the elements of achievement."

"Perhaps it's the pressure. Perhaps the loss of respect for authority. Perhaps the electronic versions of the British tabloids that has taken our society and made it so confrontational where anyone and everyone exudes an aura of entitlement…a sense of deservingness or being owed a favor when little or nothing has been done to deserve special treatment where the slogan *'Ambition makes more trusty slaves than need. There's always room for improvement until the day we die.'* Could never be more apropos."

"When I was a boy even on the farm, men went to work with one goal in mind, to retire from where they started. You went to work, did your job, played politics and then, when you reached 65, your pension kicked in."

"Today, men who have been even in the same line of work, let alone for the same employer for more than three decades are dinosaurs. There's no loyalty because there's too much politics resulting in 'us against them' and the feeling, *'I'll screw him to get ahead and get that great big raise'*. Why? Because the disparity in the workplace in terms of money, status and perks has become so great and those who have it, flaunt it! It's no wonder why American companies have such a difficult time competing."

"It's easy to compare dollars. They are all the same physical size, all use the same ink and many have images of some of the guys I think I went to college with. What's different is how many of those you have. Where the more the merrier we all dream. Underneath is the concept where quantity is equated to worth. 'I must be better because I earn more.' Good old ego! *'I better take this job, because it pays more!'* In reality, money is a lousy reason to take a new job."

"I learned the hard way and if there's one thing I pontificate, *'Work hard but keep it in balance with the rest of your life.'* Whether it's your family, friends or health, absolutely no job is worth sacrificing them for it. No one!  Not you! Not your family! Not your friends need to be pulled into the frustrations of the office! Tomorrow all those issues will be waiting and we don't need to bring them in the house with us. This is a TOUGH thing to do! The only thing worse is to take all the work baggage with us on vacation. Shut off the phone! Turn off the computer! Forget the email! Quite honestly, we're not that important that the world won't keep spinning for a few days without us being there."

"Success is really a journey of perseverance in spite of failure. In our society failure is a dirty little secret no person or business ever wants to talk about because we're all like circus clowns wearing happy masks to cover our shortcomings, thinking we're the only ones with self-doubt and misgivings about ourselves. We're not all John Wayne - in fact neither was he! His real name was Marion Michael Morrison who was not related to Jim Morrison of the Doors!"

"As Booker T. Washington once wrote, *'Success is to be measured, not so much by the position that one has reached in life, but the obstacles which he has overcome.'* I would like to humbly add that success is measured by the number of lives changed and not the number of zeroes in a person's checkbook. They don't build hearses with trailer hitches on the back!"

"The world is full of givers and takers. Takers receive value from the lives of others. We're all takers to some degree because this is what allow us to become more than we would otherwise be. If we go back to Newton - (I know, let the poor man rest in peace) for everyone taking there must be someone giving. In the end, the good guys are the givers. We must all add value to those around us. Sadly, our society seems to sanctify the takers - some of the celebrities and some star athletes who have a unique skill set that sets them apart, making them believe others should willingly give to them because they're 'special.'"

"We're all not super stars and, yet, we all can make a difference. When you're a giver you may never know the impact you're having on someone who's looking up to you because of your character, life's work, family life or, perhaps, just because of your friendship. When you're a giver, people respect you, believe in you and trust you. When this happens you can truly touch another person's life and make it better and that's good!"

"The Hochunk medicine man was simply superb! Intelligent, articulate, passionate and funny. He told me that there are only two things to look for when judging the performance of an employee… attitude and aptitude. Does someone have the skill set necessary to do the job and do they really want to do it?"

"'People who fail do so because of one of these two factors,'" he noted and then made one of the most profound statements that I carry with me today. He stated that the antitheses of attitude and aptitude would be incompetence and indifference which to me is the combination that foretells failure and appears to be malignant in American society where so many have become cynics."

I thought about his pronouncement for a long time and then retorted that I felt there were actually four critical elements…. opportunity, ability, desire and dedication and the dynamics of these four elements, with varying degrees of criticality, determine whether someone reaches any specific milestone. Whether the objective is physical, emotional, educational or financial, one can quickly see that these four elements need to be in place for anyone to perceive a degree of accomplishment and therefore 'success.'"

"In today's world, sadly, we measure 'success' primarily in the form of accumulation...of wealth and status or most recently, notoriety and its subsequent celebrity. We all perceive that success equates to independence and subsequently social 'favor', where one moves beyond the masses to a position of being treated differently in a manner that recognizes their stature."

"If you 'test' the system by reviewing extremes, you'll quickly see that this hypothesis works. Probably one of the most commonly used examples is our proclivity to dream of instant-wealth through the lottery - gamble a little, be rewarded tremendously. Some might not think this would work and, yet, we see all that has happened is that we have simply transferred a great deal of the equation to the opportunity and ability elements, where our ability to gamble a few dollars generates the opportunity of profound reward. When there's no money, the opportunity simply isn't there because the ability has been forsaken. While it all seems like a wonderful idea to 'strike it rich', one study, conducted by the National Endowment for Financial Education, found that seventy percent of lottery winners go bankrupt within seven years of winning. The study also found that lottery winners are more likely to declare bankruptcy than the average American."

"Opportunity is about more than just money. It's about being, doing, seeing and feeling, about recognizing opportunity and accepting the challenge. So many people have opportunity knocking at their door and the problem is they don't hear it. Opportunity should be the force that allows us to grow and prosper financially, emotionally, spiritually and physically. It's the opportunity, when held in balance that nurtures our being, enhances our self and expands our horizons of growth, freedom and sustenance. The preamble to our Constitution talks about life, liberty and the pursuit of happiness. Pursuit...recognizing the opportunity, when it's there but NOT guaranteeing it!"

"Once the opportunity is there and someone has seized the moment the next critical element is ability. Other than blind luck, there are four types of abilities… physical, mental, emotional and social, where the level of exception above the norm in any of these elements is what allows one individual to stand out from the masses that's both God-given and learned. Ability reflects inherent traits that have been honed to allow for a repositioning above the masses and begins to differentiate the good from the bad and then the great from the good."

"There are so many people who think they have the ability to do something who really don't! There are so many people who've talked themselves into sincerely believing they're accomplished, when they're not! There are so many people who profess to greatness who don't even understand what it means, or requires and the price they must pay for such a lofty level of achievement. There's always someone better than the next person! Someone who has more talent, more skills and more capability and yet they don't win. Why? In our world, ability alone gets us nowhere!"

"I told 'V' we must also have the desire to achieve your objective. We must want it! The problem is that desire can distort reality and warp our sense of propriety. We must desire something only if we're willing to invest in its acquisition. However, we must also temper that desire to fit onto the plane that keeps all things in perspective."

"Now comes the really difficult part…realizing there are others with the same set or even greater skills, who have the same levels of aspiration. It's here that the dedication kicks in, where each level of accomplishment requires an even greater level of dedication until, finally, your life becomes focused on a single point, attribute, or facet that eradicates the breadth of joy that can only come from a myriad of experiences."

Once the opportunity arises and the level of desire reaches a point of motivation, then and only then, do we begin the process of allocating time to its accomplishment. Once again there's a risk where the dedication becomes so great, reason is usurped and we call it addiction. From this perspective we as observers sit and watch accomplishment oblivious to the hours, days, weeks, months, years and decades needed to reach the pinnacle placed before us… unaware of the sacrifices made in all other aspects of life to hone one skill above all else so that it's exemplary."

"What makes this a true challenge is that the dedicated are not alone…their drive is not singular and they become mesmerized by those striving to attain the same lofty position of accomplishment. The child prodigy! The incessant professional! The one-dimensional individual who has sacrificed a breadth of life for a profound level of depth in a singular field! From music, to sports, to entertainment the celebrities we look up to all had to make sacrifices to accomplish their level of achievement. Sacrifices that took away the breadth of experience so many others know and enjoy!"

"When one is a husband and/or father or a mother and/or wife the challenge of achievement at work, or even maintenance, can become so profound we allocate and inordinate amount of time to our employ. What happens? The hours become longer and distance greater between first our children and then our spouse! We justify it by rationalizing our spouse can take the children here, take the children there, have dinner with them and tuck them in at night as we strive to advance our careers."

"I just spent several pages talking about the dynamics of the relationships between husband and wife, parents and children and why it's necessary to see that absence **doesn't** make the heart grow fonder. Instead, we dedicate family time to work time. We take those precious moments that should have been spent with our families and allocate them to getting ahead simply because we fear the guy in the next office is willing to make that sacrifice."

"We allocate our time to our job. We allocate our thoughts to our job. We allocate our emotions to our job. All of sudden the time we didn't have with our spouse or children is gone. The children are grown and they don't like us because we weren't there for them.

The stranger we sleep with has changed and we don't know why. We're alone except, of course, for our job!"

"When the job gets all encompassing it becomes our lover and moves in to affect our relationship with ourselves. First, it's the physical part that's challenged. Our nerves are shot and we can't sleep. Next, it's the mental part that goes and we can't think of anything but work and never ever seem to be able to relax. Those things we promised to do with the children or our spouse are periodically done but we're only a shell sitting there thinking about our next project or challenge and whether we'll succeed at work."

"Finally, when we've given everything else, we give our soul to our job! We think of ways to get ahead we lose our conscience and concept of what's right and wrong. All that matters is the job. It has become the narcotic that we must sniff, shoot or ingest so that we continue to have that euphoric feeling permeate our veins."

"We reach the pinnacle and stand there…alone, isolated with no one to share our satisfaction with. We have dedicated our life to something unable, unwilling and unresponsive to our needs. We've taken the concept of dedication and aimed it in the wrong direction and it has violated the sanctity of parenthood and marriage and we will regret it, if we already don't."

"No matter who we are, rich or poor, unknown or famous, we all have one very integral thing in common…a minute is a minute, an hour an hour, and no matter who or what we are, it's the common denominator that bonds and binds us all to the reality that time spent in one action is time lost on another. I personally learned the hard way to never forget the risk of achievement and to ascertain a critical balance that allows us to not only to bear the fruit of your endeavors but have those around us to share it with."

"The American dream can become the American nightmare if we're not careful! Don't let any job get between us and our children, spouse, or physical, mental or spiritual health!"

It was four in the morning. My eyes were blurry and, yet the thought of my son, our CEO who's 'ladder of success' literally only had one giant step, made me continue on as I wondered how the pressure was slowly squeezing the life out of him, making him a walking shadow. I was about to type my last words when the following poem crashed into my brain.

Concrete canyons of corrugated cries!
Contemplated whispers, contaminated lies!
Perforated promises provide a steady pace.
Of headless horsemen hunting for the perfect place...

Our life's a walking shadow of men and men and men.
Searching for the date that marks the endless, endless end!
Of hopes and dreams and promises in blocks of embers gray.
Our meek, meek monster's madness moves on its merry way...

While the bounties of starvation are the victories of defeat!
We wallow in a nation irreverent of those we meet.
We find today's tomorrow is still another day.
In a Freudian existence that keeps our minds at bay....

We've come to go asunder and leave upon the face.
The madness of our blunders...our philosophic space...
So when the day comes finally that marks the end of ends.
There'll be nothing more to grasp for and nothing to defend.

We'll gaze upon the looking glass and simply ask the question why.
Our lives could be so worthless as we wave our last goodbye.
We beg to do it over, with so much more at heart.
But would we really do it if we had the chance to start?

And so, our concrete canyons make us corrugated clowns.
Who play life's game of football and only marks the downs.

I yawned a deep yawn. Rubbed my sore neck, took a deep breath and wondered if anyone would ever read what I was writing while realizing I really didn't care. This was my catharsis – my testament to all I thought about as I lie in the hospital bed staring at the ceiling, wondering if that day would be my last one on earth while wondering if I died, would anyone really care.

My thoughts turned back to those dark days where the presence of death had me praying that if it was to be my last day, there was truly a heaven and I would meet up with mom, dad, Great Grandfather, Dr. Williams, the Duke, Sir Francis and my little buddy Jake, who would be standing there with open arms or paws and great big smiles, reciting just a few hoped-for words…*'You simply did your best.'*

**Family and Friends:**

Amy was off to work or wherever she went every day and I to the deafening silence of tick/tock, tick/tock that was getting to me. I'd written all I could the day before that provided a yearning to go to the Forest. I sent a text to Amy and told her where I was going but didn't get a response. I figured she was probably in a meeting as I got out the Corvette and headed towards Madison and the half-million people who called the Metroplex home.

I went south on the Interstate and exited at Highway 51 west, traversing the always-crowded Beltline to the Verona exit. The road was double lane and traffic was light. It wasn't long until I made it to Shake Rag and headed into Mineral Point. When I reached Highway 23 I turned left and made my way past Jack and Melia's and onto the farm.

Tommie and Su were in Europe at the Belgian Farm Research Convention and I knew the house would be empty. I drove past the farm research center where Francis had been trained and down the hill to the Foundation building. I elected to visit and went in through the front door. I hadn't been there in a while. There was a young girl at the entrance. We'd never had a receptionist before.

While still the same things seemed different. Peter and Luke had both retired, along with all the MadCity Boys. The entire crew were financially secure and had no need for the pressures of existence mandated by the government.

As I reached the entrance, I saw a sign stating 'Building under surveillance.' I walked into the front pod and saw a wall between me and what I'd built.

"May I help you?" the young girl inquired.

"Just thought I'd stop by," I replied.

"Do you have an appointment?"

I grimaced at the thought and replied, "no."

"Are you here to see anyone in particular?"

My scowl was forming as I countered, "I'm George Terrill."

"And?"

I was incredulous and replied, "The founder of the Derrick Williams Foundation".

There was no response.

"Sir. What can I do for you?"

"I thought I'd stop by and see what's being developed."

"Sir, you can't just *'stop by'* you have to have an appointment and security clearance from the government."

"What?"

"Yes sir, we're no longer allowed to just let *anyone* into our facilities."

I was getting a bit tempestuous as I asked, "Who's in charge?"

"Sir, I'm not allowed to provide that information. If you'd like to fill out an application, I can make certain someone reviews it and we'll then contact you about making an appointment."

"Contact me? Make an appointment? I started this foundation."

"Sir, I'm sorry, but I have my rules that state no one is allowed in the facility without prior clearance and authorization. Now, I'm going to have to ask you to leave or call security."

My foundation! My blood, sweat and tears! My battles with the government! I shook my head and realized what was going on. Once again, Newton! We'd defeated them in the court of law and public opinion and they were responding in the slow, deliberate way simply because the bureaucrats had power, money and above all else, time on their side. They'd determined that Simon and the projects were of 'National Interest' and created a labyrinth of rules and regulations making it impenetrable to even the founder himself.

I took a deep breath and realized there was no way I was going into my own building to see what my foundation was working on. Jesus! Instead I retreated and made my way down the cinder path to the bench by Great Grandfather's obelisk. I took a deep breath and sat thinking about life in general and the Cancer growing within me. We were six days from surgery and I was getting anxious.

After a spell I got up and followed the path to the springs. I knelt down and took the small tin cup from the weathered wooden compartment and filled it with water. As I was about to take a drink 'he' appeared – the great buck who'd been there since God knows when.

I looked at the majestic beast and he at me. For the longest time I was mesmerized by his presence and demeanor. There was no fear. There weren't any trepidations. All there was consisted of acceptance of each other as had been the case since we first met.

We stood motionless and then he nodded as if affirming my presence while a strange feeling came over me. For the first time in a long time, I was at peace with myself, my wife and my life. Had he brought this upon me or was it just coincidence?

I looked beyond the buck and into the bog and saw the small cloud of fog but knew to go within his domain could have other consequences. Instead I stood completely still as the trees slightly rustled and the incessant hum of the insects became eclipsed by tranquility. So often I'd come to this spot in times of trouble. So often, he'd been there, simply to assure me that life was all right. I took a deep breath and closed my eyes.

Before me, in my mind, was a space so beautiful I could hardly imagine it existed. I heard the laughter of children and the barking of the dog they were playing with. I dug deeper and realized the children were Tommie and me and it was Jake who was barking. We were probably eight and ten and simply having fun. As Jake stopped barking my head turned towards the farm house and I saw mom opening the screen door on the porch. I smiled and she smiled back. I looked towards the barn and saw dad walking towards the house with what appeared to be a newborn kitten in his arms.

I turned towards Tommie but he was gone. I turned towards mom and she, too, had departed. I looked for dad and all that remained was the farm house with the family cemetery in the foreground. What was the message I was receiving? Why now?

I opened my eyes and the buck was gone. I placed the tin cup to my lips and drank earth's nectar. How many times had I been here before? How many times of trouble or joy had I come here only to have my wants and worries diminish such that I could simply go on - on with living - on with life?

I carefully placed the old tin cup back where it belonged. I turned to retrace my steps and began the trek from whence I came. One again I stopped at the obelisk as the leaves shuddered and then were calm. Great Grandfather had spoken telling me that it was going to be all right.

I made it to my car and was about to leave when the urge was upon me to stop and visit the family cemetery. I made my way to the old wire gate that sang sounds of sadness to a melody where today to only meant yesterday.

Slowly, I made my way from gravestone to gravestone, reading the names I knew so well wondering how their lives really were so long ago. Were they happy? Did they mean something to someone? Did they want to go or glad they went?

At the end of the line was Francis and my little buddy Jake, his headstone glistening in the sun with a slice of earth reserved next to him where someday I hoped to reside. I knelt down and reflected on the joy Jake put in my life…tail wagging, just glad to see me…my God, I missed my friend.

The spell was broken and it was time to leave. I got back in the car and headed home, I had a lot to write before I could sleep again. Ninety minutes later, I entered to solitude of tick/tock, tick/tock and went to my folio and began again.

"Extended Family and Friends in the concept of relationships means we're moving away from the intense day-to-day scenario to the secondary levels. This doesn't mean these relationships aren't important. Hardly! Only that they're not in the inner core of things we do and relationships we have on a daily basis. To put it a different way we inherit our extended family and choose our nuclear family and friends! It's as simple as that. Yet, both groups become inter-woven in terms of our relationships."

"The extended family refers to parents, grandparents, aunts, uncles, nieces, nephews and cousins. A strong relationship with your extended family can be just as rewarding as close ties inside the nuclear family. However, building those bonds inside the extended family can be a little more difficult because, obviously, everyone doesn't live under the same roof. Add to this different interests and ages and we have the challenge of communicating with and caring for people we might hardly even know only because we have some sort of genetic link either to them, their spouse or offspring. Yet, with the separation, we still have an important bond that makes us share special moments, simply because 'they're our family.'"

"Families, friends and life are all about transitions from one phase to the next. As we age, there comes a point in our life when our head begins the eventual turn and we start looking back on how we got where we are as much as looking forward to where it's we think we're going. It's not a part of youth! Youth is only about tomorrow and the assumption of immortality! It's not a part of being old when the reality of mortality makes one peer back at yesterday, grasping at memories of what was and what could have been. Somewhere in between these two crossing points is the zone called middle age - when there are still more than enough of both yesterdays and tomorrows to keep both interesting."

"I guess we all reach that point - sentimental about the past, anxious about the future, thriving on today's today. Yet, like those who passed through these gates before, our head has started its gradual turn and we feel an urgency to bank our memories before too many years paint too many coats of experiences over the details that were once so clear - leaving us with only fuzzy generalities of what once was and perceived to be."

"There are many chapters that could be written - some funny, some sad, some filled with anger and frustration - all filled with lessons learned and forgotten. So many people, so many times have promised themselves they would record their lives just in case some day, somewhere, someone should care."

"In the end, for most of us, there are only five generations to our immortality - the two generations that proceeded us and two who will follow. Beyond that, in either direction, those before us and then ourselves, become nothing more than a name, associated only by a set of lines to someone curious enough to want to know. Gone are the friends! Gone is the family! Lost forever, the tales of the elements that made up a life!"

"When we were young our great grandparents were probably already gone. If they were still around, we were much too young to remember them. Their stories, like so many photographs stored in a bureau drawer have faded as each storyteller eventually stops telling their tales. Soon the pictures are of strangers, peering out from behind some frozen face. The names are gone! The stories gone! They preceded us on earth and we're bound genetically to them forever, yet they're lost in so many yesterdays."

"Woefully, unless they were someone great or some great scoundrel, all we have is a dotted line to someone whom they conceived and nurtured who probably mourned their passing. Nothing more! Nothing less! Just a name and an image frozen in time and space! How tragic that we can't contact these people and share their stories - what made them happy - what made them forlorn - what they feared and what they loved - what would they share with us to make our lives better, happier - more productive. I'm very lucky, Uncle Will took one side back to before the birth of Christ. Few people are as fortunate as that."

"Three generations behind us, we too will be lost! Our names and images will be all that is preserved by unknowing strangers. How sad and yet how true! As heartbreaking is the reality that for many of us, we also won't share of all that we explored, discovered, learned, loved and feared. Instead, all that we are and have done will be dispersed like so many leaves in the autumn wind."

"Two generations and its grandparents or grandchildren with even the most distant of memories beginning to come into focus -

as so many small bits and pieces of another day, another era, when everything was bigger, slower and a lot less complicated. As we march toward that day when that second generation is following us, I wonder how we will be remembered."

"Will grandma and grandpa be seen as kind, generous, patient and loving as ours were? Will there be a continuing increase in life's pace so that our lives, problems and worries seem as quaint? We can only hope to be remembered, as we romantically remember our grandparents - full of love and pride - common people, with a dignity that made them strong!"

"If we're truly lucky we shared our lives with our parents until well into our own adulthood. We had first-hand knowledge of their happiness and comforted them in their times of sorrow. We were the recipient of their unrequited love and nurturing, allowed to grow and mature."

"We experienced ever increasing independence from them from that point when our actual life itself was reliant on their love and care to some point in time when the relationship changed. We realized that our parental leaders had become our parental followers, whose love and compassion for us provided them with the ability to look past our shortcomings, consider us special and willingly accept the fact that there is a natural inability that comes with age to fully adjust and comprehend all the change that comes with time."

"As the years pass, in many instances, our parents become more and more like our own children - reliant on us to protect and nurture - defend and oversee - to comprehend the changes in life's rules so that they can at least, marginally, play the game. This is a natural evolution of the family. This is the way generations before and generations after should reside. One generation alongside the other - interwoven, yet, distinct, reliant, yet, independent - sharing the joy and fabric and the concept called family."

"If we are truly lucky, we'll share the lives of our children well into their adulthood. Hopefully, we'll have first-hand knowledge of their joys and excitements, sustaining our role as protector from the scrapes and bruises, both physically and emotionally, we call life."

"If we've done our job and have done it properly, we've filled them with the confidence that only comes from feeling loved . This isn't a temporal confidence but one that's inherent simply because they sincerely believe they're accepted for what they are, not for what they want to be. A confidence that they will always be loved, honored and respected. A confidence that, as their years pile up, they too will be allowed the freedom and independence to journey the road that beckons, unbridled by the vestiges of their ancestry, capable of assuming their position center stage. And finally, a confidence that allows them to willing to accept the risks of life - along with the rewards while remaining assured that, when it's their turn to play the role of parent, they do so willingly and with grace - sustaining all that's necessary to provide the same environment for their children they had provided to them. In today's world, this is a difficult challenge. The world isn't as nice as we believe it once was!"

"When the day comes that we move to the wings and our final curtain is drawn, we must hope that we're remembered for who we were, what we were and above else for our living legacy - our children. Our houses will fall - our money spent - our possessions disbursed and eventually consumed. However, our family, through our children, and its character, can carry on forever. It must be our deepest wish that we precede all of our children to the end and we truly rest in peace for doing so."

"While looking backward appears to be a gradual trend, all of us endure a point of paradox and challenge when one's head is violently jerked backward - the assumptions of eternity coldly shattered -  leaving us grasping for the past as if it were the seeds of a dandelion abruptly scattered in the wind."

"For all of us there are times, people and events we will always cherish. When we wake up one day to the news of the passing of a special person - a parent, aunt or uncle, who was the last member of their generation and realize the bridge to yesterday is broken, not only with the loss of the person but the reality that there's no longer a path of communication to the past that makes us shudder in realization. The questions never asked. The stories never told. They're gone, forever."

"As our heads begin to turn, we owe it to ourselves and our children and their children's children, too, to simply write down who we are and how we got to be that way - to share with the unknowing the heritage that made us who we are, what we are and where we are going. It need not be long or profound, only a brief outline that will keep those interested locked into reality, capable of understanding a little more about who they are, why they are and how it is they got on the path on which they journey. I believe in this so much that on those days when I'm exhausted, or really in no mood to continue to write, I travel on, not for me, even though it is a catharsis, but for those who come after me so they learn who I was and more important why I existed."

"Beyond our genetic family are our friends. We don't get to pick our family. We do get to pick our friends. It's incredible how close some families remain while how distant so many others are. It's also profound how, within the same family, there can be emotional bonds between some members but not others, due to a lack of association or respect."

"In trying to correlate the key ingredient that allows us to take this group of individuals and differentiate them from the rest of society, I came down to one word… caring! That, with our family and friends, we have a higher concentration of caring than anywhere else!"

"While this probably seems a bit simplistic, let me take it a few steps further. We all must choose our friends wisely for the sake of friendship. We can make more friends in two weeks if we genuinely show interest in them than we will have in two years if we try to get them interested in us. True friends are those whose values parallel ours. When they are common, friendship is easy. When we force ourselves to their level either way, we don't have true friendship."

"Friendships are dynamic. They come and go based on a degree of common interest. But what happens when there's disagreement?

"There's no need to take it personally or emotionally. Conflict is at its best when it creates an opportunity for us to understand a different perspective than our own. There's nothing wrong with conflict as long as it leads to resolution that's not taken personally. Conflict can be a great teacher. Conflict can be an equalizer. Conflict can be one of the many ways we can learn about life."

"The friendships we have that are the deepest are based on time spent together, sharing experiences. Today, this electronic age we live in has brought us closer together but further apart. We write but don't communicate. We stay connected but are far too distant. If we need more than one hand to count our friends, we're lucky. Once we retire, the word singular becomes more paramount as those we toiled with, cheered with and moaned with through the glory of victory and agony of defeat are simply gone...scattered by time and space to distant lives no longer shared. Beside Rodney I have few and his life and mine are distant where we see each other when we can, which, sadly, isn't that often."

I leaned back in my chair and re-read what I wrote. I closed my eyes and realized that caring is an emotion like love and hate that's taken to a personal degree. My only hope was that my family realized how much I cared for them. It's the caring that allows me to forget the small stuff and permits what many people wouldn't tolerate. It's the caring I hope and pray people see in me every day...caring about them, about our world and enough to give more than I get for no other reason than it makes me happy...happy to participate and to be alive."

**Mineral Point:**

On the farm, I was raised with certain values which included never borrowing anything, your word was your bond and, if you offered something, you fulfilled that promise. When I was in the hospital and talking with Father Pat, I'd offered to take him fishing. We set the day and had everything arranged except one minor thing...the weather. I knew he was looking forward to it and so was I. I needed a break from my solitary confinement. However wind gusts of thirty miles per hour, a long fetch, and the depth of the water, meant six-foot waves would make fishing on Lake Michigan less than appealing.

I called Pat, as he asked me to call him when he was in civvies, and he understood. I could hear the disappointment in his voice. I paused and asked him if, instead he'd like to take a ride to Mineral Point. Sadly, like so many others, he'd never heard of my home town. To entice him I offered to bring my new Corvette and the fact that Mineral Point was the first city in Wisconsin to be listed on the National Register of Historic Places.

The combo package piqued his interest as I noted. "Normally, I'd take the chopper, but with the wind gusts, there's no way, we can do that."

"That's OK." Pat replied as I told him I'd be there in a half hour."

I got out the Corvette and rode to Pat's place as he called it, which was actually a rectory he shared with some other priests who's mission involved social work. I hoped he wasn't in priest clothes and was relieved when he opened the door and came out in jeans and tennis shoes. The only thing I didn't like was the Notre Dame sweatshirt.

"Nice shirt!" I offered as he opened the car door.

"Nice car!" I he retorted.

We headed for Madison and talked about anything and everything. As we got close to John Nolen Drive, I made a quick decision and headed for Camp Randall Stadium and noted, "I can't take you to Mineral Point wearing that sweatshirt, the folks don't take kindly to folks with Notre Dame written on them. The only thing worse would be if it said Iowa."

We pulled into the stadium parking lot, got out and went into Bucky's Locker Room. I told Pat to pick out anything as long as it was red and said Wisconsin on it. Pat selected a red hoodie and was reaching for his wallet when I said, "My decision and my gift," as I slapped my Costco Visa card on the counter and imagined my two-dollar rebate accumulating in my annual spending spree.

"You don't have to do that." Pat replied.

"I'm too old to have to do anything. I'm doing it because I want to."

It was just 9:00 o'clock and so I asked Pat what he had for breakfast and he said a cup of coffee. We pulled out of the stadium parking lot, made it all one-hundred feet to the corner when I spotted an empty parking space across the street from Mickie's Dairy Bar on Monroe Street, famous on campus for its breakfasts.

"Time for a Madison treat." I offered as Pat looked at me and simply shook his head.

In we went and a half hour later, out we came with our gullets full with Pat downing the Scrambler with three scrambled eggs, sausage, cheddar cheese all smothered in gravy and toast.

"Now we can make it to Mineral Point," I offered as we walked out the door.

"I don't know if I'll be able to get the seat belt on," Pat replied.

We drove west on Monroe Street, past Glenway golf course, out Mineral Point Road to Midvale Boulevard. I explained how Madison had grown from this sleepy little city in the 1950's to the Metroplex of a half million people because it had one of the most stable economies in the nation based on government, education, medicine and insurance. I think Pat was impressed I knew so much.

We made our way down Highway 18/151 and, after we passed Dodgeville, I pointed to the spot where Jeepers Creepers and I had our little issue that almost sent me to meet his big, big boss. As we were between Dodgeville and Mineral Point, I noted

283

the Dodge-Point golf course and Uncle Hanks apartment complex and recited how my Uncle Will traced our family back to 65 BC and that I was related to Saint Arnoul, Bishop of Metz, who was the Saint of Beer, as well as Charles Martel, Charlemagne and William the Conqueror which Pat thought was really cool.

When we could see the water tower, I offered. "Mineral Point was founded in 1827 and is the third oldest city in Wisconsin. Nestled in the rolling hills of Southwest Wisconsin, called the Driftless Area, the glaciers of the last ice age missed the area and left behind the ridges, river valleys, limestone bluffs and minerals that were easily accessible at the surface."

"It's beautiful here!" Pat exclaimed.

"The name Mineral Point comes from its mining history. Initially, Native American women mined lead to trade with French fur traders. In the early 1800's the lead ore was easy to mine and my great, great, great grandfather, George Terrill  emigrated from Cornwall, worked his way up the Pecatonica River from Galena and came to the area."

"Instead of traveling back the thirty-two miles to Galena, George, along with other miners, simply dug temporary caves that resembled badger holes and that's how Wisconsin earned the nickname 'the Badger State'."

"Mineral Point has been named the most Cornish village in the United States because of not only those who came, but the availability of the same minerals the miners dug back in Cornwall, where Cornish mining activity dates back to the Bronze Age when tin was literally taken out of river valleys, in what was called 'Open Cast Mining'."

"With Cornwall and Devon providing Britain's only indigenous tin resources, by medieval times, Cornish tinners were renowned to the point their industry was subject to special laws, taxes and privileges granted by Royal charter where the mining practices were based on what was called Stannary law that took into account customary traditions."

"I've never heard of Stannary Law," Pat offered.

I smiled, and was quite proud that I'd remembered my Mineral Point and British history. I outlined. "The word Stannary was derived from the Latin *stannum,* for tin, and was and remains English law that governs tin mining in Cornwall and Devon. Special or Stannary laws pre-date written legal codes in Britain where ancient traditions exempted everyone connected with tin mining in Cornwall and Devon from any jurisdiction other than the Stannary courts in all but the most exceptional circumstances."

"Subsequent to the Magna Carta, that was signed in 1215, King Edward the First established the Stannary Charter with a monopoly on all tin mining in Devon. Ninety years later, the miners were provided a right of representation in the Stannary Parliament and jurisdiction exclusively in what were called Stannary courts. Although there's very little tin mining still done in Cornwall the Stannary laws remain part of the law of the United Kingdom and represent some of the oldest laws incorporated into the English legal system thereby representing the enormous importance of the tin industry to the English economy during the Middle Ages."

"Around 1827 Cornish tin and copper began to peter out and this caused an economic collapse. Because of this miners began emigrating and, as word spread of not only the quantity of zinc and lead, but how easy it was to mine, settlers including my ancestors, arrived in Mineral Point in the early 1830's to the point that, by 1845, roughly half of the town's population had Cornish ancestry."

I glanced at Pat and he was smiling, realizing our fishing trip was catching more than carp. It was providing a full limit of something he had no idea existed.

I continued "Along with their advanced mining skills, these early immigrants also possessed expertise in stone building construction and I think you're about to be surprised when you see their legacy reflected in the number of buildings built in the 19th century that still exist."

I turned off Highway 151 and onto Shake Rag. Pat smiled at the name and so I explained that the miner's cottages were on west side of Laxey Creek which is a 10-mile long tributary of the Mineral

Point Branch of the Pecatonica River while their diggings were on the other side. For safety's sake there was always one miner outside the mine in case there was a cave-in. When it was time for dinner, the wives would come out of their cottages, place a white rag on the end of a stick and shake it, thereby telling their husbands it was time to come home to eat."

As we slowly made our way down Shake Rag, I pulled into a small parking lot in front of a large limestone building tucked into the hillside and detailed. "This was one of, if not Wisconsin's first breweries, constructed in the late 1840s, by my great, great grandfather, William Terrill. Grandpa Will, chose the site because there's a spring beneath the building that provides 50 gallons of pure limestone filtered water per minute. For the building, Great, Great Grandpa Will had the limestone excavated from the hills behind the springs creating caverns to store the beer in. In this one location, he had all you needed to create a brewery...fresh, filtered water, the building and a place to store the beer. Construction was completed in 1850 at a cost of $4000 which would be about $150,000 today that great, great grandpa then rented to Jacob Roggy in 1851.

"Pat inquired, "Is it still a brewery?"

As we began pulling out of the lot, I replied. "It remained in operation until the brewery closed in 1961 and was converted into a pottery studio."

"Darn. I would have liked to had a brew," Pat lamented.

"Think of Spotted Cow today and you've got Mineral Spring beer back then."

We drove a little further down Shake Rag and stopped in front of three small cottages as I detailed. "In 2017, *Smithsonian Magazine* released their list of the *20 Best Small Towns to Visit in America* that included Mineral Point. The magazine praised it for its 'natural beauty, historical architecture and the art scene.' What put Mineral Point on the map are these three buildings restored by two men named Bob Neal and Edger Hellum."

"Bob was living in London and came home to Mineral Point in 1934 to visit relatives when he heard that the Works Progress Administration, or WPA, was bulldozing the old Cornish mining cottages for materials to build the bath house at the swimming pool. Bob had long been fascinated with the old stone cottages and was determined to buy one. At the site he met Edger Hellum who was harvesting stone, shutters and other salvageable items for his house in nearby Cooksville."

"Bob and Edgar formed a lifelong business and personal partnership and began developing plans to rescue three miner's cottages from demolition. They purchased the first abandoned cottage for $10.00 in 1935, removed the porch, replaced rotting timbers and roof shingles, re-pointed the stone walls, and restored interior doors and windows and named it 'Pendarvis' which means *'the dweller at the end of the oak trees.'*"

"Originally built in 1845, Pendarvis opened as a restaurant where they served traditional Cornish pasty dinners, tea, saffron cake, and pastries with clotted cream and was named one of the top seven restaurants in the United States by several national magazines and was also a favorite of Mr. Duncan Hines, who visited twice and listed it in the early editions of his guidebook, *'Adventures in Good Eating.'* Story tells that, at one time, the dinner reservation list was limited to one year. This meant you had to call a year in advance to make reservations and had better come that day, or you wouldn't get in. What makes this even more impressive is that this was during the Great Depression."

"Oh my God, was the food that good?" Pat inquired.

"I don't know. Pendarvis closed in 1970 when Bob and Edgar retired."

I pointed at the house next door and added. "Bob and Edgar bought their second Shake Rag house in 1937 and named it Polperro. Built in 1842, it was used as their initial residence. Polperro is the name of a fishing village in Cornwall and means Pyra's Cove. Bob and Edgar stripped the siding to reveal the log and stone structure underneath and removed a two-story addition that had been constructed earlier. They used the first-floor as an antique shop and mining museum while the second floor was turned into a Wisconsin history library from early southwest Wisconsin settlers full of all kinds of letters, memos and posters from the 1800's that the Wisconsin Historical Society now have.

I pointed at the next building and noted. "The third building was named Trelawny which means *settlement* or *homestead* in Cornish that Bob and Edgar bought and restored in the late 1930s that became their home for thirty-seven years. One of our cousins was named Richard Thomas and records indicate he built the house in 1843. Bob and Edgar expanded the original four rooms by adding a kitchen located in the back of the house that serviced the Pendarvis restaurant. Probably more than anyone else, Bob and Edgar helped make Mineral Point into the vital hub for the arts, preservation and tourism it is today."

"This is incredible," Pat offered with sincere awe.

We drove a little further and I pointed to what today is called the *Rowhouse*, consisting of three adjacent stone structures. I pointed and said. "The first house was built as a free-standing building around 1841. The second was also free-standing and built around 1844 or 1845. The final house, was built around 1852 in between the other two, thereby connecting them."

Pat simply smiled and shook his head in disbelief.

Near the corner we stopped again and I pointed out the Phillips House that's also known as the "Mousehole" that was built by William Phillips and Francis Carter. At some point, a small two-story stone and frame house was added to the east side that was demolished, but there's still the 'ghost mark' you can see if you look closely."

"I've never heard the term 'ghost mark' before," Pat replied.

Proud of my memory, I replied. "A ghost mark is a faint outline of a previous wall or other feature that can be seen on a newly constructed wall. It's caused by the presence of moisture in the old wall, which causes the plaster or paint to flake off or stain the exposed lumber. The original house was designated as *Cornish*

*Miners House Number One* in the *Historic American Building Survey* in 1934.

Pat simply sat shaking his head at the integrity and longevity of what Shake Rag had to offer.

I had to make a decision and decided to go down Commerce Street. Two blocks down, I pulled into the parking lot of the railroad museum and continued. "Mineral Point was one of the most important communities in the Wisconsin Territory due to the mining of lead. To tell you how important it was the Great Seal of the Wisconsin Territory is an arm holding a pick axe over a pile of lead ore."

"While the lead was plentiful, transporting the ore to Galena by oxen made the entire process challenging. To address this the Mineral Point Railroad was formed in 1851 connecting Mineral Point with the Illinois Central Railroad at Warren, Illinois with the depot built in 1856 which has survived to become Wisconsin's oldest standing depot."

"From 1880 until the 1920's zinc mining allowed the Mineral Point Zinc Company to prosper as it became one of the largest zinc facilities in the United States. During the late 1920's, zinc manufacturing declined rapidly and by 1929 the Mineral Point plant closed. With it railroad traffic was no longer needed and the railroad was abandoned in 1930. In 1984 the rails were taken up and the depot sat vacant until it reopened as a museum in 2004."

Pat commented, "You really know your history."

I proudly replied, "I lived it and my family helped create it."

I turned the car around and headed back to the corner of High and Commerce and asked Pat if he'd like to walk a few blocks as I pointed out the buildings. After over two hours sitting in the car and the Scrambler gurgling in his gut Pat thought it was a great idea. We parked at the base of High Street and walked up the south side. I pointed out how most of the buildings were built in the mid-to-late 1800's and were as sturdy as the day they were built. We made it to the Red Rooster and I mentioned Cornish Pasty. Had it not been for the Scrambler we would have stopped but I promised

Pat I'd bring him some pasty next time I came home or went to Miles Teddywedgers in Madison.

Pat smiled as we walked past the Ben Franklin and mentioned he hadn't seen one of those in a long, long time. I told him that some guy named Sam Walton got his start with a Ben Franklin as did Michaels Crafts founded in 1983 by Michael J. Dupey. Pat noticed the dog statue standing attention across the street.

I detailed. "That's Pointer who's made of zinc. He was created by the J.L. Mott Iron Works in 1889 and originally stood in front of the Gundry & Gray department store. When Mineral Point was booming all the Cornish merchants used some sort of statue to identify their buildings. At one time the town was the most affluent community in Wisconsin."

We kept walking west on High Street to Doty Street and then left past the Methodist Church that I mentioned my great grandfather helped build. We headed west on Doty Street to Ridge Street and the Jones' Mansion. I noted to Pat, "The Jones' house is a spectacular building with a glass cupola on the roof and a huge porch. It was built in 1906 by William A. Jones. The three-story structure is made of limestone and features a number of decorative elements, including turrets, gargoyles, and stained-glass windows and was the first house in town with electricity and indoor plumbing."

"The Jones family maintained the house until 1972 when it was purchased by the Mineral Point Historical Society and today is one of the most popular places to visit in town and can actually be rented for weddings and special occasions."

"How'd he make his money?" Pat asked.

"Jones grew up in the area and got a degree in Platteville to become a teacher but never taught. Instead, he made his money by starting the First National Bank of Mineral Point, then serving as mayor and finally a state assemblyman. Mr. Jones and his brothers purchased the Mineral Point Zinc Co. in 1883 when times were bad and sold it in 1897, when times were good, for a huge profit. They took their profits and made extensive land purchases in southwestern Wisconsin for mining and got rich. When Mr. Jones died in 1912 his family moved to Chicago."

"Bet the family wishes they were still here." Pat interjected.

We cut back to Madison Street and took a look at the restoration of Orchard Lawn that was built by Joseph Gundry who emigrated to Mineral Point in 1845. I told Pat. "Gundry was the merchant who purchased Pointer and also a miner who made a fortune and completed the mansion in 1868 as an eleven-acre working estate on a hill overlooking Mineral Point. Orchard Lawn had gardens, an orchard, a tennis court and outbuildings including a barn, carriage house, woodshed, icehouse and even a greenhouse, surrounding the Italianate style mansion that was made of locally quarried stone that matches that of Pendarvis. Three generations of the Gundry family lived, worked and played at Orchard Lawn and did so in grand style."

"When the last Gundry to live in the house passed away in 1936 heirs tried to sell or even give the estate away, but to no avail. In 1939 they were forced to hire a demolition contractor. After most of the outbuildings fell and the wrecking ball was poised to destroy the house, eleven local citizens intervened and raised $800 to buy out the demolition contract and took ownership for one dollar, while forming the Mineral Point Historical Society."

We then walked east on Fountain Street past the Moses Strong Mansion where I told Pat that Strong made his money in land speculation and was in cahoots with Judge Doty on the development of Madison. "Mr. Strong was selected by Judge Doty to represent Iowa County in the State's first convention to draft a constitution and his house, which was built in 1839, remains as solid as the day it was constructed as it's also made of limestone."

We continued our walk down Fountain Street and just past Jerusalem Park, where a small red brick house resides with white lace curtains on the windows and flower boxes. I pointed to the brass plate by the front door indicating that the National Register of Historic Places detailed the house was built in 1844. We stopped in front of the house next door and I lamented that it had belonged to

Luke, who took Amy and I on our balloon ride around the world that changed my life in many, many ways.

We made it to the corner and climbed back up Chestnut Hill aside the Red Rooster then east past the old Hotel Royale and back to the car. To say Pat was impressed would be an understatement.

I noted. "Mineral Point has around 2,500 residents and twenty-five art studios. Besides the architecture and the ambiance, it really has become an artist colony. Probably, the one who should get the most credit for the art revolution was a guy named Harry Nohr. He became nationally famous after World War II for crafting vases from empty ammunition shells.

Harry was Mineral Point's postmaster when my great Uncle was the mailman. As a hobby he took up wood turning from burls which are growths of a tree that form from unsprouted bud tissue creating large, knobby-looking growths on the base and trunk. Because of the deformation the rings are never concentric and the bowls Harry made were incredible. If you can find one today with his distinctive HN logo on the bottom it can be worth up to fifty-thousand dollars."

"Wow!" Pat exclaimed.

We climbed into the Corvette and I looked at Pat with one last thought. "Mineral Point has also been recognized by the National Trust for Historic Preservation as one of their 'Dozen Distinctive Destinations.'"

"You love it here, don't you?" Pat asked.

I smiled and shared with him that I'd been all over the world and nowhere did I get the same feelings I get when I came home. It's probably true for a lot of people. However when your town hardly changes during your entire life, the memories you had as a child remain in the present tense and not something in the distant past and you have a greater appreciation for your memories.

I added. "I get this really warm feeling when I'm here. I can't tell you what it is. All I can tell you is that it's there."

"Have you ever thought about moving back?"

"Every single day and, yet, I wonder if I did, would it remain special or would I acclimate and begin to take it for granted?" I paused, took a deep breath and then recited. "When times are tough. When I feel all alone. When I find myself unhappy about something or anything, I come home and those feelings seem to disappear."

"That's what I feel when I go to church," Pat offered.

I looked at the clock and it was only 3:30. I turned to Pat and offered. "I'd like to take you to **my** church, if you don't mind."

"The Methodist church?"

"No. Do you mind if we go? It's only a few miles from here."

"Not at all."

"We drove out Highway 23, went past Melia and Jack's house to the farm. We parked in the driveway as I outlined the research lab, pointed to the family cemetery and mentioned Francis and Jake and how much they meant to me. We walked down the path to the Foundation and I shared how it started, why it started and how blessed I was to have Luke, Peter and the MadCity Boys help me accomplish all that I dreamed.

Pat and I continued walking into the Forest as Pat's mouth dropped open. All that I hoped would happen was beginning.

We stopped at the obelisk and I shared the story of Great Grandfather and why his ashes were spread upon the land. I spoke of my love for my friend, Rodney, who was my 'big brother' and why I was called 'Little Spirit'. For me, it was like going to confession. However, instead of sharing my sins, I was sharing my love. I could tell that Pat was immersed in my emotions.

We quietly made our way towards the spring as I watched Father Pat's face begin to contort in one of profound disbelief. We made it to the springs and I took the small tin cups from the little wooden box and dipped them in the cool water. I held them high and then offered one to Father Pat.

He took a small sip as tears welled in his eyes. He looked at me and recited...*"The LORD **is** my shepherd; I shall not want. He maketh me to lie down in green pastures: he leadeth me beside the still waters. He* *restoreth my soul: he leadeth me in the paths of righteousness for his name's sake. Yea, though I walk through the valley of the shadow of death, I will fear no evil: for thou art with me; thy rod and thy staff they comfort me. Thou preparest a table before me in the presence of mine enemies: thou anointest my head with oil; my cup runneth over. Surely goodness and mercy shall follow me all the days of my life: and I will dwell in the house of the LORD forever."*

I stared at Father Pat as his eyes lifted towards heaven. He took a deep, deep breath and then a strange look came over his face. He nodded and I looked. **HE** was there, the great Buck, simply standing, watching. The buck's head turned as he nodded a gentle nod as if to indicate my guest was welcome.

It was only for an instant and then, what I'd seen only in those times when I grieved or my life was in turmoil, he simply turned and walked into the bog and out of our lives. I looked at Pat and he at me and we both knew we'd seen eternity. For the first time, I understood the buck was not a figment of my imagination. He was a representation of all that can be good in life if you let it be.

My hands were shaking, the silence deafening, as neither of us spoke, simply absorbing the instant. I closed my eyes and finally realized my elusive friend was merely a statement that death is not a destination but a transition from here to *there,* that Steven Hawking was wrong, the universe continues to grow, not in a physical sense, but one of spirit that only comes when you realize there truly is a God.

The spell was broken as Father Pat looked at me and nodded. For an instant, he closed his eyes and the recited, "He was here. I could feel Him."

We quietly made our way back to the house. Words were not needed. We got in the car and headed home. We arrived at the rectory and the silence was broken as Pat offered. "My church is built of bricks and stones begun by a man who changed the world simply by dying for all of us. Your church goes beyond humanity and encompasses everything God ever made without form...without structure...without interpretation. I simply can't thank you enough for sharing your world with me."

We shook hands and he slowly closed the car door. I watched him enter his world of rules and traditions as I wondered if, or how, my world had affected him. I slight smile crossed my face as the majesty of the day entered my soul and took its place amongst my most precious moments.

## Hobbies and Interests:

It was now five days before my surgery and I needed one last set of tests including a bone density scan. I was informed that the scans are done to see if the Cancer has metastasized to your bones as it is one place that prostate Cancer seems to matriculate. Stage four prostate Cancer has a way of doing that, metastasizing from the prostate to the bladder and then making its way to one's spine as it slowly eats away one's energy and will to live. I'm told the pain is excruciating as the malignant cells squeeze the spinal cord and make life miserable. I hope and pray not to go that way, jokingly telling those who will listen, my goal is to be shot at the age of ninety-five by a jealous twenty-one-year-old husband.

I arrived at the hospital and while I waited was told to drink several glasses of water. By urinating frequently after the test I would remove radioactive material that hadn't collected in my bones. The pamphlet said the amount of radioactivity in my body was safe for others to be nearby and I wouldn't have the glowing disposition so many people aspire to have as it was less than the amount from a normal x-ray.

I entered the exam room and was told to lie on my back on the table as the technologist placed a large scanning camera above my body and directed me to remain still to prevent blurry pictures. Doctor Jackson, who was a specially trained and certified nuclear medicine specialist, would read the results created by injecting a very small amount of a radioactive substance called a tracer into my vein. The injection was easy, simply a warm rush that went through my body to be absorbed in different amounts in those areas that became highlighted in white on the screen. I learned that when cells and tissues are changing, they absorb more of the tracer which may indicate the presence of Cancer. It was easy, or so I thought.

During the scan the camera moved slowly around my body taking pictures of the tracer in my bones. Periodically, Ron, the technologist, asked me to change positions to help to get pictures from different angles and made me feel like what it was like to be the Playboy centerfold, without the staples in my stomach, that is. The entire procedure took about an hour and wasn't painful. However, I did feel some discomfort from staying in the same position for a long time.

The next day Doctor Goodman called and said they needed to run some more tests because there appeared to be some damage to my bones. That afternoon, I was back at Milwaukee General for a computed tomography or (CT) scan and then a positron-emission tomography (PET) scan and finally a magnetic resonance imaging (MRI). Between cats, pets and MRI's, I was beginning to think I was at the Vet's office and not the hospital.

We were now three days from surgery when Doctor Goodman's Physician Assistant called and asked, "George, the Radiologist saw some irregularities in your ribs, did you play football?"

"Me? Yes, I played two positions...halfback and left out."

"What do you mean 'left out'?"

"Unless we were up by twenty or down by twenty I was normally left out. Slow, skinny, white kids don't fit the profile of football players."

"How about accidents?"

Holy shit! I'd never mentioned the accident with Jeepers Creepers and detailed what happened. To Doctor Goodman's P.A., it was like a light turned on as she realized the glowing white spots from the density scan were all the bones I'd broken in may accident.

"That's good news," the P.A. offered.

"Not if you were the Jeep or me," I retorted.

I had one more pre-meeting and that was with Doctor Sternberg, the psychologist. At first, I thought they considered me a wacko and then realized my trepidations were such, they concluded I needed to talk through things one more time. I'm beginning to realize the brain can help a person heal as much as all the technology.

I entered Dr. Sternberg's office and was escorted into the inner sanctum and directed to sit on a couch and was offered coffee or water. I chose water. The walls were covered with photos of trees and lakes and anything that wasn't personal. The furniture was oak and expensive and highlighted by the beige carpeting which reminded me of our office in Hartland. There were light beige drapes on the windows that allowed me to look out at a park across the street.

"How are you doing?" Dr. Sternberg inquired.

"I'm OK," I replied.

"Any concerns?"

"Sure, wouldn't you be concerned if your life was about to change?"

Dr. Sternberg looked at me with a wry smile as I think he appreciated my candor as he asked, "Afraid?"

"Yes."

"About what?"

"Tomorrow."

"What do you mean tomorrow?"

"First what happens if I don't make it?"

Dr. Sternberg frowned and then assured me. "The procedure is quite safe and shouldn't be something to worry about."

I countered. "Second, what am I going to do if they find out it's worse than they believe it is?"

Sternberg again. "Then they'll implement a different protocol. You need to realize what you have is very common and treatable. Prostate Cancer is the second most common type of Cancer in men there is."

Sternberg paused for a moment and then got serious. "Do you think it would be better to ignore it and face a potential horrific death?"

I'd heard all this before but was still worried and so I continued. "What am I going to do with my time?" We were getting down to the nitty gritty.

"Hobbies?"

I thought for a minute and realized I didn't have any and simply shrugged my shoulders.

I'd serendipitously included the subject in my treatise on life but realized I was a victim of too much work and too few interests.

Dr. Sternberg paused and then elicited, "Hobbies and interests are what adults do to play. It's what gives us a respite from what we have to do. It allows us to expand our horizons and meet people with common interests with whom we can share experiences and create new friends. It can be any activity, interest or non-professional pastime that people do for pleasure or relaxation that's normally done during leisure time."

He paused for a moment and then continued "It's amazing what some people like to do. Whether it's sailing or swimming, skiing or hiking, flying kites, travel or even being deeply involved as a spectator in a college football team, these voluntary exercises allow us to move beyond here and now and explore a world that piques our interest that's common with others. It's even more amazing when you consider the different levels of interest and expertise people can have in the same fields."

"How about writing books?"

"If that's what floats your boat, go for it!" as a smile crossed the good doctor's face and he added. "There can be huge advantages in having a hobby as it can provide time to relax and reduce your stress level. Physical hobbies also release endorphins which will boost your mood and awareness and can also help you to find new skills and uncover hidden talents. For some selecting a hobby may be a natural and easy process. For others it can be confusing regarding where to start since there are so many options out there."

Doctor Sternberg continued. "For many, the hobby is sports. Sadly, we've turned them into an extension of work. Sports should be about enjoyment, cooperation, team building, learning to deal with adversity, building character and pursuing excellence. Life's always affected by how much you allow things around you to affect the direction of your path."

I thought for a moment and looked inward. I was never good at any sport and guess that's the reason I shied away from so many as Dr. Sternberg continued. "Did you know there are nearly 250 different hobbies you can get involved in? Hobbies can sharpen the mind, create physical challenges and/or adventure, reduce stress, increase one's interaction with science and nature, expand one's knowledge of history, establish creative projects, increase social networks, music, travel and spirituality."

The doctor leaned back in his chair and continued. "What I find interesting is how some people cherish their hobbies and interests to the point of protection. I remember many years ago visiting a fellow doctor in New York and being shown into his office. The walls were literally covered with some of the most beautiful, intriguing photographs I'd ever seen. I simply stood in awe at the beauty and expression that surrounded me. I asked the gentleman who took the photographs and he responded he did. I asked why he wasn't a professional photographer and he noted that photography was his passion and if he did it for money, it would become his job."

"I was thunderstruck by the concept and, yet, after all these years, I recall the man, his photographs and logic and think back at the people I've met who've cared so much about something they were truly passionate about what they did and I admire them!"

"Is that where the photos on your wall came from?" I asked.

"No, he motivated me and I began taking photographs and these are some of my favorites."

"So you took them?"

"Yes."

"They're really good."

"Thank you. I have them here to remind me that there's more to life than work. To be passionate about something is a God-given gift. To watch someone's eyes light up as they share their knowledge and their intrigue, is a true point of wonder. To simply listen to them expound on something they're profoundly interested in generates great joy and wonderment about why everyone isn't passionate about something. To be able to focus on something you want to do and not something you have to do is what makes anything and everything become a hobby."

What's sad is how many people are passion-impaired…unable to get excited about anything in life. Not people! Not places! Not events! Not activities! Not circumstances! Their world is simply vanilla!"

"In what I do for a living, it's made me often wonder why people are passion-impaired and finally I realized that with passion comes risk. When you have strong feelings the loss can become greater, disappointment more profound and emptiness even deeper. When something for which we have passion suddenly disperses, we feel pain and today's plastic world tries to minimize pain whenever possible."

The doc stopped and then added. "One MUST be passionate and caring and enthusiastic. Without these attributes, once again, we're only a shell, walking, interacting and functioning in a world like that plastic snowman sitting on a neighbor's lawn at Christmas. There, but not really…glowing, but not really…dynamic and three dimensional, but only as what they represent and not what they truly are."

Boy, did that sound familiar. Perhaps it was on page fifty-three of the psych book I read but was still a great metaphor.

Doc looked at me and asked. "Now that we're through the bullshit, how are you really doing?" He'd seen right through my façade.

I shrugged and looked down at the carpet.

He began. "Within the five categories of consequence of a nerve sparing prostatectomy, ED and sterilization appear to have the greatest psychological effect that may result in both temporal and long-term depression and potential PTSD. Cortisol, which is a hormone released in response to stress, is released in order to save available blood sugar for the brain, thereby generating new energy from stored reserves and diverting energy from low-priority activities such as the immune system. This happens in order for the body to survive the perceived immediate threats or prepare the body for any type of stressed-filled experience."

"OK."

Doc continued. "While too high and too low levels might seem like opposites, researchers have found that people suffering from PTSD can end up having abnormal levels in either direction, where the lower level may be caused by the body responding to periods when it had too much cortisol such as after surgery. While ED results in a visual affirmation, awareness of sterilization happens when the man is intimate and there's no seminal ejaculation. It's absolute and nothing can be done about it. The ramifications, psychologically, are rarely detailed. However, articles recently have begun to be printed that address the subject."

"Men often describe prostate surgery as 'life-changing' and, although they recognize the trade-off involved between survival and post-operative complications, these complications appear to be the greatest subconscious source of distress. Linked to this, men often anticipate the future, worry about the potential return of the disease and whether post-operative complications… especially erectile dysfunction…will improve over time."

Doctor Sternberg continued. "Many men feel there's a lack of information about what happens after surgery, despite their efforts to identify this information, which is why you're lucky to have a urological group who understands there's more to it than simply removing the Cancer. Lack of information results in men feeling psychologically and physically ill-prepared for, and sometimes surprised by, the complications they experience."

"George, you need to accept that physical changes are common after surgery, contributing to negative emotions in many men including anxiety, depression, embarrassment, frustration and/or shock which impacts their interactions with family and friends. However, some men describe these physical changes as leading to positive psychological changes such as re-evaluating life and improving communications with their families, which is where I hope we can get you."

I took a deep breath and didn't know where to start. While the outside of the Terrill cake looked glorious to many because of the wealth, it was only the frosting. The actual cake inside had all kinds of issues no one knew about that challenged me more than anything else.

Doc. continued. "Men normally struggle most with erectile dysfunction as it contributes to a feeling of a loss of masculinity, guilt towards their partner and lower self-esteem. Some men are able to discuss sexual problems openly but others struggle with embarrassment. Some men find it easier to manage and adjust to the physical changes they experience than the psychological aspects."

"George, it's not the end of the world. Any and every sexual activity can still result in a climax. Don't let it serve as a false testament that you're no longer a man. If there's one thing I want you to walk out of here with today, it's the attitude that you're still you… the same person who is loved and revered, honored and esteemed who has done more for the world than so many of us will ever know."

I nodded in shy affirmation as Dr. Sternberg glanced at the clock and I knew my time was up. In forty-five minutes he'd planted a seed to help eradicate some of my trepidations and alleviate some of my concerns while making me realize I wasn't alone. As we stood and shook hands he suggested that Amy and I do something or go somewhere to take my mind off next week. I'd been to the forest and seen the buck and believe I know what he meant and, yet, I still pondered. "Was the buck there to lead me to heaven or was he there to console me and tell me it was going to be all right?"

It was our last weekend before the surgery and I knew it would be the last time out for several weeks. I asked Amy where she'd like to go and when she said it was up to me, I said Madison. Being 50 miles away meant less than an hour and so we made dinner reservations at Graze. Being less than a block from the Capitol, after dinner I asked Amy if we could go for a walk and wandered into the rotunda where I'd proposed and the kids got married. It was as resplendent as ever. What a majestic edifice!

We both looked up at the ceiling dome painted by Edwin Howland-Blashfield entitled *'Resources of Wisconsin'* that shows a female figure as *'Wisconsin'* enthroned upon clouds, surrounded by others and wrapped in the American flag.

This was the exact spot where I'd proposed, enveloped in the power of love. We paused and I repeated what I still sincerely believed and had said so many years before. "Until I met you, this was the most beautiful thing I'd ever seen."

A soft smile parted Amy's lips as we hugged and simply walked hand-in-hand back to the car and drove home. I think we both needed a break from what lie ahead. Our world was about to change in many ways and, quite honestly, I was scared of what it all meant.

## Preparation:

The day before the planned event you're required to drink a gallon of medication. Let's politely just call it 'swill.' It's intended to simply clean your entire gastro-intestinal system while giving you the worst possible drinking experience you could imagine.

If you've had a colonoscopy you know what it is. If not, you'll quickly learn why I called it swill. I looked at this huge jug of clear, foul smelling liquid and the instructions to complete the process in six hours. I can just image how many hoots and howls of laughter the pharmacist gets every time they write up those instructions! A plan of attack was needed! I determined what six equal amounts were and began with one 'treatment' planned for every hour on the hour.

After nearly gagging on the first phase, I developed a procedure that worked for me. I calculated how many gulps I could chug without taking a breath and swallowed hard. With each measured amount, I placed a small glass of grape juice next to it. When I completed drinking the swill, I gasped and then let the grape juice eradicate the God-awful taste of the medication. For me, it worked!

I read the side of the bottle.

*"**Warning!** Do not attempt to be more than 20 feet from the bathroom at any time and after the third 'session' make certain you leave the bathroom door open, light on, lid up and seat down for your next visit. Time WILL be of the essence!"*

As noted my surgery was scheduled as the last one on Thursday. This meant I needed to report to the hospital at 12:45 PM, which also meant a morning without liquids. To this end, they said do not drink any liquids. 'The best thing to do is swirl water around in your mouth and then spit it out. It kept my mouth satiated and the day tolerable. Bourbon would have been better but I made it!'

The entire registration procedure and event planning was like a fine-tuned watch. They make you feel welcome and important…

right before they make you impotent...at least, hopefully, for a while anyway! They answered my questions and kept me attuned to all the preparatory events that needed to take place. They were kind, considerate and professional.

After the day before and no liquids all day, I was surprised that I really had to pee. At first, I thought it was strange until I was reminded that I had an IV filled with liquids dripping into my veins and that was 'natural'. Twice the urge arose and twice, I asked if I could go. It would be the last time for nine days...might just as well stop for one last *'pause that refreshes'*!

After what seemed like an hour, a young woman opened the door and walked in with a pan and razor. Terror filled my mind!

"What's that for?" I asked

"The doctors believe your Cancer is contained within the prostate. However, they need to be prepared in case something unforeseen is determined."

"Unforeseen?" Gulp! "What then?" I asked.

"If need be, and there's a very small probability, they'll need to do a full retropubic procedure and you need to be prepped in case that's the decision."

I'd read up on the pre-computer method and knew it meant getting slit from your navel to the top of your penis instead of five holes around your rib cage. With that, the young lady nonchalantly pulled up my gown, took the electric clippers and began trimming my pubic hair. I cringed.

When the aide was done with the clippers, she splashed water, added shaving cream and began the process. I could tell by her level of ambivalence she'd done this before and it was simply a procedure to her and nothing more.

By the embarrassed look on my face she could tell I needed some form of assurance and added, "Under non-surgical situations, manscaping is done by nearly ninety percent of all men and whether you decide to remove your pubic hair should be of no one's concern. It's your garden, if you find it pleasing and beautiful to keep your body hair, do so. However, no one in the operating room today or later on is going to think less of you if they examine you and find you have chosen a different option."

I guess I was surprised by her elocution as she rattled off reasons for manscaping as she called it. "First, pubic hair removal is more hygienic as they gather dirt when left for a long time without shaving."

The thought went through my mind and I realized that in a few hours reference to my sex life would be in the past tense as she continued, "The eccrine and the apocrine glands produce a fluid that comes to the skin surface that is often odorless. Eventually, the fluid  combines with the skin's bacteria and begins to smell bad and is the primary reason why many men shave."

"You mean a lot of guys really do this?" I offered incredulously.

She looked at me and smiled. "I read an article that said one-in-six of all men are totally bare and only 10% are unkempt like you."

"Really…and no one's going to laugh or think I'm….I'm…you know?"

"Heavens no!" She replied as she pulled down my gown, folded the towel and headed for the door.

I let out a sigh of relief as Amy entered and smiled, asking, "How are you doing?"

"Well, I just had my crotch shaved and wasn't expecting that."

"And?"

"And what?"

"George, you're in the hospital and being prepped for surgery, not the beauty parlor."

"But!"

"But what?"

"I suppose next you'll want me to get a tattoo down there." I half-heartedly joked.

"Perhaps a rose to match mine?" Amy replied.

I didn't know if she was serious or not.

The door opened and the anesthesiologist, who I immediately called Doctor Goodnight, appeared to explain his part of the procedure…he gives you something and you go to sleep…ZZZZZ!

Seemed like a good guy! I noted that I am somewhat claustrophobic and he indicated he'd take that into consideration, especially when I told him I KO'd a small nurse at another hospital when waking up from orthopedic surgery a few years back!

Next, Doctor Thompson appeared. Having met with him on three other occasions I was familiar with his demeanor… totally confident, with 600+ successful DiVinci surgeries under his mask, he knew what he was doing…thank God!

Soon it was 'show time'. This tiny girl rolled me on this huge gurney into this bright blue room. They positioned the gurney next to the operating table and assisted in sliding me onto the slab. I looked at Mr. DiVinci in the corner and noticed his arms were covered in clear plastic sheaths. I asked the nurse to remember to take the seat covers off before they began and she said that they were there to keep Mr. DiVinci sterilized for my procedure.

'Gee, just like me when they're done,' I thought.

I reminded her again to take off the seat covers, thinking of my grandma's living room that had plastic covers on the couch that we either stuck to on a hot day or slid to the floor when it was cold!

Remembering my only concept of an operating table being from an old Frankenstein movie, I was surprised when the mid-section of the table felt like it was being lowered and flat arm rests appeared. My arms were extended and the lights above me seemed to grow brighter. I only hoped this was an illusion! But then, in my heart, I knew He was with me!

Doctor Goodnight appeared and noted my claustrophobia, stating he'd be careful in putting on the mask that would pump oxygen into my lungs to clear anything out. I wasn't asked to count back from ten. In fact, I wasn't asked anything…ZONK! I was gone! I don't even remember the mask. I guess the claustrophobia threat did the good Doctor in!

Who knows what happened! During surgery I was there, because I have the six scars and a big bill to prove it. They weren't there before the lights went out. I went through the procedure, then recovery and finally, my room, in a state of total obliviousness.

When I awoke, it was late evening and Amy was there. Huh? It was nearly eight hours later!

As my senses came back, I could hear the constant beep, beep, beep of all the machines and the hideous glare of the computer monitor across the room. I was totally awake, in VERY little pain, and it wasn't even bar time. The night consisted of nurses checking on me and then the change of command at 7:00AM as the night nurse left and the day nurse arrived. The white board reported his name who, in the next few hours, became my buddy.

I peeked beneath the covers and saw the five incisions that were promised. Four small horizontal incisions no more than the width of my little finger and then 'Bubba' who was a vertical incision about the length of the top joint of my thumb, right above my navel!

Instead of stitches, they'd used metal staples. I imagined Doc Thompson with an old fashioned Swingline stapler doing the deed. Kerchunk! Kerchunk! Kerchunk! They didn't look nearly as pretty as they had on that buff illustration guy on the DVD, but they were there. Why they didn't use an old skinny guy instead of Mr. Universe for reality in the illustration is beyond me! Buff, young, guys normally don't get prostate Cancer! We're the ones who should be used as models!

Doctor Thompson had indicated there'd be a small sixth incision for drainage. He'd informed me they 'pushed' saline solution into the abdominal cavity to irrigate any internal bleeding from the lymph node biopsies and the hole allowed the drainage to escape from the body more quickly. The drainage mechanism looked like a clear tennis ball with a tube and a drain on it. Every so often someone would come in and suck what looked like Hawaiian punch out and it would go flat.

By 8:00 AM the noise of the nurse's station just outside my door was driving me crazy. I buzzed my nurse, and asked if I could go for a walk. Magically an aide appeared amazed that I was ready to take my first journey. She helped me up and got me a chair and asked me to sit for a few minutes just to make sure I wasn't rushing things. With her help, the stanchion with the IV was rolled nearby and the catheter or 'pee bag', hence called "PB" was positioned.

I was shocked! Just like they advertised, there was very little pain! I was up, alert and ready to roll. My aide walked with me the first lap and then I told her to go take care the sick people. I did six laps of about 300 feet each, went back to my room and rested in the chair for about 30 minutes and then went for six more, repeating the process four times in two hours. I walked a mile... hooray!

After not eating for two days, I was famished! The lunch was cream of chicken soup, raspberry Jell-O, chocolate pudding and orange sherbet... Yummy! The food ladies were shocked I was so alert and full of fun for someone who just had a four-hour operation. They said 'no' to my request for red wine or even some Sprite as they said the gas would be bad for me.

Whereas Doctor Thompson had already left on vacation, one of his associates appeared. I thought it was Doogie Howser's little brother! He asked how I was doing, checked my chart and was off. I learned later he was a whiz on DiVinci. Being an old klutz, I promised never to play video games against this guy. He'd kill me!

It was agreed that I could be released after removal of the drainage ball. Little did I know it was connected to a 15-inch-long drainage tube! That's right a 15-inch-long tube. When my buddy, Harry the nurse, asked if I was ready to have it taken out, macho me replied 'Sure.' With that first tug and first extremely loud yelp, Harry stopped.

I accused Harry of attempting to turn my 'you know what' inside out to the roar of all the ladies at the nurse's station as things fell to the floor and convulsions of laughter permeated the otherwise quiet hallway. 'Holy s—t!' Harry assured me that the first tug was the worst and with all the aplomb of a dedicated professional, he had me clench my fists while he quickly provided one of the weirdest sensations I've ever felt and hope to never feel again...the clear tube slithering beneath my skin, like a slimy snake wanting out from within! Harry slapped on the bandage, and it was done!

An appointment was made for a 2:00 PM meeting to go over the proper care and treatment of the patient…namely me! All aspects were reviewed and the obligatory wheel chair arrived. In 23 hours I was going from incision, to decision, to liberation! My only wish was that some of the verbalized things like what to watch for such as abdominal pain, coughing, etc. would have been written down. My day had been too full for me to remember everything…make that anything! Having never been catheterized before, I was worried that the line out of my almost-inside-out, you-know-what would fall out.

Amy informed me that a Foley catheter actually includes a line within a line and that on the end of the outer line, inside my bladder, was a balloon filled with saline solution so that the outer balloon is larger than the urinary tube entrance. As long as you didn't pull on it, it was going anywhere! Trust me! I wasn't going to pull on anything! Harry had scared me enough!

I slid into the passenger's seat with my trusty PB next to me and headed for home. I'll warn you, that ride is **NOT** fun! Even if you have a luxury car, bring a pillow or get one of those inflated rings to sit on as every single bump is pure torture. When we came to a set of railroad tracks, I thought the lights were going to go out! I swear Amy took that route to get even with me for something! I made it home and slithered onto the couch in the family room.

**Daze at Home:**

The biggest post-operative risk is always infection. Abiding by the application of the required ointment around where the catheter came out, keeping the PB somewhat empty and avoiding outside contact so that I didn't catch a cold meant I was somewhat sequestered.

My sojourn consisted of ever-increasing walks to the mailbox. Oh, what a joy! Me and PB in a bathrobe and slippers in 25-degree weather sashaying all the way to the road and back! Meals became soft foods consisting of soups, Jell-O, pudding and ice cream to allow my digestive system the chance to regenerate itself without straining anything. Do not eat corn! During the day I would rest, watch television, call my business associates and answer e-mail. Thursday and Friday all seemed to be going well. In fact, Friday night I switched to a leg bag and we went out for dinner! It was a challenge and in retrospect, I wouldn't recommend it!

Saturday afternoon I began feeling a warm sensation between my legs…my catheter had begun leaking at that point within my bladder where it should have been sealed. I thought something major was happening. By Sunday, the amount of leaking had increased and so I called the doctor on duty. He indicated that a leaking catheter was VERY common and was not a cause of concern. He noted that one cause could be an irritation and so he prescribed some little blue pills that he said 'might' help.

I was told I needed to adjust to the situation and that paper towels worked well. The little blue pills didn't do the trick. My personal nurse (Amy) monitored both the output quantity in the PB and the clarity of the urine to make sure that was no problem. I continued to discharge the same amount, which remained clear. Instead of switching to the leg bag, I elected to retain good old PB and lived with it for the week.

They'd warned that I *might* have a few 'hot flashes'. Holy S—T! I had no idea what a hot flash was until they slammed into me! I had a total of four…three little ones that saw me want to take off all

312

my clothes and run around naked, catheter hose and all, and then a REAL DOOZY that lasted about a half hour when I wanted to simply sit in a bucket of ice water because there was no snow in the yard! No wonder why menopause can be such a bitch!

I celebrated the seventh day of recovery and awaited my appointment with Doc. Thompson. On Thursday, we met and the wonderful news was given that all of the tests confirmed the original diagnosis. The Cancer was contained within the prostate and was completely removed with no additional invasion of the lymph nodes around the gland. The conclusion was they'd removed all the cancerous cells and, yet, it would be five years before I was officially Cancer clear and ten until named a Survivor.

The Swinglines were removed and my 'beloved' catheter balloon deflated so that it, too, slid out with ease!

Looking the good doctor right in the eye I told him that ever since the surgery I had these weird cravings.

"For what"?

"To go out and buy a Cadillac?"

Doc had a perplexed look on his face and then smiled when I offered "If you're going to be impotent, you need to drive a Cadillac." This got the totally serious surgeon cackling while putting a smile on my face simply because I got him to laugh!

I quickly learned that the 'involuntary urination' was going to last a while and that, at about 85 cents apiece, they would be cutting down a small forest to keep me dry. Instead, a strategy was developed....using paper towels inside the Depends to soak up the pee! I also learned that I could take two paper towels and fold them in half and then fold them again and stuff these in the front on my Depends. This meant eight layers of absorbency! It also meant FREEDOM! I could stick two extra towels in my back pocket and go into any bathroom stall, deposit the wet towels and be on my way. No changing Depends! No disposal problems! What a wizard!

We'd been considering a new leather couch for our family room. We drove to one of them hoity toity furniture stores. You know where the salesladies are all in evening gowns, dripping with diamonds that match their aluminum clip boards. We wanted what we thought would be a really, really big! Really, really fancy! Really, really expensive mother! You have no idea the cheap thrill of looking at this gorgeous beast (the couch) and talking to the sales lady, while all the time, peeing my pants! Normally, high prices scare the s—t out of me! Not this time! Nope! Pee, all the way!

I learned that, within reason, more recovery is done when you're sleeping than at any other time. I also learned that a consistently good night's sleep will shorten the recovery period. When the first few nights were the antithesis of this objective, I was distraught until Melia pointed out I 'd gone cold turkey from all medications and my body was probably in withdrawal.

Melia was right about the cold turkey! Three nights and then my circadian sleep routine returned…hooray! Anyway, as much as what you would consider normal for a guy! God! I remember going out to bars later than the time I went to bed! I set my schedule so that I would go to bed at 10:00 PM with lights out at 10:45. Instead of an alarm I determined to let my body naturally awaken me.

I was told by Doc Thompson that it would take at least four days for the urethra to begin returning to normal size and then several more days for the Kegel exercises to begin to take effect at giving me bladder control. He forgot to tell me that coughing or even turning your head would, could and did lead to the 'squirts', as I began calling them….Little Squirts! Big Squirts! Just enough squirts to keep me heading for the Bounty!

After the surgical maelstrom had settled and life for the rest of the family returned to its former self, I sat alone and finally realized my life had changed. After a great deal of consternation I went on the Internet and ordered a copy of 'Lady Chatterley's Lover' by D. H. Lawrence. The classic novel is a story about love, passion and the human spirit personified through Constance Chatterley, a young woman, married to Sir Clifford Chatterley, a wealthy landowner paralyzed from the waist down after being wounded in World War I.

Constance is frustrated by her husband's physical and emotional distance and she begins an affair with Oliver Mellors, the gamekeeper on the Chatterley estate. The affair awakens Constance's sexuality and helps her to find true love. In my darkest hours, I feel as if I'm Sir Clifford, not paralyzed, but no longer proficient. I stare in the mirror and see the profile of a man...namely me, no longer a man, simply the casing holding everything together but one thing and therefore feeling I'm nothing. I think of Constance and want to tell Amy she's free...either way...any way, I can no longer be a restraint from her needs, but I can't. Why? Why can't I be like Sir Clifford and set her free?

The recovery process became a drag.

February 13th or two weeks after surgery, was the first time I actually sat on the pot and got to control the pee coming out of me. It was one GRAND experience! Ahh! Potty Power was on its way…I hoped!

February 14th. Valentine's Day made me bold enough to increase my fluid intake to its former 64 ounce per day plus level. Oops! Too much! Can you say bathroom about 25 times? I'd gone through an entire roll of paper towels in 2½ days! God, hurry up and let me gain control…peeing one's pants gets real old real fast.

February 16th. Reduce the fluid intake and reduce the trips! Still too many but better! Can't wait to get out of the Depends but then that really depends on me!  Up to 250 Kegel exercises per day. I sincerely believe I could pick up a 12-pound bowling ball with my butt cheeks!

February 18th. God I'm sick of having wet pants, smelling like a two-year-old and having to focus on the location of every bathroom in every place I go. This is getting old VERY fast. For the first time in my adult life I began to worry about diaper rash!

February 20-21st. Same old! Same old! Yet it seems like I'm getting more control. Still the dribbles and drips but more peeing on command! Moving past the age of two! I had very little stored volume and still a somewhat weak stream but I'm beginning to control things! God, it's funny to be so aware of something I had taken for granted for so many years! I got brave and wore khaki pants for the first time. Whew! Made it through the day! Tomorrow, my second post-op appointment! Hopefully, I'm recovering on schedule. We leave on vacation in a month and I don't want to spend all vacation standing in our swimming pool!

**The Visit:**

I presented Doc Thompson's staff with a copy of my summary regarding everything that preceded this point in time and listened to their laughter as I sat in the examining room! Seems some of the stuff must have hit home! Doc Thompson came in and asked how it was going. I told him I was tired of peeing in my pants! He informed me, politely and professionally, that it came with the territory. He indicated that bladder control came in phases that each phase seemed to last about two weeks.

After potty power and the dribbles and drips began, there would be five key phases...

- Phase I...Not peeing while you sleep! Got that one down!
- Phase II...Not peeing when you're sitting. Got that for the most part!
- Phase III...Not peeing when you're standing...Working on it but still have a way to go!
- Phase IV...Not peeing when you stand up!
- Phase V...Not peeing when you sneeze or lift something heavy!

It all made sense! Lying down, there is no compression of the bladder! Sitting, the bladder has some support. Standing, the bladder has the weight of the girth above on it! Finally, going from sitting to standing, compression takes place because you not only have gravity but are using muscles to realign yourself in a vertical position which adds pressure to the bladder. Those who have it the easiest are the young skinny guys! Us old guys lose out again! Can't get the pretty girls when we're young and pee our pants longer when we're old! Who said life would be fair?

As part of the plan to get me back to normalcy, I was offered the opportunity to go on Cialis for erectile dysfunction. One small pill per day and the additional blood in the area would not only help heal me faster but get the 'other' part of my life back on track. I asked if I needed to go out and purchase two old bathtubs to put in the yard.

One of the nurses said having the bathtub would make life easier because when I peed my pants, it could run out the drain. She must have forgotten what winter was like in Wisconsin. Nothing worse than pee-sickles hanging off the drain! If you think it's tough getting your tongue stuck to a cold pipe think about having your you-know-what stuck there instead. OUCH! If I elected to skip the Cialis I had the option of a vacuum pump around my you-know-what to get the blood to flow. I asked if I could use the Dyson. Doc Thompson didn't seem amused. He said that if that didn't work, I could have needle injections which sent a shiver up my spine! Needles there? I shuddered and opted for the little pill each morning!

Doc Thompson asked me how many Kegel's I was doing per day and macho me noted between 400 and 500.

"Too many!" Was the response! "Cut back to 200 in four sets of 50 of the quick pulses and then begin working up to 50 of the long pulses that are to be held for 10 seconds each for stamina! You'll get there but that's going to take a while!"

In the end, I really believe I'll be able to hold that bowling ball between my butt cheeks and was warned not to minimize the magnitude of the surgery.

"BE CAREFUL! No lifting of anything over 15 pounds! No climbing ladders or foolish things! Take it easy! Not too heavy on the work schedule! You just had a major operation!"

Meeting adjourned as I promised I would be a good boy and headed for home!

**You Want to Do What?:**

I was offered the opportunity to work with a physical therapist and thought why not? Her name was Megan and she was cool! Effervescent smile! Great laugh! Totally professional! Still, it seemed weird talking about peeing in my pants with a lady!

We began and my socially induced reservations were simply thrown out the window as everything, and I mean everything, became topics of conversation…Impotence, Erectile Dysfunction, Urinary Incontinence, Penile Length Shortening and PTSD and then what could and could not be done about each and what "exercises" should take place to minimize the consequence of each.

With my first visit she told me to go in the examination room and take off my clothes. I did as I was told and she walked in and asked "Why didn't you put on the gown?"

"You never told me to," I replied.

"It's right there on the hook."

"Again, you said 'take off your clothes.'"

Megan became oblivious to my nakedness and responded in a quite professional tone. "George, when they removed your prostate they took out the prostatic sphincter that controls your bladder. The reason you're here is to learn how to use your perineal muscles to take over bladder control."

"OK."

"These are the muscles between your legs that assist in keeping your balance, help your body lift things and assist your diaphragm whenever you sneeze. We're going to teach you how to use those same muscles for bladder control and do so until it becomes and autonomic response."

It was all logical and so we went through what I called butt crunches and she called Kegels. She said this was the most important exercise I could do and actually had a device that measured my butt strength. I wondered who invented this device and thought of some engineer going home to his wife with her asking him 'What did you do today?' to which he replied, 'I worked on my butt crunch machine'. 'Oh, that's nice dear' she said as they sat down for dinner.

Unfortunately, the preponderant smell of stale urine permeated the room as Megan discretely inquired, "Did you take a shower this morning?"

"Yes, about four hours ago," I replied in a somewhat penitent tone, wondering where this was going.

"Do you ever wear a hat?"

"A Badger baseball cap at the football games and a stocking cap in the winter, why?" I replied, now in a somewhat perplexed manner.

Megan continued. "When you wear a hat, is your hair the same afterwards?"

"No, it's flattened. What's this got to do with my surgery?"

"Well, George, to be quite honest, you've got a hygiene problem and that's probably the reason why."

"Wearing a baseball cap?"

Megan smiled and replied. "No, George, wearing a Badger hat doesn't make you…uh, have a body odor problem."

I was total baffled as she continued. "Here's what I think is going on. The cuticle, or outer layer of your hair, is more permeable than normal and, so, when you have the normal post-operative 'leaking issues', the urine is soaking through the cuticle and absorbed in the cortex or inner layer of your hair that provides strength, moisture, color and texture."

Megan smiled at her now-attentive student as she added. "The key here is the word moisture. Oil or other bodily fluids are getting imbedded in the cortex. Regular shampoo is designed to remove oil and dirt from outside. However, the PH of the shampoo has to be controlled so that it doesn't damage the cortex.

"In other words, while I'm cleaning the outside of the hair the shampoo isn't getting rid of any residue inside?" Even the wizard-like me was understanding.

"That's right. Now you could use a conditioner but then your hair would be really oily and the term *'greaser'* would apply."

"In other words greaser or pisser, that's me?"

Megan giggled before adding, "In cases like yours the hair retains the urine and you end up with what we call *wino syndrome*."

I just shook my head…imagining the short, skinny, old, impotent wino and asked, "What are the other solutions?"

"Obviously, the shorter the hair, the less absorption. In your case, my professional opinion is the only way to be assured of no lingering problems is to trim or remove the hair."

"You mean…bald?" I cringed thinking surgery was one thing but now?

"For how long?"

"Well, that's up to you."

"Huh?"

"How long will that take?"

"Depending on the person, from four to six months for the autonomic system to be in place."

"You mean I'm going to have to…to you know keep myself trimmed or *bald* for that long."

"That's the primary phase."

"What do you mean, primary?"

"Bladder control is secondary to the primary functions of the perineal muscles and any time you use those same muscles to lift something, laugh too hard or sneeze, if you're not ready, you can get the proverbial dribbles and drips."

"Jesus!" I said, obviously feeling sorry for myself.

Megan looked at me and seriously inquired. "Would you rather be in an urn on a closet shelf, smelling like a wino or having a little alteration? Life's not perfect and things aren't the same as they used to be but at least you're on the road to recovery."

I still had my pants down when Megan asked me if I wanted her to do it. I thought 'What the hell.'

As she was about to leave to get the clippers, shaving cream and razor, she handed me a pamphlet and said, "Read this while I'm gone, it discusses exercises for both the UI and ED. Focus on the urinary incontinence first."

Sure enough, the pamphlet said it would take a minimum of four months before downstairs started getting messages from upstairs and, because I was using different muscles, I'd always be prone to dribbles and drips. The pamphlet also noted that 'massaging the downstairs area would not only increase blood flow but begin to get the phone lines working sooner'. This made my eyebrows arch wondering which operator I called. Sadly, the eyebrows were the only things that arched.

Magen returned and did her thing. Before the surgery, it probably might have been kinky and that probably would have…uhh showed. Now it was a clinical procedure where, for the second time in my life, I was manscaped. So much for reticence and self-awareness. I watched Megan's eyes through the whole process and there wasn't a single instance of exhilaration in her. This was just another day at the office and after I left, she'd be on to the next guy. What away to make a living!

After the shave, Megan went through the exercises I needed to do to increase all the muscles and motivated me to be her star pupil. I stopped at the drug store and bought a Braun electric shaver, went home, explained to Amy what happened and she thought nothing of it, simply replying "Welcome to the club." I vowed to become diligent with both the hygienic aspect and my exercises and strived to attain a degree of physical accomplishment I probably wouldn't have done a few years ago.

WRONG THING TO DO!

It seems that old, decrepit legs are NOT supposed to be pulled all the way up to your chin! Then, I slipped on the ice and fell on my keester! Ouch! When you do, and pull your hamstring muscle…not a little…but HOLY SHIT, a lot, it hurts…like really, really hurts! On Monday, I woke up unable to walk! It took an hour to crawl to the bathroom. I was in TOTAL misery!

For the first five days, I was in a wheelchair, then a walker with one on each floor of our house. When lying flat, or even sitting, there was no pain. But standing or walking! OUCH!!!!!!

I went back to see Megan and she was dumbfounded! "My God what did you do?"

I told her and she just shook her head! Once we got over my stupidity. She asked about exercises and I told her that I was still doing the Kegels and holding off on everything else. We talked about Mr. ED and nothing was happening but then how could it, when there was so much pain on the back porch, the front porch wasn't going to turn on the lights! She asked about the 'wino syndrome' and I relayed I'd bought the Braun and continued removing the carpeting all the way down to the 'hardwood floor' proudly announcing, like a little kid, that the smell was gone, which got a giggle out of her.

Still in excruciating pain, I visited my orthopedic surgeon who had sliced and diced me so many times you would think his last name is PoPeil! He looked at me and shook his head. Amazing, a brilliant physician who had gone to medical school, worked for nearly 40 years and rebuilt my body and his comment was…"You have a real pain in your ass!" and ordered an MRI.

The good doctor prescribed Percocet for the pain, forgetting to tell me they caused profound constipation. How profound? Well, it was like pooping charcoal briquettes! If you want to know the truth! The MRI was done on Wednesday and it was cool showing that all I had was one big, bad m-----f------g pull.

No TEAR! Hooray, as that would have meant more surgery. The good doctor recommended deep tissue treatments on the hamstring using ultrasound. Once again, another new physical therapist with her hands in my pants! Once again, a totally professional situation where she found the spot that was causing all the pain at the base of the right butt cheek and did her deed. By Saturday I'd ditched the walker and on Sunday was able to get rid of the compression sleeve but was told that it would take UP TO NINE MONTHS to get rid of the pain in my a--!

Wednesday, two weeks hence and my follow up with Doc Thompson was filled with another surprise! There were now three goals in my recovery…. elimination of both the urinary incontinence and Mr. ED and now Cancer prevention.

I kept doing the Kegel's and was down to one pad a day. The next change was increasing the daily dosage of Cialis to 10 mg because it increases blood flow to the lower abdominal region, which not only helps in surgical recovery but regeneration of the nerves needed to send Mr. ED on his merry way.

The Cialis probably helped with the surgical recovery but there was no 'boing', except, of course, when you saw the price of the prescription. It seems insurance companies consider Cialis to be a 'recreational' drug and not something to help you get back to normal life. I was shocked at the cost and realized how they could afford those fancy bathtubs and commercials all the time.

On a more serious note Doc Thompson noted he'd just read an article that stated that the more you weigh, the greater the chance you'll get more Cancer. One little joke about Cadillac's and he had to scare the s—t out of me again! The doctor said using a BMI of 25 as a base equal to one, a BMI between 26 and 30 increases your chances of Cancer 300%. When your BMI is greater than 30 the chance of Cancer increases by 800%. As I learned later, BMI indirectly measures excess body fat which is the real culprit behind a variety of illness and a high BMI level correlates with future health risks. As a skinny runt, it was his way of warning me about adding weight, which is quite common in post-surgical patients.

Beyond BMI, there are other types of composition measurements. These measurements include *bioelectric impedance*, which measures how much water a person contains by sending a small current of electricity through the body, *densitometry* which is calculated by a device that detects how much air and water the body displaces, and measuring the concentration of fat on the abdomen with skin-fold calipers that tell men they needed to watch their weight. I promised to start eating a healthy diet when we and if we got to go and then return from vacation! He scared me! 'Recurrence' had not been part of my thought pattern.

**Metamorphosis:**

Amy and I decided to head to the 'Lighthouse' for a few days. We were scheduled to fly down on Amelia[X] which was our plane of first choice. We boarded and began to taxi when the pilot identified a mechanical problem and returned to the hanger. They inspected the issue and determined we needed to take one of the other jets. It was no big deal except the flight was going to take a little longer.

On our flight, Amy asked me how I was doing.

"OK," I responded.

"You're not yourself."

"Well, if you had your sex taken out, how would you feel?"

"Grateful I was still alive."

"But, I can't...we can't."

"It's OK."

I was getting a bit perturbed with both the topic and her demeanor. I never liked what I considered to be a condescending tone in anyone's voice and replied. "You don't know what it's like to no longer be a man."

"But you are in every other way."

"But not *that* way," I countered.

"We can do other things!" Amy replied.

I let out a deep sigh as my interest in *that* just wasn't there. I'd been informed, instructed, monitored, counseled and warned but no one told me about the hormonal changes that would take place. I was told men have different feelings after surgery and even rapid mood swings. On one hand, there's relief the Cancer has been removed, surgery is over and you've gone home. But I certainly wasn't prepared for the emotional roller coaster that found me irritable, angry, frustrated and sad to the point it was physically and emotionally draining.

I looked across the airplane aisle at Amy and said something I never thought I'd ever utter. "Look, I know  you've done everything you could to be...uh, loyal...but I also know you have needs I can no longer fulfill. If you need someone to satisfy them, it's OK with me."

Amy just stared at me in disbelief, not knowing how to respond, and then replied. "You're the only man I've been with and the only one I want to stay with for a long as I live."

I was honored by her words but wanted to make certain she completely understood and responded. "If you have *other needs*, go for them. It's not fair that, just because I'm no longer a man, you can't be satisfied."

Amy sat for a moment as her eyes squinted. I didn't know if she was frustrated, angry or enthused. She took a sip of her drink and then replied. "George, you're the most noble man I've ever met."

She paused for a moment as I realized she said man and continued. "Even though things are going to be different, you're still my husband and my lover. I won't deny, there haven't been those *other* urges, nor can I promise I can always withstand the temptations. What I can promise is that you will always be the only man in my life."

I took another deep breath and looked at my wife. "Amy, I want you to be happy and be… be satisfied. When we were on Saint Martin the very first time and sat in the parking lot at Rancho Del Sol, remember what I told you about Amelia Erhardt and what she vowed when she got married? If we're to continue to have an existential relationship we both must accept the foundation of free will and the ability to think, act and be what we truly are!"

Amy looked at me and frowned as I asked, "Why are you frowning?"

"Because," Amy replied.

"Because you're physically attracted to other persons and enjoy their company? Because those people are women? What difference does that make? Two people who have feelings for each other and share each other. What can be more beautiful than that?"

"But you don't…"

"Don't what?" I was getting a little perturbed. "There's no difference, Amy!" I interrupted. "You have your  boundaries and expanded them. I would be a hypocrite if I judged you on that."

"But," I softened my voice and added, "Society, religion and government assume that heterosexuality is the default normal, and therefore, all other sexualities must have been caused by something going awry. Nothing *causes* bisexuality any more than anything *causes* heterosexuality. And to be very clear, nothing went wrong or awry with you because you're bisexual. It's the way God created you and for you it's natural."

I took another deep breath, looked into Amy's eyes and added. "It's not bad! It's not evil! It's simply you. You can't let society, religion, the government or me determine how you feel and, above all else, determine right and wrong. You have a level of freedom that you feel comfortable in and as long as you don't try to force your ways on the unwilling, there's nothing, absolutely nothing, to be ashamed of, embarrassed by or something you need to ever regret. In fact, I've always thought more of you because of it."

"When you...you satisfy those needs, you experience ephemeral things I could never duplicate and now can't even come close to replicating. All I know is that for all these years, you've chosen ME and I will always be profoundly grateful for that. Of all the men and women in the world, YOU CHOSE ME! Instead of half the world, it's the entire world and I'm the one who's lasted forever."

What she'd done before and during our marriage wasn't any of my business. After our wedding, at first I was miffed until I formally accepted her for what she was and vowed to support her. We all have indulgences and proclivities our partner, society, religion or our family would want to change but can't.

I remembered back to our conversation as if it was yesterday. Before marriage! Before kids! Before all the excitement became mundane and offered the same explanation. "Sex is really only touch...the closest of all touch, and it's the touch we're all afraid of. Yet to touch another person can be the most rewarding of all emotions when there's commitment and passion involved. It doesn't matter who the person is as long as both people sincerely care for each other. Now that I can't provide that and readily accept you still have deep-seated needs, I'm setting you free with no anger, frustration or recriminations on my part."

I looked across the aisle again and, in an effort of equanimity, looked deeply into Amy's eyes so that I could feel her soul close to mine and continued. "There'll always be negativity in our world and pushback, just as there are always going to be people out there who chastise our relationship and won't like you or me...people who are talking behind our backs about who we are. Those people really don't matter. It's about whether we like ourselves and love each other. If we like ourselves, nobody else matters. If you love yourself as much as I love you, we're going to continue to live a wonderful life."

My head cocked to one side as I continued. "The world will go on. The weak will fall and, yet, we ...you and I...will still be standing. Our world is, more or less, a fixed thing and externally you and I must adapt ourselves to our changing world and not be frustrated when we can't change the world for us! We can please ourselves or we can please others. Emotions will constantly change ... but our life together will always stand as one!"

I turned and looked out the cabin window at the ocean below. "After all you went through all I can ask is that you stick to living life to the fullest as far as life sticks with you."

I paused and looked back across the aisle at Amy and continued. "Always remember...We must please ourselves because no one else ever will. Because I love you so much, it's what I want you to do... please yourself, with no concern about any potential recriminations from me. I can't totally sense your frustrations. I have no idea what it's like to by half-trapped by consequence. I can only imagine what it's like to have tendencies and urges that you're forced to constrain simply because of society or your concern that I'll be upset or your own sense of self-defined dignity doesn't allow it. As of right now, I give you my word, I won't be upset and it's totally up to you."

Amy looked at me, took a deep breath and responded. "I try. I really, really try to keep those…those feelings out of my life but they're there and no matter how hard I attempt to block them, I can't. I can go days feeling 'normal' and then they come back when my guard is down and simply over-power me and make me feel inadequate and wanting."

Amy continued "He or she doesn't matter to me. Simply put, exquisite doesn't have gender and neither does love. I married you because you're exquisite. Like you, my libido is piqued by those who I see. Unlike you, there's no delineation. I acknowledge I'm attracted to more than one sex - not necessarily at the same time, nor in the same way or the same degree. I've been loyal to you and only you. You're the only man I've been with since the day we met. Sadly, it's only half of me and the other half remains unrequited for which I feel I've always let you down."

I looked out at the ocean again and replied. "I once wrote that rarely can one's soul rise up, gasping through the fathomless fathoms under which we live. I still believe we're all nothing more than fish swimming in the sea, endlessly swimming, as we seek our own true joy in the mucky murk called loneliness. To find someone...if only for an instant...can provide hope that others will allow us to breathe the sweet nectar of acceptance and, yet, through it all you and I have had each other where the gift of yourself to me has been so much more than mine to you. You've completed me and, yet, I know I've never been able to complete you."

Amy's closed her eye as if to shut out reality as I continued. "I've known since we met that I could never provide everything. I've accepted it and done my best. For all these years you've done everything you could to restrain that inherent part of you that's always been there. Now that I've changed, I want to give you the opportunity to complete yourself by removing any reservation you might have so that you do what you need to do, when you need to, with whomever you feel will complete you in a way I never can or could."

"What about my lack of inhibition?" Any inquired.

"Once again, it's something you're comfortable with. You don't flaunt it. You're just ambivalent to it. You're one of the most passionate people I've ever met and is one of the many reasons I fell in love with you. Extreme inhibition can eradicate or impede the desire to make room for passion—to keep your spark and your life-force intact. All the forces of repression, from within and without, can easily rob your vitality if you let them. I've read that repression of the lifeforce is what drives most people into therapy. Inhibition isn't necessarily the enemy and exhibition is certainly not the nirvana where all passions should be acted on. And yet, we all still need inhibition to have a conscience."

"I've known and loved you for over two-thirds of my life. There are days when you're simply incredible in many ways, both good and bad. When we come to Saint Martin I see a different side...someone not so tied-up by propriety and limited by expectation, afraid to be yourself for fear it will have consequence. I've often wondered why you're so much more liberated than at home. I keep coming back to what you once told me about how people would look away when you walked the beach when you came here to die. I began to realize that beneath it all there remain the pain and scars when death wrapped upon your door and you told it to go away. Perhaps, just perhaps, your...uhh...physical liberation is simply a subconscious way of showing the world you didn't die and those who visually rejected you they were wrong...completely wrong."

I looked across the aisle at the tear stained wife who was the love of my life. She asked. "Do you mind?"

I replied. "Not at all and continued. "Hans Christian Andersen told it so eloquently in the story of the ugly duckling. After a mother duck's eggs hatch, one of the ducklings is perceived by the other animals as an ugly little creature and suffers much verbal and physical abuse. She wanders from the barnyard and lives with wild ducks and geese until hunters slaughter the flocks. She finds a home with an old woman but her cat and hen tease and taunt her mercilessly because they say she's different and, therefore, ugly and once again she sets off alone."

"The duckling sees a flock of migrating swans. She's delighted and excited but cannot join them for she's too young and unable to fly. When winter arrives, a farmer finds and carries the freezing duckling home, but she's frightened by the farmer's noisy children and flees the house. The duckling spends a miserable winter alone outdoors mostly hiding in a cave on the lake that partly freezes over."

"The duckling, now having fully grown and matured cannot endure a life of solitude and hardship anymore. She decides to throw herself at a flock of swans feeling that it's better to be killed by such beautiful birds than to live a life of ugliness. She's shocked when the swans welcome and accept her only to realize by looking at her reflection in the water that she had been, not a duckling, but a swan all this time."

"Amy, you are my swan...beautiful, graceful and we share the life-long bond of the swans where both partners play a crucial and fiercely protective role in the upbringing of both their cygnets and their mate to the point that, when they are under threat, they'll use all their might and fight to the death if need be to protect those they love."

I reclined my seat to allow the whitecaps of emotion to gradually calm. Had I gone too far? Had I really meant what I said? When your body and mind are in turmoil, you have a tendency to evoke thoughts and promises that have been sequestered for a very long time. When you feel inadequate you try to make compensations you might not mean. Like a glass shattering on the floor, there was no way of turning back. My only hope was that Amy understood and put everything in perspective. Only time would tell.

Our introspection was broken by the pilot announcing we'd be landing in fifteen minutes. I looked across at Amy who was peering out the window wondering what was going on in her head. We landed and Uncle Frank was there with his infectious smile as we all got in the Rover and headed for the 'Lighthouse'.

"How was the flight?" Uncle Frank asked.

"Fine," I replied.

"How are the kids?"

"Fine," I replied.

"How are you, George?"

"Getting better every day."

Amy rode in total silence.

We made it to the house and took the tram up the hill. It seemed like it had been forever since we were there and, yet, it had only been a few months filled with more than anyone could ever want to happen.

We went to L'Auberge Gourmand for dinner were greeted warmly by Mary and Pasquale and, as always, found it to be spectacular. Sadly, the evening was lifeless, defiled by the abyss created with an offer I really didn't know I meant.

We had our celebratory gourmet breakfast of freshly squeezed orange juice and Frosted Flakes. As afternoon arrived, I got out my tan swimsuit and pulled it on as we were anxious to go down to Orient Beach.

As we were about to leave the house, I sneezed and it happened. They'd warned me and I'd been doing my Kegels but when you sneeze and are using the same muscles for bladder control, accidents can happen. I looked down at the expanding dark spot on the front of my shorts as an embarrassed frown crossed my face.

I looked at Amy as if to ask, "What now?"

Amy looked at me with a mournful grimace as she felt my embarrassment, frustration and anger that had ricochet off me like so many pellets of sadness.

I went back up to our bedroom, opened my dresser, found some old black gym shorts and made my way back downstairs. Not a word was spoken as we got headed for Orient Beach and Melia's famous tag…'Ozone' for clothing optional strip of sand.

We made it down past the big restaurants to the Wilco compound with the sports activity center, Le String and Lucille's. I knew I was no longer impervious to the feared 'dribbles and drips' and needed to buy a dark bathing suit so that, if accidents happened again, it wouldn't show.

We went into Lucille's and her warm magic began. I told her I needed a new bathing suit. Lucille nodded and went to the wicker basket on the floor, pulled out several options and directed me to the dressing 'room' if you wanted to call it that.

I slipped into the suit and tried to pull it up. The inseam was cut to ride as low as possible. The front was cut as narrow as possible. The sides were as thin possible as well. In other words, the only thing covered was *possible* and even that was barely disguised leaving nothing, and I mean nothing, to the imagination, as I thanked myself for maintaining the hardwood floor.

Amy was standing outside the changing room, which also served as the breakroom, storeroom, closet and everything else room and beckoned me out. I slid back the drape and Amy's mouth dropped open and a big smile crossed her face before she began to giggle.

I opened my hands, palms up, as if to ask, 'Well?'.

Amy reiterated, "Well, big boy, I'll certainly know when you're excited to see me."

I laughed for a moment until reality struck. It would probably never happen again. I took a deep breath, caught leave of myself and, with no mirror in the changing room, went to the display area, looked in the mirror where all I could say was, "Oh my God!"

I turned, faced Amy and asked…"What do you think?"

"Everything's covered," Amy replied.

"Barely," I offered as I turned around and realized the word BARELY had a new meaning in the rear.

"What size is it? Amy asked.

"Medium."

"Try on a size small," Lucille urged.

"Are you kidding me?"

"Why not?" as she handed me the same suit but smaller and off I went into the 'changing' closet.

I slipped into the suit and found that, while the cut seemed the same, the suit rode even lower and the drawstring was a little shorter with 'possible' literally *out*. I slightly opened the curtains as Amy's eyebrows arched and she laughed a silly laugh. We'd crossed the line and so it was back to size medium, which was still only one-fourth the coverage I'd ever worn in my life.

There are times in your life when you have to justify the decision you make and this was one of them. I had to make a choice…run around in what I now considered nearly naked or sit at the house and do nothing. What would the folks in Mineral Point think of me now? Wait a minute! I'm not in Mineral, I'm on Saint Martin and it's where the French play and no one, anyway I hoped no one, would care.

Lucille, talked Amy into a little yellow number before we could escape next door for lunch. Between my 'here comes hop-along' and being nearly naked, I thought there would be stares until I saw other guys in literally the same suit and realized, other than the limp, I blended in. We had lunch and several drinks and then a few more drinks until my attire reservations were gone and the motto evolved into 'who cares?'

On Monday, Amy began her daily routine of walking the beach at sunrise and, with no one home, I spent time checking my email and sitting out by the pool. Amy returned and smiled, reminding me about both Shirin Yoku and Mindfulness as we lay catching rays. For lunch, it was back to Orient Bay and lunch at Bikini Beach. I wore shorts. No need scaring the patrons with 'how low can it go' and debasing their gastronomical endeavor.

I really needed to understand why it was that what was once special through repetition became commonplace while what was once commonplace became mundane. I Googled it and found no definitive answer and developed my own social philosophy called *'The Theory of Acclimation'* that simply states 'repetition has a way of taking something unique, special, thrilling, embarrassing or exciting and evolving it lower and lower in terms of being different, exciting, embarrassing or special into something common or even mundane.'

Ask a smoker what they smell like and they don't know, simply because their olfactory lobes negate the smell. Ask a person who lives near an airport about the jets and their auditory senses mentally erase the noise. Visit someone whose house has a spectacular view and, after a few months, sadly the thrill is gone. The same thing can happen wherever something unique – both good and bad – becomes commonplace.

On Tuesday my acclimation set in, my level of braggadocio increased and I no longer felt weird in barely-there. We had lunch at Wai and went back to Le'String where we met a young lady from Paris named Michelle whose husband had just been hired at one of the Dutch hotels. She noted they'd rented one of the condos with the new post-Irma, blue roofs on the north end of Orient beach and said she knew no one.

Michelle was in typical French attire for someone in their twenties or early thirties…baseball cap, oversized sunglasses, bikini and thought nothing of it. She looked at me and smiled. I wondered whether she was thinking my garb was a bit extreme for someone my age or the most liberated man on the beach. Whatever!

Amy looked at Michelle and her brows arched. I knew we'd both found this young lady visually appealing and, after my rant on the plane, internally vowed it wouldn't bother me that Amy did.

On Wednesday morning, I joined Amy with a goal of walking the beach.

Amy began to take off her clothes, looked at me and said, "George, remember how you felt on Sunday? Once you acclimated didn't you see it makes no difference to anyone?  The next step is simply the mental aspect of going naked in public. Once again, this requires a little internal fortitude and willingness to take that first step. Rest assured in fifteen minutes it won't seem like a big deal."

Now, wearing almost nothing is one thing. Wearing nothing…was something else. I shook my head "no" and Amy didn't push it.

I think, out of respect for me, Amy remained attired. I made it about 100 yards and couldn't handle the pain. I let Amy take her walk as I simply sat on one of the lounge chairs the crew was setting for another day in paradise. Amy made it back at 7:55. We went to Good Morning for breakfast, then headed back to the 'Lighthouse'.

"How about tomorrow? Will you try it?" Amy asked.

"Ok. Maybe," I replied with a great deal of trepidation thinking she was referring to walking the beach but wondering if she was inferring being naked.

When we got back to the 'Lighthouse' I Googled public nudity and found out 52% of American respondents said they weren't offended by public nudity if it was socially acceptable and 28% of those who never had, said they'd give it a try under the right circumstances.

It was three and time to go back to the beach for Happy Hour. I looked at my tan swimwear, remembered the pee stain and thought 'forget-about-it' realizing I'd rather have skin showing like so many others than the proverbial pee stain.

Perhaps it was my mindset that I was no longer a man. Perhaps, it was the crazy emotional roller coaster I was going through. Me, the conservative one, evolving, becoming indifferent to who thought what.

We went back to the beach as alcohol and laughter took away any remaining reservations, inhibitions and embarrassment. Michelle was there and the three of us settled in to talk about anything and everything. As the afternoon was ending and it was time to go Michelle mentioned that Claude, her husband, was working the late shift and wondered where a good place was to go for dinner, as she was all alone. Amy looked at me and offered to have Michelle join us at Le' Taitu which was just down the hill from Michelle's condo.

"Is it a long walk?" Michelle inquired. "Claude has the car."

"We'll pick you up," I offered.

"Why don't we go somewhere in Grande Case?" Amy offered.

"Bistro Caribe?" I inquired.

"Great," Amy replied. "We'll call and make reservations."

"Do I need to get dressed up?" Michelle asked.

"No, not at all," Amy replied. "Wear something light and lively."

It's a little over a mile from Le' String to the condos and so we offered to give Michelle a ride back to her condo and that way would know where she lived. While driving Amy called Uncle Frank who made reservations for 7:00 PM. We dropped Michelle off and went back to the 'Lighthouse'.

I jumped in the pool as Amy took a shower and got dressed for dinner. When I got ready and came down to the great room I simply smiled and told Amy she looked nice. We drove to Mont Vernon and arrived at 6:55. Michelle was standing outside, smiled and waved. We went for dinner and both the food and service were impeccable. Two bottles of Pinot Noir evolved and we were all loose as a goose.

Michelle asked where we lived and Amy detailed the 'Lighthouse' and our reasons for building it. Michelle commented that it sounded beautiful. Amy offered to take her on a tour and so we headed for home.

Michelle loved the tram and said it reminded her of skiing in the Swiss alps. I thought it certainly couldn't have been that tall of a mountain and a little rough sledding through all the brush.

I offered to pour us each a nightcap as Amy took Michelle on the house tour. The girls came back and Michelle noted that she'd never seen any house as beautiful as ours. We retired to the deck just as the pool lights clicked on. Amy detailed how the color of the LED lights ranged from red, to gold, green, blue or white and asked Michelle which color she preferred.

Michelle replied, "gold," as Amy asked me to change the lights and I did as requested.

"The water looks like champagne," Michelle observed.

The bottoms of our glasses came quickly as Michelle shared her life story regarding how Claude always wanted to manage a property and this was his big chance. I inquired whether anyone wanted another drink and both reluctantly said yes. To the kitchen I went and poured another one and took them back to the pool.

Amy and Michelle were discussing the weather and Hurricane Mariah and how we'd been here with Reggie and Sam and rode out the storm.

"Are they friends of yours?" Michelle inquired.

"Well, sort of." I offered. "I was in the hospital for an extended period of time and they were one of my nurse teams."

"Oh, my. I hope it wasn't anything serious," Michelle offered.

I wanted to minimize the issue and simply replied. "I had great care and made it."

Amy was feeling no pain as she added. "George almost died. He had 70 blood clots in him."

"Oh, my God!" Michelle responded.

"A close one," I added

Amy continued, "Then he had Cancer and that's why we're here…to celebrate his recovery."

"Cancer?"

"Yes."

I looked at Amy and gave her *the stare* and she knew it was time to stop the discussion. The last thing most men want people to know is that they've been neutered.

The topic became walking the beach and Amy outlined the basic eight o'clock rule and said she tried to go every morning and how it all began when she came to Saint Martin to recover from Leukemia.

Michelle changed the subject by offering. "Your pool looks so inviting. Our pool was destroyed by the hurricane and they said it could be six months before it's replaced. That's the reason we can afford the rent."

"Do you want to go for a swim?" Amy asked.

"I don't have my suit," Michelle responded.

"It's just the three of us. I don't think George will mind, will you?" Amy offered.

After sitting with her at Le' String where she was wearing virtually nothing, I thought 'What the hell?'. I guess she thought the same as Michelle responded. "Well, if you don't mind. Perhaps the water will take away some of the alcohol."

I opened one of the storage areas and took out three towels and went to refill our drinks as Amy and Michelle slipped into the pool.

"Come on George, join us!" Michelle urged.

Instead, I simply joined them and, for the first time, other than in medical situations, found myself naked in front of another woman other than my wife, as we spent the next half hour talking and more importantly, sobering up. What felt strange was the fact it was neither erotic nor embarrassing, it just was to the point within a few minutes, I no longer cared.

"What time do you think it is?" Michelle offered.

"I don't know. I'll go check." Amy replied, stepping out of the pool and walking into the great room, returning to announce it was almost eleven.

"I think I'd better go home. Claude will be coming soon."

"George, why don't you clean up and I'll take Michelle home?" Amy offered.

I wrapped a towel around myself as Amy and Michelle dried themselves off and climbed into their clothes. We went to the door and Michelle gave me Faire La Bise, and offered, "Thank you for a wonderful evening. I get very lonely when Claude is at work."

"You'll have to come again," I offered.

Michelle stepped back, smiled and replied. "I'd like that very much. Perhaps, I'll see you tomorrow."

Amy opened the door and I heard the tram depart as I began putting the glasses in the dishwasher. About a half hour later I heard the tram arriving as Amy walked in.

"Well?" I asked.

"It was a wonderful night. She's such a nice person."

"And?"

"And, what?"

"Well…"

"Nothing. I gave her a ride home and we talked about meeting tomorrow. She's really lonely."

With that, I closed the doors, shut off the lights and we went to bed.

"Goodnight, moon!" I whispered, reflecting back to reading the story to the kids hundreds of times.

In the moonlight, I saw Amy smile as it was my way of telling her I loved her and, yet I wondered what if anything had transpired, somewhat angry with myself for not keeping my airplane promise.

Thursday morning came early and I took a sabbatical from the walk. There certainly was a hitch in my giddy-up. Amy was gone until nearly ten. At first, I didn't think anything of it. When she returned she seemed flustered?

"Are you OK?" I pondered.

"Yes! Why?" was the curt response.

"I don't know, you just seem a little…a little perturbed."

"I'm fine." Amy offered as a scowl of irritation clenched her eyes.

"It's nearly ten o'clock."

"Now you're questioning what time I get back to the house?"

"No! I was just wondering."

An exasperated looked crossed Amy's face as she offered. "I was down by Le' String and ran into Michelle. She was heading for Mont Vernon and we started walking together. When we got to the rocks, she invited me for coffee. What's the big deal?"

"It's not a big deal and I'm sorry I asked," I replied in a tone intended to express my apology.

"Well, I feel like I'm under some kind of microscope."

"Geez! All I did was try to understand why today was so different than any other day. I'm sorry."

"George. You know I don't like being probed."

"Sorry!"

The silence that pervaded allowed for cooler heads. The last thing I wanted or needed was her to get in one of her 'moods'. Not today. Not now! Not under these circumstances.

We spent the morning isolated in our own worlds reading. At one o'clock, cooler heads prevailed and we simply took the tram down the hill to Anse Marcel Beach restaurant. We always felt we needed to limit our visits. If we ate there every day they'd need to send a cargo plane to take me home and my Theory of Acclimation might set in. God that food is great!

At three, we went back to Orient beach with me now totally comfortable in my Lucille attire. There was no sign of Michelle and I really don't know who was more disappointed or relieved, Amy or me.

Dinner was at Astrolab and so we got a little dressed-up with Amy in one of her designer outfits and me in black shorts and a white golf shirt. I wasn't taking any chances.

Friday. Well, to paraphrase Neil Armstrong…"One small strip of cloth from man, one giant leap of faith in his behind." We walked and not a single person gawked and, while still feeling like I was no longer a man, I really wouldn't have cared if they did. Vive Libération!

We made it down to the Mont Vernon end and then back where Amy gave me a hug and whispered "From a caterpillar to a butterfly," as we slipped into our clothes.

We went back for happy hour and Michelle was there but seemed a distant.

"How are you Michelle?" I asked.

"I'm fine," She replied in a somewhat structured way.

"I'm sorry we missed you yesterday afternoon." Amy offered.

"Well, some things came up."

"Would you like to have a drink?" I offered.

"No, thank you."

I went and retrieved drinks for Amy and me and asked for the chaise lounges at the shoreline. I turned to see what looked like and some sort of chilled conversation between Amy and Michelle and felt I'd better let it be between the two of them.

After what appeared to be a break in the action, I approached and announced. "I've reserved the chaise lounges. Would you like to join us, Michelle?"

"Thank you but I've got my chair back there." Michelle responded, pointing over her shoulder to the Ozone. "Would you like to join Giselle and me?"

"I think we'd be intruding, don't you George?" Amy replied.

"Thanks, anyway." I replied as I raised my glass and said "Cheers" while Amy said "À la nôtre vôtre tienne."

Michelle nodded and offered a polite smile and said "Au revoir".

As Michelle walked away I looked at Amy wondering that was all about. Had Amy made the first move or Michelle? Thirty minutes to go from the 'Lighthouse' to Mont Vernon and back again wasn't that long. I then wondered why Amy didn't get home from the beach until nearly ten the next morning and if it was just coffee that transpired. I silently vowed to keep my thoughts to myself. Nothing was offered and so it ended.

We drank our drinks and were heading for the Rover when I saw Michelle and Giselle walking back towards the condos in their typical young-French nearly-nothing attire. Who knows?

We went to L' Piment for dinner and returned early. There was still some wine left from the previous night and it was one of those pristine, cloudless nights where the stars sparkle as we sat out by the pool and simply enjoyed the light show and each other's company.

That night, for the first time, the urge returned but that was it...just an urge!

Amy sensed my disappointment, frustration and embarrassment and gently kissed me on the cheek. As my eyes closed, I slid my arm beneath Amy's head and we both fell into a deep sleep as I dreamt of being a man...a man that I am...NOT!

The six days had zoomed by. Amelia[X] was sent to pick us up. The respite from all that had transpired did us both good, even though, once again, the vacation was too short. On the plane home Amy looked at me and inquired, "Were you serious about our discussion on the way down?"

I thought for a moment and nodded in the affirmative.

"What if I don't want to?"

"You're free to do whatever you want, with whomever you want."

"I want to be with you." Amy replied "You and only you."

I smiled and thanked God for understanding. Unless you've been there and suffered from post-surgical depression, you have no idea all that goes through your mind - the anger, fear, frustration, humiliation and embarrassment - they're all there, like some sort of emotional stew that boils over and sticks to the stove in a dark circle of regret. In six days, my wife had attempted to show me it wasn't the end, just the beginning of a new and different chapter. I was grateful but still despondent.

**Peek Sneaking:**

The following Tuesday, I went to see Megan for a follow-up. I was prepared for the ritual...Kegels, pain in the butt, hygiene and how to pick the right penis pump. Megan had been on vacation the same week we were. I showed up and waited my turn and she walked in all golden brown.

"Down with the pants," She instructed.

I offered to take off my shirt too but she said no.

As she bent over to check my legs for swelling, I got a peek all the way down the front of her smock. She didn't have a bra on or tan lines! My God.

"Nice tan!" she commented.

"You, too," I replied, wanting to add 'No tan lines for either of us', but afraid to let her know I'd sneaked a peek. Dirty old man!

"Where'd you go? I asked.

"Jamaica, man!" was her reply.

"Where'd you stay?"

"A place called Hedonism Two."

I'd heard about the place and offered in a very poor British accent..."*A four-star lifestyle-friendly, clothing-optional resort that offers guests an adult playground experience that's famous for its lascivious living.*"

"You got it," Megan said with a smile.

It's not what I would have guessed. Yet, after what she did for a living, I realized she was more liberal than I thought.

"Wanna see my lack of tan lines?" I jokingly ask.

Megan smiled at my bravado and inquired, "Did you get tan all over?"

"Our house on Saint Martin is very private and Amy even convinced me to walk the beach with her."

"So your hang-ups evaporated?"

"Guess so."

"It happens to a lot of my patients. Some go overboard, but most begin to accept it's just skin."

"Well, do you or don't you?" I cajoled.

"What?"

"See my lack of tan lines."

"That's OK", Megan said, smiling, accepting that it was becoming another private joke.

"Darn! I've been wanting to show someone all week. I tried at the airport but security was there. You know, boney butts are off limits."

Her exam was done and it was time to change the subject as she told me to wait. I wondered where was I supposed to go with my pants hanging on a hook?

Megan returned with two pumps and told me she needed to make sure they fit properly.

"You mean they come in different sizes?" I ask incredulously.

"Small, medium and large."

I was afraid to ask which size she brought thinking that if I was running the marketing department, I'd have them labeled large, extra-large and jumbo for psychological reasons.

Megan proceeded to show me how they worked and I was certainly glad I left those inhibitions at the front desk. I was instructed to slide the pump on and began squeezing the ball, of the pump that is.

"Tell me when it's getting uncomfortable"

A few weeks ago, I wouldn't have been thinking about something like this, now she wants me to tell her when to stop as my you-know-what begins to grow.

She smiles. "You're a grower, not a showier!" which put a little swagger in the old two-step.

My you-know-what got ginormous…anyway for me, it was!

Megan deflated it…the pump that is, along with my ego…slid it off and put what looked like a rubber band around the base! Hello!

"You can leave this on for up to thirty minutes" Megan offered.

"I don't think I'll be able to button my pants" I replied.

Before she could say another word I added, "Besides, there aren't any people out in the waiting room, I'm that excited to see."

Now, she had a real smirk on her face.

I'm standing there 'at attention,' as she said, "This is what you can do with your wife."

I asked in all earnest, "Where do I put the rubber band on her?"

Another wry smile, shaken head and then, "Smart ass!"

"What do you know about how your penis works?" she asked.

Like any typical guy. I had no idea.

She proceeded to point out all the different parts and what's called the frenulum that would still send electricity through my body.

"Oh my God!" I'm thinking to myself.

She was cool as I asked. "What's that?"

"It's a man's version of the clitoris." She replied. "It's your pleasure center."

"You mean I don't need to go to McDonalds anymore?"

Megan just shook her head and, in a very professional tone, she instructed, "It's where all the sympathetic nerve endings are. When you had your prostate removed, the nerves affected were only the parasympathetic ones that allow blood to flow into the corpus cavernosa, which are literally fleshy caverns in your penis that create the erection. The sympathetic nerves remain intact and allow for neural pleasure and orgasms."

"Parasympathetic? Sympathetic?" I repeat.

"The best way to remember is - parasympathetic represents point" as her index finger extended out like the barrel of a gun, "sympathetic equals shoot," as she lifted her thumb and blew the end of her index finger like cowboys did in old movies.

She smiled and asked…"You get the picture?"

"Point and shoot!" I took my right index finger and aimed it at her and said "point" then blow on the end and said "shoot" while realizing – or at least hoping - there could still be some physical gratification in my life and regretting I didn't have the lesson before we went to Saint Martin.

Megan instructed me to undo the rubber band and practice as she left the room to meet with another patient. For fifteen minutes, I repeated the process – pump up/down, pump up/down, band/on, band/off - until I had it down, or would that be up?

There was a knock on the door and Megan returned.

"Are you getting the hang of it?" she asked.

Once again, I thought it was the wrong choice of words as I stood there, smiled and shrugged in disbelief. She had absolutely no trepidation and went about her business as if I'd been trying on shoes.

"Do you want the battery-operated or the hand pump version?" she asked.

"What's the difference?" I inquired.

"About $300" she replied.

"For $300, I can give myself a hand job instead of having the machine do it for me." I replied with the double entendre well in place.

We were done for the day and so I got dressed. As I was about to walk out with my new friend, - the pump that is, - a wry smile crossed my face. I stopped, turned, looked back at Megan, stuck out my index finger, raised my thumb and said "Pow" while pretending to blow smoke from its end, and laughed.

Not to be outshined, my outlandish friend stopped in her tracks, laughed and repeated my motion, blowing smoke as well. I don't know who giggled the most as we both grinned at our private joke while I returned to reality and a new secret code intended for whenever we met.

As I was walking to my car I realized my transformation. Something that was so…personal and embarrassing a few weeks ago, had been professionally addressed in a manner that left me at ease.

Thanking Amy and Megan for reducing my inhibitions, I realized it was just another day for Megan to be quickly forgotten by the next man up, as our lives moved on.

## And the Results Are….:

Life comes in segments. From youth to adulthood, middle age and then being a 'senior citizen'. Along the way, you're supposed to acquire things to do when you get old. Never having been a hunter, fisher or camper, my world revolved around travel and work and travel for work. Ideally, you and your spouse have some common likes or interests. When you don't and all your friends are work-related, one certainly does become the loneliest number.

Once you have *one of those 'moments'* when life hangs by a thread, your world changes and with it, your focus. Gone are the assumptions as you look at a blank calendar and fill in the spaces with doctor appointments intent on keeping you live.

When you don't hunt, fish, or camp and can't travel, you need something besides the tick/tock, tick/tock of the mantel clock to look forward to. My initial goal was to simply write my philosophy of life, which I hope I'm doing. In the meantime, I started posting notes in my appointment book concerning all my doctor schedules which, in retrospect, has provided insight into my emotional state as I navigate from cancer patient to cancer clear and then survivor.

*Friday, the 13th…Great day for a critical test…what was I thinking? I had my PSA blood work done. I guess, deep down I was terrified that the surgery didn't work and there were rogue Cancer cells multiplying within my body. So here I was…a grown man living in fear of a simple blood test, scared to death the PSA comes back greater than zero!*

Amy is working more now than she did before she retired. She's gone when I get up and is rarely home for dinner. One is certainly the loneliest number.

*April 17….The results came back…I got a call from Thompson's office saying my PSA came back at 0.1 and panicked! "Oh my God, the end is near! Go pick out your best suit. You can't be cremated because they are afraid you'll start a fire with all the alcohol in your system." 0.0 would be perfect. 0.1 doesn't sound like much. But as I soon learned anything above zero could mean something is still in there! The question that strikes fear into your heart and soul then becomes…At what PSA level does it indicate there's been a recurrence of Cancer?'*

I went to the Internet and sought reliable sites and this is what I learned…The key element I had to remember was...  regardless of what my initial PSA had been, just because I won the battle the war was NOT over. I need to keep track of my PSA and do so at frequent intervals.

***April 20:*** *Having the numbers and relying on the Internet created an emotional maelstrom where I was certain rogue cells were already banding together for the next onslaught. I visited the doctor's office and quietly - which for me is virtually impossible - sat in the examining room, alone…immersed in my fear…0.1!…Oh my God, what happened?*

*This wonderful man walked in with a big smile on his face. "You had a GREAT report," he said.*

*I looked at him and responded 0.1 meant that I was on the threshold of recurrence at which time the tears welled in my eyes and he realized I wasn't kidding. He saw I was as serious as a heart attack and quickly reported that I'd missed the key element…<0.1…"LESS THAN 0.1". Life is good! He gave me his shoulder to cry on and the tears flowed! Tears of joy! Tears of profound relief! Tears of exceptional gratitude for finding my malady early, directing me to act promptly and visit Doc Thompson...for being kind, considerate and compassionate… and for simply being a wonderful man who's helping me retain and sustain my life for which I will always be grateful.*

***June 16*** *– Graduation from physical therapy. My hamstring still hurts and 'it' won't grow without the pump. All I do is give Megan a hug and thank her for all her help. She comments, "Hang in there."*

I reply, "That's the last thing I want it to do".

***June 30th*** *- As the days evolved into weeks and then months, the paramount 'operational' issues that permeated my psyche began to dull.* I'm beginning to wonder about my wife. She's never home and when I bring up going to Saint Martin, she changes the subject.

*August 10*...*Another milestone! Time for that all-important, six-month check up with Doctor Goodman! The six-month check is the biggie! If there were rouge cells, they would have multiplied and begun showing up. They say there's as much trepidation about the six-month exam as there was having the surgery. Trust me, there is! Why? Because you know so much more than you did going into the tunnel.*

*August 14*...*The weekend was over and what were once my fingernails consisted of a few chewed stumps! I guess I was nervous! After waiting all day, I got the call....PSA is still less than 0.1....HOORAY! Hoots and hollers in my car as I was driving home! Time to celebrate! Yahoo!*

*August 15*...*I meet with Doc Thompson and savor the moment. Things are looking good. All quiet on the fearsome front until he tells me he needs to see me in four months. Man! This guy can take you down lower than a snake in a wheel rut. Twenty-one hours of joy and then back into the world of fear. December 12, come and see me again. It takes ten years to be considered a survivor!*

So, six months were over! What was once thought to be nothing more than 'a little' operation has turned into a life changing set of circumstances. Unless you never have had Cancer, and I hope you haven't, you have no idea how tone word can change your life.

*December 12: Time for the proverbial "check-up" which consists of Doc Thompson filling in his computer report.*

- *Yes...No...Yes...No...Yes...Maybe!*
- *It's like Christmas and you already know what's in the box.*
- *Are you feeling good? Yes!*
- *Are you peeing in your pants? No*
- *Are you getting over your depression? Some of the time!*
- *Is your dick getting hard? No!*

- *Do you want it to?  Obviously! Yes!*
- *Do you want to stick a needle in your dick?*
- *Are you f---ing kidding me? No!!!!!!!*
- *Let's give it a few more months with the bathtub gin!*

You get to his waiting room and look around and all that's there are old guys. The receptionist is simply super. Her left handedness shows her attitude... simply funny and she makes you feel welcome all the way! Of course, they call it a waiting room because that's exactly what you're going to do. You wonder how many other guys have 7:45 appointments. You strike up idle conversation with the guy next to you about traffic, weather and even property taxes.

I guess when you learned to whisper in a saw mill, the other old guys - Beltones and all - are listening in. Not long before one of the elderly gets up and walks over and sits RIGHT, and I mean RIGHT next to me. Our arms are touching. Yuk!

He's alone and lonely and wants into the conversation! Weather – traffic - the government! Yup - all the way! Then he asks the question - "What are you here for?" It sounded like a newbie in prison!

I told him a prostatectomy! He asks what my Gleason's were. I say, "Jackie" and he doesn't crack a smile and so I tell him the truth and he corrects me. "Can't be that." You would think he was writing a fricking book and not me!

He asks what my PSA is and I tell him, 'Less than 0.1'

He says, "Mine was that and then went through the roof. Now I've got bladder Cancer and I'm on...some fancy drug, whatever you call it and I'm going to die!"

If I could get it hard with relief (don't worry, there's a happy ending to this story) before I met this guy, it would have puckered and hid from sight. What a way to start the day... feeling good before this clown decides to take you down to his level of oblivion! Merry Christmas! I hope that the coal Santa brings you is used as an enema!

Back to the good doctor! I'm studying everything I can on the Internet because I can't find out about what I want to know anywhere else and I have questions. However, at $500 per hour they'd better be brief as he has a whole bunch of other old guys to ask yes – no – yes - no questions to.

He answers my questions that I...yes, inquisitive I find out that I'm  the first ever to ask if the nervous structure on both sides of the prostate are the same...I'm the first ever to bring a nerve response schematic that outlines the entire neural structure of the reproductive system... "just remember...point and shoot!"

He's cool, until he says, "See me in three months."

I thought it was going to be six! Shit! Now what?

Between the waiting room scrooge and three months, the euphoria is gone...zip, zero, zilch! I did score 60 days of Cialis on the way out the door, which covers the co-pay of the visit. Put the emotions back in the zip lock bag! Hide those fears buddy boy! Another 90 days until the next round!  Will the tension ever end?

***January 31***...*Happy Anniversary…One year down. I hope a lot more to go. The day never meant anything before. Now it's branded into my psyche as the day they took my sex away…and probably saved…or at least, extended my life.*

*While some would look at the day with anger, remorse or fear, I looked at it as just another day…a milestone…a mini event in the remainder of my life. Having taken it upon myself to learn more than 99.9% of all non-medical people on earth I think, I believe I have a better perspective on what happened, what's happening and what might happen.*

Learning can be liberating…liberating of the fear, trepidation and anxiety that comes from simply not knowing. They say that the second greatest motivator is fear...the greatest motivator is hope! Right now, I working on the greatest one. The day passed without incident. One down and nine to go!

For this first time in a long, long time, I have started thinking about long term goals instead of short-term objectives! For the first time, in a long, long time, thoughts of demise are becoming secondary instead of primary! For the first time in a long, long time assumptions of good have begun to erode fears of bad!

I guess I'm tired of sitting home alone. I call Wilco and arrange for a flight to Saint Martin. I make it to the 'Lighthouse' and it seems quiet and empty when you're all alone. I last four days and then head home. I guess I'd rather have communal cold than solitary sunshine.

***March 6…*** *It's almost 8:00 PM. The phone rings and I wonder who's calling me at night. I reach for the phone and it stops ringing. I look to see who it was….the doctor's office! Fear pummels me, knocking the wind out of my gut. I MUST know and yet fear the worst.*

*I return the call and get the receptionist. I ask for the nurse. She comes on with her always pleasant way to tell me that my PSA was, once again, less than 0.1…negligible!*

I have yet another respite from the grim reaper! The pressure begins to subside! The spring begins to uncoil and I shudder with relief. Deep, staccato breaths reduce the tension with each repetition. I lean against the kitchen counter and close my eyes as tears trickle down my cheeks and thank God for the respite. It takes nearly an hour for the tension to leave my body. In sixty minutes the pressure subsides, the breathing returns to normal and thoughts again focus on tomorrow instead of yesterday.

***June 13…****I have the urge to stop in and say hello to my favorite physical therapist. I walk in and there's a new receptionist. I ask if my friend is available and am informed she's relocated to Atlanta. Huh?* Amy and I have another disagreement about her working too much. She tells me Derrick needs her help. I feel isolated. Shit!

***September 16…****All clear. PSA less than 0.1 and the questions are the same…Yes! No! Yes! No! Yes!. Watch your weight and see me in six months. Whew! Good until the next time.*

You can only spend so much time alone until you begin talking to yourself. The sad part is, I've begun answering and actually arguing as well. This isn't what I want out of retirement. I think of Reggie and her Experientialism and find myself envious."

"One truly is the loneliest number when you're a captive in your own home where facades of contentment build walls of isolation. I think about the lady across the lake sitting by her pool all summer and wish it wasn't getting cool. Now I'll have nothing to peek at and wonder if she's as lonely as I am.

*October 19… I'm in France. I leave my phone on and during the night I get a phone call. It's my doctor's office, telling me to call them. A cold chill fills my room and my mind is rampant with fear. I attempt to call back and get a recording. "We're closed for the day and will be for the next five days". My confidence is shattered like a delicate glass upon the floor! It seems almost imperceptible to think that confidence can evaporate by such a profound magnitude based on a very few meaningless words. For five days I ponder what is wrong! Why have they called?*

*October 24… I call the doctor's office as soon as it opens to learn there was a billing error and they had a question. Five days of fear! Five days of trepidation! Five days of wondering what in hell is going on, only to learn that it was a billing question. I do my best not to rip the proverbial head off the young lady on the other end. My vow of tolerance grabs holds of my anger and I indicate what the five days had been like, reporting that two years previously they had called to tell me I had Cancer. She was profoundly sorry…almost to tears! I told her that this was between her and me as long as she promised that the next time she called a patient she noted she was from the billing department. She agreed. Case closed! Fear subsides but the white caps upon my mind still did not subside. God, what a state of emotional existence. Confidences shot by a simple phone call. Two down! Eight to go!*

I spend time with our gardener and get rip roaring drunk. I stagger home and fall into bed. At least I have a pillow to hug.

*February Year Two: Time to make the appointments. First the blood work, then the urologist. The tension spring begins its slow, tortuous wind…tighter, tighter, tighter.*

***April 11...****A few drops of blood in a tube! The spring begins to override my emotions. Fear! Trepidation! Been there! All initial indications should be consistent and yet the fear is there.*

I spend my days wondering where has time gone. I await Amy's return from work with both anticipation and anxiety, not knowing what kind of mood she'll be in. Will she smile and make me feel as if she's glad to see me or will it be the now persistent glare of inconsequence I seem to be to her.

***April 15...****The entire day is spent waiting for the phone call. At 6:09 PM it comes. "All results are good." The spring begins to unwind! Zzzzzzz! (sound of spring unwinding. ) It takes several minutes of deep breathing and thanking God before I can walk, talk or think. The same routine as before and the same results and, yet the pressure is still the same.*

I'd like to celebrate. Sadly, there's a text telling me she's delayed. I sit and eat a can of pork and beans. I like them. Amy doesn't. They're my treat.

***April 19...*** *For the first time in a month, the pressure is gone. I feel alive! A respite for another five months! Thank you God! With each day, with each week, with each month, with each year, my confidence grows! I'm still here! I still have a long way to go but by God, I'm not in an urn sitting on the closet shelf!*

I want to go out and celebrate, Amy says she's got meetings and won't be home early. I'm beginning to wonder if my 'release' has motivated her to find someone a little more exciting than an old man sitting home watching his hair turn gray.

There's something about solitary confinement that has a way of warping reality. I always remembered that farmers seem to have a tendency of being that way simply because they're alone so much. As I sat and commiserated about my fate, I began to think of how life was passing me by. As I perused the internet an article regarding tattoos caught my eye.

I learned that 26% of American adults have at least one tattoo. The most common age group for people is 18-34, with 40% of this age group having at least one. I wondered what it would be like if I had one. My wife has one as does my daughter. I learn that the most popular design is a flower located  on the arm or wrist. What surprised me was only 10% regret getting theirs.

When you've almost died and then had prostate Cancer and are in an age group beyond the 30's...ok, make that 50's, I wonder if I should get one myself. I decide it's something I want. I had to decide what and where. When you've survived Cancer, you begin to recognize and respect the zodiac sign and, at first, I thought that was what I wanted. Then I began to feel it was too generic and so I took the international symbol for men which is the circle with a plus sign attached, began to play around and created a symbol for prostate Cancer. The logic being, it's a type of Cancer that only affects men. In the end, I developed....

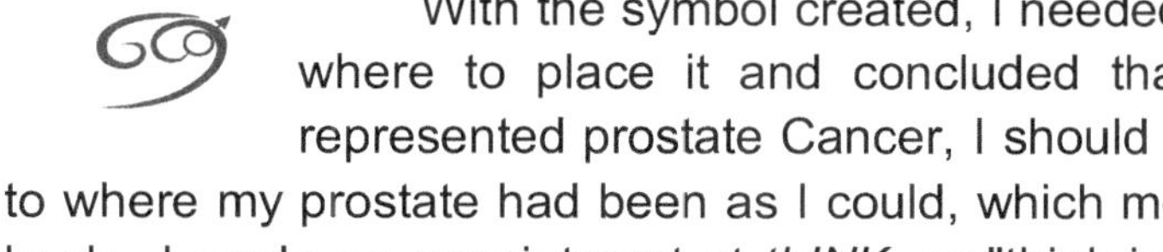 With the symbol created, I needed to determine where to place it and concluded that, because it represented prostate Cancer, I should put it as close to where my prostate had been as I could, which meant my lower back.  I made an appointment at *thINK*  or "think ink" in Delafield and had it done without ever conferring with Amy.

Was I crazy? I don't think so! I just wanted something to remind me of my condition. As the ink dried and tape removed, I waited until what I thought would be the right time to show Amy while somewhat reticent about her reaction.

It was nearly nine when Amy got home, exhausted, flustered and in no mood for anything except a stiff drink. I poured her three fingers of Terrill Bourbon and handed it to her.

"I've got something to show you."

"What's that?" Amy inquired with a pensive look on her face.

"I hope you won't mind."

Now the look was one of concern as I took off my shirt and turned around. Amy looked, realized I'd been inked and questioned. "What is it?"

"A tattoo."

"Gee, no kidding!"

"I created the design?" I proudly report.

"You did?"

"Yes."

"Well, it's really unique. What does it mean?"

"It's the symbol of Cancer and men...in other words... *'men's Cancer'* or prostate Cancer."

Amy nodded and smiled before offering. "I never thought you'd do it."

"Do you like it?"

"I think it's great. You're strong enough, brave enough and man enough to wear a badge of courage and I'm proud of you for doing it."

"You don't mind?"

"Hardly! I think it is what you needed to write the final chapter in your transition."

"No one's going to see it." I offered.

"That's up to you." Amy replied. "It's your body and making a statement is quite noble."

I was relieved as it allowed me to make a statement to myself that I wasn't a victim, just a participant, not someone who'd lost something, but gained a new sense of being I could share with those I wanted to.

**Surprise, Surprise:**

June 11th, the phone rings…ring-ring, ring-ring, ring-ring. You get the idea. The area code is 404…Atlanta. Normally a robo call but I pick up.

"Hello!" I offer.

There's a pause on the other end and then, "How's the hardwood floor?"

It's Megan. I smile and spend the next hour learning all about life in the south. The topic arises about what all I'd learned. I mention I'm planning on writing a book on men's reproductive health.

June 17th, it's Megan again. "Heh, Hardwood, how would you like to come to Atlanta and make a presentation to wives of men who are about to have their prostates removed.

I pause.

Megan adds. "We'll pay $1,000 plus expenses."

Gee, things just got interesting.

I reply. "I will, if you donate the money to cancer research."

On August 12th I fly to Atlanta, am picked up at the Dekalb-Peachtree Airport and make my way to the clinic. I walk in and am greeted by the receptionist and given the magical mystery tour of one of the largest urological practices in America.

We end up at a door that has one of those push-button key locks on it. My tour guide indicates it had been the medical supply storeroom until Megan converted it into a classroom. The guide presses some buttons and the lock releases. She opens the door and turns on the lights. The room is small and yet comfortable but has no window. My claustrophobia begins to kick in. Against the long wall and away from the door is a large monitor. Below it is a long table and next to it a podium that has a laptop on it. There are landscape photos on the walls and six chairs set in a classroom style.

The tour guide excuses herself and indicates Megan would be there in a few minutes. I examine the room and it has Megan's imprint all over it, tidy with nothing out of place. To take a former storeroom and turn it into a classroom meant that was the way it had to be.

A few minutes of silence goes by and Megan walks in, points her finger giggles and says, "Pow".

I raise my right hand, point my finger and go "Pow" in return and giggle as well.

Megan's changed for the better. More professional or make that cosmopolitan I guess. Gone is the plain brown hair replaced by light brown with blonde highlights. As she smiles, I see the results of having her teeth whitened. Not too white but enough to make them radiant. Remembering her in scrubs it was nice to see her in a cream-colored pantsuit that emphasized her summer tan while covering a white silk blouse discretely unbuttoned, but not too far, all emphasized by a thin gold necklace, matching earrings and black pumps.

I smile and offer, "You look great. I mean, really great."

Megan smiles and says, "Thank you. How are you doing?"

"I'm fine." I reply in a somewhat discordant way.

Megan senses there's more and probes. "Really?"

"Yes, sure!" I lie.

"How are things at home?"

She's hit the hot button.

Right now, I just don't know, Amy's never home and when she is, she's like a stranger...so distant...making me so alone."

"Have things changed since...well you know, since the procedure?" Megan inquires.

"Yes!" I forlornly reply.

"I'm sorry."

"It's tough being alone all the time...literally a stranger in the company and foundation that defined who I was."

Again Megan offers her condolences.

"I have my writing and that's about it." I offer, almost as a form of confession. "The kids have their lives and when they call, they talk to Amy. I feel like a spectator and not a participant in this thing called life."

Megan glances at the wall clock and points to a light gray plastic tub on the table containing a set of navy-blue scrubs and indicates I should put them on.

"What?"

"Well, George, it will make you look more…uhh…official and if we need to show or demonstrate anything, it'll be easier than wearing regular street clothes."

I finally see the logic and ask her where I can change.

Megan says, "How about right here? It's just you and me and there's nothing I haven't seen before."

Gulp. Years have ways of rebuilding modesty but I do as directed. Megan pays little attention while preparing for the class.

Because of the limited room size and Megan's attention to detail I knew that having street clothes piled anywhere was against her nature.

"I'll be right back," Megan reports as she takes the tub with my clothes and offers, "I'll put these in my office."

Megan returns and it's now thirty-minutes before 'show time' and I've got some notes prepared.

Megan, has a different idea. "You've never been too bashful, why not just show them what this is all about?"

"Huh?" When we were just one-on-one it was one thing. In front of a group, that's something else. A strange feeling begins to override my enthusiasm.

"I'll be the moderator and we can go through the basics, procedures, results and consequences," she replies.

"Basics?" I ask.

"Anatomy and physiology" she replies. "All of the attendees have signed the same affidavit you did outlining the presentation and what's included and have accepted the content matter. The document is very specific and no one should be surprised by what they see or hear."

I really never examined the agreement and now understand it's probably going to be a lot more explicit than I thought. I realize I can't back out.

I've agreed to the meeting, flown to Atlanta, have a group of ladies whose spouses are about to go through what I did, who've all signed the document that outlines the contents of the meeting to which I reluctantly think...'Sure, why not'? Ahh to be in show business!

The ladies finish their tour of the facilities and enter the room at precisely four. There are six of them, all in their fifties or sixties and casually dressed. Megan introduces me as simply 'George' and informs them I was previously one of her patients.

Megan goes through the prostate cancer statistics. Twenty-five percent Caucasian, forty percent African American, fifteen percent Asian and it's the second most common form of men's cancer there is. When caught early enough it's highly treatable. Megan goes through all four stages and then outlines the fact that cancer recovery is measured in three phases.

Phase One: Immediate belief that all the cancer cells have been removed.

Phase Two: Five years, when you're considered cancer clear.

Phase Three: Ten years when you're classified as a cancer survivor.

We spend the next hour doing show-and-tell and going over all the basics as Megan goes through the power point with graphic images of the entire male anatomy. Not being used to photos of naked men with large, erect penises makes me a bit uncomfortable and feeling a bit inadequate...make that quite! For Megan, it's just another day at the office.

Megan gets past the physical stuff and into the physiological aspect. Topics such as the function of the parasympathetic and sympathetic nerves and the actual penile structure including the frenulum and corpus cavernosa, that would have been embarrassing a few years ago, become nothing more than clinical statements.

Next, Megan shows a short video of the robot and how it works and finally the five surgical consequences...impotence, erectile dysfunction (ED), penile length shortening (PLS), weight gain and stress that could lead to post-traumatic stress disorder (PTSD).

I do my best to make my interjections humorous, even though it's a life-changing scenario in a lot of ways. We urge the ladies to make certain their husbands understand the fact that, even though the incisions are small, this is a major operation. Megan also warns them that not following the timetable in terms of physical activity could risk immediate life-threatening and permanent damage that may minimize any chance of full functional recovery.

Finally, it's time to go into the post-operative procedures that all male patients need to partake in and the formal presentation comes to a climax. (*Sorry I couldn't resist*)

Megan begins with, "We've covered the anatomy and physiology and how the system works, reviewed the pre-op, operating and post-op procedures and I wonder if you have any questions.

"How big are the scars? Lady Number One asks.

Megan suggests I show them.

I take off my scrub top and the ladies are somewhat confused by the fact the scars are barely visible.

Megan looks at me, holds up a medical Sharpie and I nod approval. She takes the marker and 'draws' where the incisions were made along my rib cage.

The ladies are all surprised by how small the incisions are and laugh when I do my very poor muscle flexing imitation of the Hulk.

Lady Number Three asks about the pre-surgical preparation as she seems to have a high level of consternation. I remember back to the shock when the girl came in and did her...uhh...alterations.

Megan offers. "Even though most procedures incorporate the minimally invasive laser, standard surgical protocol requires necessary steps for all possible situations which means being prepared for any and all complications. The robotic procedure being planned has been done over two-thousand times by our surgeons such that it includes the **VERY slight** chance there will need to be a full incision called a radical retropubic prostectomy. I want to emphasize that the preparation is a standard *just in case* procedure and doesn't represent anything more than that.

There seem to be frowns about retropubic. Megan asks whether I'd be willing to show where the incision would be if I'd had a radical retropubic procedure.

I hesitate and slide my scrub bottoms down as far as possible as she draws a line from just below my navel to the top of what's still hiding. There's a surprised look in the faces of all the ladies.

Mouths drop open as the sixth lady hesitatingly asks. "Why have you… uhh…you know, remained so…uhh…bare?"

Megan responds. "After surgery, there will be a period of four to six months of gradually improvement from urinary incontinence because bladder control switches from the prostatic sphincter to the perineal muscles. Even after the adjustment, there can be urinary leakage."

"Some patients find that the cuticle of their hair is too permeable and the net result is that it absorbs all types moisture resulting in hygienic issues. By electing to remove the hair, you eliminate the potential problem. It's totally up to the patient. It's private, personal and beyond any stigma formerly associated with the choice."

I add, "I happen to be one of those individuals. At first, I was somewhat embarrassed and then, as I got used to it, I realized it didn't matter, validated by the fact I no longer have the issue I was having."

Magen adds, "As a social animal, we all have a series of parameters that create how we judge others. The big three are sight, sound and smell. Too tall, too short, too thin, too fat…too loud, too sharp of laugh…too strong of body odor."

"When you meet someone who smokes, you can smell it but they can't. Why? It's called olfactory fatigue where their brain cancels out the smell of cigarettes. The same thing can happen with the smell of stale urine. When it happens, the colloquial term is 'wino syndrome'. The person's olfactory lobes have adjusted and, yet they have a strong odor about them."

The ladies all nod in agreement as it appears each one has a person or an instance when it's happened to them.

I retake the presentation. "No one wants to smell like they peed their pants, especially if they can't smell it themselves. It's really frustrating when you take a shower and the smell's still there. Megan and I discussed this when I was her patient and tried everything from different types of shampoo and conditioners to even tomato juice and nothing worked. Finally, the decision was made to simply remove the hair for hygienic purposes.

I pause for a moment to allow the thought to be considered and then continue. "At first it seemed weird and then, as time went by and articles written about trends in male grooming, I'm no longer reticent about what I've done, especially when I know that, had I not been willing to show you, you'd never known."

There's a pause and then it's Lady Number Six again. "So you…uhh…shave every day?"

I reply in a clinical tone. "There are five ways. First, you can use a razor. Second, you can use a chemical depilatory. Third, you can have them waxed. Fourth, you can have electrolysis. Finally, you can have them permanently removed with a laser. They all have advantages and disadvantages."

Lady Number Five asks, "So you remove ALL the hair?"

I reply. "Yes, I have very permeable hair and it's necessary."

"Should our husbands do that?" Lady Number Three inquires.

Megan interjects, "The pre-op removal will do the inguinal area. The balance is up to the individual and duration can be for hygienic or cosmetic reasons."

Lady Number Six smiles, looks at me, raises her eyebrows and bashfully admits. "I shouldn't say this but I do like the look," to which the entire female ensemble nods in the affirmative with smiles and raised eyebrows.

I look at the lady and seriously ask why she *shouldn't* say it. I add "if you don't add moral support, your husband will be embarrassed or ashamed, which will do nothing more than extend the depth or duration of his depression. Remember, he's going through a really rough period in his life. He's been told he has cancer, then told he has to have surgery. Finally, he realizes that, other than time, the one subliminal thing that all living beings have in common is being removed and even though the urges are there, the cold reality is, there's nothing he can do about it and he's reminded time and time again that the one and only thing that allowed him to realize his masculinity no longer works. For the longest period I no longer considered myself to be a man…just a eunuch whose purpose in life had changed and with it my own self-concept and sexual identity."

Lady Number Five askes, "What does your wife think about this?"

I look down at the floor and contemplate my response. "My wife is a cancer survivor. She had Leukemia when she was in college and lost so much weight she was down to around seventy pounds. With all the prodding and poking she went through and so many people uncomfortably looking at her simply because she was considered anorexic, she became liberated and is actually the one who urged me to follow the regimen I've chosen."

Lady Number Six. "Any regrets?"

"Not doing it sooner."

I stop, take a drink of water and continue. "Because we're here in a clinical setting and I committed to share virtually everything, you got to see another side of me…a personal thing that helped me reduce my stress level by eliminating one potential social stigma."

"Under normal circumstances it's a private, personal matter no one knows about and I no longer have the condition I had before. We all have enough stress in our lives than to worry about smelling like a wino and stress can kill, not only in terms of elevated blood pressure and lost sleep but as a carcinogen, as well."

Megan changes gears and begins to outline the post-op exercises that need to be incorporated. She outlines Viagra and Cialis and massage therapy and why the increased blood flow can speed up the recovery process. She then begins to outline attempts to regain sexual function and discusses the fact that the parasympathetic nerves are literally the diameter of a human hair with the consistency of wet Kleenex. I know that Megan has added this to soften the blow regarding the highly probable ED situation.

Megan begins reiterating how the system works and how the parasympathetic nerves actually are the key to increased blood flow to the corpus cavernosa showing a diagram of regions of penile tissue that become hardened when filled with blood. She notes that after a radical prostectomy there's a heightened probability the nerves will not function properly and will result in the loss of erectile rigidity. Megan then notes that, like any of the part of the body, failure to stimulate the area will result in atrophy, thereby, reducing not only the size, but the probability of any post-operative functionality.

Megan states, "The objective is to regain blood flow to the corpus cavernosa." She outlines the chemical options and injections. She looks at me and notes they should be integrated with the post-operative use of what's called a penis pump that creates a vacuum to increase blood flow to the area.

She continues. "Research shows this type of therapy helps regain sexual function and retain penis length after a radical prostatectomy, especially for men who use it in the weeks immediately after surgery. It's not clear which treatment – or combination of treatments – is best. However, our surgeons and therapists recommend using a penis pump along with ED medication."

Megan produces a penile pump from beneath the podium that looks like a clear cylinder with a rubber edge around one end and pump on the other. The ladies look on with keen interest as Megan continues. "While it might seem a bit *different*, it can begin the recuperative process and assist in retaining prior functionality."

"Lady Number Four asks, "How does it work?"

Megan interjects. "With this treatment, you position a plastic tube over the penis. A hand or battery-powered pump attached to the tube helps pull more blood into the region to gain an erection. Once the penis is firm, you periodically press the bulb to sustain the vacuum or slip a band, called a constriction ring, around the base to help maintain the blood in the corpus cavernosa."

Megan looks at me and I realize she wants me to audition the pump for the ladies. She then asks, "Would you like a demonstration?" to which all ladies nod in the affirmative.

I cringe!

Megan feigns handing me the pump and waits for my response. Formerly, I would have been mortified, now I'm resolved that I'm helping six guys who otherwise wouldn't have the inclination to even consider the practice. Instead Megan presses a button and there's a video demonstration of the entire process with some guy doing the deed.

I glance at Megan and there's a mocking smile on her face as if to say 'Gotcha.'

The audio plays the hum of the pump and slowly the air in the cylinder is removed as the ladies watch the penis begin to increase in both length and girth.

Lady Number Two comments. "My goodness, it really does change."

Megan responds, "They're available on-line in both manual and battery-operated configurations.

I note that Amazon has nearly fifty different models to choose from.

Lady Number Four asks, "What's the difference?"

I reply, "About three hundred dollars."

"How long do you keep it on?" Lady Number Five asks.

Megan again, "Your husband should incorporate the pump two times a week for 5-10 minutes each time."

"Are there any risks?" Lady Number Five, again.

Megan replies, "The chance of side effects with a manual pump is lower, compared to other ED treatments but side effects can include changes such as bleeding under the skin, known as petechiae, temperature and color differences caused by the constriction band, as well as pain and bruising if the vacuum is too strong or the pump or constriction ring is left on too long."

Another lady raises her hand and asks. "Can you still be intimate?"

Megan responds. "The sympathetic nerves are not affected by the surgical procedure. This means, that, although the erection is impaired and there's no seminal discharge, there can be a male orgasmic reaction."

The ladies look to me and I reply. "It's different, but there can be intimacy."

The second lady offers, "Do you miss it?"

What a dumb question! I swallow and respond. "Yes, of course. But I don't miss agonizing about being ashes in an urn sitting on a closet shelf."

Lady Number Three asks. "Did you go through a period of depression?"

"Most certainly." I reply. "It comes with the territory and is always somewhat in the back of my mind. You're making both physical and psychological changes that go against inherent nature. The natural urges are there but reality takes over and you have this lingering feeling of inadequacy and the absurd conclusion you're no longer a man."

"How has your wife dealt with it?" Lady Number Four asks.

I think to myself about the always absent Amy and simply reply. "My wife's been wonderful. She's understood there will be good days and bad days, happy days and sad days and helped me learn to love myself, which I don't think I did before."

By now, I'm no longer uncomfortable and totally ambivalent as the next lady raises her hand. "Have you always been so…so open?"

"Hardly!" I reply. "I was very conservative and quite squeamish until I realized, in a clinical setting, I needed to check my modesty at the door. My only goal is to help you understand so that you can help your spouse recover both physically **and** emotionally. I never intended on making my… ahh… situation public. I've seen what prostate cancer can do to a man and how, through education and counseling we…you and I…can help others go 'through the tunnel' as I call it."

The next lady asks, "How has your experienced changed your perspective on life?"

I pause for a moment and then answer. "We all make assumptions that life will go on and then something happens that changes that perspective and opens our eyes to just how fragile life really is. For me, eighteen months before my cancer diagnosis, I collapsed with seventy bloods clots in me. I was rushed to intensive care, totally immobilized and given less than a five percent chance of living three hours. For the next six days I was on a respirator and could neither move nor talk and simply stared at the ceiling."

There's a gasp in the audience as I continue. "That changed everything and I now consider every day a bonus day and something special. I survived the blood clots and, so far, the cancer. In reality, the two of them saved my life. You see, like so many others, I took life for granted and now I cherish each day, each moment and each new experience."

"Five years ago if I'd been asked to come here and share my story, I wouldn't. First, there was no story. Second, I was too busy living life to realize it might abruptly end."

I pause for a moment and then decide I need to explain what happened. "I was in the hospital with the blood clots for nearly a month. The first six days, I was strapped to a bed and totally immobilized. I could only move my right thumb to call for a nurse. I was on a ventilator and could only communicate by blinking. For the entire period all I could do was look at the ceiling and count the tiles. Needless to say, it gave me a lot of time to think."

"As I progressed I began a mild exercise program consisting of walking the hospital halls. One day, I peeked in a ward room and saw eight elderly ladies who were all stroke patients…too sick to go to a nursing home, where the room they shared was the last place they'd ever be."

"I was simply taken aback by the sadness I saw reflected in their eyes. They knew this was the end. Few had any family left and so they were alone, without smiles, without anything to look forward to except dying. I took it upon myself to go every day and meet with my 'lady friends', as I began calling them, simply to brighten their day and try to make them laugh."

"For the first time in my life, I was giving of myself and, quite honestly, it was one of the most rewarding things I'd ever done. I'm here today because of those ladies. I'm here because I want to give of myself simply to see if I can help you and your husbands have an easier time than I had and hopefully reduce the stress they are now experiencing."

After an extended period of silence, I continue, "A German doctor by the name of Hamer did research and determined that cancer can be caused by profound instances of stress due to death, job loss or life changing situations, like having blood clots or a loved one with cancer. His premise was, 'By reducing stress, the body can naturally fight the rogue cells that come about and help minimize any further onslaught of cancer.'"

"Do you have ways you use to reduce stress?" Lady Number Four asks.

I look at the group and reply. "Thanks to my wife, I've developed a different perspective towards my body based on three exercises. The first is called Mindfulness, which is a breathing exercise we can teach you in a matter of minutes. Second, is an environmental process called Wim Hof where you let your body adjust to the environment instead of modifying the environment to meet your comfort level. Finally, is a Japanese exercise called Shin Yin Roku or forest bathing."

"Forest bathing? Lady Number Five inquires as I immediately sense she thinks you're out in the woods taking a bath when in fact the practice of interaction with nature can decrease stress and depression. Forest therapy might help stress management for all age groups and may help with depression and other mental health problems of PTSD, abuse, lonely elderly people, drug or alcohol addicts, blind people, and other people with special needs. Nature therapy could also improve self-management, self-esteem, social relations and skills and may reduce aggression and improve relationship abilities.

I look directly at her and offer. "Research estimates that eighty percent of our perception, learning, cognition, and activities are mediated through vision. By closing our eyes for extended periods of time, our other senses become accentuated which can have a calming effect on the entire body."

There are frowns amongst the sextet as I continue. "By closing your eyes and participating in Shin Rin Yoku your body opens your ears, nose and taste buds as well as your entire body. This allows you to reap the sensations from the world around it and the overall neural responses have both a soothing and calming effect."

"Do you have to be in the woods?" Lady number one asks.

"You can do it anywhere. Being in the woods simply surrounds you with nature. However, you can practice it anywhere. My wife does it on the beach in Saint Martin. The key is connecting with nature."

"What do you wear?" Lady Number Four asks.

"From anything to nothing." I reply. "The less you wear, the more senses are exposed. Therefore, you have an opportunity to enjoy your aggregate sensory information. When you cover any part of your body, that part's blocked from the natural neural sensations. If you want the optimum sensory experience you simply stand naked outdoors so that all but the bottom of your feet are involved or go for a walk."

"In other words, be a nudist!" Lady Number Five concludes in a somewhat negative tone.

I look directly at her and seriously reply. "The terms 'nudist' and 'naturalist' are often used interchangeably but there's a difference between the two. Nudists are people who enjoy being naked in a social setting while naturalists are people who believe in living in harmony with nature. Nudists typically practice for recreational purposes, such as swimming, sunbathing, or hiking. They may also attend nudist clubs or resorts."

"Naturists, believe that being naked is a natural and healthy way to live. They argue that it allows people to feel more comfortable in their own skin. Forest bathing is intended to generate solitary tranquility and internal peace. If you have some private place outdoors where you can disrobe, you can reap the benefits to a much greater degree but it's simply not required. The key is allowing your other senses to communicate with your soul."

"You do that?" Lady Number Four asks.

I smile and nod in the affirmative before adding. "At first I thought it was a bunch of hokum. When I got over the titillation, I started to relax and my sensory awareness began to develop. After a few times, I began pushing myself to keep my eyes closed and think peaceful things such as pleasant memories of our children, my parents, my favorite place on earth called 'The Forest', even my dog Jake and how much I loved him. It wasn't long until I began to experience all the things my wife told me I would. It's not sexual! It's sensory liberation!"

I smile again at the ladies and add. "When I do eyes-closed Shin Rin Yoku, I can focus on any part of my body instead of having it be one amalgamated sensation. What's neat is how much more I hear and smell….birds chirping, the smell of fresh cut grass, a bee simply pollinating a flower…they're all there and now part of the world I formerly took for granted. I've been able to naturally lower my blood pressure, breathing, heart rate and stress level and improve my sleep patterns to the point I feel more refreshed than I have in years."

"How has all this changed you?" Lady Number Three inquires.

"First there was the acclimation. What began as somewhat risqué and uncomfortable became commonplace until I began to realize the total immersion of my body was releasing me and allowing me to be free. Through repetition there's no more titillation and I'm comfortable in my personal universe. For some, it will never happen simply because they've been socialized to think that it's wrong and I understand and respect that as it was the way I was until I was set free."

I paused for a moment to let my thoughts sink in and then continued. "Beyond the physical aspect the psychological and emotional facets have also changed. I'm not a nudist nor an exhibitionist. Yet, after six days strapped to a bed unable to talk or move, I now look at my body as nothing more than the superstructure for my being. As such, I'm no longer hung up on who sees what. I don't go around intentionally exposing myself. However, I really no longer care who sees what, IF they willingly see it. I'm neither aroused nor embarrassed. However, I'm also very conscious that those I'm exposed to are allowing it to happen, which is why we all signed the affidavit that outlined today's curriculum."

I look out at the bobble heads moving up/down as the ladies realize this isn't a peep show, it's a tutorial on how to assist their spouses in transcending physically, emotionally and psychologically, to help regain their health and minimize the depression or worse, PTSD that will take place.

I pause for a moment as I feel the need to assure the ladies this is intended as a serious medical presentation. I sit on the edge of the table and note. "I didn't come here today to thrill you, embarrass or even titillate you. I came here to help you better understand what your spouse is about to go through. Would I have done this before meeting with my lady friends and then Megan? Absolutely not!"

"I'm glad I came. I also commend you for being concerned and open enough to help start this program. When I had my surgery there was nothing like this. My wife and I went in blind and I came out scared, scarred and despondent. With this program you have an idea of what's going to happen and how you can help."

"At first I thought this would be couples but now realize that would be a mistake. Because of her compassion Megan developed this program for women only to allow for more in-depth discussions without all the reservations if we were in mixed company. We all know most men are a lot more… uhh… inhibited than women and so the topics and questions wouldn't have been as open."

I look at the ladies and then offer. "My only goal has been to help minimize confusion and, most importantly, help you reduce the depression that's going to follow. Trust me, the depression **will** be there. Sadly, most men are too reticent to talk about what's going on. Depression and PTSD are real and oft-times debilitating circumstances. It's only through compassion and support that men can recover and begin to relive their lives."

It's Megan's turn. "Scientists evaluated the prevalence of anxiety and depression in nearly 4,500 patients with prostate carcinoma. They studied clinical anxiety and depression as a result of prostate cancer treatment. The analysis identified the prevalence rates in post-treatment, on-treatment and pre-treatment depression. Based on the results, pre-treatment depression had a 17% frequency rate, 15% during treatment and over 18% post-treatment. For anxiety the pre-treatment incidence was 27%, 15% during treatment, and 18% post-treatment."

Megan continues. "You might be asking yourself, 'what's behind this high level of depression?' The fact is, there's a range of different elements causing the problem. The first one being the qualities that define a man's role in society that venerates men who have physical strength, control, toughness, and dominance. When a time comes for them to ask for help many men believe they're showing signs of weakness."

"Psychologists presume men don't want to appear weak or emotionally vulnerable so they end up concealing these emotions without asking for help or support. However, without emotional and informational support, it becomes challenging to deal with prostate health."

"The reason for that is relatively simple, prostate cancer impacts the gastrointestinal, urinary, and reproductive systems. With these problems men tend to feel ashamed and embarrassed in front of their romantic partners or family. Due to their weakened state, they then display extremely high anxiety levels. Sadly, the greater the magnitude, the greater the odds patients will hide their feelings and emotions. When someone refrains from expressing themselves and divulging these emotions, the mental stressors only keep piling up."

"You're here because you love your spouses and want to help them. You need to be aware of the symptoms that may include disturbing thoughts, feelings  or dreams related  to  the  events, mental or physical distress, alterations in the way they think and feel and an increase in the fight-or-flight response. These symptoms can last for more than a month or more after the event and will remain somewhat latent for a longer period of time."

Lady number one raises her hand as Megan nods to her and she asks, "what's the difference between depression and PTSD?"

Megan offers, "Depression is a mood disorder that's characterized by persistent feelings of sadness, hopelessness, and worthlessness. It can also cause physical symptoms such as fatigue, changes in appetite, and difficulty sleeping caused by a variety of factors, including genetics, brain chemistry, and life events."

"PTSD is a mental health condition that's caused by a traumatic event. The traumatic event can be anything from a natural disaster to a car accident to a violent crime or prostate cancer. It can cause a variety of symptoms, including flashbacks, nightmares, anxiety, and avoidance of anything that reminds the person of the traumatic event."

I take over. "Fortunately, most people who experience traumatic events don't develop PTSD. Those who experience prolonged trauma, where they can't accept the changes, may develop what's called complex post-traumatic stress disorder, or C-PTSD that has a distinct effect on a person's emotional regulation and core identity."

Back to Megan. "The main treatments for depression are counselling and medication. Our surgeons and physician's assistants are all trained on identifying the symptoms and implementing post-operative programs to resolve any ongoing issues."

I chime in. "While many people don't think it's that prevalent, in the United States about twelve million adults have PTSD in a given year, and over thirty-million Americans will develop it at some point in their life. Sadly, the rate of PTSD in the United States is seven times greater than the rest of the world and it's more common in women than men."

I pause for a moment and wonder if should make a political observation and figure 'why not?' as I add. "I believe one of the reasons for the increased levels of American violence stems from stress. In the *'land of the free'* to have more than one mass killing every single day indicates there's certainly something wrong."

Another pause to let the numbers sink in and then implore. "Perhaps you can see why I'm such a proponent of relaxation therapy."

The ladies all seem impressed by my candor and, after 'seeing' me, I don't think there's much left to cover and we're all comfortable with that.

There's a pause and then I make an offer. "Ladies, I have a proposition for you. Please write this down."

Each lady obliges as I give them an email address and add. "Look, what we've been discussing is something most men don't want to admit and fewer want to talk about. I'm a long way from being medically trained. However, I've been through what your spouses are about to go through. If they have any questions please have them e-mail me and let them know I've been where they're going. However, I do have some requirements."

The ladies stop writing and wait for the shoe to drop.

"First, no last names. Second, no photographs. Third, I don't want to know where they live or care about their race, religion or orientation. I'm only here to help."

The meeting ends to a warm round of applause. In ninety minutes I've personified the malady and given hope, while potentially, minimizing both concern and confusion.

## Lead Us Not...:

The office is closed and so Megan escorts the ladies to the front door. I sit in the now-quiet room and ponder what all we accomplished as a glow of self-satisfaction overcomes me.

There's a long pause and then the silence is broken by the sound of the 'click' of the lock opening. Megan has discarded her suit jacket and looks ravishing in her cream-colored slacks and white silk blouse, while carrying the plastic tub with my clothes in it. I try not to stare when I realize she's either removed or was never wearing a bra as I realize I never forgot the peep show in Milwaukee.

Megan's hand touches my arm and she looks directly into my eyes. "George, you're so down to earth."

I take yet another deep breath. I haven't been touched by another woman in over thirty years and nervously reply, "That's the farmer in me." My mute mantra becomes, *'If things were different.'*

I pull off the scrub top and look at the circles on my abdomen and wonder how I'm going to remove the ink. Megan smiles and hands me one of those foil wrapped handi-wipes that come immersed in alcohol that she's put in the tub.

I quietly tear off the edge and try to see all the ink on my torso. Megan realizes there's no mirror and no way I can see what I'm doing.

"Here, let me help you," Megan offers as she sits in one of the chairs, has me face her, takes the alcohol wipe and begins gently erasing the marker lines along my rib cage. I watch her eyes and observe her focus on what she does. As she completes the seven circles, she slides my scrub pants down and begins wiping my lower abdomen and adds. "I think all the ladies would have liked seeing a little more," referring to the meeting content.

I, in turn, reply, "Well, there certainly wasn't much more for them to see."

Megan's attention shifts from removing the marker to my eyes as she casually offers, "I really appreciate  you came today?"

Megan pauses and nods at what's been hidden. I take a very deep breath and ponder what she is inferring.

My mind says....'Don't.'

My conscience says....'Stop.'

The roaring hormones within me scream 'Don't stop, don't stop, don't stop!'

Megan looks up at me and there's a different expression on her face....cat like...almost like looking for her next prey. I've never seen her look like this before....teeth locked in an artificial smile as if she's about to pounce.

Megan pauses and whispers, "You know the ladies were right," as she focuses on erasing the retropubic line with her fingers sliding across the exposed area.

"What?" I whisper through staccato breaths. .

"I *like the look*. More important, I love how soft your skin is."

My head tilts back. How do I respond?

Megan finishes and stands before me. Somehow, someway, she's unbuttoned more of her blouse until only the bottom two buttons remain closed. "I can never thank you enough," as her hands clutch the back of my shoulders and she pulls me in for a hug of gratitude.

Megan pulls back and looks at me with an arduous expression that I believe isn't pressure, but yearning.

My head tilts back. How do I respond?

Images of Amy smash into my brain. The vows made. The abstinence on my part with the knowledge and, quite, honestly, pain that it hasn't always been that way for her. I know I gave her permission but what about me? Thoughts of the cool ambivalence that now permeates our house enter my mind. Alone together! Alone apart! No one has made me feel like this in years. Amy and I sleep in the same bed and most nights she doesn't even say 'goodnight.'

Every nerve in my body is screaming yes...yes...yes. Every ounce of my conscience is shrieking no...no...no. My logic is becoming emotional gumbo intermingled until they are no longer segregated, mixing one-ounce pride with one-ounce titillation and one-ounce regret.

Megan unbuttons the last two remnants of her modesty and gently slides my hands upon her breasts. I hear her breathing deepen as my hands slide softly across what had once been hidden in all but my imagination.

After what seems like an eternity where neither of us wants to relinquish the other, Megan's hands go to my lower back and she pulls me in as I feel her body pressed tightly against mine.

We're in contact from our thighs to our shoulders with nothing serving as the tactile border between us.

I don't want it to end.

Finally, I lean back wanting more than anything else to feel her lips and wait for her to respond.

Megan whispers…"please."

It's the most sensual whisper I've heard in years and wonder what it means.

We stand enmeshed in each other.

I close my eyes and listen to her whispered breaths of anticipation.

My mind clears and I can feel her against me and sense her excitement.

I'm awakened and alive.

Oh my God! Make me stop!

I breathe deeper and try to imagine how she tastes and feels.

Staccato envelopes my soul as my nerves tingle in every possible way.

My rasps punctuate the air as I feel her hand on the back of my neck.

She whispers in my ear, "Please, let make me make you happy!"

I lean back against the table, while trying to stay attached.

Megan follows suit as she pulls the string my scrub pants and they fall to the floor. Her hand slides down and presses against what had been hidden. Now she's kneeling before me and begins addressing what had just been covered. With no stimulating response capable, I feel profound inadequacy and yet, Megan continues to accelerate my pleasure until I'm breathing deeply, having reached the point of no return. No matter how much guilt, how much regret or how much I want to, I can't stop simply because turning back has become emotionally dangerous, physically impossible and prohibitively beyond my carnal self.

A bolt of energy slams through my body making me quake in bliss. What she had once assured me could happen was profoundly true. There can be pleasure... incredible pleasure... pleasure that takes you beyond here and now to a point the eclipses reality and launches your body to a completely different plane.

Megan stands and I glance at her expression only to witness the predatory look supplanted by a soft glow of satisfaction. Once again, we embrace. I pull her in until we are pressed against each other.

My hand slides down as it seeks the button on her pants.

Megan whispers in my ear..."next time you're here".

Instead she glides my hand up and I fondle what had only been a dream a few moments ago.

Megan leans in and whispers again, in my ear, "thanks for cumming."

Her lips purse, as do mine.

Her tongue slithers across her upper lip and then our lips meet.

I feel the softness I've only imagined.

I slide my tongue in her mouth and taste her as a hint of peppermint enters my brain.

For a longing instant, we breathe as one.

My tongue retracts and her tongue touches mine as she melds the taste of her with me.

Reality strikes and our embrace settles in a clumsy puddle of propriety.

We catch ourselves.

Inevitability returns.

We both take deep breaths, elicit forsaken smiles and quietly, reluctantly, acknowledge we need to end.

Our bodies release, seizing our somewhat unwilling selves.

Megan steps back and watches as we both catch our breath.

She looks deeply into my eyes for any clue.

There's none.

Veracity rears its reluctant head as we grudgingly, physically and emotionally detach.

Our eyes disconnect as I reach for the pool of scrubs on the floor and then quietly garner my street clothes and begin to dress.

Megan's blouse remains open, ambivalent to my glances. I yearn to touch and feel again what lies shamelessly exposed, simply to make her share my passion, but know we can't continue.

She takes a deep breath of reservation, folds the scrubs and places them in the tub from whence they came.

I'm overcome with guilt and dig deep into my soul for justification.

It's not there.

Reality strikes.

We quietly pick up the empty coffee cups and soda cans as Megan casually announces she's being named General Manager of the practice and everyone, except the doctors, will be reporting to her.

I believe the day will come when even the doctors will be answering to her, as well.

I stop, look at Megan and say. "We have a house on Saint Martin. You and your husband can use it anytime you want."

There's a substantial pause as Megan replies. "We're not together anymore. Rick didn't want to leave Milwaukee and **really** doesn't like what I do for a living. He moved back to Wisconsin and I'm moving on with my life."

"Sorry to hear that," I reply.

"It is, what it is. No kids. No problems. It just wasn't working out."

"OK."

Megan stops for a moment and then adds. "I love my job and they're making me a junior partner. Money shouldn't be an issue. I really want to…to find myself, if I can."

"What do you mean?" I inquire. "You're on your way to a phenomenal career."

"There's other things I want to discover that I've been reluctant to try. Now that Rick's gone, I just want to find out who I really am."

I don't know where the conversation is going and don't think it's any of my business to ask.

My glance at the wall clock is intercepted.

"What time's your flight?"

"When I get there."

A frown comes across Megan's face as she surmises, "I don't understand'.

"We have company planes."

"Planes?"

"Yes! Wilco."

"You mean THE Wilco?" Megan inquires with a look of profound surprise.

"Yes."

"And they let you use one of the planes?"

"We own the company."

"You own Wilco?" Megan gasps.

"Well, the family does, or should I say, Wilco own's us.

Megan realizes she's bringing out some deep-seated discomfort and offers. "I always thought you were just this funny guy who made my day. Now I find out who you really are."

I simply shrug my shoulders.

A point of inquiry evolves across Megan's face. "So, you're also the George Terrill who won the Nobel Peace Prize?"

I nod in the affirmative.

"I never put one and one together."

"I really don't like letting people know. I just want to be like everyone else."

Megan shakes her head as if totally surprised. "You're a wonderful man, Mr. Terrill…"

"George, just George."

I'm reluctant and yet press the Uber App, calling for the return.

The response indicates the driver will arrive in seven minutes.

I look at Megan and she at me.

There will only be seven more minutes together.

I don't want to leave and it appears she doesn't want me to.

I take a deep breath and mentally convey…*'lead us not into temptation…again'.*

Four minutes pass and legitimacy comes into play.

I quietly nod as does she.

Megan's hands begin the slow process of buttoning her blouse. I watch and yearn for another touch.

She senses my yearning and faces me once again.

Her lips meet mine and they linger as if trying to curtail the eventuality.

Reality strikes as I gently brush the misplaced tendrils of hair from away from her cheeks.

We walk hand-in-hand to the front foyer, just out of sight of the security camera and glance out, reluctantly anticipating the maroon Uber Camry with Georgia license plate number AB-115-BA.

I feel her rapid pulse through the sides of my fingers and wonder if she feels mine.

Uber's pulling in the parking lot.

Megan squeeze's my hand and provides one last polite hug as nothing more than a silent declaration of goodbye.

I feel her pressed against me and ask myself why am I leaving.

My conscience supersedes as I walk out the door.

I stop, turn and offer, "I can come back, if you want me to."

Megan smiles and nods in the affirmative and whispers, "Perhaps, stay a little longer."

Megan points her index finger and mouths "Pow" as a retiring smile transects her face.

My body tingles as I point my index finger and repeat the gesture, while blowing imaginary smoke from its end.

Megan sensuously slides her pointed finger entirely in her mouth surrounded by the lips that had just caressed mine and slowly, deliberately, lets her finger slide from within as the tip of her tongue slowly glides across her upper lip and she smiles.

Oh my God, I really don't want to go!

With that, the spell is broken as I reach for the Camry door and turn simply to see Megan wave a gentle goodbye.

I smile and attempt to memorize all of her, only to wish it didn't have to end.

I'm driven back to Chamblee with a sense of contentment in my mind and angst in my heart.

Amelia III is waiting.

I climb aboard and settle in.

I reflect on all that's transpired in the class and surmise I did a good job…anyway I hope so.

I shake my head when I realize what I've done. Not the content or the exhibition but allowing myself to become so…so desirous.

Amelia III takes off and heads for home.

I peer out at the countryside below. To my right, I see the edge of darkness as the sun sets. To my left, the last vestiges of a day I'll never forget and hope I never regret.

I reflect on how both Amy and Megan have transformed me and realize I no longer care about so many things that once mattered.

Perhaps it's an amalgamation of what's been done to me and the training.

Perhaps, I'm just responding to my subconscious.

Perhaps, something latent within me has surfaced.

I don't know.

All I know is I'm profoundly different and, in many ways, more indifferent than when I awoke this morning.

Strangely, I feel somewhat liberated knowing I can be more of the real me while really not knowing what that means.

I sit back, close my eyes and contemplate Megan's ever-present smile and wonder if it's real.

I relive the last vestige of her fingers slowly sliding down and wonder what she's trying to communicate when she offers…*'stay a little longer.'*

I think of Amy and wonder if she'll sense anything as a maelstrom of guilt rumbles through my mind like midnight thunder.

I challenge my growing fondness for a woman young enough to be my daughter and remember Steven Sondheim's "Send in The Clowns".


*Isn't it rich?*
*Are we a pair?*
*Me here at last on the ground*
*You in mid-air*
*Send in the clowns*

*Isn't it bliss?*
*Don't you approve?*
*One who keeps tearing around*
*One who can't move*
*Where are the clowns?*
*Send in the clowns*

*Just when I'd stopped opening doors*
*Finally knowing the one that I wanted was yours*
*Making my entrance again with my usual flair*
*Sure of my lines. No one is there*

*Don't you love farce?*
*My fault, I fear*
*I thought that you'd want what I want*

*Sorry, my dear*

*But where are the clowns?*
*Quick, send in the clowns*
*Don't bother, they're here*

*Isn't it rich?*
*Isn't it queer?*
*Losing my timing this late*
*In my career?*
*And where are the clowns?*
*There ought to be clowns*
*Well, maybe next year...*


I become introspective and wonder if the lyrics are referring to Amy, Megan and/or me. I ponder Megan's career and combine it with my theory of acclimation and deduce the combination must have some effect on her outlook on life and liberation. I add in the politics of business and the challenges that come with big incomes and wonder if it's made either Amy or Megan artificial…simply veneers, created to make anyone, everyone, feel special until they get what they want.

My mind goes back to her comment, *'uncovering things I want to discover that I've been reluctant to try.'* I  ponder its meaning. Perhaps, her goal is to be more adventurous than her persona let's on. Perhaps, her former life was like Amy's, constricted by what she felt she had to be. I wonder…have Megan's experiences widened her parameters or has she always been *adventurous* and now simply has the latitude of finding out who she is and where she really fits. I ask myself, will the journey end up in contentment or simply a dream and fantasy that doesn't come true? I finally ask myself, where do I fit in or, for that matter do I fit in at all?

I ponder again*….'stay a little longer….'*

I open my eyes and wonder why am I thinking these things.

I look out at the cities below. It's evening. I contemplate what people are doing, thinking, eating, saying, oblivious to me peering down on them.

I flash forward to home and the solitary life that has become my norm. Perhaps this is my justification. Perhaps, it's my way of getting even for the years of pain knowing I'm all alone. Perhaps…perhaps…perhaps.

My eyes focus on the bulkhead as if it's a wall between my thoughts and reality.

I take another deep breath and realize we're all very much alike. I ask myself, "isn't this what we all really are?… Sondheim's clowns.

I shut my eyes as tight as I can when I realize I'll never know.

The flight is short and, as we land in Milwaukee, my thoughts become usurped by the authenticity of the immediate and now I feel profoundly remorseful.

Carefully, I file my introspection within my secret soul, stored for another day, another time, another whatever that just might replenish my lust for life. I glance at my extended right index finger, smile and whisper…"Pow!"

## Keurboom!:

I reflected on my presentation, thinking that none of the ladies or their husbands would e-mail me. Wrong! At first there are a few and then, as word spread, a torrent began that I responded to. With each question I needed to make certain I have the correct response beyond noting that I was a patient and not medically trained. With not much on my plate I realized I hadn't finished the last chapter of my hypothesis concerning the universe, and so I opened my folio and began writing.

"The universe is not just rocks and gasses, atoms, protons and electrons. It's simply everything **and** nothing. In 1985 cosmologist Edward Harrison wrote 'where there is a society of human beings, however primitive, we find a universe, and where there is a universe, of whatever kind, we find a society. Both go together. One does not exist without the other.'

"A universe unifies a society, enabling its members to communicate and share their thoughts and experiences. Each society determines what is perceived and what constitutes valid knowledge, and the member of that society believes what they perceive and perceives what they believe, so that, each culturally imposed framework acts as a filter, constraining our concept of the universe while enabling our explorations."

"Human existence is founded on our interaction with other humans. It's the part of our universe that we cherish most - family, friends, co-workers and neighbors who represent just a few of the interactions that take place on a daily basis from which we define 'who' we are. Because socialization is so critical to our wellbeing it isn't surprising to find that the most stressful experiences in a person's life center around those that strain or break social interactions."

"The health benefits of being socially active and the health risks of social isolation are not limited to how many people one interacts with but the level of satisfaction these social relationships provide. When a person feels  their relationships are inadequate to satisfy their intimate and social needs, loneliness can happen even when they are with others.

"For some loneliness leads to actions the lonely person hopes will generate positive responses from others. Unfortunately, these actions can have the opposite effect than what the lonely person intended thereby exacerbating the singularity the person was trying to escape. For this reason loneliness can be characterized as feelings of social isolation, absence of companionship and rejection by peer groups with feelings of an isolated life in a social world forming the dominant experience."

"What stops us from reaching out to others and expanding our relationships? To me, the answer lies in one word – prejudice! Now before you go, 'Oh my God!' here is my rationale."

"As I lay in the ICU thinking this was the end my mind wandered back to all that had transpired and the people who had been a part of my life and I wondered - would I be fondly remembered and truly missed? As the thoughts lingered, I began to realize that what made me happy weren't the baubles and places but the relationships created and the sadness incurred when they ended. It was then I began mentally outlining what I wanted to express, with hope it would not only rectify the mistakes I'd made along the way, but assist those who took the time to read what I wrote and help them as well."

"It's funny what sticks in your brain besides events and circumstances. The one term I remember from college was ethnocentrism. It was from one the anthropology courses I took and, as I lay there, it came front and center. Of all things to think about when you're hooked up to a respirator with IV's in your arms and feet believing each breath could be your last."

"Obviously, I didn't die. They don't know why. I just didn't and to this day they call me Wonder Boy at the hospital. The experience has obviously stayed with me as has the title except in my mind, the word 'wonder' doesn't refer to awe but to my questioning so many things I formerly took for granted."

"Quite honestly, I had to look up the formal meaning again as the years had painted over the definition I memorized so long ago where 'Ethnocentrism is used in social sciences and anthropology to describe the act of judging another culture and believing that the values and standards of one's own culture are superior – especially with regard to language, behavior, traditions and religion. These aspects or categories are distinctions that define each ethnicities unique cultural identity."

"I wondered how all this fit into the relationships I was trying to define and then it hit me. Our country is not a unified nation but an assembly of cultures – racial, religious, geographic, sexual, socio-economic - to name a few. Just as we judge other countries we also evaluate the different sub-cultures within the United States and have personal opinions about those who are "different" than we are."

"But what is culture? Culture is an umbrella term which encompasses the social  behavior and norms found in our sub-societies, as well as the knowledge, beliefs, arts, traditions, capabilities and habits of the individuals in these groups. In America the only thing that ties us together are the laws which, theoretically, are supposed to apply to everyone but hardly ever do."

"We acquire culture through the learning  processes called enculturation. This is the procedure by which people learn the dynamics  of  their surrounding culture and acquire  values  and norms appropriate or necessary in that culture and how it looks at the world. It's amazing how the different races, religions, ethnicity, socio-economic and orientations in the same country can examine the same subject and have profoundly different opinions."

"Each society has common laws and commerce along with specific cultural  norms that  codify  acceptable  conduct in  each group. These factors serve as guidelines for behavior, dress, language and demeanor in situations both within and outside the specific culture. They also serve as a template for expectations within   that   social   group   and   as   points-of-reference   when considering the cultures of others."

"As part of this process the influences that limit, direct or shape the individual (whether deliberately or not) include history, parents, other adults, peers, laws and society, in general. If successful enculturation results in competence in the language, values and rituals of the culture and socialization, which establishes right and wrong, good and bad, honorable and dishonorable and is periodically labeled 'morals'."

"Individual views on morality are influenced by the society's consensus and usually tend toward what that society finds acceptable or 'normal.' Socialization provides only a partial explanation for human beliefs and behaviors. Research has shown that people are shaped by both their social influences and genetics, as shown by the diversity of American subcultures that transcend our societies."

"What's important to remember is that the morality of American subcultures are dynamic and in constant throes of change. These gradual changes result in constant modifications to social behavior called 'cultural repositioning' that may accompany ideological shifts and other types of social, moral and ethical change, as well."

"Cultures are internally affected by forces both encouraging and resisting change. These forces are related to both social structures and natural events and are involved in the perpetuation of cultural ideas and practices within. As an example, within America the influx of Hispanic people because of economic or political issues in their native countries and the belief life will be better here, has resulted in huge changes, both good and bad, within resident cultures."

"Cultures are also externally affected via contact with other cultures, which may also produce — or inhibit — social shifts and changes in cultural practices. An example was school integration where white and black students from the same community, who never really knew each other, began to see that the other side 'wasn't really that bad.'"

"Cultural ideas may also transfer from one culture to another through diffusion or acculturation where diffusion moves from one culture to another such as rap music moving from African-Americans to popular status and acculturation being the process of social, psychological and cultural change that stems from the balancing of two cultures, while adapting to the prevailing culture of the society."

"The development of acceptable behavior within a culture is deeply tied to the biological and cognitive changes one is experiencing at any given time. When this happens the concepts and ideas of one subculture can transcend to others and begin to create a more common set of opinions on a particular subject which is called cultural assimilation. A case in point is sexual orientation that has transcended from one being considered limited to social outcasts to one accepted by many today as a form of human existence. In so doing, it has begun to create general patterns of social behavior that are more tolerant and accepting than previously recorded in the history of the United States."

"While racial prejudice has sadly always been a part of American history, today we see a tectonic shift away from abject delineation along racial lines to one more concurrent with prejudice along socio-economic levels. Here, typically the higher the level of individual development educationally, financially and/or socially, the lower the level of racial reticence as race becomes a secondary component - never forgotten - but  minimized. Whether it's the medical, professional, business or political leader, entertainer or athlete the higher the level of attainment the lower the level of racial delineation."

"Contrarily, the greater the disparity in socio-economic levels, even within the same racial culture, the greater the disdain, distrust and denigration of the levels above and below. Today, values, expectations and morals have a much broader spectrum than ever before as exemplified within just the Caucasian culture where the spectrum ranges from the elitist rich to poor white trash and everything in between.

"Americans are not alone! Humanity is in a period of globally accelerating cultural change that is resulting in the homogenization of differences that were once sacrosanct. Everything from attire to religious expression, that were once traditional are being blended into common denominators throughout the world. Driven by the expansion of international commerce, mass media - particularly the internet - and, above all else, the human population explosion and resulting massive societal relocations, changes that once took decades are now happening in years and even months. Look at images of people from around the world and the young have two things in common… blue jeans and cellphones."

"The net consequence of the American set of sub-cultures is the need for everyone, from all races, ethnicities, religions and orientations to simply stop judging other people for **what** they are by openly learning **who** they are. Beneath the color of skin, the way one seeks God's guidance or with whom they have emotional ties, lies a person who has the same desires as the rest of us where the ultimate goal is to sincerely feel wanted, needed and loved and, given the opportunity, have a better tomorrow than today."

"As a member of this universe, as a participant in this thing called life, we all can reach out to the lonely and let them realize they're not alone. We can touch their hearts and move their souls. We can look them in the eye and put a simple smile on their face and perhaps, just perhaps, help them break the cycle of singularity that permeates their soul and let them see and feel there are people who care."

"We can make them believe there are people willing to take that first step to allow them to feel as if they, too, are wanted, needed and loved. If we cherish these feelings, we need to take the time and dignity to reach out to someone who doesn't. Take time to be kind and gentle and forgiving. Take time to be patient and understanding and, above all else, take time to show our love, respect and honor for those who are sharing this thing called life."

"The challenge today lies not in existence as much as in following the right path to happiness. Any viable relationship within the universe begins with the belief that beyond our self, family, co-workers and friends is the thread called life that binds our tapestry together. We must then remember that it's NOT the only thread that we must sustain because we, as humans, are but one small component of the entire universe and WE have a responsibility to Mother Earth and all her inhabitants - humans, animals - every living thing, to help save it from ourselves."

"How do I share my thoughts on something so profound as the universe? I pondered long and hard about where we all fit in beyond humanity and what really makes up this thing called the universe. I went back to the teaching of the Greeks and looked at their concepts and then examined all types of contemporary thought to see if there wasn't some way to put my hands around the entire idea of where humans fit in. What I found was quite disturbing!"

"Let me take the liberty of digging a little deeper so that I hope I can better make some sort of rational basis for my deductions. By definition the universe is all of space and time (spacetime) and everything that exists therein. This includes the planets, stars, galaxies and all the contents of intergalactic space."

"It also goes all the way down to the smallest subatomic particles plus all matter and forms of energy. The size of the universe is currently estimated to be about 46 billion light years in diameter or about 270 trillion miles, give or take a few light years and a few trillion miles. The question then becomes what lies outside the universe? Is our perception nothing more than a component of a megaverse and what lies beyond that and that and that?"

"Mathematically, our universe is normally interpreted from a geometric perspective called the 'Euclidean space perspective' which regards all forms to be consisting of three dimensions - length, width and height regardless of form. The most popular concept of the universe perceives it to be spherical in shape so that, departing in any direction, we would eventually return to the exact same spot, if given enough time."

"Contemporary cosmology takes Euclidean geometry and adds the concept of time. Here time consists of one more permutation called the 'fourth dimension.' Time allows for the development of any point of physical reference as it refers to any another body at a specific instant. By combining space and time into a single entity, which is called Minkowski space, cosmology physicists have been able to simplify a large number of physical theories as well as describe, in a more uniform way, the workings of the universe from both the super galactic and subatomic levels which they call 'events', such as the big bang theory."

"Time is the one absolute component that ties every animate and inanimate being together with a common bond, regardless or all other variables. All people, plants, insects, animals! Everything that is alive or innate has this one common denominator regardless of who, what or where they are in the universe."

"While this one concept might seem a bit basic to many people, the concept of spacetime is so profound it remains the heart and soul of all of our social, political, intellectual and religious thinking! Simply, that all beings live in the same present. What makes the concept incredible is that the entire structure of time is manmade and malleable. The actual perception of time has been altered, modified and rearranged to reflect our social, environmental and humanistic conditions and continues to be modified as the human species evolves. From an ethnocentric perspective, humans have used the structure of time and society to adjust, modify and alter social, environmental and metaphysical propriety to fit our own cultural needs reflective of man's self-anointed position in the universe."

"With each generation humans have progressed, leaving behind parity with all other species - differentiating themselves with profoundly greater degrees. With each differentiation has come the reduction of natural enemies. With each millennium, those that had been the hunters became the hunted. With each millennium, man's predominance within his universe has increased, expanded and repositioned itself until today man's only natural enemy is himself."

"As humans evolved the species began to split into cultures predicated by what many have called institutional 'facts'. These 'facts' represent beliefs and attitudes where the culture organizes and defines itself by imposing those 'facts' on every member of that culture who then accept the 'facts' as truth that are modified by members of the culture until they become part of the culture itself."

"While my reference has been to historical evolutions we all can see that alterations in culture even today are changing the individual and their 'facts' socially, morally, ethically, and empirically, whose members are then changing the culture. The result is that the next generation's point of reference is totally dichotomous with the previous generation. This next generation will then accept or reject the 'facts' presented and will either abide or rebel against their existence in a never-ending cacophony of variances."

"How important is change and culture? One theory is that without change there would be no need for our concept of time and if there was no concept of time, would we have no culture or personal definition. While the entire question of time seems a bit ludicrous, it's a philosophical treatise that dates back to before Plato and Aristotle who pondered the consequence of change and, therefore, time as it affects man's relationship with man and his universe."

"The current digital era is realigning the entire world as we reshape our most personal experiences. Gone is any form of anonymity, replaced by a time and geographic stamp that reflects where we are, when we are and whenever we are, ensuring that we're always linked, resulting in a new culture whose benefits are yet to be determined. There are no secrets anymore!"

"Marshall McLuhan's concept of the 'Global Village' pontificated in 1962, when describing the effects of broadcasting on society is being enhanced by the profound global migrations of millions of peoples of different ethnicities, heritages and religions that is homogenizing what were once distinct cultures and challenging their cornerstones. With them regional identities are being melded into a global stew."

"It was only 70 years ago that the US Interstate System began and with it the erosion of local dialects traditions and ways of life. In the past 20 years, this has been happening on a global scale. Had it brought peace and understanding it could be seen as the cornerstone of the elusive evolution of mankind to stop wars and killing each other. Sadly, it has not. Today, globally, we see a time of profound social and political turbulence and upheaval as traditional thoughts, customs and beliefs of both the migratory and the inherent populous clash."

"We can pound the American flag in the sand and preach how great it is to live here. Sadly, so many people in America don't have the basic skills needed to not only survive, but prosper in this land of the free. Add to this the total degradation of any knowledge concerning a sense of decency, propriety and environmental responsibility and it isn't difficult to see why our country and society is slipping as badly as it is and why so many other nations really don't like Americans. Generations ago we stuck out our hands to help others. Today many simply stick out their hands and ask 'what's in it for me'?"

"I find it profoundly interesting that the only time the words 'middle class' are mentioned in America are around elections where the politicians pontificate about 'middle class values' like some Norman Rockwell painting. Middle class values are faith-based, regardless of religious belief...humility, compassion, generosity and forgiveness and a sense of equity and propriety that includes respect for others and their right to life, liberty and the pursuit of happiness, which, by the way, is not a God-given component!"

"Today we find a government that's almost at a stalemate, unable to function, unable to act, unable to provide what we all so dearly need - leadership. What happened? My opinion is that it has become too lucrative to be a politician - not just financially - but with all the perks associated with the task - those special favors, those special accommodations - that go beyond the norm and make the job so narcotizing."

"Our leaders propound health care and, yet, have their own special health care program. Our leaders propound individual retirement and, yet they award themselves pensions. Our leaders ask us for sacrifice and, yet, they lavish perks and awards upon themselves in the name of equity. Ideally, politicians should work for the good of the electorate and not for the good of themselves. Let them participate in the same health care program! Let them save for their own retirement! Let them experience the challenges of raising a family on a single income and see how the laws would change."

"I believe in equity! Equity for all in terms of certain basic rights…life as it equates to good health, liberty as it equates to the acquisition of knowledge and the pursuit of happiness…not the guarantee but the ability to achieve it through sacrifice and effort!"

"I could preach about our culture and society adnausium but have elected to stop right here with one final statement - We cannot stop social change! However, as a dominant member of the universe, humans MUST have reference to where we are culturally, physically, socially and environmentally."

"As Julian Barbour, a famous cosmologist once noted, 'It's change that provides the illusion of time, where each individual moment is a whole, complete and existing circumstance in its own right - called 'Nows'. As we live, we seem to move through a succession of 'Nows' which are nothing more than an arrangement of everything in the universe at that instant…Never to be exactly duplicated again - where the only evidence we have of last week and therefore time, is our memory. Erase the memory and you erase time'."

"As society changes people, so people change society. We, as members of a society can grab hold and try our very best to retain what is good and change what is bad. We, as members of a society, owe it to ourselves and to our children and our children's, children's children to ensure that we retain those values and beliefs that have made our society and our culture what it is and what we hope it will be. We, as members of our society, must interact and respond to those elements that challenge what we believe to be right."

"Whether it's health care, immigration, education, drugs, sexual orientation or any other social or political flash point, we all must work towards the good of all. As the preamble to the Declaration of Independence notes, *'We hold these truths to be self-evident that all men are created equal with certain unalienable rights to life, liberty and the PURSUIT of happiness.'* This is what our society is founded on. These are the cornerstones of our democracy. This is what our culture must hold dear for which so many millions have died."

"The list of issues seems to grow on a daily basis and, yet, beyond our human needs, there are the needs of the world. We are in an incredible period of change as our species travels on. We, as humans, continue to differentiate ourselves from all other species leaving behind all other living beings in our wake of technological innovation as they fall victim to our 'progress'. Sadly this transformation is resulting in horrific consequences that are simply killing the rest of our existence."

"To this end, we turn to those we perceive to be leaders. Yet there's a profound difference between leadership and authority. People lead others because the others want them to. People abide by rules established by authorities because there are consequences if they don't. The challenge we all have is determining who to follow and why."

**Winding the Spring:**


It's September 16th and one of my prescriptions cannot be renewed without a medical revisit. I get a call from the urologist's office and am told I need full blood work for my semi-annual PSA check. The date is set and already, the spring begins its slow, torturous wind...Click! Click! Click! With each day the pressure re-emerges and the void of confidence begins to fill with the dark, murky fluids of fear. It's over a month before the blood test and I'm already feeling the pressure.

October 10th  Happy Anniversary! The third anniversary since learning I had Cancer. Now pretend everything is normal...like nothing ever happened. SURE!!!!!!!!!!!!!!

October 27th  Time for the blood work. You would think that after five times, I would be used to the drill....NOT!

Blood pressure...180 over 102! Holy shit! White coat syndrome? No! It's fear! The spring is wound tight. "See me in three weeks! Your blood pressure is at a dangerous level!

October 28th I make my thrice-weekly visit to the "health" club...or senior citizens center as I believe it is during the day. I run into a woman whose husband is stage four prostate Cancer and ask how he's doing? There's a weary smile. "He had bone Cancer in his spine and the tumor had to be removed. The Cancer was the really aggressive type and so the chemo would have been terrible. He went into hospice last week and is finally at peace that the war is over."

My spring winds even tighter! The day drags on! I intentionally leave my phone in the car so that any message I get will be recorded. After dinner I go out to the solitude of the garage and press the button. "Your test results are back and everything looks good". Once again there's a flood of relief! Once again, I feel the strain seeping from my body! Once again, I sense a reprieve and thank God for all that I have.

October 4th Amy takes my blood pressure in the morning…126 over 76. The sun is shining and there's a smile upon my face! She says she'll be late. I can't remember when the last time was she was home early.

Megan and I have kept in contact through e-mail. All the ladies from session one reported they appreciated the presentation and it helped their husbands recover faster.

"Will you do another session?" I'm asked.

The bubble has burst and I say reluctantly say yes, anxious and yet also yearning, rationalized by the $1,000 bucks for Cancer research. I head to Atlanta assuming the same routine. There's been a change in plans. Megan wants to add what can be done when someone has ED. In other words, different practices.

The program begins and we go through the anatomy and physiology and once again I put on my 'show' except this time, there's no video of the pump, it's me. I simply don't care as the nerves and inhibitions simply aren't there as the Theory of Acclimation seems prevalent. The meeting is extended and we get to the 'satisfaction' part of the presentation.

Megan gets out some devices.

I figure it's show and tell.

It was! She shows and I supposed tell what they're like.

Not what I planned, but I'm brave and full of B.S. as I'd never seen half of what she provides.

Same questions. Same response. Same everything.

The meeting ends and the ladies leave.

Time to erase the marker lines.

Megan takes the alcohol wipe and begins. Gone is the effervescent smile! Gone are the glances! Gone is the, 'Pow.' Instead, I feel like a porterhouse steak that's been put in the butcher's display case. She reaches my thin strip of modesty and stops. I stand waiting, hoping she will continue her downward journey.

Instead Megan offers with a dispassionate tone. "Too bad you didn't show the ladies what all the devices do."

"I've never seen half of them in my life," I reply.

"That's unfortunate. You don't know what you're missing."

"You mean, you have?"

There's a quick lift to her brow as she offers. "Too bad you've got to go home or I could show you."

Gulp!

I nervously whisper. "I can send the plane home and have it come back tomorrow."

"You can do that?"

"They're my planes," I offer in a very confident tone.

"Can you stay the night?"

"If I want to."

"Do you?"

Jesus, Mary and Joseph! The temptations are so great and yet I don't think I could forgive myself. I'm still reeling from the first experience, now torn between lust and languish, unable to overcome the consequences that may appear.

I mentally try to justify staying. Amy is so engrossed in the company, I feel like extra baggage…nothing more than someone to come home to where she can vent her frustrations, who's gone before I get up in the morning, absent all day, arriving home, tired and depleted, indifferent towards me. I sense I'm taken for granted, deserted in the name of commerce physically, mentally and emotionally, never accepting that my day, make that, every day consists of nothing more than the tick/tock, tick/tock of isolation that's invading my soul and eating away at my sanity.

Megan is waiting for an answer.

My mind snaps back to 'now.'

Megan looks at me with yet a different, almost lecherous smile, raises her eyebrows and whispers. "Just you and me and we can… uhh…rehearse and you can… uhh… see what all these things do."

Reality strikes.

I catch myself and back off.

The temptation is great, yet, I know the answer must be 'no.'

I look at Megan and simply say, "I can't".

The spell is broken.

The realm of woulda's coulda's, shoulda's takes over.

Megan nods and smiles, an austere smile to reflect her disappointment.

She turns and departs, only to return with my clothes.

I begin to undress and she departs again.

I take out my phone and punch in Uber.

They say it will be five minutes.

I breathe deep and wonder if I made a mistake.

Megan returns as I look at her with a forlorn glance that she emulates.

We arrive at the front door just as Uber appears.

I give her a hug that's met with a stiff reply.

She whispers, "Thank you."

I say, "You're welcome."

I crawl into the back seat of the car and look back.

The office door is closed and the lights are off.

I ride back to Chamblee and Amelia III in total silence, climb aboard and we take off. I sit and my mind goes back, back, back as the emotional catacomb opens and questions arise.

My mind reverts to her comment, *"Uncovering other things I want to discover that I've been reluctant to try,"* and ponder its meaning.

She's different but I can't seem to place it…smoother, more detached and perhaps an inkling that she's being more adventurous than her persona is letting on.

The bond is still there and, yet, it's different…not quite so innocent.

Has she been politicized?

I close my eyes and wonder why.

I open my eyes and look down at the backdrop of humanity going about as, yet, another profound sense of singularity pervades my mind.

I'm sequestered in my emotions, wondering, questioning, analyzing the day and experience, realizing just how far she'd lured me until I'd reached the point of my regret.

My eyes focus, once again, on the bulkhead as if it's a wall between my thoughts and reality.

Have I been duped?

I take a deep breath look inward and sadly challenge Megan's sincerity.

Do I dare question whether Megan's ever-present corporate smile through her perfectly bright white teeth is real or just a façade that hides pain and loneliness, sadness and sorrow or some conniving trick to make me do what she needs done, pushing my bounds beyond where I thought they would ever go?

I take a deep breath and realize we're very much alike.

I ask myself, 'isn't this what we all really are?'...Shakespeare's Macbeth...'*nothing more than a walking shadow...a poor player... that struts and frets his hour upon the stage, and then is heard no more.*'

I shut my eyes as tight as I can when I realize I'll never know.

Once again, we land in Milwaukee.

My thoughts become cluttered by those who greet me.

The journey is over and I realize I don't want to do it again.

I glance at my right index finger, simply shake my head and whisper, 'No'.

April 7th Same tests! Same results! Yippee!

July 3rd - Father Pat died today. He was 61!

Three years ago, I asked Pat to do me a favor and get his PSA checked. He said he felt fine and never went to the doctor. He hadn't been to one in over 20 years! Pat had stage four prostate Cancer that spread to his liver, lungs, spine and brain. Such a wonderful man!

Such a waste!

A single drop of blood three years ago and perhaps, just perhaps, I wouldn't be writing this about him.

SHIT!

January 30th: Ten years have passed and I'm officially a Cancer Survivor. The emotions are gone but a deep sense of gratitude still remains. There's no one home to celebrate with. I go to the store and buy two Hostess snowballs and say 'whoopee'.

Megan and I haven't communicated in a long, long time.

Too bad!

But then, maybe, not.

Send in the clowns!

**The Rude Awakening:**

Tick/tock, tick/tock, the year rolled by as it melded into this thing called yesterday. It was December and the gray winter sky was underscored by the black branches reaching out like an old lady's fingers trying to grasp any sense of warmth and resurrection. The holiday decorators had come and filled the yard and house with the reds and greens to make us merry. Sadly, forlornly, it wasn't working. Even the Christmas songs had become nothing more than anvils of angst intended to do nothing more than make one feel guilty for not being more, giving more, doing more with the underlying promise that material things equate to love and more than a just feeling. So much for the Christmas spirit.

It was Sunday and breakfast time which had become the only opportunity Amy and I had to sit silently facing each other. My, God, we'd grown distant. As I sat eating my eggs, the phone rang and I watched Amy's expression morph from one of inquiry…to concern… then to one reserved only for profound distraught. Tears welled in her eyes as she simply nodded at the receiver and finally offered, "Thank you for calling" before collapsing in total emotional terror.

"What?" I asked, irritated and somewhat impatient.

"Uncle Frank."

"What?" I inquired as my tone morphed to one of concern.

"He died."

"What?" I exclaimed, now almost incredulous.

"He had a heart attack last night and died."

"Oh, no!"

Amy rushed to my arms and I held her as she sobbed. Her parents were gone. Her brother was gone. Aunt Julia was gone. Now, the last vestiges of yesterday simply evaporated and she was singular… alone, empty of the past. There's no good time for death but to do so right before Christmas seemed profoundly cruel.

"Arrangements?" I asked.

"Not yet and why now?" as Amy's hands went to her face in terror, as if I would have the answer.

There was a pause as Amy turned to me and said, "I think we need to talk."

I knew this was serious. I thought it would be about 'us'. Instead I was about to find out how bad things really were at Wilco.

We sat at the kitchen table as Amy began. "George, things at Wilco aren't going well."

"What do you mean?" I inquired.

"When the Duke was alive, everything he touched turned to gold. In the end the company over-extended into things we should have never started.

I felt like an ice pick was being jabbed into my soul.

Amy continued. "When the initial team began to retire, we didn't have the same wisdom as my dad and the leadership we put in place didn't have the drive and expertise it should have. As we grew, other specialists came along who duplicated our efforts in every single arena and, instead of being great, we became good. As we attempted to compete, we began cutting corners and evolved from good to average as those competitors began eroding both our business and passion until we evolved into mediocrity."

Amy took a deep breath and continued. "Derrick thought the best thing to do was sell off some of the assets and expand into different areas. In the end we over-extended the company to the point that right now the assets are less than the net worth of the corporation."

"But things are going to be Ok, aren't they?"

"I don't know. We've pledged everything, and I mean everything, to keep the company afloat and it's like we're playing Monopoly with pup tents when everyone else has hotels."

"Is there anything I can do?" I inquired.

"Not really, unless you can come up with a few billion dollars."

Oh, my God!

"What's at stake?" I inquired.

"Everything."

My hands trembled in frustration as I requested, "Define everything."

"Wilco, France, St. Martin, Pine Lake…everything."

"What?" I challenged as I slid back in my chair, incredulous to think that all the chips were on the table as I selfishly asked, "What about Terrill B&B and the farm?"

"They're part of Wilco."

I took a deep breath and, as I exhaled, simply whispered "Jesus".

Amy continued. "Things have been bad for a long time.

"Why didn't you let me know?" I demanded, now churning in a maelstrom of anger and pain.

Amy looked at me with tears welling in her eyes and simply said, "After all you've been through I didn't want you to worry."

"But!"

Amy saw the look of frustration on my face and offered. "George, you've had blood clots and Cancer. You've been at risk and all the material things we have will mean nothing if you don't have your health."

"Why now?" I asked.

"Derrick got involved in one of those Ponzi Schemes. He wanted to take the company public and show profound growth. Instead the scheme collapsed and with it all our money and now the company.

"Oh, my God." I felt as if I'd been hit in the chest as I sat in disbelief. The deafening silence was broken by the ringing phone. It was the Emerald Funeral Home in Saint Martin. Amy took the call and discussed arrangements. Cremation? Yes. No funeral. No memorial. Just as Uncle Frank wished.

Amy looked at me and inquired. "George can you go down there and take care of everything? I really need to stay here and help try to save everything…anything!"

I quietly nodded in the affirmative and asked when she wanted me to go. Amy indicated they wanted me there as soon as possible as they needed someone to pay for the cremation. I really didn't know if she wanted me out of town to protect me from the pressure or because she was so ashamed of what was happening.

I indicated I would go the next day.

Amy hung up the phone and I called Wilco Ops and told them what was going on. The flight was scheduled for the next morning. I didn't sleep well and drove to Mitchell Field with the plane sitting on the tarmac. I was told Amelia[X] was in for regular maintenance and I'd be taking Amelia III. I climbed on board and opened the liquor cabinet only to find it empty.

My flight was solo and I was alone to think about life. While the remainder of the folio sat at home filled with the thoughts I'd read many times, I took some Wilco letterhead from the bulkhead and added one more section which seemed to culminate all that came before.

We landed at Princess Juliana and I looked at the spot where the Rover normally would be waiting and realized I already missed my dear friend. I went through customs and took a taxi to the 'Lighthouse', reflecting on the joy of life for those who came to visit but never have time to actually experience Saint Martin."

"As a tri-national who repeatedly traversed between Wisconsin, France and Saint Martin, I've become 'blended' in terms of my outlook on life and hoped I was able to take the best from all three and mix them together in terms of lifestyle, social standards and tolerances…yes, tolerances, as each has its freedoms and limitations…socially, politically and ethically.

From America I took the enthusiasm that comes from being in the land of opportunity. From France I took the joy of the moment where clocks tick slower and life's more casual. From Saint Martin I took the expanded parameters of acceptance, physically, socially and ethically. In so doing, I thought back to my first comments about assumptions and how the one thing I've learned, above all else, is that you never should assume anything. In so doing, each day can be filled with the majesty of something new and exciting to store in your memory drawer you carry in your mind, heart and spirit.

I made it to the 'Lighthouse' and stood on the deck and looked out at the ocean below and listened to the afternoon plane take off for Saint Lucia and then the deafening silence of singularity. Tick/tock, tick/tock. I made my way up to our bedroom, opened the closet and took out a pair of dress shorts and golf shirt.

I got in the Rover and made my way to Auberge Gourmand. I rationalized. 'If I'm going to have dinner alone, it will be at my favorite place, filled with so many memories.'

I arrived and the staff, who are my friends, were all there and made me feel welcome. I sat alone at table number one as Pasquale poured a glass of wine and we toasted Uncle Frank and his memory. Word spread fast that he was gone.

I ate my dinner staring blankly at the quivering candle and realizing it's a metaphor of life that will slowly burn down and finally flicker out or suddenly be whiffed out before its time. Either way, the cold, dark pallor of death will ensconce itself, as it does us all.

My trance was broken when the check arrived. I opened my wallet and offered the Wilco card. Mary smiled, took the card and returned with an embarrassed look on her face.

"Mr. Terrill, the card has been refused."

A look of surprise and then embarrassment flushed across my brow.

"There must be some mistake," I offered.

"I tried three times and it wouldn't go through."

I opened my wallet and offered my rarely used personal American Express card.

Mary accepted it, went to the desk and returned with the same look on her face, telling me there was a problem, as my heart sank.

Pasquale, came over and offered. "You and your family have been good to us for so many years. Tonight, the meal is on us."

"I'll send you the funds. I just don't know what's going on."

Pasquale waved his hands as if to indicate it wasn't necessary. I shook my head in an apologetic way and slowly walked back to the parking lot only to see the Rover being towed.

"My God what's going on?"

I hailed a taxi and went back to the 'Lighthouse'. The tram wasn't working and so I made my way up the stairs as despondency crept into my soul. Sleep did not come!

The bright sun greeted me and I made my way to the funeral home. Uncle Frank's remains were there but the cremation needed to be paid in advance. We'd always kept cash in the 'Lighthouse' vault and, after dinner and the Rover being towed, I knew there was an issue and so I paid the three thousand dollars needed for a proper cremation with directions and agreements that Uncle Frank's ashes would join Grandma Marie, the Duke and Aunt Julia in Bae Marie.

I made my way back to the 'Lighthouse' only to see a strange car parked in front of the driveway. I asked myself, 'Who would be so inconsiderate as to park there?'

I made my way up the stairs only to find the door open.

"Can I help you?" I asked the two gentlemen standing in my living room.

"Mr. Terrill?"

"Yes."

"We're here to serve eviction papers and escort you off the property."

"What?"

"Yes. The property has been foreclosed, as well as the 'House on the Hill', auto dealership and property on Orient Beach."

"What?" I offered incredulously.

"Sir, here are the documents. We know this is an unfortunate surprise and we will work with you to remove your personal belongings but we need to have you vacate the house as soon as possible."

"Let me call my wife, if you don't mind."

I picked up my cellphone and the line was dead. It was my Wilco issue and I realized things had gone terribly wrong. I sat down at the kitchen table, took a deep breath and asked to see the documents. While not a lawyer, I could tell the gentlemen had every right to be there and I needed to move out.

I took another deep breath and asked if I could use one of the gentlemen's phones. They nodded in the affirmative and called Wilco Corporate only to have that line dead as well. I called Wilco Ops to schedule a plane home and it too was dead. Jesus!

I had no other credit card and only $800.00 left after paying the funeral home. I asked for one more phone call and contacted Delta Airlines and made arrangements for the next flight from Princess Julianna through Atlanta and back to Milwaukee. I told them I'd pay when I got to the counter. Airfare was $786.00. I needed more cash, but there was none.

"Gentlemen, here's what's going on. I just made arrangements for a flight home and need a ride to the airport. I'm willing to trade four bottles of some of the most expensive wine in the world simply for a ride."

The men looked at me and frowned and so I added. "Obviously, something has happened that's affecting my credit cards, as well as ownership of our property here on Saint Martin. All I'm asking is for the dignity of leaving. Is that too much to ask?"

They realized I had a quandary as their position softened as one offered. "Mr. Terrill, we know how generous your family has been to those in need here on Saint Martin. We also have our instructions. You don't need to give us wine for the ride. We'll call a taxi and make certain it's paid for.

I went to the guest bedroom closet and got the only suitcase and placed a few personal belongings in it before I asked, "Do you mind if I take one last tour before I go?"

"Ok."

I went up to the tower and looked at the ocean and pondered if I needed to simply follow Uncle Frank and go to Bae Marie.

I wondered what was happening at home.

How's my wife?

How are my kids?

What's going to happen?

I stopped in our bedroom and realized that someone else would be sleeping in my bed, not realizing or accepting their world could someday come crashing down.

Finally, I made it down to the main level and offered to show the two gentlemen the control center and provide the code for the vault. They already had it. It came with the settlement, along with everything, except what I was carrying in one small, brown suitcase. They checked to make certain it didn't contain anything that now belonged to them.

"I have one last favor."

"Yes sir."

"Would you mind calling my daughter in a couple of hours at this number? It's my daughter and she can let my wife know my schedule."

"Yes sir."

"Thank you."

## 34B:

I slowly walked down the steps to the waiting cab and took a silent ride through Marigot to the airport. I went to the economy line and waited my turn to pay. I placed eight one-hundred-dollar bills on the counter and received $14.36 in change. I made my way through security and out to the gate. No seat was assigned until everyone else had boarded and I was given seat 34B…the center seat of the last row in economy.

I boarded the plane, stuffed my bag in the overhead and sat down in a place I'd forgotten existed and, yet, there was congruence that pervaded my nature. We took off and I listened intently to the safety instructions and then, as I peered out on the memories, the man sitting to my left, pulled down the shade, as if to draw the final curtain on a life once lived. We became airborne and I simply stared at the seat back a few inches in front of me.

I closed my eyes and thought of all that had transpired. I wanted to write a few sentences but had no paper or pen. Instead I began reiterating my thoughts over and over and over and this is what transpired.

"The universe is large to the point of being beyond comprehension. Mankind has evolved taking it from a point of being a member of the universe to being its guardian. Along the way humans have fouled, despoiled and profoundly upset the delicate balance that has been in place for millennia. Our progression now sees mankind consuming itself socially and environmentally - changing our culture, changing our society and changing our world - homogenizing it and reducing its scope and luster to a single finite point called 'now'."

"We must respect all living beings who share this universe with us. We must honor their dignity and ensure their survival. We must lead others and those with the power to change and rearrange the world to the same point of acceptance that we're **not** alone on this planet or in this universe. We must realize and more importantly admit that we're here on an interim basis to share the graces of God and all the He or She has provided and assume that today is our last and make of it what we can for we never know what tomorrow will bring and always, always, always cherish the moments for they, too, are fleeting."

**Our World:**

I made it through the Atlanta Hartsfield maze to my gate and got in the Basic Economy line on Delta Flight 7125 to Milwaukee. A sense of relief flowed through my veins when they told me I'd been 'moved up' to 28E. I was still in a center seat and my knees were still against my chest but at least the guy at the window left the shade open.

I regretted not calling Megan to at least say hello. Maybe next year...send in the clowns. The guy next to me was reading a book by someone named Jordan Peterson. He got up to use the bathroom and left the book face-down on his seat. I glanced at the back jacket and read 'The book's central idea is that suffering is built into the structure of being' and although it can be unbearable, people have a choice either to withdraw, which is a suicidal gesture, or to face and transcend it. Living in a world of chaos and order, everyone has 'darkness' that can turn them into the monsters they're capable of being to satisfy their dark impulses in the right situations. Scientific experiments show that perception is adjusted to aims, and it's better to seek meaning than happiness.'

My seatmate came back and I pretended not to have noticed his book. I was offered a soft drink for free and beer for $6.00. I took a pass. After wearing $2,000 shoes I'd forgotten the empty feeling of having no money and nowhere to get it. With $4.06 in my pocket, no telephone and no one to call, my next concern became getting to Pine Lake and that had me anxious.

I opened my little brown suitcase and took out a sheet of paper. I knew what I wanted to simply outline of my thoughts on relationships while realizing they were the only thing that really mattered if a person REALLY wanted to have a joyous life.

I thought back to Dr. Haugen and realized what a jerk I'd been and yet, he lit a fire within me to summarize the difference between happiness and joy realizing there was a definite progression that needed to take play to truly experience joy.

**Oneself:** Physical, Mental, Spiritual

**Spouse:** Attraction, Association, Communication, Understanding, Trust, Compromise, Forgiveness

**Children:** Teacher, Counselor

**Job:** Opportunity, Ability, Desire, Dedication

**Family and friends:** Mutual Trust, Respect, Reward

**Hobbies and interests:** Relaxation, Stimulation, Socialization

**Universe:** Leadership, Compassion

As we were making our final approach over Lake Michigan my thoughts turned to Amy and how she was enduring all that had transpired. I glanced at the Wilco terminal and saw all the planes parked on the tarmac and wondered what it felt like when you're to blame. I wondered how do you comprehend going from everything to nothing? I asked myself what are the consequences and what about tomorrow?

We landed and I made my way down the terminal escalator towards the exit door with my mind hidden in thought about how I was going to get home. I looked up and wondered if my eyes were deceiving me. It really couldn't be, could it? I saw the smile and knew it wasn't a dream. When friendship turns to love and love to brotherhood those in need are magnificent in the glory of those who care.

I looked and a soft smile creased my lips as tears gathered in my eyes. The person who'd always been by my side was there. I walked up to him and simply nodded.

"Little brother, let's go home." Rodney had heard the news about Wilco's default and called 'V'. My dear friend simply stopped his world and came to mine. His big hand was placed upon my shoulder as he spiritually carried me back to my reality. We drove to Pine Lake and I was allowed to gather a few personal belongings. I offered my keys to the man who watched my every move. He indicated the locks and security code had already been changed. I looked for the family photos on the fireplace mantle and it was bare.

We'd already been removed…wiped clean in the name of commerce.

I took one last look and understood that, gone would be all the trappings of wealth… the fancy shoes, fancy clothes and perks we'd come to expect. I entered Amy's study and looked at the almost barren shelves.          A dejected frown crossed my face as I realized that my first gift to Amy…Amelia Earhart's model Lockheed Electra 10E I'd made as a kid, sat austerely alone where it had always been as a reminder of a time so long ago when only tomorrow stood before us without the chains of yesterday.

I took the Lockheed down and carried it with me, like a child hugging their most-loved teddy bear and made one last pass through the great room where the professionally decorated Christmas tree sat alone… isolated, abandoned in the corner, a dark, stark reminder of the counterfeit way in which we lived.

I wondered if Wang Huning's hypothesis about America was correct when he wrote that America had traded its soul—the connective tissues of community, tradition and family—for the glory of wealth and power. Strong but weak-spirited, individualistic but lonely, rich but decadent - a paradox headed for disaster.

I turned to Rodney and simply ask, "What now?"

"Well, my friend, thanks to Melia purchasing the condo in Madison and having it in her name, you have a place to start over. The structure has been foreclosed but not the apartments."

"What about the research foundation?"

"The foundation is under the control of the government as well as the rights to Mediglove."

"And the forest?"

A smile crossed Big Brother's face as he looked at me and said. "The Forest is still ours…yours and mine and will be forever."

We headed west towards Madison with me sequestered in the wretched silence of defeat. As the drive progressed I thought back to when Rodney and I met…working at the casino, the cottage, Jeepers Creepers, Amy as the UPS driver, proposing to her in the

Capitol rotunda and the glow of memories that started it all that made my life worthwhile.

I had a hollow feeling in my heart. All my dreams were shattered. So much work! So many hours! One assumes it will last forever. Poof! It's gone! Yet a strange sense of peace shielded me as I paused and thought about the blood clots and how death really did save my life.

My eyes sought something – anything that would give me a sense of now and, yet, it was all a blur. Like life, *now* is forever progressing - minute-by-minute, hour-by-hour, day-by-day - until it's only a rear-view mirror filled with reflections called yesterday.

From my brush with death I'd changed. I know I had! First, I learned that when you fly you need to stand up periodically to prevent blood clots. Second, I learned that a simple PSA blood test can save a man's life.

From that day forward, I did everything I could to abide by my own prioritized mantra and did so in that order and no other. It hadn't been easy! With each contemplation, deviation, consternation, I attempted to see if I could derive another way…some other set of dynamics or different order that would create a greater level of happiness and satisfaction.

In the end I always came back to the same series and always in the same sequence  realizing that death not only saved my life but gave real meaning to the concept of tomorrow - no longer assumed - no longer taken for granted - allowing me to cherish each today as if it were my last. I remembered glancing at the reflection in the passenger window and observing an old man looking back who readily admitted he's not perfect. I pondered if there's anything that actually is.

My mind wandered as I accepted the treatise that the net sum of the universe is zero and believe it's true for each person...good and bad, happy and sad...resulting in the same consequence, namely an individual with strengths and weaknesses, aspirations and foibles, where the only constant is time… something everybody and everything shares, until there is no more time, except the time to go.

The only sounds within the car were those of the tires humming on the frozen, Wisconsin winter road and the incessant wind pressing against our destination. I realized life's like that…cold at times, with wind that makes nothing easy, yet, makes us stronger.

Rodney turned on the radio to divert the deafening silence. I glanced at my dearest friend and silently nodded. It was as if divine intervention had come into play as Simon and Garfunkel's 'Bookends' began. …*'Time it was, and what a time it was. It was a time of innocence, a time of confidences. Long ago, it must be! I have a photograph! Preserve your memories, they're all that's left you.'*

I took a deep breath to thank God for what he'd provided…a life, unlike many others. Affirming I'd been loved and hated, admired and admonished as a leader and a fool beyond my wildest dreams. Yet, in the end even at the top of my mountain or down in its deepest valley, none of it mattered…not the money, perks or material things. Had it not been for the people who gave my life meaning, I would have been nothing…done nothing… accomplished nothing.

Rodney took his eyes off the road for an instant and glanced at me before his attention returned to the blackness ahead as he simply stated. "You're a great man, Little Spirit. While there are dark clouds on the horizon, your sun will rise again."

Rodney's soliloquy entered my heart compelling me to bathe in the warmth of his compassion. It had been a long, sad day - from the funeral home to Atlanta and then Milwaukee and not knowing how I was going to get home, then Rodney and Pine Lake and now the ride to Madison tightly grasping my little plastic plane.

I closed my eyes to hide my sorrow as exhaustion overtook me. I sat, ensconced in the obscurity of my grief until Rodney pulled up in front of the condo and, in the softest, quietest, most gentle way, offered, "Amy's waiting for you. She has a Christmas tree and wants you to help decorate it with popcorn strings and handmade chains of red and green paper links."

**The Waldwick Series:** The ten-book series spans nearly 200 years and are independent yet intertwined in several ways including, characters, location and thematic objectives that examine current social issues from different perspectives. Regardless of the time period or the characters in question, the core component - judging people by who they are instead, of what they are, remains paramount.

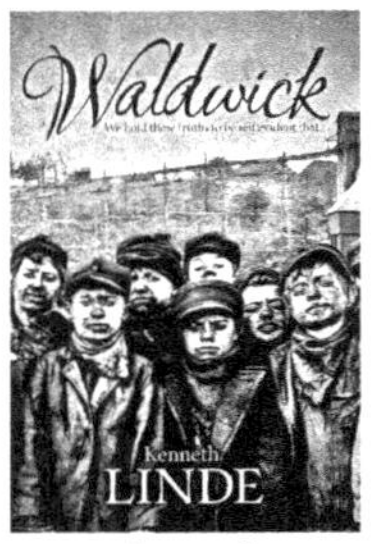

*Waldwick* addresses the subject of physical, social, economic and political oppression in the 1800's. Set in Cornwall, England, Virginia and Southwestern Wisconsin, *Waldwick* frankly discusses what one family was willing to do to overcome oppression, as told through the eyes of the narrator, George Terrill. *Waldwick* then summarizes what happens when the oppression is removed and opportunity arises. Integrated into the story line are actual events and people and how the main characters are affected by their existence and their interaction with these people and events. Above all else, *Waldwick* is a love story … love of the land, love of one another and the love of freedom, woven in a tapestry of acceptance, tolerance and justice. *Award Winner*

*War of My Brothers* examines America of the early 20th century and how and why it changed as seen through the eyes of Hank Terrill, great grandson of George Terrill from the original Waldwick. Ride along as Hank witnesses World War I, the Spanish Flu, the 19th Amendment, that gave women the right to vote, the Great Depression, World War II, Korean War and Viet Nam and how life changed, people changed and those who govern changed, as well. Experience the traumas of life and the joys of the living as you thank God that it didn't happen to you.

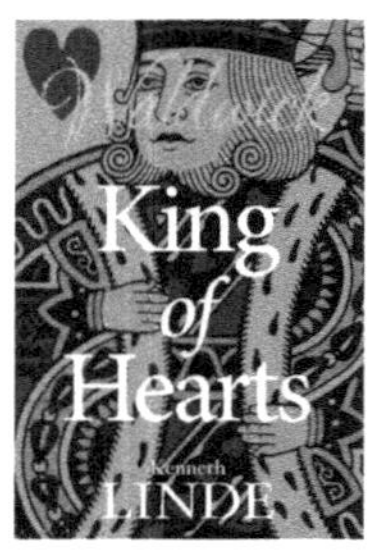

*The King of Hearts* has been reviewed as *"ambitious, extensively researched and deeply engrossing"*…a story that traces the actual Terrill family through 60 generations as it learns the consequence of wealth, power and prestige over 700 years only to have it all collapse around them. Using a blend of magic realism, lyrical prose and imagery *The King of Hearts* weaves a complex tapestry of a family's history from 65 BCE through sixty generations. Beneath it all, the book is about friendship and the deep, mutual bond between people based on trust, support, and genuine connection that goes beyond just companionship—it's about understanding, loyalty, and being there for each other through life's ups and downs.

*Little Spirit* Based in contemporary Wisconsin, *Little Spirit* examines the concept of eminent domain and the taking of land and dignity, first from the Indian's perspective and then today, as seen through the eyes of George Terrill IV a descendant of the original George Terrill. Using flashbacks through a 94-year-old, blind, Ho- Chunk Indian elder, named Great Grandfather, George learns about the feelings and challenges of the Ho-Chunk nation and the taking of their land and also how contemporary America hasn't changed that much in terms of citizen rights.

*Driftless* revisits George and his wife fifteen years into their marriage. Reflecting on the challenges they face when their marriage becomes mundane while examining the profound question of which is worse… having nothing or everything. As the mystery of the Forest is revealed *Driftless* examines the consequence of technology and the power of special interest groups to control the status-quo for their financial gain, while addressing the issue of individual rights in time of personal need, where the one thing all people have in common is … time!

*The Hayflick Limit* addresses the challenges of parenthood, while discussing a person's rights to live and die. When affected by an incurable malady the question becomes *"Would you choose five-to-seven years of normal mental acuity, at which time you would abruptly expire, or risk everything and allow for the slow, gradual decline with hope that a different, longer-lasting cure might come along?"* *The Hayflick Limit* addresses the role of government in establishing the validity of the Hippocratic Oath?

*Let Go* examines the consequence of bullying as Melia Terrill is affected by the verbal onslaught and her commitment to the only friend who has shown her the beauty of acceptance for who she is. The books examines the perks and perils of extreme wealth, the solitude of loneliness and frustration of achieving one's goals only to realize that all dreams can become nightmares when one risks everything for perhaps nothing as it delves into thoughts, emotions, joys, sorrow and consequences of being a captive of one's own past and fleeting fame.

***Survivor...How Death Saved My Life*** looks at the consequence of an altered set of priorities and how it can take a near-death experience to "right the ship". Totally immobilized for six days, George Terrill examines his life and it's mistakes and vows, if he survives, to make things right. *Survivor* addresses the psychology of fear, the challenges of being told you have less than a 5% chance of living three hours and what you think about when you sincerely believe you're going to die.

*Greed* is a thought-provoking literary tale of ambition gone awry, exposing how the pursuit of wealth can fracture family relationships. This intense novel, explores the intricacies of human nature and the pursuit of meaning. It serves as a critique of modern society's obsession with wealth and status that challenges readers to reconsider what success truly means, making this book not just an exhilarating journey but a profound reflection on the human condition.

*And/Or* Using Newton's Third Law as a lens to explore relationships where every action sets off a chain reaction, *And/Or* journeys in ways no one can predict or control while asking difficult questions about resilience, identity, and redemption. As such, it ponders deep philosophical reflections and existential questions by drawing sharp connections between science and human nature, asking such profound questions as...Is it possible for a person to truly recover from betrayal? Can love survive after it's been broken? And when one loses everything, what's left? *And/Or* is a gripping, thought-provoking read that will linger long after the final page.

**Disclaimer:** This book is pure fiction. Some of the events detailed herein may be true and have been faithfully rendered as researched by the author to the best of his abilities. The information contained is intended to provide helpful and informative material on the subjects and events addressed and written as an interpretation of his learning. It does not guarantee accuracy or social integrity and has been written for the purpose of education and entertainment.

There are towns called Waldwick and Mineral Point, Wisconsin where the author's childhood was filled with magical moments and marvelous memories and a village called Waldwick that remains nearby and is the birthplace of the author's grandmother and mother. There are many Terrill's and Harris's in the area who are the author's relatives and he hopes and prays he has done the family names justice by what he has written for they, are the kindred spirit upon which our country was created. There is no reality to the names used as they are all of consequence.

There is a wonderful island called St. Martin that is filled with love and life where smiles come easy, the food is superb and the memories can last forever. The names of the restaurants are real and the food is GREAT and the author only hopes that he's done them all justice with his descriptions.

There is always the risk of blood clots. 35% of all people who have one, find it terminal. Prostate Cancer is real and does affect men in many ways. BOTH CAN BE PREVENTED! I am a survivor of both the blood clots and prostate Cancer and thank God for giving me these extra days.